P9-CAO-554

Praise for
DAVID WILLIAM ROSS

"He writes with grace, he writes with power"
Westport News

BEYOND THE STARS

"As broad in scope as *Lonesome Dove*
and as fulfilling"
Arizona Daily Star

"Excellent . . . Honest . . . Unsparing . . .
A western with a difference"
Philadelphia Inquirer

"Masterful, dramatic . . .
Filled with heroic deeds . . .
A sweetheart of a story, expertly told"
Macon Beacon

"Well-written . . . Engrossing . . . Few who begin
these pages will choose to turn away before learning
the fates of those who live within them."
Publishers Weekly

EYE OF THE HAWK

"Powerful"
Tulsa World

"A good read, and well-written"
Kirkus Reviews

Other Avon Books by
David William Ross

BEYOND THE STARS
EYE OF THE HAWK
WAR CRIES

Avon Books are available at special quantity discounts for bulk purchases for sales promotions, premiums, fund raising or educational use. Special books, or book excerpts, can also be created to fit specific needs.

For details write or telephone the office of the Director of Special Markets, Avon Books, Dept. FP, 1350 Avenue of the Americas, New York, New York 10019, 1-800-238-0658.

SAVAGE PLAINS

DAVID WILLIAM ROSS

AVON BOOKS ◆ NEW YORK

```
VISIT OUR WEBSITE AT
http://AvonBooks.com
```

SAVAGE PLAINS is an original publication of Avon Books. This work has never before appeared in book form. This work is a novel. Any similarity to actual persons or events is purely coincidental.

AVON BOOKS
A division of
The Hearst Corporation
1350 Avenue of the Americas
New York, New York 10019

Copyright © 1996 by David William Ross
Published by arrangement with the author
Library of Congress Catalog Card Number: 96-96167
ISBN: 0-380-78324-X

All rights reserved, which includes the right to reproduce this book or portions thereof in any form whatsoever except as provided by the U.S. Copyright Law. For information address Avon Books.

First Avon Books Printing: September 1996

AVON TRADEMARK REG. U.S. PAT. OFF. AND IN OTHER COUNTRIES, MARCA REGISTRADA, HECHO EN U.S.A.

Printed in the U.S.A.

RA 10 9 8 7 6 5 4 3 2 1

If you purchased this book without a cover, you should be aware that this book is stolen property. It was reported as "unsold and destroyed" to the publisher, and neither the author nor the publisher has received any payment for this "stripped book."

To Sol Levine
lifetime friend.
You brought compassion and companionship to our youth
and left memories to gladden our years.
Thanks, old pal.

It was near dawn when they reached the border. The frightened slaves clung tensely to their mules, riding double, whispering to each other, searching the darkness with furtive glances that kept swinging uneasily to the dim figures of white men riding behind. There were eight Negroes; two young women who rode together, and six men, only one of whom looked over twenty. They had come from a large Missouri farm, forty miles from the border, and were finally nearing Kansas and freedom. Yet the anxious blacks had been sensing a difference between the grimly bearded man and his two companions guiding them, and the cold silent figures said to be protecting them from the rear.

Nor were they alone with their worries. Cole and Dennis Sadler, riding beside the leader, Noah Crolly, were worried this waspish, stubborn old abolitionist had badly misjudged these border ruffians he had hired for protection. More time should have been spent checking character and reputations. They particularly didn't like one who had kept back most of the night, keeping counsel with others who dropped behind to join him. He was a tallish man with a round full face, his piercing blue-gray eyes a peculiar tint, the upper lids falling too low, leaving a malign look that intensified as he stared at you. On arrival and being asked he had muttered his name was Charlie Coyne.

Yet if dour old Noah was irascible and preachy, he was also fiercely dedicated to his mission. He visualized himself as grasping the torch from the dead hand of John Brown, as that dangerous fanatic entered history on the

1

gallows. It meant nothing to him that Brown murdered in cold blood or that insanity, which had raged for generations in Brown's maternal family, had finally claimed him. He was convinced that that strange seditious zealot, like himself, was answering a call from Heaven, and those divinely summoned could never be evil.

A thunderstorm far to the west was throwing up lantern flashes of light that traced a hilly horizon ahead before quickly fading away. A breeze, coming with a musk of rain, began rustling through the trees.

The first hint of trouble came as they hit the creek running up toward Shawnee Mission, assuring Crolly he was back in Kansas. In spite of the threatening weather it would soon be dawn and he would no longer need an escort. Arrangements had been made to start these Negroes north where other abolitionists would see they reached Ohio and offered places to settle. The New England society that had sent Crolly into the field provided him with money and a few "Beecher's bibles," rifles smuggled into the territory as religious texts, but his real problem was dependable manpower. Like all Free-Soilers these Sadler brothers were against slavery, but few like them were willing to cross into heavily armed Missouri, defying well-publicized laws to rescue slaves. Crolly had once considered using Jayhawkers, bands of Kansas men who raided Missouri in retaliation for terrifying onslaughts made from across the border. But these nocturnal guerrillas were often as lawless as their counterparts, and tended to steal horses and cattle and kill resisting Missourians before liberating slaves.

A great table rock, a well-known landmark that the creek gently circled about, was empty, and there was no sign of guides to lead the fugitives north. Crolly scowled at the barren stretch of shale, just visible in the graying light. The trials that bedeviled his mission were endless. Only an infinite faith in the divine overseeing of his work kept rising rage from distorting his face. Cole Sadler reached over to nudge him. "Want me to scout about some?"

Cole, a tall man with dark, even features and a voice that commanded respect, was known for his level head and way with a gun. His younger brother Dennis was a slim towhead, a high-spirited lad who was there against the advice of their older brother, Troy. But the Sadlers needed the money Crolly paid and, because of several scrapes encountered on this venture, even old Noah felt they were earning it.

"Might be best you do," allowed Crolly after a moment's thought. "Take Dennis and try both sides of the creek. Can't imagine what's keeping Lame Fox. He's always been here waiting."

Lame Fox, a local Shawnee who sometimes did clandestine work for Crolly, was the best tracker on the border, but he had enemies, among them escaped prisoners he had tracked down for the army at Leavenworth. His signal was to be two quick owl hoots.

Cole and Dennis, keeping their horses to a trot, were almost a mile down creek when they heard a shot. Cole stopped and stared back across the murky plain, its stunted foliage beginning to take form in a meager light feeding in from the east. Across the creek he could see Dennis had stopped to look his way. After a few moments he signaled his brother to continue searching along the creek bed while he turned back to retrace his steps. Something told him that shot meant trouble.

As he drew near the table rock he dismounted. The very stillness before him smacked of danger. Taking advantage of some heavy brush rimming and drawing nurture from the creek, he began to move closer, grimly forcing his way through almost a hundred feet of tangled thicket before hearing voices. Then, edging up, he had to stare at the scene for several heartbeats before he grasped what had happened. Crolly had been shot. His body was on the ground and two men were going through his pockets. The man called Charlie Coyne was waving a gun at the Negroes and hissing to the men around him. "Be quick about it! We're on Kansas soil now . . . makes 'em sure enough runaways. We'll take 'em to Caldwell's . . . keep 'em out of sight till we settle rewards." He glanced down the creek where Cole and Dennis had disappeared. "Now move out before those two farmhands get back . . . Selgany and his outfit will finish 'em like always."

Cole saw there were ten of them, revealing some had been waiting in ambush, too many for him to take on. Caught in this bramble, they'd kill him with their first volley. The men started hurrying the blacks away, taking Crolly's horse and turning around to backtrack toward Missouri. He heard one of the toughs calling over to Coyne as they left. "Quick as we 'uns get to Caldwell's them young nigger wenches gonna be mighty handy for some funnin'."

Restless Troy Sadler, if nagged by bad luck, was a determined man. Not built for sympathy and too assertive to draw warmth, he viewed life like a veteran gladiator scouting the arena, taut but secretly convinced of victory. Yet in spite of this hard exterior Troy had the great protruding eyes of a dreamer, a man who saw visions in clouds and dreamt of conquests that would spark history. He was a tall man with broad shoulders, his forearms thick and visibly muscled, his face masculine, roughly hewed, his head shaped for a helmet.

He had been scrutinizing a well-worn text, left to him by a long dead mountain man, when his eyes were pulled away by the sight of Silas Cheatem coming down the river trail. Cheatem was his nearest neighbor, a strange, secretive man, but not one to be taken lightly. He watched Cheatem stop and gaze toward the river where Cathy Jo was bathing. His sister-in-law, Cathy, Cole's wife, usually slipped down to the river in the late morning to a small cove where water eddied in, forming a pool. There, shielded by the brush, she slipped off her clothes and quickly washed. Cathy, a buxom if still shy girl, stood out on a frontier where every woman was noticed. Normally she had a happy-go-lucky way about her, while most females on this troubled border, surrounded by ever-rising violence, were grim with worry. Nor could they be blamed. The issue of slavery, like a volcanic fissure in the bedrock of the nation, well beyond the power of law or religion to suppress, was surfacing where it was easiest to contest, along the lawless western borders. Night raids, arson, looting, and even murders were becoming commonplace. There was a growing rash of widows, many already soured by hardship, facing the added affliction of loneliness. Some with ragged children could be seen in the settlements struggling through the day, their hair unattended or primly pinned up, their overworked bodies looking shapeless in drab burlap or wool. Cathy made her own clothes or cut down her husband's, and while always looking presentable, if a little boyish, there was no concealing her ample breasts and shapely hips.

Silas Cheatem, though prudently concealing it, was a sensualist, a man given to succulent thoughts, toothsome foods, and fleshy females. He was a heavyset man, the top of his body seeming slightly larger than the bottom. But for all that he was powerfully built and the noticeable bulge around his waist as much muscle as fat. He had been watching Cathy for some time now, not that he had any hopes of bedding her, for she was married to a formidable gunman, but the thought of it played well in his fancy. Yet Silas was a man who never underestimated what time, money, and a little luck could do. Cathy had not noticed him stopped on the trail and innocently stood up, revealing her full breasts. From his distance he could just make out the red nipples. It was Troy's voice breaking out from the doorway that ended this enticing tableau.

"Got a reason for coming by?" he shouted. At the sound of his voice Cathy dropped down and Cheatem turned to face Troy, managing a smile.

"That I have." Cheatem's smile slowly receded, replaced by a businesslike firming of the mouth. He waited until he was a little closer. "Was wondering if your brothers had hired out yet."

"Got some reason for asking?"

"Maybe offering them a job."

"Job? What kind of job?"

"Need some lumber brought over the line, thought they might be interested in the work."

Troy considered his answer for a moment. "Best wait till they get back . . . you can ask them yourself."

"Where are they?"

"Wouldn't know."

"Hope they're not messing with that damn fool, Crolly. There's enough goddamn trouble around here without fetching more."

"Like I said, I wouldn't know."

Cheatem gave him a doubtful look, then rubbed his mouth. "Well, I'm pulling out . . . moving west . . . figger on claiming some land out there while the claiming is good. You folks fixin' to stay here?"

"Ain't decided."

Cheatem stared in the direction of the border. "By Jesus, things are getting worse every day . . . if war comes calculate all hell is fixin' to break loose."

"Reckon it is."

Cheatem sucked his tooth for a moment. "Well, I'll be going along. Tell Cole and Dennis to come by first chance."

Cheatem turned about and started back. This time he didn't stop to gaze at the brush where Cathy was bathing.

Troy watched him go. He often wondered where Cheatem got his money. He had heard he had left a business in Ohio and was heading west to claim some land and start a cattle or horse spread. Looking down the trail, watching Silas disappear, he felt a growing irritation. Cheatem was the sort of man who would succeed too. Something about him made you think he could see ahead and act accordingly. Troy was aware he, himself, needed a plan, a better one than he had managed to put together so far. Cole and Dennis were counting on him, accepting his belief in the old mountain man's story about the Shining Mountains and the secret they held. When Cheatem arrived and settled next to them on the banks of the Kaw, he remembered Silas immediately talking of continuing west, openly predicting eastern Kansas would soon be a holocaust of trouble that any sensible man would avoid. Problem was the Sadlers didn't have the money to outfit up, and there was hardly any work a man could put his hand to. On the frontier folks mostly did for themselves.

His mind turned to his brothers and how they might be faring. He had always had grave doubts about Crolly. He had heard abolitionists rail against slavery before but old Crolly was ready to defy the federal government, even shoot it out with state militia to liberate slaves. Most people by now were wary of him, knowing his bold forays across the line were fraught with danger. Had he worked more quietly he might have gotten a few volunteers, but his fanatical pronouncements were reaching the ears of Missourians hanging about the border, many aware of why he was soliciting help. His only real advantage was money, a seemingly inexhaustible supply being pumped in from religious organizations in the east. It was money that finally persuaded Cole and Dennis to risk this raid with him. But now they'd been gone for several days and it was growing harder for Troy to hide his fears from Cathy. Secretly he was hoping they'd be back by nightfall.

Catching Cathy toweling her hair as she came up from the river, he began to think that perhaps Cheatem was right, maybe they should be heading west. Summer was almost here and the season for finding and setting up diggings in that lonely country, where reports of Indian trouble were continually trickling back, would soon be passing.

Shy or not, Cathy Jo Sadler was anything but a simple girl; in fact, she remained a puzzle to many around her. Still, in her own mind, she was firmly convinced of two things, what she loved most and most hated. By far she most loved being Cole's wife. By far she most hated Kansas. Married at seventeen, now in her nineteenth year, she was experiencing a growing frustration that her womanly body, which had turned strikingly shapely since her marriage, seemed to arouse every man that looked at her. Not being flirtatious, and married to a man not given to jealousy, she still sensed men were peculiarly aware of her, oft times seeming to be quietly musing about her, both their shyness and boldness hinting at intimacy. At times it proved unsettling. She was reasonably sure now it wasn't vanity. She used to think she was having illusions, even laughing at herself for ridiculous conceit, but then something always happened, like Cheatem, a man she detested, sneaking up and peeking at her nudity, raising again her old irritation. There had even been a few incidents when she was sure her husband's reputation kept men from taking liberties that might have gone well beyond mere words or looks.

In truth Cathy was more striking than pretty. Her eyes were a cool, pale blue, her long, soft hair gave off a dark tint of gold. High cheekbones gave her face a classic look. Only her mouth, which seemed to fit the sensuous cast of her body, gave any hint of her warm nature and, as Cole knew, capacity for passion. Yet it was her strangely graceful movements that caught most people's eyes, for Cathy unconsciously had a smooth-flowing yet delicate step that unthinkingly caused a provocative sway of her body. Cole, half smiling, had called attention to it once or twice, but Cathy couldn't seem to change the way she walked. Troy and Dennis, secretly proud to have such an arousing female in the family, urged her not to change.

In spite of his attempts to seem casual and unconcerned, Troy failed to fool her. She knew whatever her husband was doing was dangerous. She didn't dislike this restless, dominating brother-in-law, but she objected to his hold over Cole. She hadn't wanted to come to this raw, bitterly contested strip of land. She hated violence and was appalled to find it continually mounting about her. But Cole insisted on following his older brother.

Intermittent thunderstorms had been roiling overhead since dawn, and though both managed during daylight hours to find ways to be alone, darkness and coming to the dinner table always raised tensions between Cathy and Troy. She shook her head, frowning as she put down the pan used to fry fish taken earlier from the river. "Troy, how long we going to stay in this dreadful place? Never a night passes but I don't 'spect we'll be murdered in our beds."

Troy ran a quick hand through his hair, an early sign of unease. "We're fixin' to head west real soon."

"Why not now . . . tomorrow?"

"Got to outfit up first."

Cathy sighed. "If it's money you're after, can't see any to be made around here . . . a man has only what his claim or livestock will bring . . . only time cash comes up."

"Figure there's still some to be earned."

"How?"

The sound of hoofbeats coming up to the cabin door brought Troy out of his seat. He snapped up the rifle he kept handy after dark and moved to press his eye against a large crack, where planks making up their makeshift door had dried, warped, and partially split.

An Indian dressed in dark buckskins, with his head shaved down to a single braided scalp lock, jumped from his horse and approached the cabin.

"Jesus, it's Lame Fox," muttered Troy, half turning to Cathy. The Shawnee, a familiar figure along the Kaw, though more tolerated than accepted, moved freely about only because very few, like Troy, knew of his secret ties to Crolly.

Troy pulled the door open but the Indian made no attempt to enter. He stood several feet away, pointing to the west. "You go!" he said, as though those two words conveyed a message easily understood.

"Go where?" answered Troy.

"No stay here!" responded Lame Fox. "Much danger now."

"What is it?" demanded Troy. "My brothers in trouble?" Cathy appeared behind him, a lamp lighting her pale face.

"Yes." The Indian swung back to his horse. "Crolly dead."

Troy's chest came up like a man holding his breath. "What about my brothers?"

"They come back, but you go now." Again the scarred, painted arm swept toward the west.

Troy stepped outside the cabin, trying to move away from Cathy, but she stayed with him. "You're saying

Cole and Dennis are in trouble for helping Crolly?" he almost shouted, anxiety making his voice sound high and strained.

"Yes, plenty trouble!"

"Come on now, dammit, sure as hell others have helped him before?"

"Yes."

"Well, what about them?"

The Indian mounted his horse and turned to stare at Troy for a long moment. "They all dead!" he almost whispered in a cold, tired voice. There was something akin to defeat in the Indian's expression. It convinced Cathy, at least, this warning might be coming too late.

Troy, his face drawn and now cramped with concern, could only stare into the night as the troubled Shawnee pulled his mount about and rode off.

2

Cole quietly worked his way out of the thicket, aware he and his brother were now marked men, candidates for murder. But his mind wasn't on himself or even young Dennis, it was on Cathy Jo. Proslavers would stop at nothing to halt this covert traffic of slaves northward for freedom. Poor sermonizing Crolly was dead, yet Cole knew his slaying was only one in a crucible that had destroyed whole families, even communities. Had not the old preacher sent him and his brother searching for Lame Fox, they too would have been lying sprawled on that rocky surface, now becoming clearer in the growing light. A man named Charlie Coyne was the sinister leader of this deadly ruse; it was a name Cole wasn't likely to forget. Somehow Coyne had passed himself off as a ready gun, available for hire, with no ties to either North or South; not a difficult thing to do when many people on the border kept their feelings hidden, sensing danger lay in declaring for either side.

Twenty-three-year-old Cole was a man who rarely acted on impulse or allowed himself fanciful notions about his plight. But the facts here were too stark to dismiss. Men who knew the country well and lived by the gun had watched both he and Dennis aiding this flaming abolitionist, who Missourians knew was sent by self-righteous northerners to steal their property and destroy their way of life. The thin crevices on Cole's darkly tanned face deepened as he glanced westward, where the storm could be heard rumbling closer. His metallic gray eyes, always intense, narrowed as he thought of his family and grappled with building fears. Many thought Cole resembled his brother, Troy, but his features were more refined and his brow lacked the stress lines that betrayed Troy's search for something life kept denying. But like brothers everywhere they saw in each other qualities both envied and resented. For Troy, Cole was a vital anchor to reality. Once Cole made a stand, or committed to a point of view, he could not be easily swayed or scared off. If he lacked Troy's imagination or gift with language his word was as dependable as the coming sunrise. Steady, reliable Cole, a man not given to loud talk or assertions of power, but when forced into a stand folks allowed he could back it up.

Yet Cole, himself, was the first to admit he lacked Troy's ambition and fiercely enterprising heart, his air of excitement, his ability to seek out endless promising, if not always profitable, ventures. For Cole, and even the young carefree Dennis, Troy brought fervor and warmth into a drab world by coming up with ideas that promised riches or, at least, escape from the drudgeries of farming or their father's tanning yards. Troy easily dreamt up adventures that neither Cole nor Dennis could have matched in a thousand years.

Suddenly there was light enough to see Dennis coming back along the creek bed, with still no sign of Lame Fox. Cole couldn't believe the Shawnee simply failed to appear, more likely he was here earlier and spotted the Missourians waiting in ambush. That luckless Indian faced the most perilous future of all. Unlike slaves, considered private property and at least protected by law, forces on both sides readily killed Indians caught taking sides in white men's quarrels. Redskins under suspicion had a way of disappearing on the frontier.

Young Dennis, startled by his brother's hushed but hurried reporting of Crolly's murder and the threat now facing them, looked around anxiously, as though another attack was imminent. "What we gonna do?"

Cole remained silent, struggling to think of a way out of their predicament. Some things had to be done before racing back to warn Troy and Cathy Jo, things that took time. Decency said they had to bury Crolly; left lying here in this isolated spot his body would go to scavengers or soon be infested by vermin. Though they could do little to avenge him, Cole felt they should at least get word of his murder to his sponsors. Approaching the body, Dennis began to groan as he saw Crolly's pockets turned inside out, the money gone. He started to whine; now they would never be paid. The cash they had risked their lives for, the hard-earned coin Troy was counting on to get them to the Shining Mountains, had vanished.

Cole silenced him by gesturing with his hunting knife to the one Dennis carried. "We'll have to use these to dig with . . . better get started, there's some soft ground yonder."

Half an hour later they had Crolly's body in a shallow grave, covered by a thin layer of rocks carried from the creek bed. It was all they could do. Cole stuck a crude cross into the ground, but his mind was already on the town of Lawrence, the only place he could think of to leave word of Crolly's death. He reckoned the growing town's post office was their best bet, though perhaps risky for either of them to be seen there today. Lawrence was a settlement supposedly dominated by antislavery sentiment. It was there that Crolly did his recruiting, but there he had also recruited Charlie Coyne.

The storm thundering across the plain brought little rain; instead it was now stalling and shifting around, beginning to pass to the south. It was typical spring prairie weather. By the time they left, the sun was working its way through, its rays like golden shafts spearing into hill country to the north. Cautiously they headed northwest for Lawrence, but immediately began losing time, trying to avoid wagons and riders heading south for Ottawa or points below. But Cole didn't want any witnesses to their riding away from the vicinity of a murder.

It wasn't until noon that they pulled up on the outskirts of Lawrence, Cole telling Dennis to leave the note with the postmaster, returning as quickly as possible.

Dennis, at seventeen, six years younger than Cole, felt closer to Cole than he ever did to Troy, who seemed ancient at twenty-eight. It was all because Cole treated him like a man, while Troy, though forever smiling at him, treated him as something less. He was happy to find himself riding into town alone; it was a sign Cole thought he could handle a task involving some risk. Yet he had to fight against a strange weakness in his knees when the postmaster, taking the note, turned to regard him queerly, eyeing the boy closely after frowning at the folded sheet marked *To anyone asking for Crolly*.

"Crolly?" repeated the tall gaunt figure, cocking his head to one side to better study Dennis. "Ain't that funny, someone just asked for him . . . believe the gent is still here . . . yeah . . . that's him over there, standing by the door. What d'you say your name was?"

"Didn't say, but gotta go!"

"Hold on a minute." The postmaster was leaning against the heavily littered counter. "Hey, mister, you looking for Crolly? Got a note from him here."

A distinguished-looking man, dressed in dark clothes and sporting a well-trimmed beard, broke off his conversation with a seated figure who wore a star and was chewing on the wet end of a badly mangled cigar.

"Me?" said the stranger turning toward them. "You say there's a note for me?"

"You asked about Crolly, didn't you?"

"That I did."

"Well, here's a young fellow brought a note marked 'anyone asking for Crolly.'"

Dennis wanted to charge out of there; icy-cold fingers had started working down his spine. He knew the note said that Crolly was dead and where he had been buried, but neither he nor Cole expected to be about when it was read. Cole had warned him that as soon as the contents of that note were known the one delivering it would be wanted for questioning. It would be assumed he knew more than the note revealed about Crolly's death—there might even be more dangerous assumptions. Dennis measured the distance to the door; he would have to get by that figure with the star. It didn't look promising and when the bulky figure stood up to block the exit it didn't look possible.

The stranger, approaching the postmaster with his hand out, gestured for the note. The postmaster's face lowered a little, his eyes narrowing slightly, betraying a stab of curiosity. "Mind if I ask your name?"

"Quarles, Henry Quarles," said the stranger. As the postmaster handed over the note the man glanced at Dennis, murmuring, "Thanks, young fellow."

Dennis shifted around, bringing his right hand nearer his gun. He had no idea what to do but he couldn't allow himself to be held here. Something told him that note was about to spell disaster for him and his brother. He made up his mind; no matter how badly they dealt with him, he wasn't going to reveal Cole was waiting outside of town.

As Quarles's eyes scanned the note Dennis held his breath. He watched the man's expression, figuring that would be the first sign of trouble. But Quarles's face remained fixed as his eyes followed the few lines. He ended by folding the slip of paper in his hand and smiling at Dennis. "I'll be happy to carry out Mr. Crolly's wishes," he said blandly. Dennis was too shocked to answer. He stood there as Quarles, taking him by the arm and nodding at the postmaster, began walking them both to the door. "Let me buy you some coffee, young fellow," he said genially enough. "You look like you've come a long ways and could use some."

Dennis was too confused to resist. All he knew was he was getting out of that office and seizing the quickest way back to Cole. At the stranger's prompting they crossed the street and entered a little shack that proved to be a restaurant. While Quarles ordered two coffees Dennis began to muster courage again. There was nothing threatening in this man's manner, but the way he concealed the fact of Crolly's death had its sinister side. Quarles's expression was clearly meant to reassure him, but after sipping his coffee the man started asking questions that had Dennis's stomach muscles tightening.

"You didn't come here alone did you, son?"

"Ain't saying," answered Dennis.

The man smiled. He could have been trying to be kind, but Dennis found his cool, assured manner unsettling. He tried a sip of coffee but had to struggle to get it down. He wanted to leave.

"You got to stop worrying about me, young fellow," said Quarles almost gently. "I figure you to be Dennis Sadler. Where's your brother, Cole?"

Dennis had the coffee cup to his mouth but the second sip he took was sputtered back in the cup. "Who the hell are you?" he gulped, his heart picking up its beat.

"I'll introduce myself in due time. But come now, where's your brother?"

"Ain't saying."

Quarles sat back and studied him for a moment. "Noah Crolly was carrying quite a bit of money when he died . . . any idea what happened to it?"

Dennis almost shouted back, "We didn't get any!", mutely swearing at himself for saying "We." But Quarles didn't seem to notice, or more likely he already knew the truth and didn't care.

"Too bad," mused Quarles, drawing up his mouth and fingering his beard. "Perhaps we can work something out. Where do you live?"

"I ain't saying." He pushed his chair back. "What's more I'm leaving!" Dennis got up. Staying there longer only risked blabbing something that would lead to real trouble. Though displeased, Quarles didn't try to stop him. Silently he followed him out and as Dennis mounted and rode away he turned and nodded to a slim, wiry man slumped against the shack's far corner. Nonchalantly this man, whose dark, weathered face looked like he'd never been indoors, took a horse from the hitching post and without looking back at Quarles began trailing Dennis down the street.

It was after midnight when Cole and Dennis reached their cabin. Noticing a light still showing, unusual at that hour, they stopped the horses a short distance away and walked them to the yard. As they drew near, Troy and Cathy Jo could be heard arguing. So loud was their quarrel neither heard the horses approaching and turned to stare with startled expressions when Cole appeared at the door. Cathy, rushing into his arms, was suddenly sobbing, "Thank God you're back! You're safe!"

Troy, quickly circling the two, grabbed the pale-faced Dennis by the arm, half shouting, "What the hell happened?! Is Crolly really dead?! Is it true?!" Dennis, his shoulders slumped in exhaustion, nodded.

Cole, hugging Cathy, swung to his older brother. "Damn right he's dead! Shot down at the creek . . . and likely we're wanted by the law to boot."

Troy, making a fist of one hand and gripping it with the other, held Cole's eyes for a moment. Cole, knowing he was about to ask the critical question, grimly shook his head as part of the answer. "No, we didn't get any money. The bastards that shot him robbed him before they rode off . . . nothing we could do."

"Jesus!" breathed Troy, his fingers going up to press against his temples. "Now what the hell do we do?"

"What do we do?!" screamed Cathy. "You, the great planner! The great thinker! You get us into this unholy mess and now you're asking what we're gonna do! You'd best have a way out of this, you . . ." Cole began to shake her gently, hushing her by pressing her down into a chair.

"Cathy, this is no time to be fussing people out."

"No time to be fussing . . ." she cried, grabbing his hands, pulling his face closer to hers. "Cole, that wretched-looking Indian, Lame Fox, was here tonight, saying we got to leave! Leave quickly! Go west! What's he talking about? Are we in danger?"

It was several minutes before Cathy could be convinced whatever danger they were in, getting panicky only increased it. Still, it was hours before their plight was soberly measured and grimly accepted, and deep anxiety was etching every face when finally, as birds began chirping at a hint of dawn, one by one the Sadlers tried to sleep. But that sunrise, as Cathy lay in Cole's arms, in the small second room of the cabin, she vowed her husband was going to have to choose between this wild-eyed, brash and gallingly domineering brother of his and her.

Henry Quarles was a man of considerable, if well-concealed, power. He controlled a widespread underground organization, assisting slaves struggling northward to freedom. It was risky, taxing work, casualties were expected, but the loss of Crolly once again proved Quarles's conviction that piety was no substitute for prudence, shrewdness, and sound judgement in handling men. The border swarmed with rootless trash, many whiskey-soaked, amoral, dangerous parasites, inured to killing and addicted to the power of the gun. Behind them, and brutally using them, were proslavery Missourians, claiming a mandate to murder any caught abetting the flight of slaves. The border was too long, with too many wild stretches, for effective policing, raids in both directions were common, deaths often at a level that amounted to a state of war. It was not a task for those whose main resource was prayer.

Tom Zacklee, known only as "Lee," Quarles's old but formidable scout, had little trouble following Dennis, and then he and Cole, to their cabin. He was a quiet, taciturn man who had spent most of his life alone in the mountains, but he had uncanny instincts and a tracking ability that made him impossible to lose. Yet he did not get back to Quarles until the following day. By then other sources had informed Quarles the Sadlers, now known to have been assisting Crolly, were slated for murder.

Henry Quarles was not a man easily upset, nor was he above exterminating the whole homicidal Selgany family, if such an act did not draw attention to himself or his work, endangering his mission. Yet, his role was a trying one; every day he faced critical decisions where life and death, not to mention men's freedom, hung in the balance. But he needed those two Sadler boys. The recent incident, tragic as it was, had proven they were acting in good faith, were at least trustworthy, a qualification very few he could reach out to had. Most of his organization was now far to the south, seeking out courageous Negroes, starting them on their way north. But at the moment he had a pressing problem. A small, newly arrived group was holed up only twenty miles from the border, and with Crolly gone no one to spirit it across. He had lost so many slaves to double-dealing "sympathizers," he had become wary of any with southern accents or seemingly drawn chiefly by money. Rewards being posted for escaped slaves had gotten so high, even he, with his financial backing, was finding it difficult to compete. He badly needed those Sadler boys to help him out of his fix. The desperately waiting blacks had only a day or so before their presence at the limestone cave would be discovered and their fate sealed. There were ugly rumors that slave owners were publicly hanging runaways as a warning to those still in bondage.

The following morning he set out for the Sadler cabin, grimly aware no plan he could fit together removed the menacing problem of the Selganys. He wondered what would be a fair price to offer for what he was asking. But

no figure he could manage at the moment seemed
adequate for running the risk of murder. All he had
gathered about these Sadlers, whom he had discovered
came from Indiana, was that they were all fairly young
and one a fetching female whom every man queried
remembered with a smile.

After a few hours' sleep Troy sat over his coffee,
looking at a rude map and gesturing to Cole on how they
could make their way westward toward the Shining
Mountains, with only one temporary stop along the way.
Cole and Cathy sat across from him. Cole, aware Cathy
was deliberately avoiding Troy's eyes and sensing what
was on her mind, decided to broach the issue before she
did. Since awakening he had become aware of a deep if
muted anger stirring in his wife.

"Troy, you know we can't travel without we get some
supplies . . . 'specially some victuals." He shook his
head, affirming their plight. "We need shot, rope, some
cutting tools, and heavy stretches of canvas. We ain't
gonna find those west of here."

Cathy's fingers tapped the table's edge as she unexpectedly spoke up, her eyes still avoiding Troy's. "We're
near out of flour, bacon, even beans . . . you're drinking
the last of our coffee." She finally turned and stared
directly at Troy. "There's only half a cup of salt left and
hardly any honey. What you figuring to eat out yonder,
grass?"

"We can hunt," offered Troy defensively.

"You can hunt, slaughter, and hold it over a dung fire
all you want," said Cathy Jo, her eyes suddenly flaring,
pinning Troy with sudden rage. "Hear it's how them
savages live out there—reckon it fits you!" She turned to
Cole as though Troy's response no longer mattered.
"Don't expect me to live out of a wagon, eating raw meat
while this idiot traipses through mountains he ain't
never seen and ain't sure he can find! Listen, Cole, I'm
frightened enough, hearing what I did last night. Don't
ask me to go out there without some way to live decently
and safely. Right now I wish to God I was back in

Indiana, we've followed this addle-headed fool long enough!"

Cole motioned to Troy to leave them alone. Troy, resentment clouding his face but realizing only Cole could quiet the now furious Cathy Jo, rose and made his way to the door, but Cathy's threat had shaken him. He quickly sensed she was forcing Cole to decide between him and her. Concern tightened his expression as he crossed the yard. Much as his brother respected and appeared devoted to him, he had no hope of winning that battle. Cole would never give up Cathy Jo, no man in his right mind would.

Cathy Jo, her hands gripping the table before her, was declaring she had had enough. Unless Cole came to his senses and started a new life, one that would provide for them better, and offered at least some promise of a future, she wanted to go back to Indiana. Cole, in spite of several attempts, couldn't move or dissuade her. Instead he found himself in a quandary. Without warning she was forcing him to a decision that felt like a crossroad in his life. Young as she was, experience had taught him to take this wife of his seriously. Cathy Jo wasn't given to craft or guile; her pale blue eyes alone testified to the cold import of her words. Internally he was slipping into such a turmoil he actually felt a weird sense of relief when Troy reappeared, saying a fellow named Quarles had arrived. Wouldn't state his business but was anxious to speak with Cole and the still-sleeping Dennis.

Silas Cheatem was a careful, cautious, but still impatient man. All signs pointed to war and he had no intentions of being embroiled in it. He kept thinking about the lush open lands along the river valleys to the west, and intended to be safely settled on his share of that fertile range before any violence broke out. It was part of his religion never to take risks he could avoid. To build a proper and permanent shelter on his claim he needed lumber, lumber that could only come from a sawmill across the border in Missouri. But Missouri was dangerous territory these days, particularly for travelers from Kansas. Getting a wagon with a large load of valuable lumber across the perilous border involved predictable risks. It fitted his style to have someone else run them, and his mind had settled on the Sadler boys, whom he surmised from chance remarks were more than a little eager to raise some cash.

When they hadn't appeared that morning it annoyed him. Being a man constantly conscious of time, he knew, considering what he wanted to accomplish that summer, there was none to waste. As noon drew near he decided he would have to take the river trail again to the Sadler cabin, a move he resented because it made him seem too dependent on them, perhaps putting them in mind of raising their price. But with trees scarce on the plains that lumber was critical; he couldn't go west without it. He also planned to buy the long wagon it was coming in and an extra team of horses. With those costly but vital purchases his final preparations would be complete. Now safely and sensibly equipped, and having the summer season to travel, that all-important first leg of his carefully arranged plan would be taken.

As the cabin came into view he noticed a strange but impressively well-bred stallion tied outside. Apparently they had an important visitor. Well, if the boys were busy, maybe he could chat a while with that curiously shy but luscious Cathy Jo.

Hattie Boggs stood on her toes near the cave's entrance and peered across the wide stretch of tangled growth that ran toward a tiny stream, sunk from sight at the foot of a distant hill. "Dey comin'," she whispered to her husband, Ben, hunkering beside their daughter, Chloe, and looking up at her voice.

"Both of 'em?" he asked in a half whisper.

"Yeah, ah see Skeeter and deres Sam right behind him. Dey bringing water."

"Wonder can we get some food."

"Mebbe dangerous. . . . Don't want to rouse no farm dogs . . . don't want someone findin' tracks."

Ben rubbed his stomach. "We ain't eat for a spell."

"Deys a piece of turnip left, you and Chloe take it."

Ben fetched the small piece of turnip from Hattie's bag and, cutting off a tiny slice, gave the remainder to Chloe.

Chloe, watching her mother, had surprisingly light skin and near Caucasian features. At fifteen she was beginning to fill out, her body already showing the promising curves of womanhood. She was a thoughtful child, not fully comprehending this desperate passage to freedom but acutely aware they were in great danger. The damp smell of the cave had her wondering how long they would remain there. "We going soon?" She spoke quickly, as though speech here had to be held to half a breath.

"Hush, child," said Hattie.

"Now we here, reckon we jus got to wait," advised Ben.

Hattie, glancing at her child, knew they were there because she was determined Chloe was going to live a different life than her mother. When Hattie was Chloe's age the slave owner's grown sons and their friends started forcing her legs open and using her and her sisters for barnyard orgies. She never knew who Chloe's father was, only that he was white and a rapist. That wanton life soon aged her, coarsened her ways, destroyed her budding but still fragile femininity, and soon the abuse stopped. Ben came along a year or two later, after being deliberately separated from his family and sold onto her plantation from somewhere far to the south. He had taken the name of his first owner, Boggs, and after she knew he didn't object to Chloe, and was willing to help make a home for the three of them, took him in. But she had long since decided Ben Boggs was a truly good man, a mate who would follow her anywhere, run any risk for her or Chloe. If folks didn't think Ben was too smart it didn't matter, Hattie reckoned herself smart enough for both of them.

Her two young nephews, Skeeter and Sam, had gone for water. She could see them coming now, furtively slipping through the waist-high grass, aware danger lay in every direction, every snapping twig a possible warning, every bolting rabbit or cawing crow a reason to freeze, all senses quickly attuned. They were serious, hard-working young men, older than Chloe but fond of her and intent that she, like themselves, would reach freedom. It was because of her that the guns they had stolen for their escape had been left behind. Laws had been posted that any Negro caught with firearms was to be executed on the spot . . . recently amended to include all caught in their company.

As evening started to fall, hunger began to claw at them again and Hattie looked at Skeeter, her long, drawn face question enough.

"Ah dunno," he said, studying the terrain they had crossed over for water. "Deys wild turkeys over where yuh see dem hedges run out. Could be dey'll roost a little later."

Sam was quietly surveying the country beside him. "Dis possum country for sure . . . ah knows," he muttered.

"We fixin' to cook some?" queried Ben.

"Ah still gots the flint," muttered Skeeter, worry edging his voice and making it sound stressful. "But jus remember, we gots to be careful fussing wid fire."

"Build it back in duh cave . . . should help," murmured Hattie. For a moment she seemed to be talking to herself, then she reached for Skeeter's arm and pulled him around to face her. "What's on de hill back of here?"

"Ah dunno."

"Reckon we ought to find out?"

"Reckon so."

"Well, git on up there while deys light . . . no sense poking around up dere in duh dark."

Half an hour later Skeeter was back, his face set in a grimace, hard as granite. Everyone saw it was an effort for him to speak, but his message couldn't be withheld. "What d'you find?" asked Sam hurriedly, preparing himself, as were the others, for trouble.

"Ah found a dead fox in a trap. Dey's a trap line quarter mile from here. Fox wasn't dead long. Trap must have bin set dis mornin'. Man who set it got hisself some hunting dogs. Ah could see our jug lying front of dis cave standing on that trap line. We cain't stay here."

There was a long moment of silence before Hattie spoke up. "We cain't leave neither!" she snapped. "Leastways we cain't go far. Dis where they comin' fo us."

Now a long silence took over as the sun continued to drop in the sky, everyone suddenly appearing to forget they were hungry.

Quarles deliberately waited outside for Cole and the awakened Dennis, his hand braced on a tree stump along the far side of the cabin. Dennis swallowed hard at the sight of him, hissing to Cole. "It's him! It's the gent who deviled me at Lawrence!"

Cole, realizing a man with force in mind wouldn't have come alone, approached him with only a curious stare. "Something you wanted!"

Quarles pulled himself erect. "Mr. Cole Sadler, I believe."

"That's me."

Quarles smiled at Dennis, who was standing slightly behind Cole, his eyes still stark. "I've already met your brother."

There was an awkward moment as the men stood facing each other, Cole pointedly waiting for Quarles to go on.

Quarles, quietly clearing his throat and glancing at the cabin as though to assure himself those inside were beyond earshot, said, "I'm sorry for the misfortunes you've encountered assisting Mr. Crolly, it was a terrible experience for both of you, I'm sure. Also I am distressed to hear you were not paid for your services. I'm sure poor Crolly had every intention of keeping his word on that." He paused as though his mind was gearing up for more positive thoughts. "I've been searching for some way to make amends."

"Make amends?" repeated Cole.

"Yes, perhaps enlisting your services again, this time offering a reward sizable enough to make up for your regrettable loss."

Cole looked at him steadily for a moment. "And just who might you be?" he asked coldly.

"Let's say I have assisted Crolly in my own way."

"What way was that?"

"As you can imagine Mr. Crolly's work required considerable funds . . . I helped with those."

Cole shook his head and glanced at Dennis. Then with a grunt he turned back to Quarles, "Mister, if you're here to talk about going back over to Missouri, you've had your trip for nothing."

"I'm sorry to hear that."

"What d'you expect? Whoever killed Crolly ain't likely to stop with him. Our whole family is worried about being murdered. T'aint enough money in the territory to get us to try that again."

Quarles looked like a man gathering strength for some desperate bargaining when his eye caught Cheatem coming up to the lone hitching post to stare admiringly at Quarles's mount. "Who might that gent be?" he asked quietly. It was clear he wasn't anxious to have witnesses to his visiting the Sadlers.

"Just a neighbor," said Cole, turning to catch Silas nodding at him before going to the cabin door. Dennis, though remaining silent while still nervous and squirming around, had spotted Troy watching them intently from a rear window. Dennis, always a little afraid of Troy, was convinced his older brother, with his protruding eyes, could see things others couldn't. At the moment he was sure Troy knew exactly why Quarles was there, even what he wanted. It was the thing that frightened Dennis about Troy, like those wizards in conical hats that kept popping up in stories he read as a child. Troy, without being told, always seemed to know what went on in another's mind.

With Cole and Dennis stepping outside to speak with Quarles, Troy found himself alone again with Cathy Jo. She was about to flounce away to the second room when he stopped her, saying, "Just hell bent on making trouble, ain't you?"

She turned around and stamped her foot. "If getting away from you is making trouble, I ain't denying it!"

"You'll see, Cole's got more sense."

"He hasn't got sense enough to see he and Dennis have been doing all the work, running all the risks, while you squat around here like some critter a little tetched, waiting for a full moon. Could be he's fed up with your daft ideas, could be he figures it's time you risked your own hide. If you're so smart at figuring things out and all, mebbe you could figure out how to get yourself to work . . . take some of these risks . . . make this family a bit of money."

"You got a heap to say, ain't you?"

"You got a heap to hear, and if I was you I'd start doing some listening."

At a dismissive wave of his hand Cathy turned and disappeared in the other room, while Troy settled by the rear window, his eyes quickly fixed on the three men in sober conversation outside. Secretly Cathy's remarks sorely bothered him. He had wanted to go to Missouri with Cole, but Crolly wouldn't hire him, probably thinking Troy, with his outspoken ways and assertive manner, would be too hard to handle. The old man picked Dennis instead. Now, as he watched this stranger called Quarles talking to his brothers, he realized there could only be one reason why a man of his obvious means was visiting a backwoods cabin to talk privately with a family as destitute as the Sadlers. He needed something done, something only people with poor prospects, or poverty pressuring them, were willing to do. It wasn't long before he reasoned that "something" was likely connected with the border and how to get people or possessions unlawfully across. Once again his restless, impetuous, and fatefully venturesome mind began to churn.

Cheatem, met by Troy at the door, was disappointed at not finding Cathy inside, but he stood with his arms crossed, abruptly declaring he had come to query Cole and Dennis about fetching his lumber.

Troy, having trouble hiding his disdain for this testy, ill-mannered visitor, allowed they'd be free in a moment or two. He couldn't bring himself to offer Cheatem a chair and was glad Cathy stayed in her room. There was something sly and oily about this man's ways that made it an effort to be civil to him.

But Cheatem appeared not to notice Troy's lack of civility and launched into gratuitous remarks about his ordering this load of lumber, plus an additional team of draft horses, to prepare himself to head west fully equipped to properly post property lines and permanently settle a claim. His tone, starting casually enough, rose as he warmed to his subject, his hands coming up to slice the air for emphasis, his expressions implying those not following his lead were short on savvy. Troy could only stare at him, saying nothing but curious to know why this irritating braggart always seemed to have life figured out, always seemed ahead of other folks, secretly smiling at the futile efforts of luckless souls like himself. He was glad when Cole and Dennis stomped in, greeting Cheatem without enthusiasm and reaching for what remained in the coffee pot. Troy, suddenly wanting some privacy to think through his disturbing split with Cathy, a rupture that might cost him his favorite brother, Cole, stepped out the door they had just entered to discover Quarles watering his horse at the river. As his mount drank Quarles was looking up, rubbing his forehead and searching the sky like a man beset by a problem that had just taken a turn for the worse.

Troy, gripping his chin, studied the somber figure of Quarles for a few moments and then started strolling toward him.

* * *

Because Silas Cheatem was a obstinate man, used to his own way, it took nearly an hour for Cole and Dennis to convince him they weren't going back across the border, in fact if anything the family was studying traveling as far west of these parts as possible. Because he found himself offering a hundred dollars, twice the figure he had in mind when he arrived, Silas simply couldn't take their refusal seriously. "All you need to do is ride over there and fetch that damn wagon back," he argued. Cheatem knew nothing about Crolly's murder, or their involvement in it, and Cole, not wanting word to spread any faster than necessary, chose not to enlighten him.

With disgust etching his features Cheatem took a sullen step toward the door. "Damn if I can figure it out," he complained. "Thought I'd be doing you folks a favor." Cathy Jo suddenly entered the room and his eyes swung toward her, but the look she gave him discouraged his looking back. "Reckon I'll find plenty others eager to come by such easy cash." He stood in the doorway for a moment, bracing his shoulders, incredulity still distorting his face, then stepping out he slammed the door behind him.

He was starting back, swearing profanely under his breath, when he spotted Troy down the road waving to Quarles who was just riding off. His first impulse was to leave the trail and work his way back through the brush, avoiding Troy. He had had his fill of Sadlers for one day. But he quickly saw Troy was deliberately hurrying toward him, as though he had something pressing on his mind. Within a few moments Cheatem was to discover Troy did have something on his mind, and he was to hear the most agreeable part of it, but in keeping with Troy's talents for scheming, regrettably Silas wasn't to hear it all.

For a fact no one really heard it all. Cole and Dennis stood agape as Troy told them he was going for Cheatem's lumber. Cathy received a cool, wiry smile as he explained he was not afraid of the risks, he had never been seen in Missouri before and was not likely to be connected to Crolly. Lame Fox's warning was for his brothers alone. A hundred dollars was a tidy sum; it would set them up with near everything they needed to move west.

Cole shook his head. "A hundred won't cover it all."

"It will cover plenty," responded Troy.

"You're certain there ain't more to this," remarked Cathy cautiously. She was not sure how she felt about this sudden daring decision of Troy's, but something about it disturbed her. She sensed at once Cole would never let Troy go alone, and was suspicious that Troy had figured that out too. She sat down nettled, still resolved to reach some understanding with her husband, but aware Troy's bold action had complicated matters. Only young Dennis seemed relieved. Knowing Troy he was sure he wouldn't be asked along.

"Reckon we safe here?" Hattie was looking around the grove Skeeter had settled them in, frowning at the sparse brush that didn't quite conceal them all, and a stunted tree that cut off their view in one direction.

"Safe as we gonna get," muttered Skeeter.

"Cain't we find 'nother cave?"

"Cave no good if they come wid dogs . . . only trap us."

"How we gonna know when dat gospel man come lookin' for us?"

"Ah'll be watching."

It was already dark and they had just fed on a small possum Sam caught and cooked, making it sizzle and give forth a high aroma that mixed strangely with the fragrance of a pine forest. They were still hungry but no one dared mention it. Fugitives quickly learned talking about hunger only increases it.

Ben was rubbing his shoulders, feeling the growing chill in the air. "How we fixin' to sleep?"

"Ain't got but two blankets," replied Hattie. "Sam and Skeeter can take one, us three make do with t'other."

"We cain't all stretch out 'n sleep," remarked Sam. "Who's gonna watch?"

Skeeter pointed at him. "You, till middle of duh night. Den ah takes over till mornin'. Figure dat trapper most likely work de trap line sometime 'round dawn." Skeeter was one year older than Sam, a happenstance he used for his edge in rank. But Sam had a growing insurgency in his eyes and was only biding his time.

Chloe nestled down between Ben and Hattie. She was cold and frightened, but she kept remembering Hattie's promise that at a place called Kansas they would find "milk and honey." Now if only that milk was warm and the honey sweet Chloe could endure one more night of breathless hiding and desperate pleading with God for a safe dawning. In spite of endless scares and ceaseless tension, lately she had been spending nights thinking about her body, for her breasts seemed daily more prominent and Sam and Skeeter had started looking away shyly when she raised her skirts to cross a stream or work her way behind Hattie through a swamp. She had always been a little afraid of boys, particularly white ones, but to see her older male cousins looking awkward when parts of her body were accidentally exposed was a new experience. It made her smile a little to herself. She wondered if Hattie also affected men that way.

Now it wasn't Hattie who was awakening her but some premonition that caused her eyes to suddenly open and find Skeeter sitting up, his torso outlined against the faint pink sky of dawn. He seemed to be listening; it made her listen too. Almost at once she heard it. It was very distant, but it was unmistakable. Somewhere along the slope to the east a pack of hounds was racing through the underbrush, their baying seeming to gather strength every time the wind rustled through the leaves above and lowered again. Suddenly they were all awake. No one spoke, but within moments, grasping their blankets and their few belongings, they were hurrying single file behind Skeeter, who had only his knowledge of hill country to offer hope that somewhere beyond those promontories he could see breaching the slope would lie another stream. If not, the fate of runaway slaves, lashings, disfigurement, scorching brands to mar one's face or breast, and even hangings awaited them. For many escapees the prospect of capture gave death, in the spiritual peace of a piney hillside festooned with flowers, irresistible appeal.

Like fungus on a rotting log the Selganys sprung up in a backwater community where the law had suffered a long, unheeded, insidious decay, and like many parasites they and their kind were slowly destroying the rural society which was their host. Some would consider the Selganys not so much evil as amoral; they killed with the detachment of hyenas, they had the attributes without the ritual convictions of ancient assassins. They were ignorant and unwashed, dangerous and devoid of conscience, but they were lethal enemies, making even distant neighbors uneasy. For their own amusement they often killed their victims slowly, in ways that allowed for a ghoulish family competition in marksmanship to liven up their work.

Hap Selgany, the father, had come out of the mountains of Tennessee. His tobacco-stained mouth opened to show three yellow teeth in his upper jaw and four in his lower. None of them connected. He wore overalls that were fouled with the droppings of slaughtered chickens and pigs, mixed with the blood of multiple murders. A slattern woman posed as his wife, but she was known to be simple-minded and addicted to raucous laughter at the deeds of her menfolk. Three sons, from a commonlaw marriage that ended in murder, were as lice-ridden and unkempt as their father. They spent their time messing with guns and drinking home-brewed corn liquor, a concoction Hap bragged could keep the devil from finding his way back to hell. None of the boys married; Hap didn't want females pestering him about lifestyles. Their sex lives, apart from an occasional slave woman who fell into their hands, were confined to derelict Indian squaws, who came by for whiskey, offering themselves in lieu of money.

Their only source of revenue was the violent acts they were paid to commit, acts that even in most lawless lands would have long since brought vigilantes with a rope. But killing abolitionists, and those serving their cause, was hardly a crime in proslavery Missouri.

When Charlie Coyne left the Selgany ramshackle farm, he was relieved to be gone from the smelly surroundings that housed this clan of degenerate slayers. But he was far from content with the sullen way they greeted his request for the Sadlers' extinction. The Selganys survived because they were far more crafty and cunning than many suspected. They were deadly on land of their own choosing, but recent experience had taught them the Kansas side of the border was increasingly hazardous terrain. Their reputation as killers needed no embellishing. They had spilled enough blood to draw the attention of local militias, even high army officers at Fort Leavenworth. Jayhawkers had once set a trap for them which only Hap's nose for trouble enabled them to avoid. They had no illusions about what being captured on Kansas soil would mean. Their position was plainly stated. If the Sadlers crossed over into Missouri the Selganys would see they were vulture bait within the hour, but Coyne would have to say just when and where they would appear.

In spite of the increasing rewards offered they coarsely repeated their condition until Coyne became irritated, incensed, and finally secretly enraged. He was not worried about the Sadlers coming back to Missouri; if they did, he would find ways to eliminate them himself. His problem was elsewhere. His work demanded he be free to come and go in Kansas; spies like himself, pretending indifference on the slave issue, slyly watched for signs of "rescue raids," as the northern press now dubbed slave stealing. It was a vital key to their success. He was presently flushed with the reward money he had collected from the Missouri authorities for Crolly's hapless slaves. The work certainly paid well and the risk to himself should have been nil. But a disquieting fear nagged him. Those Sadler boys had seen him with the Crolly party, surely they knew now he had disappeared with the slaves, leaving Crolly's dead body behind. His work depended on avoiding any suspicion in Kansas, but, with both brothers able to identify him, any chance encounter would prove fatal. One way or the other Cole and Dennis Sadler had to be removed, and of all the ways possible only one could quiet the fears of Charlie Coyne.

Henry Quarles had ample reason to be worried about Troy. The man seemed quietly troubled, anxious, even a trifle desperate. But Quarles was in dire straits himself. His escaping Negroes would not be safe at that cave for long. As of now he didn't even have a plan. Troy assured him he could bring them out, apparently having a scheme he was not prepared to divulge. He was disturbed at the frog-eyed Troy's open interest in money, but since he was satisfied with Cole and Dennis's character, decided he would break a discretionary rule and take Troy on.

But their hasty pact was still riddled with problems. Troy had to make contact with the slaves and knowing the location of that cave might not be enough. Escapees had abandoned that sanctuary in the past, and valuable time was lost tracking them down in the surrounding countryside. Such work was dangerous beyond belief, for the risk of discovery mounted by the hour. He shook his head gravely, wondering what this venture was finally going to cost him, besides the two hundred dollars he had promised Troy.

Silas Cheatem, though relieved to find Troy willing to go for his lumber, was still rankled by Cole and Dennis's refusal of his offer. Damn strange family! When the required wagon came he'd be wise to get shut of them.

Curiously he saw nothing strange about Troy wanting a fifty-dollar advance on the hundred promised; to his mind it made the agreement binding. He was only bothered by Troy's insistence on waiting a day or two before starting. Yet things became a lot clearer the following morning when he saw Troy and Cole riding toward town. It confirmed his long-standing suspicion that the Sadlers were broke and the fifty dollars was for vital supplies that couldn't wait for Troy's return. He wondered how such a destitute family could attract and hold a desirable woman like Cathy Jo. Surely a man like himself could provide for her better. One day, when poverty and the unrelenting rigors of this raw country brought her to her senses, she might begin to realize it.

Breathless, nearing exhaustion, but spurred on by fear, the little group, following Skeeter's lead, finally struck a stream running down toward the valley floor. Skeeter quickly led them into the water, turning about to watch Sam rolling the two blankets together. There was no need to talk. Ways of throwing dogs off their trail, and other means by which escapees survived, had been drilled into them long before they left home. With a nod to Sam, Skeeter led the others upstream while Sam, the blankets over his shoulder, started racing down. Upon reaching the nearby valley floor, Sam emerged from the water and, dragging the blankets behind him, began to crawl through the heaviest brush he could find. Thorns and nettles tore at his skin, and branches whipping back stung his face and arms, but doggedly he drove himself forward, often on his hands and knees. It wasn't until he had covered almost half a mile that he began to circle, working his way back to the heaviest thicket he had come through. There he crawled into the middle, stood up, put the blankets on his head, and in a series of jumps made his way to the nearest tree. By swinging from its lower limbs he managed to cover over twenty feet without touching the ground, then he dropped off and raced to where he reckoned the stream could be found again. Once in the water he was careful to step on rocks just below the rippling surface until he found a limb reaching over the stream's edge. Here he swung himself as far up the bank as he could.

Then, almost paralyzed by fatigue, he slumped in a small hollow and, burying his head in the crux of his arm, he began to sob and pray at the same time.

High up the slope Skeeter kept going until he was sure he had traveled further than Sam. Trackers, coming to the stream, would follow it in both directions until the dogs picked up the scent again, then they would unite and continue their pursuit. Luckily after a draining climb they came upon an old willow collapsed over the stream. Skeeter climbed into it and pulled Hattie and Chloe up behind him. Ben managed to get one leg up and with Hattie's help crawled along the splintered trunk to the bank. They made it to a small clearing in heavy brush just before the distant yelp of dogs signaled their worst fears were about to be realized. Skeeter looked about helplessly, there was nothing more he could do. After a few moments they looked at each other, then joined hands, settling on their knees as their husky voices followed Hattie's in a short prayer. Hattie finished by wiping her eyes, hugging Chloe and pleading skyward, whispering to the angels to protect this little group of sinners and remind the Savior to keep a merciful eye on Sam.

Jeb Slaughter was a trapper whose livelihood was disappearing before his eyes. The land was being claimed, farmed, fenced; wild game was growing scarce. He knew this would be his last season. He had taken the fox pelt, which was still in fair condition, but too many of his traps were catching only skunks and possums, which were worth little, or a rare coyote, which was worth less. The dogs romped about him, nipping at each other or speeding off to explore rabbit or woodchuck trails. They were hardly worth their feed anymore, although being hounds they would track down enough game to feed themselves if one day he had to turn them loose. For the last few seasons they had been good only for treeing bears, bobcats, or even pumas. Those pelts were still worth taking and once the animal was treed a well-placed bullet made them his. But the land was getting crowded, wildlife was dying out. He would soon have to find other work.

After years of trapping his ears were well attuned to his dogs. He knew when they were after valuable game, something about their baying that was different from the yips and barks that marked their play or racing rabbits to a hutch. So, suddenly hearing them on the slope above, sounding excited and beginning to bay in unison, he scrambled up after them and began to follow their lead. It was several minutes, going mostly uphill, before he realized the dogs had stopped somewhere ahead and were milling about. Finally reaching them he discovered they were smelling the ground where the foliage lay flat as though bodies had been lying on it. Closer study turned up tiny ashes, spread by someone trying to remove traces of a small fire. The last revealing bit of evidence was the viscera of a small possum. Slaughter, after years of tracking in the wild, needed little more. He had tripped over the trail of someone trying to keep their presence secret. In this country that someone was almost sure to be escaping slaves. For a moment he looked undecided, but a man losing his livelihood is alert to chance sources of income. There was always a bounty for capturing and returning escaped slaves, sometimes a considerable one. He had his hunting rifle and a pistol, and had heard Negroes were not allowed to carry arms. He studied the ground for a moment, there were at least three here and maybe as many as five. That many could bring him a fairly tidy sum. He took his lead dog and led him around the outskirts of the recent campsite. On the second circle the dog lunged away from him and, with his nose to the ground, started running along the slope. He had picked up the departing trail.

Slaughter grinned to himself. If a puma couldn't fool these dogs what chance would slaves, unarmed and strangers to this country, really have?

* * *

Henry Quarles had no way of knowing the postmaster, who spent his early evenings gossiping at the local barber shop, had inadvertently linked his name to Crolly. Such sociable palaver normally did little harm, but in a town like Lawrence it sped through a covert communication system that, by the following day, reached the vigilant ears of Charlie Coyne.

With Cole and Dennis still above ground, Coyne wasn't about to enter Lawrence, but he arranged for a few shadowy mercenaries to do his bidding, and by sundown they reported Cole had been in town with his older brother, Troy, and while Cole shopped for supplies Troy had been spotted in the back of a restaurant having coffee with Quarles.

Promising him an additional bonus, Coyne induced one of his henchmen to track Troy Sadler and report his next move. With his talent for sensing what was in the wind Charlie Coyne smelled the imminence of a fast-forming plot. The right signs were all there. He had stolen the money meant for the Sadler boys from Crolly's body. Quarles was likely the one staking Crolly and was now offering to make amends. Could it mean another try at spiriting slaves across the border? It was more than a reasonable possibility. He mused about it for a moment, then smiled to himself. Maybe things were starting to break his way. He had better get back to the Selganys and start making some plans of his own!

6

Jeb Slaughter followed his dogs to the stream and stopped there to look up and down the slope. Had he been tracking a puma, with its catlike intelligence, it would have likely turned uphill, making it harder to follow, but almost all other animals pursued would be drawn to the heavier foliage of the valley floor for cover. Man was no exception. Jeb started the dogs downhill. After only a few hundred yards he was rewarded. The dogs raced up the opposite bank of the small stream, entering heavy brush and deep thickets where they scraped along the ground, replacing each other as leader and following a scent so strong the dullest among them ran without wavering. Jeb couldn't keep up; he had to circle one patch of heavy undergrowth after the other, the dogs leaving him further behind each time. But his suspicions were gradually rising. Five people rushing through such heavy growth would have left a visible trail of broken limbs and trampled vines. Whoever left that trail was alone and scrambling for long stretches on his hands and knees.

When he heard the dogs circling and working back to a short distance from where he stood, he realized he had been outfoxed. The dogs were stopped in a heavy thicket, yipping and whining, confused that the trail had petered out. A single person had led him astray while the others managed to conceal themselves somewhere on the wild slope. Growing angry at being duped he took his dogs back to the water and followed it upstream, but if the others escaped that way, slipping out of the water higher up, his dogs failed to discover where.

Yet anger only made him more determined. He was sure these fugitives were somewhere close by; what he needed was a little help. Luckily he knew where to get it. After all, reporting their whereabouts, if they were finally caught, would still entitle him to a slice of the reward.

Quarles watched Troy and Cole riding off with deep misgivings. By now he knew Troy was returning with a large wagonload of lumber, and had surmised Troy's plan was to try and bring out the escaping slaves concealed in it. Incredibly his brother Cole had not yet been told about the Negroes waiting at the cave, Troy saying Cole would accept this news better once they were headed home. Quarles stood whistling lowly to himself as a rare sign he was nervous. Memories of Crolly refusing to hire Troy troubled him. Crolly had felt the man was too full of fanciful notions, snap judgements, and pointless indiscretions. But now the fat was in the fire; he could only pray for luck.

Yet Quarles was not a man who felt comfortable leaving things to luck. He had decided to take a serious step, risking one of his most valuable assets to insure, if possible, the success of this chancy venture. After looping one stirrup over his saddle horn, a signal to his secret scout, Lee, that they had to meet, he waited until he saw the other glancing from across the street, then left for an abandoned stable north of town. Both were careful never to address each other in public; it was vital no one ever suspect a link between them. Lee was Quarles's eyes and ears throughout the whole state of Missouri, and even beyond, where his growing organization was slowly penetrating. Lee was more important than any local leader, such as Crolly, usually responsible for only one leg of an escape route. But Lee's value depended upon his obscurity. Once a connection was drawn between him and Quarles, not only would his life be in danger but his value, as an agent, free to travel anywhere without suspicion, would cease.

Lee listened quietly as Quarles explained the facts surrounding this hazard-ridden rescue mission, his attentive hazel eyes not quite concealing a veteran's distaste for projects thrown together in haste, and hanging on the untested abilities of cocky amateurs. But Lee never questioned his assignments, for he was a dutiful servant whose only requirement was that he be allowed to do things his way. Since he excelled at his work Quarles was more than glad to make such a concession, knowing a more dependent man would have increased his own burden, and once alone in the field be worth far less.

Once informed of the problem Lee hardly needed Quarles to instruct him; it was evident the danger lay in the fugitives not being found at the cave. For a thousand reasons they may have had to seek cover in the sur-

rounding countryside. But failing to make contact with
the Sadlers, they were as good as lost.

Lee shrugged and said he had better leave at once.
Quarles shook his hand firmly, warning him not to take
any chances that might compromise his role in their
work. It was a hard truth that both avoided voicing, but
since the risks they faced matched the risks of combat-
ants in war, each understood Lee's anonymity was
critical. It had to be preserved even at the sacrifice of
some fugitives.

Cole was riding alongside Troy puzzled at his
brother's silence, wondering why Troy disappeared
briefly in town, and starting to feel this new mysterious
air surrounding matters smacked of trouble. It was all he
could do to convince Cathy Jo this trip for lumber
carried only minimal risks and would bring badly
needed money. After listening to him refusing Cheatem
she knew he was deceiving her, was going only because
of Troy, an obvious truth that rankled her more than any
lie. He knew he was in serious trouble with Cathy. She
intended to bring her claim on him, subtly contested by
Troy, to a head. Like many easygoing men, who consider
problems between wives and male companions largely
imaginary or based upon unfortunate or wrong impressions, he found it difficult to deal with a problem he
didn't believe existed. But Cathy was in dead earnest,
she wanted an answer, warning she would be waiting for
one when he returned.

He rode along, troubled in ways he couldn't articulate,
grappling with the emotional needs of a woman measuring her mate's love. He was suffering the deep uneasiness
disputes with Cathy always stirred in him. It affected his
whole outlook. The day now had a contrary feel about it;
the squinting of Troy's eyes hinted that his brother had
more than lumber on his mind. He was in Missouri now,
a place he swore he'd never return to, but so distracted
was Cole by his worries that the precautions common
sense should have demanded be taken were partially
and, as the day wore on, then totally ignored.

The trip had taken all that day and both were relieved

when, after the irksome and stressful ride, they sighted
the sawmill which, following Cheatem's directions, they
finally found on the Blue Springs road.

That same evening Jeb Slaughter bounded into the
sheriff's office at Blue Springs, his excited announcement
quickly arousing two sleepy deputies, before traveling
next door to pull the sheriff's boot from its favorite perch
on a crowded bar. Before dawn a posse of ten had been
assembled for a manhunt, which was becoming a fixture
of life in Jackson County and its environs.

By sunrise the following morning the posse was already on the stream where Slaughter lost the trail and, at
the sheriff's hurried signaling, began to fan out. Slaughter had left his dogs in town, though not by choice. The
sheriff kept two uncommonly savage wolfhounds, used
for tracking and sometimes fatally attacking escaped
prisoners. These beasts would not tolerate other dogs
and destroyed any they managed to reach with their
massive jaws. Everyone except the sheriff was uneasy
around these killers, as all knew they had once torn an
escaping youth apart.

After an hour or so the search for fresh tracks proved
fruitless. The sun was gathering strength, making the
moist air of the valley uncomfortable. The sheriff, growing fidgety, began to reason the fugitives were surely
headed for the border. But for slaves, bent on escaping,
the border was a dangerous place. They would need help
to get across it safely. The sheriff was well aware escape
paths, set up by abolitionists and their sympathizers, ran
through his county. He had killed two Ohio traders
caught in this felonious activity last year. As he pieced
this situation together, Slaughter had simply chanced
upon some escapees waiting for a guide to see them
across to Kansas. Well, he would stake out the surrounding countryside; any strangers showing up would be
taken into custody and questioned. Those without satisfactory answers could try his jail. His jail had a way of
making people talk, making them repentant, often making them limp or suffer severe headaches for months to
come.

He sent his men out a few miles in every direction, telling them to carefully scout back roads and little used trails. He reckoned them to be about eight or nine miles southwest of Blue Springs, wild enough country but still easily crossed for one familiar with the terrain.

Two restless hours passed as Slaughter and the sheriff made conversation and stared up at the silent rolling slopes. Then near noon a wind came alive in the tree-tops, causing a scent of rain to drift down. Suddenly one of the men came galloping back, crying out a wagonload of lumber was moving westward on a overgrown dirt road a mile or two to the north. There was a moment of silence before the sheriff, spitting out a wad of tobacco and calmly digging in his pocket for another plug, turned to Slaughter. "Don't sound too likely," he muttered, leisurely scratching his underarm, "but you never can tell. Best we go have a look!"

Cole first realized how careless he had been when he caught the sawmill owner staring at the rifle he carried. It was a "Beecher's bible," an army issue abolitionists purchased in Massachusetts and smuggled into Kansas for use in their struggle against proslavers. It had been given to him by Crolly, but it was a gun that for the right eyes marked a man. The mill owner said nothing but his expression kept shifting between curiosity, concern, and doubt. The smile that accompanied his "Howdy" soon slipped away, replaced by a more unsettling expression. "Cheatem, you say? Yeah, we got that order all ready to go."

"Reckon you could show us where we can find that team and wagon," suggested Troy. "We'll be leaving in the morning, right early." The sale, having been arranged by mail, left only handing over the bank draft Cheatem had sent along to complete. But, this done, Cole still felt something was left hanging in the air. He expected the man to say where they could get some grub and spend the night, they needed both food and sleep, but the owner simply studied the bank draft, pocketed it, then turned and pointed to the other end of the yard.

"Wagon is over there, that long one fully loaded. The team is stabled in that big shed on yer left. Leave any time you're ready."

"Can we get some grub around here?" said Cole, his voice just tight enough to mark a suppressed irritation. "We ain't ate since morning." His eyes swept the yard. "Need a place to bed down too."

"Shack down the road a piece, sells victuals," replied the owner. "Back of that shed there's a stable, got a heap of hay in there . . . 'bout all I can offer."

The brothers exchanged glances and started away. Cole couldn't resist saying, "Didn't figure to trouble you any, sir. Always nice doing business with right friendly people."

The owner studied them for a moment, uncertainty still clouding his eyes. "In this country, partner, you'd best be careful who you call friend." Mumbling to himself, he turned away.

Before dawn the next morning they were on the road, Troy handling the wagon and Cole riding alongside. But after two or three miles Troy hurriedly pulled the wagon into some heavy brush and jumped down. Cole, coming up, thought something happened to the team. "Trouble?" he asked.

"No, but we got to shift this lumber around."

Cole's eyes widened and then blinked in surprise. "What d'you mean 'shift the lumber around'? What the hell is wrong with the way it is?"

"We've got to fix an empty space in the middle. One big enough to hide a few folks."

Cole dismounted and came over to stand eyeball to eyeball with his brother. "Troy, what in Christ's name are you jabbing about? You gone loco or something?"

"If you'll just help me I'll explain everything."

"Explain what?!" Cole stepped back and seized the front of his jacket. "Troy, what in God's name are you up to anyway?"

"We're gonna make two hundred dollars."

"Two hundred dollars! For what?"

"Getting some folks over the border."

"Slaves?"

"Only ones they'll pay for."

Cole's face turned three shades whiter. "You idiot! You wanna get us killed?"

"If you'll help me we'll be home tomorrow rich enough to go west in style. We can buy enough to make even Cathy Jo happy."

Cole sank back against the wagon, one hand coming up to hold his forehead like a man whose brain needs stimulating to deal with another thought. "You . . . you bastard, why didn't you tell me all this before we left?"

"Wasn't sure you'd come."

"I damn well wouldn't have!"

"Well, we're here now. Might as well make the best of it."

Cole turned and struck the wagon with his fist. "Damn if Cathy Jo isn't right about you. You're a sure enough Jonah, a stupid jackass, full of crazy ideas that spell nothing but trouble."

"We're wasting time."

"I've got half a mind to leave you here to wiggle your own way out of this fix alone." Cole's mind was urging him to ride off. His brother had trapped him in this ridiculous and perilous scheme, and, knowing what he did about border crossings, he could already feel disaster descending. But his heart refused to join in. Furious as he was he couldn't leave his brother to face danger and perhaps death alone. That he simply couldn't do and deep in his gut he knew it.

Trouble was Troy knew it too.

Lee knew where the cave was but he was careful not to get too close. He watched it from a distance till he realized it was unoccupied, the escapees had left. Though they couldn't have gone far, they might still be hard to find. Knowing there was no telling what direction they had taken, he wisely worked eastward first. The country seemed quiet and he was not concerned until he spotted riders in the distance, armed men who seemed to be patrolling along roads and trails, causing them to

rise up then drop from sight again in the rolling countryside. He could hardly have come upon a more ominous
sign. Getting as close as he could he pulled himself up
into a towering oak and, crouching behind its massive
trunk, spotted a wagon coming in the far distance, and
riders beginning to gather on the road before it. In this
wild country that wagon was almost bound to be the
rescue one, but the slaves could not yet be aboard, for it
was still several miles east of the contact point. This was
going to be far more difficult and dangerous than he
thought.

Charlie Coyne had not been idle. He didn't know the
whole story but he knew enough. For reasons not yet
clear Cole Sadler had ridden back into Missouri, this
time with his brother Troy. This was damnable luck, for
it left young Dennis still loose to identify him as a
murderer. Still, he wasn't going to miss a chance to
eliminate Cole; only one thing was making him hesitate.
He had heard Cole had a reputation as a gun hand and
that made him nervous. Like Cheatem, Charlie Coyne
never took risks he could pay others to take for him.
That explained why, after a hurried ride, he found
himself drinking their harsh corn whiskey and making a
sinister deal with the Selganys.

Darkness was descending again and they had moved
deep into a heavy stand of pine, pushing the brown
needles together for resting places and urging each other
to silence. Hattie was chewing on the last of a rabbit leg,

food taken from a feeding hawk Sam saw plunging for its kill. There had only been a bite or two for the five of them and all were beginning to feel weak from hunger.

That morning they had heard the dogs baying below on the slope, heard them circling and then finally losing the trail. For a while they thought the danger of discovery was over, only Hattie doubted it. "Dey not finished," she whispered, hugging Chloe. "Dey know we somewheres. Dey be back."

With the use of bird call signals they had made up and used as boys, Skeeter was able to guide Sam back to the group, but Sam came in cut and scratched in a thousand places, his face drawn with fatigue. Old Ben started saying they ought to be moving north or west, trying to get out of Missouri, but Hattie reminded him they had to walk, not knowing what they might stumble into and running the risk of chance travelers or even stray farm dogs picking up their trail again. "We gots to stick by dat cave . . . till help come by."

"What if it don't come?" grunted Skeeter.

"It'll come!" snapped Hattie, hugging Chloe closer.

"Why you so sure?"

"Cause we is righteous and de Lord is a'watching over us."

Skeeter looked away, he had listened to enough preachers while growing up to be convinced the Lord favored the righteous, but if that was so his record for trouble made it clear he wasn't righteous enough.

Skeeter was up before dawn, scouting down the slope, looking for a vantage point from which they could watch the cave entrance while remaining out of sight. An hour of quietly slipping through long stretches of vine-covered hardwood trees and tall outcroppings of rock was finally rewarded. He found a spot where the cave and the plain before it were in full view, while he could not be seen from twenty feet away. Dawn was breaking and he decided it was time to get back to the others and tell them what he'd discovered. As light started breaking over the countryside he decided to take one last look, and in that unexpected moment his breath stopped in his throat and his heart skipped a beat. There coming

across the distant field was a posse of men riding along
the foot of the slope and spreading out as they approached the vicinity of the stream.

Restacking the many cuts of lumber proved hard
work, made more difficult for Cole by a seething anger
he could not dispel. Like most of Troy's ideas a hidden
space sounded simple in concept but floundered on the
fallacies of his structural notions. The lumber had to be
stacked so it concealed a hollow space but looked
normally piled. Only the size of the hidden space escaped violent discussion, the obvious limitations even
this long wagon placed upon concealed compartments
left a hole Cole felt ridiculously small, especially when
he heard it was for five people. "Better hope they're
midgets," he said sardonically; even in the morning cool
he had long been sweating profusely.

Troy pulled a final splinter from his hand. "It's gonna
have to do." He breathed heavily. "We just got to get
moving."

Cole went to remount his horse. "You know where the
hell you're going?"

"Got it committed to memory. Shouldn't be no
problem."

"You'd tell a man shot between the eyes he had no
problem. When you gonna wake up and realize we're in
God Almighty trouble." He brought his horse around to
where the wagon was righting itself on the road. "How
far we got to go?"

"A piece. Figure we should be there 'bout noon."

"Noon?" Cole rubbed the remaining sweat from his
brow. "Christ! That's five hours!"

"This wagon can't move no faster."

Cole shook his head in disbelief, a reaction which
visibly added to his disgust. Spitting dust from his
mouth he turned newly infuriated eyes on his brother.
"And just how far is this goddamn place from the
border—a week?!"

Troy waved a deprecating hand. "Don't get to fussing.
You'll see . . . won't be no problem."

* * *

Lee sensed an increasing urgency to find the missing fugitives. What he had glimpsed in the distance was surely a search party, meaning their presence was known. In this wild country they could hide for a while, but in a day or two hunger, accidental tracks, or an attempt to reach the border on their own would be their undoing. His first move, as an experienced tracker, was to put himself in the quarry's position. Escaping slaves could be counted on to follow instructions as long as possible. He had often seen them improve upon directions but only in emergencies did they violate them. Lee assumed they would not go far from the mouth of that cave; somehow they would keep it in sight. It was their only hope of contacting their next guide to freedom.

With his trained eye he made a great arc around the slope, leaving the cave site as its center and noticing a few landmarks to guide his search. Then, leaving his horse hobbled, he slipped off, hurriedly moving upward from one point of scrutiny to the next, until he was high on the slope. There the cave site dropped out of sight. Then he descended the slope until it was visible again. Now cautiously watching the heavy growth beneath him, he moved slowly along its arc. A half hour passed as he crept from one point to another, holding for a moment at each to detect movement rather than form. Finally he was rewarded. He saw something moving at the edge of a stand of pines. He studied it for a moment before finally realizing it was the head of a woman moving away from some bushes and quickly disappearing among the thick grove of conifers. Breathing a sigh of relief he began to scramble down the slope after her.

Hattie never dreamed going to relieve herself in the bushes would lead Lee to their hiding place, but after her fright at seeing him coming behind her, and then discovering who he was, she thanked the Lord for giving her the urge to go.

Lee had no time to waste on getting acquainted. Skeeter and Sam, once over their initial shock at finding him standing a few feet from their campsite, bent over the map he was drawing on the ground. They were told they had to get to a trail a mile or two to the north, follow it east for roughly two miles and wait there, concealed as best they could, until a wagon loaded with lumber appeared.

Skeeter complained that there were men down below searching for them, going in that direction now was bound to get them caught. Lee patiently explained they didn't have a choice, they had to make contact with that wagon which was already coming in the distance. He had seen the men mentioned and though they might delay the wagon this wasn't sure, and if they did there was no way to tell for how long.

"What if we don't git dere?" pleaded Skeeter.

"The driver's been told to wait at that spot if he can, but with a sheriff and a posse watching he sure can't wait long."

"We sure enough gonna git caught," groaned Sam.

"If you stay here sooner or later you sure will," warned Lee. He stood up and looked at the sky. Rain clouds had suddenly appeared and the heat of the sun had fallen off. "Best you get going, I'll see what I can do about that posse."

Chloe put her hand on Lee's arm. "We ever gonna git to dis freedom place?" she asked, her voice rising with a slight tremble.

Hattie turned to exclaim, "Ah done told you, de Lord gonna see to that!"

Lee looked at Chloe and managed a smile. "We're going to give the Lord all the help we can."

Chloe put a second hand on his arm and continued to stare at him. "You think de Lord really trying to help us poor folks?" she asked.

Lee looked stomped for a moment, but then he glanced upward and managed another smile. "He's fixing to send us rain, ain't He?"

Cole saw the rain threatening too, just before he sighted riders gathering on the trail ahead. Cole was sure any encounter this side of the border was dangerous, but an encounter with unknown armed men in this desolate stretch carried a special peril. He caught Troy's eye and pointed ahead. Troy, peering over the horses, licked his lips before drawing them into a firm line across his face. "Trouble you figure?"

"You wouldn't like what I figure."

"So far we're just delivering some lumber."

"Suppose they don't believe it." He looked about himself quickly. "Suppose someone recognizes me?" Then, with a start, he saw it! That damn rifle that had raised the sawmill owner's curiosity was still stuck in his saddle scabbard, the Beecher's bible that in these parts could well get him hanged. He pulled his horse around back of the wagon, he had only half a minute to dispose of it before his action would be noticed by the men coming on. He pulled abreast of the spot where the hidden space lay. Reaching over he worked it between two slabs of heavy wood and let it slide inside. He managed to get back in front just as the first rider came up.

"Howdy," he said, noticing the first rider waited until the one behind him came up before responding.

"Just where you headed, partner?" For some reason the stranger, though halting by Cole, directed his question to Troy.

"We're taking this lumber west a ways," said Troy, tying the reins around the whip socket.

The second rider, followed by two savage-looking dogs that came to sniff at the wagon wheels before staring up at Troy, grunted as he shifted the wad of tobacco he was chewing. "Where you from?"

"Outside of Lawrence."

"Where'd that lumber come from?"

Troy told him about the sawmill on the Blue Springs road and got a quick nod in return. Then the gruff figure, that both could see now was wearing a sheriff's star, rode around the wagon and came back to stop, this time beside Cole. "See any niggers hereabouts?"

"Nary a one."

"Figure some runaways hiding out in these parts. Keep an eye out, they likely making for the border."

"We got no truck with niggers," piped Troy from the wagon seat.

The sheriff gave him a searching look, saying pointedly, "Best you don't. Best you get back to Kansas." The sheriff's mouth was slightly pursed as though something was bothering him but he wasn't sure what. "Surprised you come this far south," he muttered. "Most folks would have used the river road, a sight easier going."

"We new to these parts," explained Troy. "Next time we'll know better."

The sheriff's expression cast doubts on the wisdom of there being a next time, but, though looking like a man anything but satisfied with this encounter, he waved them on. They were over a hundred yards down the trail before the sheriff, still gazing after them, remarked, "That story don't hardly fit my liking, best we keep them in sight for a spell."

Charlie Coyne, edgy as an antelope with fire in the wind, had been receiving information from local informants all day. Alerted and anxious for the cash he was dispensing, they quickly helped him fill in the picture. He already knew the Sadlers had left the sawmill with a load of lumber, apparently heading back to Kansas. He had also heard there were runaway slaves reported in the hilly country south of the river road. He had been putting these facts together and was about to advise the Selganys where they could find and attack the Sadlers on Missouri soil. Hap, who made all the family decisions, listened to him and finally agreed. But with loaded wagons, he argued, traveling slowly, it would be almost sundown before they got close to the border. Sundown was his favorite time for an ambush. They would need maybe an hour or so to determine exactly how the Sadlers were coming across. The rest would be ridiculously easy.

Coyne doled out the largest payment he'd ever made for evil in his life, and Hap responded by fetching a fresh jug and pouring generous drinks all around. Knowing the country well but realizing they had a ways to go, the

Selganys saddled up in the early afternoon and, with
Coyne trailing along behind, were soon galloping west
toward the Kansas border, passing on the way the hill
country where escaping slaves, each carrying a cash
bounty that kept creeping into Coyne's mind, had been
reported.

8

Back at his horse Lee figured it would take the best part
of an hour for the fugitives to reach the contact point,
but he could see the wagon still had a distance to go,
although it seemed to be pulling away from the mounted
men. He had hoped the posse, once allowing the wagon
to go through, would turn to continue their search
further afield, but ominously they strung out, keeping
the wagon in sight as they drifted along both sides of the
trail. This was going to spell disaster. Somehow that
posse had to be decoyed away from the wagon or the
escapees were lost. He could ride out there, fire a few
shots, then hightail it into the heavy woods on the slope,
hoping to lose them in rough country. But he had been
solemnly warned against putting himself in jeopardy.
Quarles had pounded into him that his loss to the
organization would be a setback that would take a year
to recover from. For a moment his mind was torn with
indecision, but Tom Zacklee could never stand indecision. He began to move back to the foot of the slope,
giving the approaching line of posse men plenty of room
to ride by on his left. He watched them moving through
the tall grass, apparently matching a similar line across
the trail. He was almost close enough to see their

expressions, which appeared to be intent, watchful, like men grimly expectant. There was little doubt suspicions had been raised, and that now the wagon was a moving trap, a lure that would draw the fugitives, thinking it their only hope.

Deep in a stand of brush and absorbed by the tragedy he saw forming before him, he was almost thrown from his mount as his horse suddenly reared back wildly, flailing its hoofs in the air and plunging away in fright. Unbelievably, a massive dog hidden by the long grass had lunged up to attack him in the saddle. Only his experience with wounded grizzlies in his mountain days saved him. He pulled his pistol without thinking and fired twice at the dog's head; the beast dropped back whining as the horse shied away. But it was not over. A second huge dog came charging through the heavy brush, its great jaws open, drooling whitish saliva. This one he shot in midair. As it fell he pumped another round into its protruding rib cage. But there was no time to catch his breath or steady himself; he swung the horse around and drove his spurs into its flanks. No one needed to tell him the posse was already racing toward him. After all his precautions, by missing the presence of those dogs in the long grass he had managed to betray himself.

Hattie was the first to hear the shots ringing out. She was keeping Chloe in front of her as they hurried behind Skeeter. She turned to Ben, who was following her. "Lordy, dey coming," she rasped.

Sam, who was behind Ben, looked down the slope. "Dats too far away to be shootin' at us," he replied quickly. "Keep going."

Skeeter, who had hesitated at the shots, now held his hand up. "Hold on . . . deys horses running up yonder . . . could be some fighting."

Sam moved up from the rear. He listened for a moment. "Dey goin' by . . . best we keep going . . . we ain't got dat much time."

Skeeter looked dubious, uncertain, but he started

ahead again. "Keep up," he breathed back at them. "Pretty soon we gots to go down to dat trail."

Cole rode along beside the wagon muttering to himself. Only a fool would think they had convinced the sheriff. He didn't bother looking back to see if they were being followed. He didn't have to. He saw Troy glancing over his shoulder and knew from his brother's troubled expression that they were; not obviously, of course, but cautiously from a distance, as though waiting for something to happen. If the fugitives were to show any time soon their fate was sealed. How he and Troy would fare was not pleasant thinking either, and he was becoming convinced they had to abandon the wagon and start racing for the border. Troy's saddle horse was still tied to the rear of the wagon, and, taking advantage of a deep bend in the trail they could manage a fair head start on the posse.

He was about to tell Troy their luck had run out, it was time to race for salvation before the fugitives appeared and put it out of reach. He had just started to speak when shots rang out, making him hold his breath and rise up in the saddle. In the distance he could see the posse heading for the slope. He decided at once the escapees had been spotted and were being pursued. Afoot their capture was almost certain. Troy, still looking confused, but relieved at the posse disappearing, rapped the team with the reins and hurried the wagon down the trail. Troy knew about the cave but was told at any sign of trouble to pass it by. Instead he was to watch for a deep gully on the left-hand side of the road, only a mile or two beyond the cave. At every depression he spotted alongside the trail he stood up in the wagon and peered into it. Yet it was almost a quarter of an hour before he came to a heavy grove blocking that side of the trail; just inside its rim was a deep washout. This depression was only visible when he leaned over from the wagon seat, but while peering into its recess he thought he saw a face. A second, more intense look and he knew he saw a face, young, anxious, and black.

* * *

Lee started driving his horse up the slope, knowing he had stupidly gotten too close to that posse. That he still had a reasonably good chance of escaping did not ease the fact that he had opened the door to tragedy. All he needed now was for his horse to step into a gopher hole and himself to fall into the hands of Missouri authorities. He would be faced with questions that even if answered safely would make his face known, his activities suspect, and his value to Quarles near zero.

He could always pay for the dogs and, as long as he stayed away from the runaways, his presence there might be explained as accidental, but the thought of those fugitives put him in mind of something else. If he turned east, the most dangerous direction, he could at least pull that posse away from the contact spot. It was a tempting if risky thought. He would have liked to think it through but there was no time; hoofbeats were mounting behind him. He stopped for a moment, rose up in the saddle, and saw wild country stretching for miles in undulating waves to the east. As he hung there a vagrant raindrop came down the wind and lightly pelted his cheek. It triggered a cryptic grin that revamped one side of his face and left him slapping his knee as he swung his mount about and raced off in that direction.

Skeeter was the first one out of the washout, followed by Hattie, Chloe, and Ben. Sam lingered a moment, studying the two white men, then cautiously followed. Troy was already out of the seat, climbing the wagon, heaving the top boards off the hiding place. "Come on!" he said. "We've got to hurry!"

Skeeter peered into the hiding place. "Dats mighty small," he muttered, but his expression quickly tightened with resignation. "Come, Hattie, you first."

Hattie held her skirts down while Skeeter and Sam, scaling the wagon, helped her in. "Deys a gun here," she called out as she settled on the bottom. "Give it here," said Sam. Hattie handed the gun out as Ben and Skeeter helped Chloe in. Sam noticed Troy and Cole were staring at him holding the gun. "You want dis?" he offered.

"No. Keep it in there . . . we don't want it seen," Cole's

words were hurried as his eyes swung over to study the distant rise where the posse disappeared. "Let's get going!"

Ben, Skeeter, and Sam climbed in. As everyone expected it was a tight fit. "How long we gwine set like dis?" groaned Ben, settling Chloe's legs beside him.

"Get yo elbow out of my ribs," complained Hattie, shoving Skeeter's arm. They shifted about trying to force some comfort out of cramped and awkward positions forced by rough, unyielding lumber.

Troy was excitedly piling the covering boards back in place. He couldn't wait to get the team moving. There was no way of knowing what pulled that posse off or when they'd be back, but he couldn't believe the wagon had been forgotten. Cole, riding ahead, repeatedly glanced back with looks that mutely expressed their predicament. They had finally found the slaves and were now inescapably tied to them; whatever their fate, the two of them were surely going to share it.

The Selganys knew of the three likely trails running from Blue Springs to the border. One was heavily traveled and hardly the choice of a wagon evading notice. Of the remaining two the one to the north was plagued with wet ground and steep grades, leaving the one to the south, in spite of its overgrown and lonely, isolated stretches, the best route for secret passage. Like wolves that once roamed this country the Selganys knew their territory and the paths their prey followed to cross it.

It was late afternoon when they picked up the wagon's trail and, with some surprise, also came across the posse tracks. Hap began to curse. A posse that size could be troublesome. Most sheriffs, aware the Selgany crimes spread to adjoining counties, conveniently left these killers to neighboring lawmen. But large posses tended to make cautious sheriffs brave, young ones ambitious. It was only after his oldest son, Luke, tracked the posse up the slope and reported them gone from sight that he started his gang west again in pursuit of the wagon.

It was close to sundown when they finally caught sight

of the heavy load, laboring along still a few miles from the border. Hap was soon figuring this couldn't have worked out better. They were nearing a thick grove that surrounded a dip and turn in the trail, a spot almost perfect for an ambush. They had only to circle around, get ahead of the plodding wagon, and be ready when it slowed to make the awkward turn. Charlie Coyne, warning them again to shoot Cole first, hung back as they rode into the grove, preferring to watch this execution from a distance.

Cole was getting ready to breathe a sigh of relief. They were drawing close. Even though old Crolly was killed on Kansas soil somehow it seemed safer there. But he had been secretly and seriously worried about Troy pressing the team harder than was safe; from time to time he noticed one of the horses stumbling. They should have been rested hours ago but Troy wouldn't hear of it. He was hell bent on getting across that border. Cole could only imagine what was happening to the fugitives. Cramped in that narrow space for hours, they must be in pitiful shape. Fortunately it was only a few more miles.

In the hot, constricted space, Hattie and Chloe had finally squirmed together, Hattie's softness easing poor Chloe's plight. For a time her bottom had been pressing into Ben's chest and her face caught between Skeeter's knees. Only Sam, lying on top, could breathe normally, and he had carefully pressed two boards apart to get a limited view of the passing countryside. He would have liked to have thrown out the weighty gun, allowing a bit more space, but these white men wanted that weapon kept out of sight. Likely there was a good reason. He was just hoping it was good enough to justify the enormous risk having it held for escaping slaves. Sam knew something about guns but he hadn't seen this model before. It was a single-shot rifle which he noticed warily had been left loaded. He was about to whisper down to Skeeter that he could tell from their jerking, and pulling unsteadily at the start of every incline, that the horses were tiring, when something strange happened. They were suddenly violently rocked as the team must have bucked backwards, making the wagon swerve as though leaving the trail. Sam, with fear cramping every arm and leg, held his breath, as through his peek hole he saw a tall, malevolent-looking figure holding a gun on their driver.

Cole had a queasy feeling after glancing at the road ahead. It was leading into a heavy grove where it quickly turned and disappeared. He knew it must swing about sharply and drop down to fall from sight. Though there was no evidence of trouble the senses that guide men when normal sight deceives had him up in the saddle, staring intently in all directions. Into the grove and starting downhill, they came to a hairpin turn. Troy swung the team around, hoping the wagon would follow, but as they turned the team hit a barrier of brush stretched across the trail and heaved back to avoid being entangled in it. Instinctively Cole reached for his gun but it was too late, on every side Hap Selgany and his three sons had them covered. The faces of their captors quietly drooled tobacco juice while smiling like demons, having just tricked pious souls into hell.

9

Lee had little trouble staying ahead of the posse; he was only surprised they kept up such a dogged pursuit. He would have thought the risk of losing that wagon would draw them off after a few miles. Instead, it was over an hour and they were still trying to overtake him. Their horses must be winded, as was his, since both had slowed down, but there was still no sign of their turning back.

Of course he had no way of knowing the Blue Springs sheriff was a very stubborn man, stubborn and now outraged at the loss of his dogs. Like many lawmen depending too heavily on his badge, he wasn't entirely secure in his role, and needed the respect fear bred in people. Those dogs were part of an image he had consciously developed for his office and, by extension, himself. Whoever the dog-slayer was, his capture would bring on the worst punishment vengeful hands could devise, and if he could be connected to those escaping slaves, hanging by a vindictive posse was not out of the question.

As long as the rain lasted Lee kept dismounting and leading his horse up every difficult hill. It was an old mountain trick. Pursuers hurriedly following a trail would ride their mounts up these slick, steep slopes, thereby tiring them more quickly. At the first evidence his lead was increasing, making his escape a matter of time, he began to think of turning west again, hoping he had given the wagon a fair chance to reach the border. Surely the posse's horses were too exhausted to get back to the trail much before dark. But Lee was a sensible man, he knew he had just risked what he had been warned against. Quarles wouldn't like it. Quarles wanted his mind kept on the many slaves waiting in misery to be rescued, the organization must be held intact for their sake. Lee promised himself he would remember that hard truth from now on.

The Selganys' addiction to killing their victims slowly and in a way that tested their marksmanship was coming into play. Cole, suspecting they were all about to die, sensed pulling his gun would only precipitate the killing. Troy was staring at Hap, who, because the wagon was in the dip, was standing slightly behind and above him. He had never seen a more vile face or a more loathsome expression. Hap was looking down at them like a raunchy gargoyle gloating over corpses. The silence was almost unbearable and back in the wagon Sam was reaching down to squeeze Skeeter's arm as the only signal of mounting panic he could manage.

"Where d'yuh think you're going?" Hap's tone was almost a purr, oily and menacing.

Troy had to gather his breath to answer. "Just delivering a load of lumber. That's all."

"Well, what d'yuh know. Jes deliverin' a load of lumber." Hap half whispered. "What yuh got on that wagon besides wood?"

"Got any niggers in the woodpile?" croaked Luke. The other brothers soured the air with guffaws. But Hap was studying the trim of the wagon, his curiosity apparent. "Guess maybe you better throw off some of them top pieces, see iff'n it's all lumber."

To his left Luke spit noisily, then let out a raucous laugh. "Hope yuh got some nigger wenches in that woodpile, a young one would sure pleasure us some."

Inside the cramped compartment Hattie froze. They could hear every word and knew now they were going to be discovered. Poor Chloe was not going to escape her mother's fate, and God alone knew what was in store for the rest of them. Sam took a quick glimpse through his peek hole. Because it looked out on the right side of the wagon all he could see was Hap's figure looking down. His heart jumped at the sight. He had never seen a more wolfish-looking face.

Hap, who was keeping an eye on Cole, now ordered him to climb the wagon and throw some boards off. On the wagon Cole would be easier to watch. Cole, knowing their only chance was to fight, as these were surely the murderous Selganys, saw four guns loosely trained on him and could only obey. Nor could he see any way to delay removing the boards covering the escapees. A deep feeling of doom lodged in his chest, draining his limbs, making it a struggle to even lift the first plank.

The air around had become brittle with tension.

But for mankind the human brain is the ultimate mystery. It seeks its own line of reasoning, determines its own values, defies all logic to obey imperatives it alone comprehends. There was no time for poor frantic Sam to ponder the consequences of his act, he only knew he could not go forward into the scene breaking around him. There was no point in weighing alternatives; if an alternative existed he had to take it. Sanity would not survive seeing himself and his brother back in chains, Chloe and even Hattie being violated and used for obscenities his mind rebelled at picturing. What was hateful and undesirable was suddenly unacceptable and then impossible. He worked the gun around and fitted its muzzle into the peek hole. Then as Hap's lanky form loomed over the sight Sam firmed his mouth and pulled the trigger as something deep inside of him sprang up like a spring miraculously released.

Silas Cheatem made a second trip that day to the Sadlers. The first one had gained him nothing. He had packed most of his things in his small wagon and was trying to hire Dennis to drive the heavy one carrying lumber when he traveled west. He, himself, could handle the light rig with some personal things he wanted to keep an eye on. But Dennis wasn't agreeing to anything until discussing it with Cole and Troy. Cathy Jo had stood listening from a distance, her expressions anything but cordial, but Silas decided that might just be his problem. She might have felt left out.

Now he was back, his hand taking a fatherly hold of the young Sadler's shoulder. "Course you wouldn't be alone," he confided, watching Cathy a few feet away, bending over her stove. "I'm figuring on fetching a woman too, for cookin' and sech."

Dennis quietly backed away, suddenly aware Cheatem was looking at him but talking to Cathy. "Like I said, cain't give an answer a'fore my brothers get back. Told you once."

"All right," conceded Cheatem, "but you're getting old enough to make your own decisions. Mark of a man!" He turned to Cathy. "Reckon you can see the great opportunity here, eh?"

Cathy didn't look like she was going to answer, somehow she resented even looking at Silas, but hanging up the towel she held, she finally turned to him. "You don't seem to hear what folks say, 'specially if it don't please you. I think you'd best hear this. If you're so fired up on hiring help, go into town . . . plenty needing work there. You already got your answer here. No need for you to stay around any longer, and I'd just as soon you didn't come back till my husband is home."

Cheatem pulled back with a grunt. "Mighty damn unfriendly, ain't you?"

"Call it what you like." Cathy was starting into the second room. "Dennis, make sure the horses are tended to before it gets dark."

Cheatem, his face beginning to mottle with rage, followed Dennis out into the yard. "Pretty sassy bitch that sister-in-law of yours. Needs a good hiding."

"Wouldn't try that if I were you."

Cheatem turned to face the cabin door as though it were Cathy. He stamped his foot. "Damn women! Cole and Troy were mighty pleased to work for me, earning money a sensible way, not risking their asses trying to rustle runaways over the border!"

Dennis was trying hard not to smile, but mention of the border reminded him of Crolly's death, and his face turned sober as he looked at the sky and wondered how his brothers were faring.

Sam's single shot brought two changes in that deadly setting that were to have crucial consequences for all involved. One, it erased Hap Selgany, the satanic driving force behind a family of homicidal degenerates, and, two, it gave desperate Cole the opening he was praying for. Shock registered on the faces of all three Selgany boys as Hap fell and lay sprawled on the ground, and Cole drew and fired before any of them had a chance to fix sights on him. He knocked Luke out of the saddle, then ducked down behind the pile of lumber. The two younger boys fired over his head, then turned their guns on Troy. Troy was slow getting his pistol into action and took a slug in the shoulder before Cole, bobbing up, drove the two to flight. The Selganys were not used to shooting at people who shot back, and without Hap to rally them or stiffen their gut, they ducked away. Luke, who was only wounded, managed to reach and hang onto his saddle horn as his mount pulled him back into the grove.

Trying to think clearly, Cole jumped down from the wagon and started pulling the obstructing line of brush away. "Get us out of here!" he shouted to the wounded Troy, who, realizing Cole wanted them to get out of the dip, rapped the team with the reins and pulled the wagon forward until they reached level ground.

All of this happened inside of a minute, and no one was sure it was over. Cole got Troy down from the wagon and had him lie alongside the trail to examine his wound. A slug was buried in his shoulder but luckily the bleeding wasn't bad. Both knew the Selganys might be back at any moment and started looking for cover to make a stand. But after searching for several minutes Cole decided it would be safer to keep racing for the border. As long as they stayed on Missouri soil they were in danger.

On the wagon the five occupants of the hiding place were holding their breath, whispering from time to time to Sam to tell them what was going on. After the roar of the gun stunned everyone and left them dumbfounded, Sam had become strangely mute, with his jaw set determinedly, his eyes staring through the peek hole at the dead body beyond. "Deys nothin' going on," he said grimly. "Ah done shot somebody . . . big rascal looked like he needed shootin'. Somebody else did some shootin' too, cain't see nobody now . . . must be dey went off."

"Didn't leave us, did dey?" anguished Hattie.

"Hope not."

But then they all felt the wagon moving, not as it did before for just a few moments. This time it continued steadily until Sam let out a big breath and sighed, "Must be we getting close to Kansas, if dis keeps up believe y'all finally going to make it."

Skeeter reached up to punch his backside. "Sam, next time we gots to travel dis way you riding on de bottom."

Back in the grove Luke, shot through the arm and dangerous as a wounded grizzly, almost spit at Charlie Coyne. All he wanted was his brothers to help him attack that wagon again. But it was plain to see Luke wasn't Hap. His younger brothers didn't figure he came out of that fight with any claim to leadership, however much they shared his thirst for revenge. Coyne, rubbing his hands together, kept insisting he'd paid to have Cole killed and expected that service rendered. Luke, in pain and growing furious, made it clear they also killed people for getting in their way, and refused to talk about anything but another assault on the wagon.

After an hour Luke finally convinced his brothers they owed it to Hap to follow these men and kill not only them but their entire families. That's what Hap would have wanted. That the border had to be crossed to carry out such a slaughter no longer deterred them; without Hap's wily mind in the balance the young Selganys were beginning to act like the demented jackals they were. Coyne, deciding he might be well rid of these criminal crazies, still couldn't resist offering them an additional bonus for proof of Cole's death.

The brothers, taking time to bind up Luke's arm, finally set off after the wagon. They rode wildly even when darkness came, for Luke kept riling them with what a loss the death of their crafty old father was for them. In time the young killers, in a fury of frustration and a mania of rage, pounded ahead like rabid wolves running down an elusive stag. Hap would have been stupefied to see, in spite of his long and grim training for survival, his sons now running through the night like mad dogs, recklessly crossing the deadly border, blind to everything but destroying their prey.

≈ **10** ≈

Henry Quarles had studied for the ministry but had given it up for a career in medicine until the death of a young devoted wife brought a great change in his life. Now he was committed to relieving the human suffering that he found pervaded the world. From a prominent New England family, affluent enough to have retreated from a life that had denied him compassion, he chose instead to ease his own sorrow by relieving that of others. The work he chose was dangerous, calling for a quiet kind of courage that didn't appeal to many. But Henry wasn't interested in glory, although his powers of organization might have made him a notable general or statesman. His sole aim was to bring freedom to as many enslaved souls as possible, and he shrunk from no task pursuing it.

Anxiously he waited for signs of the wagon, but in the darkness could only guess at the way they might come. One thing was certain—the Sadler brothers would head for home, or the house of a neighbor named Cheatem, whom he discovered had ordered the lumber. But he would not allow himself to think the mission had failed, that would only diminish vigilance or weaken resolve. In this work faith in the power of a just and merciful God was needed and accounted for the many religious men and women committed to the task. Quarles was only glad he added Lee to their sketchy rescue plan. He was convinced the Almighty appreciated servants whose talents required little guidance.

It was almost midnight when the wagon finally crept into Cheatem's yard. The horses were exhausted; they halted in their tracks, heads hanging almost to the ground. Once safely across the border the escapees had climbed out of their hiding place and were now riding in plain sight on top of the lumber. Cole, who was now driving the team, looked exhausted, but Troy, sitting beside him, was pale and near collapse from the loss of blood oozing through a crudely bandaged wound on his shoulder.

Cheatem, carrying a torch out to the yard to greet them, almost exploded when he saw five dark figures atop his lumber. He had to look twice to affirm what his eyes said was there. "Great screaming Jesus!" he roared. "Where d'they come from?!"

Cole tied the reins around the whip socket and stepped down. "No concern of yours," he muttered roughly. "Here's your goddamn lumber, they go with us!" Cole went to bring up a saddle horse from behind the wagon to carry Troy the short stretch home. "Here's where you get off," he said to Skeeter, who at once began helping Hattie and Chloe to the ground. Sam, still holding the gun, looked carefully at Cheatem before slipping down. "We walkin' now?" he said to Cole.

"Not far," answered Cole, giving Sam his own horse to lead.

Hattie and Chloe stood silently, waiting to be shown the way. Cheatem, over his shock, was playing his eyes upon them, lingering on Chloe just long enough to bring anxiety into Hattie's voice. "Dis Kansas," she said in response to her hidden fears. "We free now!"

Sam and Skeeter helped Cole with Troy, and having him secured in the saddle began to follow Cole as he led his wounded brother up the trail to the Sadler shack. "We'll settle in the morning," Cole called back to Cheatem, who, scowling, began releasing the team, wondering how long it would be before they could be used again.

No one knew Quarles was watching this scene from a line of heavy brush a hundred yards away, but even he didn't know the Selganys, managing to stay on the wagon's trail, had at last come up to discover it in Cheatem's yard. Though no longer loudly exclaiming their rage, they had doggedly tracked Hap's murderers to their lair and now the vengeful killings of all connected to these culprits could begin.

Cathy's relief at seeing Cole coming through the door was immediately offset by the shock of seeing the wounded Troy and five Negroes entering her cabin. Speechless, she listened to Cole's brief explanation, cut off by his insistence they help Troy first and talk later. Troy was laid on a bed, but no one knew how to remove a bullet without painfully probing the wound. Only after noticing Troy was already running a high fever did Cathy tell herself she had to try.

Dennis, his eyes wide and tense at the excitement around him, was the first to notice Chloe eyeing dry slices of bread lying on the table. Without thinking, he lifted the plate and offered her one. She seized it and breaking it in half offered one piece to Hattie. Then both of them broke their pieces and offered quarter pieces to Ben and Skeeter. With Sam looking ruefully at the slices remaining on the plate, Dennis realized these people were starving. He offered Sam the remaining slices and in less than a minute they disappeared. Feeling awkward, he shifted over to bring some cuts of pork, the remains of his and Cathy's dinner, still sitting along the rim of a serving dish. He had nothing else to offer but within moments the plate was clean. Feeling embarrassed and looking apologetic, he didn't notice Chloe approaching him. She took his hand and squeezed it, a gesture clearly intended to thank him, but it only made him look at her shyly and for the first time realize how pretty she was.

Wanting to turn away but noticing Chloe was still staring at him, he uttered almost bashfully, "Cathy will fetch you something quick as she finishes with Troy."

He couldn't know Chloe was glad this shy young man was uneasy in her presence. It told her he was as young and insecure as she. Like women the world over, instinct hinted to her this wasn't a male to fear, this boy was as unsure of himself and inexperienced as she. In some deep mysterious way she also knew he found her pretty.

For the first time in her life fifteen-year-old Chloe was finding herself enticed by a male—and this one was white!

Troy, grimacing in pain, as Cathy had only kitchen utensils to dislodge the bullet, was close to passing out and Cathy was beginning to panic at the sight of increased bleeding. It was only the outbreak of shots in the distance that pulled them away, Cole running for the rifle Sam still carried, and Cathy to kill the lanterns, an attempt to keep figures within as invisible as possible.

Before moments had elapsed they knew the shots had come from Cheatem's place. Cole and Sam, who had snatched up Troy's removed pistol, were moving down the road toward it. Dennis, told to stay behind to guard the others, stayed in the doorway, pistol in hand while Cathy returned to press a rag over Troy's wound. In the darkness Dennis, now strangely conscious of Chloe's presence, was aware she was standing behind him, staring anxiously into the night. Not a sound could be heard in that darkened room, but at some point in those long breathless moments he felt Chloe reaching out and touching him lightly on the back.

Had it not been for Henry Quarles, Cheatem would have been dead. One of the Selgany boys had a bead on him coming back from taking the horses to a shed out back, and could hardly have missed if Quarles hadn't fired first. The Selganys, thrown into confusion by this shot from nowhere, turned and sprayed the suspected area with bullets. But Quarles was too low and too deep in the brush to be easily seen. He had only tried to scare the Selgany boy, not knowing who he was shooting at. But Cheatem, who had ducked into the house, emerged with a shotgun and began to fire at the flashes of exploding powder across his yard. Again the Selganys found themselves in a fight not of their liking. They could deal with the gun in front of them but the gun behind threw the odds against them. Though still willing to fight, the youngest now refused to move forward into the yard and become a better target. Luke, in a fit of disgust, emptied his pistol pointlessly as Cheatem ducked back into the house. Luke had not seen Cole and Troy leaving and assumed they were inside. But the Selganys were beginning to lose their nerve.

Now the youngest brother wanted to leave. "This ain't bin our day," he rasped, still warily searching for the gun that had scared him, throwing him off his aim. "Bastard is jest gonna have to be flushed out before we can do erry a thing!"

"He kin wait," snapped Luke. "We got to smoke those yellow polecats in the house out furst."

Had the Selgany brothers worked together they might have achieved something, but Luke slipped around to the far side of the house by himself, while the others squatted down at the outskirts of the yard awaiting Quarles's next move. Precious moments were lost, when the house could have been rushed, their three guns quickly silencing Cheatem. Swearing to himself, Luke pushed some light underbrush against the dry pine boards of the house and after several tries coaxed a flame in it with his pocket flint. The blaze was just beginning to gather strength when he joined his two brothers. "They be traipsing out soon," he snapped as he squatted down beside them.

"What about that bastard back yonder?" spouted the young one, beginning to realize the fire could make them even better targets. "Luke, damn if you ain't fixin' to get us killed!"

"Don't start talking rabbity," snarled Luke. "We came to do a job and we bound to do it!"

But by now Cole and Sam were nearing the approach to Cheatem's yard, and could see the flickering light of a flame on the far side of the house. "By Jesus, I believe the place is on fire!" Cole half shouted, momentarily forgetting the shots that had brought them there. But his voice and the sound of their feet on the scrabble convinced the Selganys more guns were gathering behind them. The two younger brothers, ignoring Luke, sprang to their feet and started shooting in the direction of Cole's voice. Mayhem broke loose as Cole and Sam, dropping to their knees, returned the fire. Quarles opened up again, but this time he wasn't shooting to scare and his bullet seared across the youngest brother's thigh. With a yelp the young Selgany backed into the brush and shouted to Luke, "Come on! Let's git!"

Luke turned to see both brothers were deserting him and realized within moments he was going to be trapped, outgunned, and killed. He began to straggle after them through the dark foliage, but he couldn't resist shouting behind him. "We'll be back, you bastards! The Selganys are fixin' to dance on your graves! Jus you never forget that—cause we ain't!"

It was to be a night of unending calamity.

By the time they were able to bring water from the rain barrel or run it up from the river, the fire was out of control. Skeeter and Ben, at Hattie's urgent bidding, had run down to help, but it was no use. Cheatem stood by and fumed; such crazy doings were always thrust upon him by others.

It was Quarles, emerging from the brush and trying to organize their vain efforts to control the fire, who finally realized the house was lost and suggested they all retire to the Sadlers. Cheatem, furious at his easy assumption of command, demanded to know who he was, only to be abruptly silenced when Quarles advised him, not too delicately, that he was the one who likely saved his life. It was not like Henry to talk that way, but something told him this Cheatem was a man devoted to his own appetites, and one who, though just saved from death by a stranger's gesture, was sounding arrogant where gratitude should have humbled him in thanks.

Cheatem, if not embarrassed, was at least uncomfortable at Quarles's words and turned away. "I need a drink," he said plaintively. Cole, whose mind was still on Troy and his untreated wound, started back toward their place, motioning for the runaways to follow him. Cheatem, swearing under his breath, reluctantly followed along. Quarles, recovering his horse from the deep brush, arrived last. But it was Quarles, at the first sight of Troy's wound, who, revealing his medical training, soon had the slug out and the wound bandaged, to Cathy's relief. But Quarles's mind was working even as he bent over the prostrate Troy. Only he knew the predicament they were in, only he knew a solution had to be found that night.

Cathy was aghast when she heard the attackers at the Cheatem place were well-known murderers. She closed her eyes in momentary shock upon hearing their threat to come back. Nervously she was pulling together what food she could for Hattie's family, but her words were directed at Cole. "You think I'm going to sleep another night in this place after hearing that!"

"Now don't start taking on," pleaded Cole. "We've just got to get some things settled."

Quarles had slipped out to his horse with lines of worry trenched about his eyes. What he had gathered from hearing of a sheriff and a posse in that lightly traveled country, and the prepared ambush by the Selganys near the border, convinced him these escapees were no secret, and this close to the border were still in jeopardy. He had no quick way of getting them north, and remaining here even the rest of this night was risky. Quarles didn't know Charlie Coyne, but he knew he and his ilk existed, and no act, however brazen or depraved, was beyond them.

He returned to Troy with a small flask of whiskey, offering careful swallows to the pale, drawn face.

"Damn, if'n I couldn't use me a drink too," groaned Cheatem.

Quarles, ignoring him, spoke quietly but his voice had a commanding quality that caught everyone's ear. "I think you should all get out of here, this place isn't safe anymore and the Selganys may not be your only problem."

"And just what in hell does that mean?" demanded Cole.

"It means there's more to worry about than that half-demented clan of butchers. Just remember they aren't the ones who killed Crolly."

"Who did?" cried Cathy.

"Somebody making money off captured slaves."

Hattie, her face tightening, was breathlessly following the conversation. "We in Kansas now! We free!" she declared.

"The folks Crolly was guiding were in Kansas too," said Quarles evenly. "We've got to get you a lot further from the border than this. This isn't Philadelphia . . . laws don't mean much around here."

Cheatem was on his feet, looking determined, like a man pouncing on a decision. "Me, I'm clearing out," he declared. "Ain't nothing around here but trouble." Pointedly he approached Dennis. "You want that job?"

Cole looked quickly at Dennis, then bluntly answered for him. "What job?"

"Offered him a job driving my lumber wagon. No reason to hang on here, being burnt out and all. Chance for him to make some money."

Cathy stood up to face him. "You go and we'll be left here to deal with those wicked people," she exclaimed. Stamping her foot, she turned to Cole. "I've told you once, I want out of here!"

Hattie could be heard murmuring to herself, "We in Kansas now! We free!"

Cathy's ire flared in her eyes. She stepped closer to Cole, pointing at Cheatem. "If he's leaving we're leaving too!"

"Tonight?" Cole glanced at Troy. "Can't you see Troy . . ."

"Yes! tonight! Troy can sleep in the wagon. I couldn't close my eyes for a wink around here after what I've heard."

"And wats about us?" asked Hattie, her hand rising to grasp her throat. "Wats we gonna do?"

"You're going too," said Quarles, one hand reaching out to her in a reassuring gesture.

"And just who's taking them?" demanded Cheatem.

"Might be you'd take some," returned Quarles. "We pay for that service."

Cheatem was about to refuse until he heard the word pay. He stared at Quarles for a moment. "Pay? How much?"

"Fifty dollars for each."

"That isn't much."

"Well, perhaps they can work some for you, I mean on a temporary basis."

Cheatem looked over the five escapees, but again, to Hattie's annoyance, his eyes lingered on Chloe. Yet his glance finally ended on Hattie, herself. "Can you cook?" he asked gruffly.

"Can blackbirds fly?" she answered, staring warily back at him.

"We can help with dat lumber," offered Skeeter, noticing Cheatem wavering.

Cheatem pursed his mouth up and considered the offer. He had long been aware he was going to need help; maybe he could make a virtue out of this damn disastrous night. He had only one problem. He didn't have much faith in Negroes, having heard somewhere they weren't too bright. He didn't want his wagon in a ditch. "Well, all right, but I got to get something settled first. Who's gonna drive?" He was looking at Dennis.

Had he been looking at Dennis earlier he would have noticed that Dennis was now shyly watching Chloe and was attuned to every move she made. Dennis had even caught Cheatem, as did Hattie, looking at the young girl and suddenly found himself resenting it. But Dennis's answer left little doubt that nothing anyone might say was going to stop him. "I will!" he said firmly. "I'll drive your damn wagon."

In spite of the stress and bitter arguments, Quarles couldn't help being impressed by Cathy. Her frank

demand they leave smacked more of common sense than
fear. He knew something about fear; people who readily
admitted it were the least affected by it. He could also
see why men remembered her. She moved about with a
sensuous grace, not deliberate on her part but still
curiously arousing. To his surprise he was also struck by
Chloe. This young girl, with her obvious white blood,
had an almost Grecian beauty. He avoided staring, but
had to glance at her several times to satisfy himself. It
was a blessing she had reached Kansas. That face and
figure would have brought a fortune on some slave block.

It was two hours before they were ready to leave.
Dennis went with Cheatem to bring his wagons up. They
hitched his fresh team to the lumber wagon and the
other, after feed and rest now somewhat revived, to the
lighter rig. Cheatem took along some harnesses and odds
and ends from his back shed, but the fire had left only a
primitive stone chimney standing to mark where once
stood a house.

Back at the Sadlers, Quarles helped Cathy put down
bedding in their short wagon, which Skeeter and Sam
had brought around. Cathy could tell by the way they
put the team in harness and handled them that these two
knew their way around horses. It put her in mind of
something that had been bothering her. She knew Cole,
who, exhausted, had lain down for a badly needed nap,
would want to ride one of the saddle horses, never liking
confinement to a wagon. Which meant she would have
to tend Troy if he needed help. Someone to drive could
ease the problem. She chose Skeeter, who seemed the
more talkative of the two. "Yes'm, ah be mighty pleased
to drive y'all," replied Skeeter quickly. He and Sam had
decided it would be better for them if these two families
stayed together. Like Sam, he found a worrisome quality
in Cheatem's looks and half-swaggering stance; of neces-
sity they learned a lot from gestures that might have
been missed by less watchful eyes. Cheatem was not a
man people in trouble could expect sympathy from, let
alone help. Without showing it Sam was relieved she had
chosen Skeeter. He was busy studying where the guns

were being placed. In his own mind he was determined not to be separated from Hattie and, above all, from Chloe. What was causing it he didn't know but he sensed Chloe had been acting strangely in the last hour, secretly tense as though she had something new and exciting on her mind. His father had always told him young girls didn't have a lick of sense, but Sam, having experienced a few young girls who without warning had him on the brink of matrimony, wasn't sure.

No one noticed that Quarles, in helping Troy to the wagon, had slipped the promised two hundred into his pocket, but Troy was more alert now and even managed a smile, a smile that said, "I told you I could do it." Quarles turned away. He had heard how the posse had been drawn off by shots fired by some unknown figure in the brush, and his concern for Lee had been mounting. Did his valuable right-hand aide once again forget the greater good? Henry Quarles hadn't quite settled in his own mind just how Troy had managed "to do it."

Finally they were ready to go. Cheatem's wagon started off first, heading due west along the river trail. The lumber wagon came next with Hattie, Chloe, Ben, and Sam aboard, along with a basket holding the remains of Sadler food. Skeeter brought the Sadler wagon up last, with Cole, riding his saddle horse, planning to shortly take the lead. The wagons creaked along, and Skeeter studied the sky. It was a clear night and Skeeter could tell from reading the stars that it was only an hour or two until dawn. The wind from the west smelled sweet, and he was suddenly suffused with a sense of relief, as though a burden imposed at birth had been lifted from his shoulders. Again he sniffed the air. If that was freedom he was smelling, it sure smelled good.

Inevitably the fire had been seen by settlers closer to town, and in the morning men appeared to walk about the ashes and speculate on what happened to the late occupant. In time the Sadler place was also found abandoned. By noon word of these findings were on the streets of Lawrence and Charlie Coyne, drinking in a crowded coffee shop, frowned to hear the Sadlers, whom many men recalled because of Cathy Jo, had disappeared. Muted anger drove him to make a mistake he had never made before, publicly expressing an opinion that drew attention to himself. "They wouldn't be running off like that if they weren't trying to dodge some gunplay, likely because of some goddamn trouble they caused."

"Just how you reckon that?" asked a companion turning to him.

"Figures. They wuz always sticking their nose into places it didn't belong."

A few gruff voices offered companionable rather than considered agreements, but one, seemingly out of idle curiosity, put his cup down and, stifling a yawn, said, "You sure sound like a gent who knows a heap more than most. How come?"

Coyne realized his mistake. He had talked too much, made himself noticed; now men were staring at him curiously, now he had to rectify his error. "Oh . . . just guessing what likely happened, could be they just got itchy and up and went. That breed is always shy of money . . . willing to chance anything to get it."

This explanation, hurried by a twinge of anxiety and not entirely making sense, was to some ears more indicting then his earlier comment. Had he looked carefully about that coffee house he would have noticed a single well-dressed patron, two tables away, his head down but his hearing focused on the conversation at Coyne's table, his shoulders stiffening almost imperceptibly at Coyne's remarks.

Henry Quarles left the coffee house shortly after, but it wasn't until late that day, when to his great relief he saw Lee watching him from across the street, that he met with his cherished aide and, describing Charlie Coyne, gave him another very chancy assignment.

Sometime before noon, Cole suggested they make camp and rest through the heat of the day. Cheatem had no objection and surprised everyone by producing a salted ham he said they could cook. Sam and Skeeter soon had a fire going while Hattie was busy washing the ham in a stream that ran into the river. Troy insisted on sitting up. Cathy was still in an uncertain mood and, though feeling safer, deeply annoyed at these events that had interrupted a reckoning with Cole. Resignedly she turned to change Troy's bandage. She decided he looked better, but it was an awkward setting as Troy, with uncharacteristic humility, sat silently nodding his thanks as she worked. The wind that had been brisk in the morning now seemed only to be idling and close to stifling by noon.

During the long morning Dennis found opportunities to glance at Chloe, at the lightness of her skin and the soft sculpture of her young face. He had to fight to keep from staring for he had become aware others were watching her too. Positioning himself so he would be the one to help her down from the wagon, he did not miss Sam coming up and eyeing his hands on Chloe's waist, which he released moments sooner than he'd planned. Hattie also seemed to be aware of anyone coming near Chloe and immediately reacted when Cheatem ran his hand up and down the inside of Chloe's arm.

"Git yo' hands off her!" Hattie rasped fiercely.

Cheatem, annoyed but visibly thrown on the defensive, tried to pass it off as curiosity. "Where'd she get that light skin?"

"From white pigs like you!" Hattie stood before him, defiantly, hands on hips.

Cole came up, noticed Sam and Skeeter quickly moving up behind Hattie, and decided this kind of trouble they couldn't afford. He stopped in front of Cheatem. "If you want these people to work for you, you'd best listen to her, or you're gonna find yourself alone with two wagons and no one to hear your complaints."

"Jesus, a man can't open his mouth to people he's paying to work for him without he be made to look small."

"You ain't paying for anything but work," responded Cole. "You damn well better remember it!" He nodded at the grim-looking Sam. "That young fellow has already killed one white man who didn't suit his fancy . . . likely he's gitting some notions about you already."

Cheatem managed to cover his nettled reaction to this exchange, disguising it with a complaint he thought might move minds in another direction. "Thought we was getting ready to eat! Best we get to it . . . We didn't stop here to jaw all day."

The others moved off slowly, but Cathy, sitting to the rear and smiling in spite of herself, couldn't imagine Cheatem could still be hungry after choking down that hunk of humble pie.

The houses began to thin out. There were long stretches where they saw no one. Travelers passed them going in both directions, some coming east and reporting Indian trouble in the Colorado Territory; others overtook them heading west. A few of the latter planned to turn south shortly and pick up the Santa Fe Trail. Chloe kept marveling that traveling across the countryside in the open like this was so different from the harried and fearful trip up through Missouri. Secretly excited, she kept experiencing a run of emotions that drew her hands to her heart. A young girl sitting in the sun, laughing at the splash of butterflies that occasionally covered the wagon, or a flight of chirping birds flushed by the plodding team. To her it was like traveling in a fairyland. Now with food in their stomachs and hope in their hearts her family was beginning to smile at each other, a thousand subtle messages of relief and mounting expectations passing between them. Sharing her family's run of emotions that needed but a spark to turn to merriment, she pulled her knees up to her chest and hugged her secret body, while her mind kept slipping to the tall, straight-shouldered youth driving the wagon.

It gave her a funny but reassuring feeling to sense he liked her, that his hands on her waist when he helped her from the wagon seemed to reach through her dress, feeling for her flesh. On that weird spontaneous impulse she had deliberately touched him in the dark the night before but didn't know what to do next. There was also the hovering shadow of Hattie. All her life Hattie had warned her away from white boys, had forbidden her to even walk where they might catch her alone. She had met men like Cheatem; they all found ways to get their hands on her body, but Hattie had always been there to raise such a rumpus nothing serious developed. But she realized her body was maturing, more and more men stopped and stared. Every female slave knew if a white man wanted her badly enough . . .

Yet Chloe was growing confused, she sensed this white boy was harmless, in fact he looked to be fretting that his awkward attempts to get close to her were going to get them both in trouble. She couldn't help a sympathetic twinge; she felt something akin in reverse. Chloe had never kept secrets from her mother. She had been raised to share everything with Hattie, but how was she going to say she was attracted to a white boy? Yet Chloe knew things about herself, like the kind of desires that rose in her heart and sooner or later she obeyed. Like eating a piece of candy she had promised to save for Sunday. Now she knew when evening came and darkness protected her, she would find a way to touch Dennis again, and he would know . . . she held her breath, letting the thought form . . . he would know what she wanted him to know.

But what was she going to tell Hattie?

It wasn't simply by accident that Quarles spotted Charlie Coyne in that coffee house. Dennis and Cole, once realizing he had a right to know, supplied the name

Charlie Coyne as the man who shot Crolly and made off with the slaves. Quarles found the name on the list of men Crolly had hired for that mission, but didn't know him by sight. Still, he had his own way of finding things out and soon had enough hints to lead him to that crowded coffee house, where watching carefully he saw entering a tallish man, with peculiarly tinted eyes, his upper lids falling strangely low, giving him a malign look. Aided by this one feature, supplied by Cole, Quarles's attention remained focused on Coyne until the man's uneasy and suspect remarks convinced him he was looking at Crolly's killer.

Little sleuthing was required to deduce why Coyne wanted the Sadler boys in their graves. By identifying him before a court of law they could put a noose about his neck. But Quarles wasn't interested in justice or local jurisprudence. Frontier courts, if often swift and severe, could also be uncertain, particularly where escaping slaves were the issue. He sat filling in the dimensions of Coyne's malfeasance, deciding it must have been Coyne who hired the Selganys to silence Dennis and Cole. The man had committed monstrous crimes but as he glanced at the figure across the restaurant he saw a worried face. Worried people were prone to mistakes. They were also vulnerable to imagined threats.

Quarles, anything but a gambling man, decided, as he finished his coffee, to follow his instincts here and play a long shot.

In spite of Quarles's unsettled mood it was turning into an eventful day. Before happily catching sight of Lee, ambling along across the street, waiting to be noticed, he had dropped by the sheriff's office, though at the moment there was no sheriff; the incumbent was only an acting sheriff, a former deputy bucking for the job. Frequently Quarles intentionally stopped to chat with this gabby, cigar-chewing delegate of the law. He had last seen him in the post office when Dennis rushed in with Cole's note. Visiting with this acting sheriff was Quarles's way of making his going and comings appear innocent and his pretended role as a land developer, simply cultivating the right friends, convincing.

The conversation between them was usually incidental and banal, as Quarles didn't rate this aspiring lawman's mentality very high. Yet where one's aim is to use rather than enlighten, a certain obtuseness can have its advantages. "Hear the Sadlers just up and left, eh?" Quarles began casually.

"Seems to be a fact," allowed the other.

"Don't really believe it, do you?"

The acting sheriff scratched his head. "Got reasons for thinking otherwise?"

"Maybe."

The deputy gave him an inquiring look. "Something I ought to know?"

"Well, I don't know. I was just speculating, but seeing as how they're still owed some money, I figured they'd be back tonight to collect."

The lawman looked interested, but started pulling a cigar from his breast pocket. "Well, most folks allow they did stew a bit 'bout money, but ain't no law against collecting what yours." He bit into the tobacco. "Wished I knew who torched that house out yonder, some say there were even shots fired. Got a feeling it weren't local devils, wouldn't be surprised if some of them yahoos from across the border were the critters."

Quarles's face took on the irate lines of a businessman perceiving a lack of law and order. "Be a feather in your cap if you could nail some of that trash. Running wild like they do you can expect plenty more mischief before they're finished."

Quarles was getting ready to go when the sheriff looked up, his face suddenly coming to life with new energy and interest. "You figure they'll be back soon . . . like tonight, eh?"

"Could be."

Now the lawman was on his feet, standing face to face with Quarles. "I'm beginning to think you might know a heap more than you're letting on," he said almost brusquely, whipping the cigar from his mouth.

"All I said was the Sadlers were likely to be back tonight, seeing as how they have money coming. Please don't make more of my remarks than I intended."

"Yeah, maybe so, but what I think you're getting at is whoever scared them off last might try it again tonight."

"That hadn't occurred to me but I'm grateful it has to you. You're likely to be our sheriff soon, and we need someone with a quick mind for such things . . . got to have some respect for law around here."

The lawman studied him for a moment. Quarles's reference to his being sheriff soon hadn't been wasted on this ambitious candidate. He forced a smile to ease his way into saying, "Now, look mister, I ain't asking any questions, but if you was to know something that might give me a chance to show folks around here I'm the right galoot for this job I'd be mighty obliged."

Quarles looked mildly startled. "Well, naturally, if I can contribute to law enforcement in any way, as a loyal citizen I'm bound to do it."

The acting sheriff smiled again, reached for his hand, and winked. "I'm glad to hear you say that, Mr. Quarles, we 'uns totting a star sure appreciate that kind of help."

Later, this loquacious, posturing, aspiring deputy, unable to resist using confidences to make himself seem important, as well as wanting his temporary office, the beneficiary of free cigars and drinks, to become permanent, had dutifully completed his rounds of the town's bars and its single crowded barber shop. As Quarles had hoped, rumors that the Sadlers might be back that night were beginning to circulate. Charlie Coyne heard it outside the barber shop, and, stepping into the nearest bar for a stiff drink, was soon mounted and galloped out of town.

But anxiety had so distorted his thinking, and so urgently was he pressing his mount forward, that he failed to notice a slight figure, far to his rear, appearing out of nowhere and taking up his trail.

In the late afternoon Cole shot a deer and by twilight Skeeter and Sam had it skinned and butchered. Strips of roasting venison filled the campsite with pleasant aromas as drips of fat hit the fire. Hattie had Ben busy washing and slicing onions from Cheatem's wagon, and

Troy, feeling better, was out of his berth and taking their team to water. Everyone seemed to fall into an appointed role, though Cathy was only waiting to catch Cole alone to express her feelings regarding this hurriedly planned and still confusing trek. She had no idea where they were going, only that they seemed to be following Cheatem and were counting on distance for safety.

The meal brought them all together and Cheatem, acting sulky and out of sorts since his encounter with Hattie, stood over the fire making a clumsy attempt to resume control. "Want you all to know I'm gonna get me a fine stretch of bottom land staked out, and for a spell there figures to be plenty work. But I ain't putting up with no slackers. If you work for Silas Cheatem you'll sure as hell earn your keep."

"Ain't working for you," said Cole.

"Me neither," added Troy.

"And how long you 'spect us to work for y'all?" said Skeeter, looking down.

"By rights as long as it pleasures me," spat Cheatem, his manner turning surly. "And I ain't putting up with no uppity talk neither!"

"We g'wine work a spell," said Hattie. "Don't wanna be beholding to the likes of you. But you be careful, hear! . . . We free now, we studyin' some doings on our own."

When the fire died Chloe whispered to Hattie she was slipping into the brush to relieve herself, but instead circled around to the Sadler wagon where she knew Dennis was talking to his brothers. Creeping up she could just see his form in the darkness, but as she came within a few yards he suddenly turned and looked directly at her. Her heart failed her. Shaking, she dropped down and scampered away, hoping she hadn't been seen. But the incident unnerved her and back with Hattie she couldn't help settling on her share of blanket and taking her head in her hands.

"What's ailing you, child!" demanded Hattie.

"Nuthin', Mama. Just a bitty stomach ache . . . goin' 'way now."

" 'Spect it's dat meat, weren't rightly cooked."

"Reckon so, Mama."

Dennis was furiously gripping the side of the wagon. He was sure he had seen someone ducking away as he turned. Could it have been Chloe? Jeez, he was stupid. All day he had been wondering how to get her alone, and now, because he hadn't the sense to stay alert, a golden opportunity might have slipped through his fingers.

He moved cautiously around the wagons, hoping to get a glimpse of her, but all he could see in the darkness below the lumber wagon was some huddled forms settled down to sleep.

Yet matters were to change only a few hours later, when a black bear, smelling the cooked venison, stumbled into their camp and Cheatem, rudely awakened, began firing in the darkness. The men were immediately up and racing about with cocked guns until Cole, killing the bear with his first shot, shouted for everyone to calm down before some nervous trigger finger did some damage.

It took a while for the camp to resume its composure, for everyone was seeking cover from an unknown and therefore unlimited threat, but Chloe went back to sleep content, for in the melee she had rushed passed Dennis, and the two of them, impulsively reaching for each other, had joined hands long enough for her to squeeze his and feel him squeezing back.

Unexpectedly, and still wrestling with his problems on that already taxing day, Quarles was approached by a young, studious-looking man whom he was to discover was a former schoolteacher. This youthful-looking stranger carried papers that identified him as Crolly's replacement. Since all such volunteers for this critical work were thoroughly checked before being sent into the field, Quarles assumed there was no need to be concerned about the man's qualifications or degree of dedication. His own information was that a group of eleven slaves were drawing near the border and would be ready for a night crossing in about two days. Walking with him casually back to his dwelling on the outskirts of town, Quarles began a briefing that would only end when this fresh and untested operative left on his first assignment. Henry wished he had come on a less demanding day but he supplied the newcomer with some maps and urged him to take sufficient time to study them, and if possible commit them to memory. It was almost dark when, with relief, he heard Lee riding up, and quickly excused himself to talk with his scout. The new addition to his covert operation, whose name was Ebert Devine, seemed content with a little solitude to study Quarles's maps, and Quarles, keeping to his rigid policy, closed the door behind him, making sure Devine, however well vetted, did not lay eyes on Lee.

But Lee's information had to be acted on at once. The Selganys were just across the border, surely waiting for nightfall to make a strike on the Sadler place. Quarles immediately decided it was time to talk to the man who wanted to be sheriff, for now the gamble promised to pay off.

Charlie Coyne, half drunk, swore he would bless the day Cole and Dennis Sadler were dead. He had taken his last bit of money to the Selganys, along with the news that the Sadlers were expected back that night. Although the Selganys, for their own reasons, were determined to finish off Hap's killers, Luke still pocketed Coyne's money without a word. Only the youngest put up any kind of squawk. "That means we got to cross that bitch of a border again. Damn if I like it!"

"It'll be nighttime," said Luke reassuringly. "We'll be over and back before they have time to spit or piss. Besides, we cain't let them buggers get clean away. You forgettin' what we owe Pa."

"If Pa was here he'd no more cross that border than take hog shit for gravy."

The third brother was cleaning his gun. He had been staring at Coyne for a noticeable period of time. "You coming along?" he asked sullenly.

"That wouldn't be wise," said Coyne unsteadily. "You fellows work best alone."

Coyne knew the Selganys didn't cotton to him. That he was a paying client meant little. Ruthless as they were they weren't the craven cowards which they suspected he was. It all came out in the youngest's comments. "Where you fixin' to be when we hit the Sadlers?"

"Best I slip back into town, keep an eye on things there."

"'Bout what I figured. You better be right about them Sadlers being there . . . My brother Luke likes your money but I calculate Pa would be alive today if'n he hadn't messed with a flat-eyed freak like you."

Coyne felt a cold sensation at the back of his neck, and, though half numbed by whiskey, told himself again he had to get away from these deadly cretins. He hated himself for needing them, but after tonight he wouldn't. After tonight he would be free to move about, free to plot his way to making more money. Charlie Coyne was as broke as he had been the day before he managed to get himself recruited by old man Crolly as an armed guard, protecting escaping slaves.

13

If Charlie Coyne hadn't been drinking he might have been able to scotch Quarles's plans, but Charlie, heading for the nearest bar upon returning to town, was bleary-eyed and near half asleep, his head propped on his arm, when night fell and whispers of a posse forming began to spread.

The acting sheriff, quickly assuming a self-importance that matched the significance of his new information, was busy deputizing volunteers for a posse to deal with some unidentified Missouri raiders plotting a foray over

the Kansas border that very night. Quarles was careful
not to give any hint that it might be the Selganys; he
knew the danger of seeming to know too much. But he
was prudent enough to leave two thoughts for the
lawman to ponder. One, it might well have been, as the
other already suspected, outsiders who attacked and
burnt out Cheatem's place last night, and two, since it
was known the Sadlers had some lumber dealings over
the border recently, perhaps these were the troublemak-
ing Missourians who owed them money, coming to settle
the debt with lead.

The acting sheriff had no trouble piecing these suggestions, insights, and information together and sagely
judging the old Sadler cabin to be the place to watch. He
was further strengthened in his shrewd conclusions by
Quarles's commenting he was displaying the very attrib-
ute people looked for in a sheriff. But Quarles was not as
calm and assured as he seemed. He was depending upon
another's vanity and what he perceived to be an un-
healthy inclination to scheme his way into a job calling
for men of a different stamp. Though acting this part
bothered Quarles, he turned away knowing a far uglier
task lay ahead. If this went well it might account for the
Selganys, but Charlie Coyne was his responsibility.
Charlie Coyne had killed Crolly; Charlie Coyne had
returned eight desperate Negroes on the lip of freedom
to slavery; Charlie Coyne, with the Sadlers gone, would
think himself free; but Charlie Coyne had only hours to
live, for Quarles, never shunting aside any task required
to carry out his mission, was going to deal with him.

The Selganys had been riding since sundown and it
was getting close to midnight. They deliberately stopped
on the trail where it swept past the ashes of Cheatem's
home, and now, guns in hand, were moving up silently
to the Sadlers. It appeared Coyne was right about the
Sadlers being home for they spotted a light in the cabin,
though it could only mean their victims were up and
about instead of asleep. Luke, leading the way, his
brothers close behind, hesitated then stopped warily at
fifty yards. There were no horses at the hitching post,

which meant little until, after studying the ground, he sent one of the brothers to check the shed in the rear. When the brother came back shaking his head, Luke felt a cold clamp of fear closing on the top of his spine. If there were no horses here there were no people, and that light was suddenly a sinister beacon, set by some human hand with intent to deceive. Fear, the most contagious of all emotions, struck the youngest next. "Jesus!" he blurted out. "Didn't I tell you this was tarnation foolish! Damn if Pa ain't spinnin' in his grave!" Suddenly they could feel the presence of others around them. The youngest one almost cried out, "What the hell do we do now?"

Like a base drum pounding the approach of doom, a voice roared out from the darkness behind them. "Lay down your guns before we blow daylight through your guts!"

Had wily old Hap been there they would never have surrendered. Their only chance was to draw and shoot, clinging to their fleeing mounts, praying darkness would help. But it happened too quickly. They were seized, disarmed, and with swift and callous handling had their hands bound behind them. But the worst was yet to come. The deceiving lantern was brought from the cabin and held to their faces, bringing on not only gasps of surprise, but a slow rising murmur of grim, even grisly satisfaction. Several members of the posse realized, by some incredible luck, they had caught the murdering scourges of the borderland, the notorious Selganys.

Ebert Devine proved to be an idealist, a pacifist, and a man devoted to godly works. He had long suspected he had a calling higher than history teacher in a rural primary school. When chosen for work in this daring slave rescue society, a cooperative church enterprise whose accomplishments had been reported in mythical proportions back east, he dropped to his knees in an hour of thankful prayer.

That evening Quarles, his mind elsewhere, was continuing his briefing when he encountered a problem that left him biting his lip and swinging uneasily in his chair. Ebert Devine did not believe in firearms. He was opposed to violence in any form and refused to carry or dispense the Beecher bibles routinely needed for this work.

Quarles, quietly stupefied and growing secretly annoyed, managed to regard him patiently for a moment before asking, "What will you do if people you are supposed to protect are attacked?"

"I have always placed my faith in prayer."

Quarles covered the wiry expression misshaping his mouth with a hand, but his eyes were vexed. Would the church fathers ever grasp what caliber of man was needed to pursue this hazardous work? When would they realize they had chosen to engage a well-armed enemy, supported by an entrenched society and shielded by the law? He shook his head. The briefing was over. Devine was told tomorrow he had to recruit help to escort some escapees over the border. Watching him retire with his Bible, Quarles could only think of a cloistered nun, armed with her beads, about to deal with rampaging Indians. Had he the power he would have dispatched Devine back east at dawn, but he was powerless, he had to accept the church's chosen candidates, unless . . .

The acting sheriff, once the Selganys were recognized, proved himself a woeful choice for his job. By rights he should have taken the prisoners back for trial and punishment under the legal system he was sworn to serve. But this crass though cagey opportunist sought popularity by letting himself be caught up in the mob rule sweeping the posse once the captives were identified. There was no check on lawless acts after that. The frontier's criminal code was raw, rudimentary, and reduced to basics. Those who lived outside the law got no protection from it. A long list of heinous crimes the Selganys were known to have committed were shouted out. A few men who had lost friends or relatives by their hand demanded the right to execute them. But the general consensus was for hanging. Torches were lit, revealing the pale, terrified faces of the Selgany boys, and ropes began to appear.

A tree alongside the Sadler cabin was chosen. There was no lack of ready hands to fix the noose about their necks. Bitter and profane language accompanied cries that hanging was too good for them. Fairness required they somehow be made to suffer for the many evils committed. In the end this lack of appropriate justice was cold-bloodedly made up for by some of the more vengeful faces drawing guns and shooting the three of them low in the belly before being hoisted away to eternity. Had he seen it, Ebert Devine would have gotten an indelible glimpse of the world he had just entered, a world where God-fearing men forsook the Commandments to tame the godless. This sight would have provided a lasting symbol for him. Three bodies, still dripping blood, hanging in the darkness, waiting for the probing beaks of ravenous buzzards coming to scavenge at dawn.

But dawn, rising on the breeze-swept prairie to the west, broke upon a different setting. Cathy was watching Cole and Troy, apparently deep in conversation down by the river, where the horses had been taken for water. Troy was slowly recovering from his wound and Cole finally looked rested. Now Cathy was anxiously waiting for her husband to return, feeling the issue between them had been delayed long enough. She was aware of strange forces astir in her of late, making her search beyond all familiar boundaries of her mind. She was no longer angry but her new feelings had fomented a visceral kind of determination. If she was going to put this man first at every turn in her life, she now expected no less in return. Across the camp she could see Hattie putting a coffee pot on a low fire and Dennis helping Chloe return blankets and other objects removed for the night to the lumber wagon. There was something unusual about that scene but at the moment Cathy was too distracted by her own concerns to dwell on it. Skeeter and Sam were busy slicing strips of venison from the deer's carcass to be frizzled and joined with cornbread for breakfast. Cheatem had disappeared a ways up the bank, probably to relieve himself.

In some vague way, in spite of her mental struggle, Cathy was glad she was there. She had hated that miserable cabin, detested the fear and violence that always seemed to hover over it. Amazingly, out here all threats seemed distant, somehow made smaller by space. But she knew, for discouraged parties heading east had twice reminded them, they were headed into lonely country with hostile Indians persistently reported, and living conditions at best uncertain.

Cole finally came back leading the team; behind him Troy was slowly herding the saddle horses to grazing ground. Cathy turned to face her husband but pointedly waited for him to speak. She noticed his eyes releasing a hardness they must have carried moments before.

"It's settled," he said with what she heard as relief.

"What's settled?"

"We're going to find some land to squat down on, build on, something we can call our own. If Troy wants to push into the mountains, a'chasin' that silver lode, he can do it alone."

Cathy looked at him steadily. "You're sure of that?"

"I just said it, didn't I?"

"What about Dennis?"

Cole's eyes found Dennis across the camp standing with Chloe. His expression turned curious, then puzzled. "Don't know. He's getting to be a man . . . likely he'll have his own notions about things."

That morning a broke, despondent Charlie Coyne, plagued by his hangover and experiencing both shock and relief at news that the Selganys were dead, was forced to pull his wits together when rumors of a man recruiting for some chancy mission reached his ears. With a little work he found himself talking to Ebert Devine, whose main interest seemed to be Coyne's church record. Was he a devout man? Charlie assured him he was, and was mildly amazed he was believed. Devine was answering no questions about himself but Charlie Coyne, able to read the signs, was convinced he was about to enjoy another capture of runaway slaves and a badly needed windfall of cash. Well, his luck had been running poorly lately, seemed no more than fair it should be ready to improve.

Quarles could not restrain a cynical smile when he saw Coyne's name on Devine's list of recruits. "What do you know about these men?" he asked casually.

"Good Christians, all of them. My faith has been strengthened, finding so many in a town such as this."

Quarles, breathing evenly, stared out the window for a moment. "What are your plans?" he asked.

"I've decided to leave tomorrow morning, should get there in time to meet with those poor souls. That is unless you have other thoughts."

"Just one. This gent here"—his thumbnail pressed the paper below Coyne's name—"I'd like you to have him show up at a spot I'll describe in a moment. It had better be this evening about an hour before sundown."

Devine took the list and looked curiously at the name. "May I inquire why?"

"It's a little check we make . . . find out if a man can follow orders."

"I see," responded Devine, though his tone clearly said he did not. "And just where is this spot?"

It was not a moment he wanted to remember.

From the foliage that lined the great flat rock, which the creek gently worked its way around, Quarles watched Coyne approaching. He had picked this place, where Crolly was murdered, for reasons of his own, but it also served to heighten Coyne's day-long suspicions. As Coyne dismounted and stepped uneasily onto the rock, Quarles moved out of the foliage to confront him. A moment of dread silence settled on them, two men alone in this isolated spot, where violent death had already struck once. Coyne immediately reached for his gun but hesitated when Quarles didn't follow suit. Instead Quarles was glancing about as though in quest of something. "This place look familiar?" he asked, his glance finally settling back on Coyne.

Coyne, his face noticeably pale and drawn, licked his lips. "Should it?"

"When you kill a man . . . ought to remember where you took his life."

Coyne turned sideways and dropped his front shoulder. It was a gunman's stance and his hand was back at his weapon. "Who the hell are you?" he muttered.

"Crolly's ghost—does that surprise you?"

Coyne no longer had the Selganys between him and the wrath of angry faces bent upon bringing him to justice. Now he would have to salvage himself, have to depend on his nerve and skill with a gun to keep breath in his body. He had spent an anxious day, shaken badly by this summons here. Now he knew delaying would only sap what was left of his self-control. He had to act quickly while his nerves held, his hand stayed steady.

But killing is not the simple act it seems. All raised in a Christian world have impounded into them that taking human life is a deadly sin. The Selganys had regressed to barbarism, as convinced as wolves of their right to kill, but Coyne was only a dissolute man, a parasite turned predator, killing at opportunities devoid of risk. Yet efficient killing is never a matter of will, which is open to all, but a matter of conviction, which is possible only for the few. Coyne, fighting a cringing fear of death, was experiencing a mindless rage at being trapped. Quarles was standing convinced this man's sins justified his death; continuation of his life risked the termination of others. For Quarles such a killing was near a duty. He stood alert but composed, watching Coyne going for his gun, aware he himself would be late with his draw. But Quarles's mind wasn't complicated by skeins of virulent hate, enervating fears, and unconscious guilt. Coyne was only driven by an animal rage to destroy what was trying to destroy him. In spite of his desperation and fury his first shot was near lethal; it hummed by Quarles's ear to ricochet off a boulder beyond. But Quarles's deliberate returned fire opened a hole on Coyne's face below his left eye, and Coyne pitched to the ground dead before his head struck the hard shale.

14

Cheatem, if nothing else, was a man who thought ahead. The day before they were eagerly trying for distance, but now talk of a destination and the best trails to follow had to be faced. "We ought to be making for the south fork of the river," said Silas, his tone barely concealing another attempt at authority. "Good flow of water there called Smoky Hill. It's a ways, but hear it's good pasture land . . . should take a crop."

Cole, secretly interested but looking faintly amused, swung to him. "Got your spread all picked out, eh?"

"Not exactly. Figure to do some samplin' and surveyin' for suitable ground before settin' up a claim."

Cathy's interest, which had been growing since her talk with Cole, carried new concerns. "What about those Indians? Folks say they're making trouble."

"Thought of that," grinned Cheatem. "There's a fort a few miles west of where I'm aiming to squat. Should keep 'em quiet."

If the others were deterred from further comment by Cheatem's confident, proficient preparations, for even Cathy found them comforting, Hattie's mind proved to be far from the cooking utensils she was cleaning in a pail. "Wat's dis talk 'bout Injuns?" she said, looking up.

"Figured you knowed we're heading into Injun country," said Cheatem, glancing westward, "but don't reckon they'll be a problem for long."

"Deys a problem now, dats enough!" complained Hattie.

Skeeter, worried the slow pace of the wagons might not have delivered them far enough from the border, slipped up to bend over her. "We cain't stay here," he mumbled, "right now deys more trouble behind us den ahead."

Hattie gave him a sour look. "We free . . . when we gonna move 'bout like it?"

Sam appeared and stared them both into silence. This was the wrong time for such talk; they needed the protection of an escort. His tight expression went from one to another, imparting its own message. Their time was coming.

After breakfast, with Cole mounted and leading the way again, Hattie noticed Chloe moving forward to sit near the front of the wagon, leaving empty her usual seat beside her mother. At first Hattie gave it little thought, but she was watchful by nature and in time began to grasp that innocent-looking shift could be the first hint of trouble. She stared at her daughter's light skin and near-Caucasian features and, with Skeeter climbing about the wagon, in a flash realized Chloe's coloration was closer to the sun-darkened complexion of the nearby Dennis than it was to the passing Skeeter's or even her own.

With a mother's prescience she sensed her daughter was attracted to the tall white boy, whose shyness and awkward attempts at making conversation with Chloe was enough to confirm the two already felt a physical attraction. In spite of his timid, bumbling ways this strapping youth's exchange of glances with her daughter was warning enough for Hattie; passion would soon follow. With her face a queer mixture of fear and suspicion, she turned to Ben. "You notice sumthin'?"

"Wats dat?" replied Ben, who had been dozing.

Hattie shook her head in sudden frustration. "Men! Not a one of you got a flick of sense! Wouldn't see duh sky fallin' on you."

Ben, inured to the endless demeaning charges endured

by men married to smarter women, simply nodded his head. "Reckon so." But Hattie was looking up at the sky, trying to clear her mind of a swelling apprehension and its source, her nubile daughter. But after a few minutes, seeing Chloe raise her hand to touch Dennis on the arm, she called out, "Chloe! You hurry back here! Hear me, child? You jus' best hurry!"

It was late that night when Quarles returned to find Devine readying his things for the morning. Ebert had been patiently waiting for him to return, obviously curious about Coyne. "Trust everything went well," Devine ventured quietly, his hands lightly clutching the lapels of his jacket.

"It went as expected," responded Quarles.

Devine's expression turned hopeful. "Then he's reliable."

Quarles turned to engage the other's eyes. "No, he's dead."

"Dead!" Devine seemed to lose his breath and only with effort recovered it. "Dead?" he repeated. "Good Lord!" he wheezed. "What happened?"

"I shot him," said Quarles coolly.

Devine took a step backward as though Quarles's breath transmitted a virulent plague. "You shot him." Shock made his voice sound hollow. "My God! Whatever for?"

"Because he killed the man you're replacing."

"He killed . . ." Devine managed to settle himself in a chair, one hand fumbling but finally reaching his forehead. "Mercy, can that be true?"

Quarles's faint smile tried to be sympathetic. "Didn't they tell you that before you left home?"

"Heavens, no!" He bit his lip as though struggling to remember. "They talked of hard work, sacrifice, even danger . . . but no . . . not killing."

"I'm sorry."

There was a long silence before Devine, excusing himself with a pale uncertain look at Quarles, fled the room.

Quarles sat down to write a supplicating letter to the

secretary of the society, humbly detailing his desperate need for more resolute men, those mentally prepared to meet the challenges of this work. He was aware the society didn't approve of killing either, but the society wasn't on this raw frontier, purloining the property of men whose standard solution to such problems was gunfire.

He was reasonably sure Devine was going back east in the morning and could deliver his note. What he didn't know was the startling answer to his missive would mark the end of his rescue operation and once again change his life.

Hattie was not the only one to notice the skittish tension building between Dennis and Chloe. Skeeter and Sam, young men conscious of their pretty cousin's physical appeal, soon picked up the vibrations and started nudging each other. Cathy Jo also had her curiosity perked by Dennis's solicitous behavior that morning. But Cole, who refused to react to what could only be a passing fancy, looked away. Young men at his brother's age were easily aroused; at seventeen he remembered the pressure from his gonads was merciless. Until he had Cathy to make love to he remembered having trouble getting certain comely females off his mind. Troy, as an older brother, told him that was God's way of insuring the race would survive. As long as men were driven by nature to want women, and vice versa, the human race would flower. Cole didn't always believe what Troy said in those days but he gratefully accepted this proposition, as it assured him God had a hand in a few lustful fantasies that nightly troubled his conscience.

Chloe listened to Hattie's hushed warnings about "making easy" with boys she hardly knew, particularly if they were white. But Hattie was wise enough to know that with girls of Chloe's age harmless attractions were often perversely inflamed by opposition. She limited herself to a few soft-sounding but stern admonitions. "You best stay here by me, y'hear child, dilly-dallyin' around dat way might give some folks notions."

Chloe looked at her mother with a teenager's suspicion that the autonomy that came with growing up was being spitefully denied her. But she was not yet ready to argue with her mother, for it was only recently that she sensed Hattie's protection to be a confining as well as a comforting thing. She looked back at Hattie, her subdued expression signaling compliance, but the secret excitement, ignited by her teasing exchanges with Dennis, had already spread from her breast to the flesh in other parts of her body. Nothing captivates the young like the mystery of their first attraction to the opposite sex. It is one of the milestones of the miracle called life. Unaccountable but electric emotions arise to illuminate a fabulous and unsuspected side of existence. The earth is seen in different colors and they are close enough to the fantasies of childhood to slip off into a world of incredible imaginings and golden prospects. Every new sensation is consuming, intoxicating, with their only desire that the love object not disappear. Chloe looked back at Hattie, nodding at her words, but her mind was far afield. Something was astir in the depth of her, and though it seemed innocent and quiescent she knew nothing her mother could say could match its promise. More fatefully, before long Hattie would realize no cautions or threats of hers, however well stated or intended, could match this new stirring power.

Quarles wasn't allowed to sleep until morning, when he expected Devine to depart. At 4 a.m. sand, repeatedly thrown against his window, had him up, knowing somehow it could only be Lee, standing in the shadows beside the house. At dawn he had expected to search for Lee to take over the assignment Devine was to handle that day, but he had no idea why Lee sought him out at this unseemly hour.

Lee came out of the shadows, looking behind him at some dusky figure resting against a tree. Quarles, keeping his voice close to a whisper, omitted any greeting. "What is it?" he began.

"Lame Fox," answered Lee. "Found him drunk . . .

scared someone is trying to kill him. He's been living in the brush for days . . . got boozed up and is talking a lot, don't think he should be allowed to fall into the wrong hands in his condition."

Quarles signaled him and the Indian into the house. With his finger to his lips he led them down to a cramped cellar and pointed to a pile of burlap where the Shawnee sank down and lay wheezing like a wounded animal. "He can sleep it off here," said Quarles resignedly. "What we can do, I don't know. Let's see in the morning."

Lee grunted agreement.

Quarles then pulled him over to the opposite side of the cellar. "I'm almost afraid to tell you but there's work for you again today," he began.

Lee held back a wiry expression that was rising and at the last moment he managed to work into a smile.

Henry Quarles was not a proud man, but he had given himself to a cause and that cause had become his destiny. To have killed Charlie Coyne at an earlier stage of his life would have been unthinkable, but fate had led him to this world of shadows. Watching dawn break that morning he was oppressed by a sense of impending and calamitous change, like the change that shattered his life at his wife's death. He was hardly different from other men. His mood was that which grips the mind when a meaningful span of time has passed, when one whispers to oneself one is aging, a stage of life is finished, a long sequence of days has slipped behind a tangle of memories and ill-connected scenes, constantly recurring but out of clear focus. Even the piety of Ebert Devine had pulled him back for a moment to the youthful Henry Quarles, with his bride and their childlike faith in a radiant future. He shook his head. That seemed so very long ago; was it only rising now to add to his premonition of fateful change?

Henry was an educated man. He knew the stresses the nation was suffering over slavery, knew the centrifugal force of conscience must one day overcome the malevo-

lent gravity of brutality, racism, and greed. He even
foresaw the cauldron of violence that would be required
for a nation to cleanse itself, restore itself, enable its
spirit to go forward again. He knew inevitably bloody
days lay ahead, but he would not know for many weeks
how prophetic this weird mood of his was. For Quarles
was not the only one watching this dawning with troubled eyes; his was not the only straining face marking a
sleepless night. Forty miles to the northeast at Fort
Leavenworth three officers sat around a table, surrounded by stained coffee cups and stamped dispatches,
received and studied or still in preparation. The men
had been there all night, a colonel, a major, and a
captain, career army men, whose long quiescent role in
this frontier post was coming to life. The colonel was
deciding dispositions and issuing orders, the major was
recommending alternative actions, reporting on available resources or the lack of them, the captain was
standing by to set the command in action. It had started
the evening before when a highly classified dispatch
arrived from Washington. Actually it came at the end of
a series of warnings, but was shocking just the same. The
army had been closely watching the floor of congress, for
the grave issue of secession carried critical implications
for a military facing divided loyalties. At first the secretary of war held his breath and hoped. The political
decisions of South Carolina were always retrievable but
the cannonballs falling on Fort Sumpter were not. Civil
war was breaking out. The government, desperately
fighting the southern fever to secede, was striving to keep
the loyalty of whatever slave states it could. Missouri
was clearly a crucial state. All activities tending to
alienate the slaveholders of Missouri, thereby increasing
the appeal of secession, had to be suppressed. Army
intelligence, aware of Quarles's organization, which,
because of church influence they pretended not to notice, was now a hazard; its role had to be eliminated or
radically reduced. A grim dispatch, that would arrive
two days after Ebert Devine started eastward, was on its
way.

⚑ 15 ⚑

By late the following afternoon they had reached the growing Topeka settlement. Because of a recent influx of southerners this was reputedly troubled territory. They drew the wagons close together, took the horses for water, then roped them in a grassy stretch nearby. Ben, who had been given no steady chores, perched on the low limb of a tree to stand guard.

Before starting a cooking fire Cole took Cathy Jo into the settlement, hoping some supplies might be available. What they found was expensive and of poor quality. They did better dealing with discouraged families heading back to civilization, anxious to raise money with goods they no longer needed. Cheatem, who appeared at the tailgate of a wagon they were dealing with, was busily buying more guns, striking bargains that soon impressed Cole. Twice Cole looked back at Cathy and shook his head. That Silas was surely designed for business. He had a cutpurse's eye for quick profit and the accounting skills of a loan shark. He walked off with two expensively engraved and leather-covered rifles for a fraction of their worth. Cole settled for some ammunition for their stock rifles and pistols.

Unnoticed, except by Hattie, Skeeter and Sam slipped off for a swift trip around the outskirts of the settlement. They were looking for friendly faces but they saw no blacks and the whites they approached greeted them with suspicious stares. Their few inquiries about work were rudely rebuffed. One woman, her head appearing from the rear of her wagon, half whined, "Where d'you two rascals come from? Don't make no mischief 'round

101

here . . . Ah'm warning you! Hear?" The southern accent rang like a tocsin. They went back to Hattie shaking their heads. "Dis sure ain't duh place," muttered Sam. "We gots to keep going."

"Bound to find better," mumbled Skeeter.

"Hope so . . . and mighty mighty soon," responded Hattie, her eyes now almost continually scanning the camp area. She saw Chloe peering into a piece of mirror propped on the wagon, tucking her hair in and turning to see her profile. This preening was becoming a constant thing. It made Hattie frown. She saw Dennis leaning against the wagon, whittling a piece of wood. But he wasn't looking at the wood, his glances were skipping lightning fast from Chloe to herself and back. This white boy had discovered Chloe's mama was watching. Would it make a difference? She knew a bit about white boys. She shrugged, clicking her tongue. She reckoned it wouldn't.

Henry Quarles brought the wretched Indian some hot coffee and food. He knew the Shawnee was living in fear of his life. Bribed into serving white men in ways that angered other whites, death now hovered over him as either punishment or a way to seal his lips. Lame Fox looked haggard and ill. He had stolen the whiskey he had gotten drunk on the night before and his stomach, outraged at the amount consumed, rebelled even at coffee and completely refused food.

But Quarles was patient and little by little Lame Fox nibbled at the nourishment and began to recover. What he could do was another story. Staying under cover, even hiding for a year, solved little; the frontier had no statute of limitations on rogue Indians. Lame Fox had to either flee this corner of Kansas, where he had spent his life, or die.

Quarles had little chance to think of Cheatem or the Sadlers since they left. Too preoccupied by events or troubled thoughts, waiting at the edge of consciousness to disturb every attempt at rest or reflection, the Sadlers came to mind only because they were fleeing from danger, as was this Shawnee. Was there some way Lame

Fox could reach them? Moving to the thinly populated west was surely one of his slim chances for survival. Turning thoughtful, Quarles left the Indian to rest, then, whispering to himself, as though composing some quick explanatory lines, he consulted his watch and hurriedly made his way to his desk.

Dennis Sadler was neither a brash nor very self-confident young man, in fact he was shy and given to worrying what others, particularly Cole, thought of him. He discovered his attention to Chloe was drawing disapproving looks from Hattie, and maybe Sam and Skeeter. But why he didn't know. He found the girl pretty, amiable, and, best of all, like himself a little unsure of things, qualities that made her easy to be with. There were no Negroes where he grew up and he had never thought much about race, though Chloe hardly looked different from girls he once had as neighbors in Indiana. But he could feel tension rising in the camp. What he was doing must be wrong.

Still Dennis couldn't believe liking Chloe was wrong. In fact he had secretly decided it didn't matter if it was. He and Chloe had been getting by on subtle touchings but the touchings only made them want more.

Cole wasn't totally surprised to find his younger brother motioning him aside to ask questions a worldly confidant would have smiled at. But Cole listened indulgently and seriously offered advice he knew wouldn't or couldn't be taken.

"You've got your eye on that girl and they don't cotton to it . . . figure you're up to no good."

"I haven't touched her."

"That comes in time."

Dennis looked at him ruefully, kicking the ground and fretfully rubbing his forearms. "What should I do?"

"Depends."

"On what?"

"How much you like her."

"So far, plenty."

"Then don't fool her. If you find yourself in a rutting mood make sure you mean it."

Dennis winced in distaste. "Why you got to put it that way?"

"That's the way others gonna put it . . . it's what's got 'em stewing."

Later Cathy Jo, having noticed the two talking, smiled at Cole, whispering, "Big brother is giving advice on matters of the heart, eh?"

Cole, mildly annoyed, wanted to turn away. "He'll grow out of it."

Cathy's eyes took on a faraway look, an expression he had come to realize usually meant feminine intuition was at work. "I'm not so sure," she murmured.

Cole simply grunted but took her hands in his, talk of Dennis and Chloe had turned his mind to some privacy with his fetching wife. Tonight after dark he was going to suggest they take some of their bedding and slip into the brush.

Skeeter and Sam saw Cheatem bringing his new impressive guns into camp. They eyed them with respect, Skeeter even remarking, "Mighty handsome shootin' irons!"

Cheatem swung around with his usual flair for postures of authority. "Figure one day they'll come in handy. Besides we got to start bringing down game and living off the land. Supplies cain't last if we keep digging into 'em." He took a few steps toward his wagon, then turned to them again. "Can either of you fellows shoot?"

Both seemed to be suppressing smiles, but Sam said quickly, "Tolerably well, sir." Skeeter realized the "sir" was to flatter Cheatem, but it also measured how much Sam wanted to get his hands on a gun.

"Well, we'll see," concluded Cheatem. He continued to walk to his wagon, but now with a stiff, almost military step. That "sir" did wonders.

It was not a night they would forget. There was gunfire in the settlement and horses were heard racing off into the night. Cole and Cathy, returning from their tryst, quickly lost the pleasant relaxed feelings they had been enjoying when they found Cheatem nervously pacing up and down between the wagons. "Damnedest country!" he exclaimed, seeing them approach. "Mighty foolish for you to be out there by your lonesome!"

Hattie, perched beside the lumber, called out, "What we needs is guards . . . folks to look out . . . cain't hardly sleep wid dat much fuss goin' on!"

Cole saw Troy coming from their wagon carrying a pistol. "I can watch this end," he said quietly, "but someone better keep an eye to the horses."

"Damn if that ain't right!" spat Cheatem, his glance falling on the watching Skeeter and Sam. "Hey, one of you fellows take a gun and get over there beside those horses. If we lose 'em we're in a hog pen of trouble."

Sam came quickly forward, and, getting a rifle from Cheatem, was soon grimly sitting on the same limb Ben had occupied that day.

In Topeka they heard it was several days' travel, beyond the mouths of the Republican and the Solomon, to the Salina settlement a hundred lonely miles to the west. It would be the last outpost they would hit before striking Smoky Hill country. Yet the trip started without trouble. Sam found an excuse to fire the new rifle at a tree stump, noticing the slug hitting slightly high and to the left. With only this chance zeroing in he was able to bring down a startled and swiftly scrambling deer at nearly a hundred yards. It happened so unexpectedly Cheatem was impressed. "Good shootin', boy!" he called from his wagon seat. "Glad to see you're real handy with that thing. Figure to make you my night guard from now on."

Sam didn't answer but he and Skeeter exchanged glances while Hattie sighed to herself. She had always regarded Skeeter as peaceably inclined but had never been real sure about Sam. She covered her face with her hands, muttering to herself. Here they were free, yet helpless without a way to support themselves. There would always be danger until they found a place where they could settle safely. She had thought they were heading north, perhaps even to Canada, but something had gone wrong and now they were traveling west, at the mercy of folks, some of whom seemed kind enough. But this Cheatem, though no longer pestering Chloe, was clearly only interested in himself. Hattie hoped her two nephews wouldn't do anything foolish until she and Chloe were somewhere safe. She was not opposed to getting Chloe away from this party; in fact, it was beginning to seem her only hope. Cheatem had been easy to warn off since Chloe despised him, but Dennis was another matter. Now it was Chloe who needed warning. During the day her daughter persisted in sitting forward in the wagon and Ben, his head propped on one arm, lying beside Hattie, pursed his mouth up in the knowing way of the old when sizing up the young. "Believe Chloe got chiggers in her bottom," he commented almost philosophically.

"You hush yo' mouth!"

"What d'you expect. A young gal . . . it bein' spring and all. Hattie, you forgetting' wat it wuz like bein' young?"

"Stop dat foolish talk. How you 'spect ah'm gonna forgit bein' young . . . bein' a gal . . . bein' black?!"

Ben shifted uncomfortably. "Mebbe different here."

"Only difference is ah didn't have to listen to yo' foolish talk back den. Now like ah said, hush up!"

Ben said no more until dark, when night fell on that fateful setting where trouble first struck.

Quarles had little difficulty convincing Lame Fox his only salvation lay in flight, but flight to where was the question. He was in danger, surely courting an unmarked grave. The Shawnee looked about him with the ravaged eyes of the damned. In a white society fugitive redskins needed white friends to survive, but only whites likely to consider him useful could be safely approached. Quarles's mind had settled on the Sadlers, but was far from certain they would agree. He had written a reassuring note to Troy and Cole, citing the Indian's value and only obliquely referring to Lame

Fox's need for a safer haven than Douglas or any of the surrounding counties.

By day's end Lame Fox was forced to accept Quarles's plan, as neither could think of another, and that night they made their way to the vacant Sadler cabin. Quarles pointed to the heavy tracks made by the wagon loaded with lumber. He asked one of the best trackers on the border if he could follow that sign until he overtook them. The Shawnee was in no mood for smiling but he looked at Quarles with that curious expression Indians reserve for whites who find it hard to believe Indians can read the earth as they themselves might a second-grade primer. Quarles pressed his hand and, warning him not to dally, wished him luck as he galloped off into the night.

If long stretches of deserted land made Cole occasionally think of Indians he knew it wasn't Indians he now saw approaching in the distance. They were white men, heavily armed and curiously halting as they approached the little wagon train. He watched them stop and dismount while still half a mile away.

Instinct warned Cole to halt too.

"What's the trouble?" demanded Cheatem from behind.

"Don't know," responded Cole. "Aiming to find out."

Troy came up, his shoulder still bandaged but now giving his arm free movement. He joined Cole, who was still staring ahead. "What do you think?"

"Hard to tell."

"Trouble?"

"Could be . . . I figure to stay here, let 'em come to us."

Cheatem, listening behind them, turned to signal to Skeeter and Sam. "Best you boys get up here." Sam came up holding his rifle and Cheatem, nodding at it, reached behind him and brought out a second gun for Skeeter. "Don't know what the hell this is all about but best be ready."

A long silence ensued until Cole, looking at the dropping sun, made a motion to Cathy to bring her wagon up. "Late enough to make camp," he said, affecting a nonchalance he didn't feel.

But it didn't fool Cathy. "Who are those people?" she asked.

"Don't know . . . suspect we'll find out a'fore long."

Hattie, alerted by the halt, was peering toward the distant figures. "Lordy, ah smell trouble . . . trouble like de Lord got to protect us from. Ben, get up and help . . . dey fixin' to set up camp."

"So early?"

"Dats right! Deys sinful-looking folks out dere, jus squattin' and conjurin' up Lord knows what, deys things we gots to do before dark."

⚔ 16 ⚔

It was still light enough to see the far horizon when two riders detached themselves from the strange group and slowly cantered toward them. Cole, glancing around the campsite, was on the verge of warning Cathy and even Chloe to stay under cover but was reluctant to further alarm them.

Cheatem, standing in his wagon, was the first to make out the oncoming riders. "Sure as hell don't look like no preachers," he muttered. "Funny, just two a'coming. I calculate there be eighteen to twenty of 'em."

"They're fixing to palaver," said Cole, moving out to keep the visitors as far from the wagons as possible. Troy and then Cheatem joined him. Dennis, Skeeter, and Sam, all armed, watched from the far side of the lumber wagon.

"Howdy," Cole called out as they rode up. One was a thin-faced man with a straggly beard and a mouth that opened to reveal several front teeth missing. The other was heavyset and grossly fat, his belly pressing against his gun belt and overflowing around the saddle horn. The thin one wore a slouched hat, the fat one had a shock of red hair held in place by a filthy headband.

They were both smiling but their smiles lacked animation, as though painted on their faces. Almost immediately Cole could see they were studying the campsite.

"Howdy," answered the thin one. "Figured you might have some horses to sell cheap."

"Figured wrong," said Cole. "Going to need every head we got. Sorry."

"Where you folks headed?"

"West," said Cole, making it clear he didn't intend to say more. He was striving to look casual but a feeling of imminent danger was beginning to chill him. He didn't like the way these two were sizing up their party; they were looking curiously hard at Sam and Skeeter, who now had guns visible before them.

"You lettin' niggers mess with guns?" grunted the fat one.

Troy who, like Cole, could feel the rising menace, blurted out, "That's right! And either one of them boys can shoot warts off a toad."

The thin one suddenly began to look doubtful, as though wondering if this bunch would be as easy to deal with as expected. Small parties, badly outnumbered and beyond the pale of law and order, usually gave dangerous-looking gangs stalking the trail whatever they wanted. Occasionally a party, defying the odds, would fight, usually to be overpowered, robbed, and often murdered. But these dubious characters had about concluded this particular outfit looked too able to inflict damage and wasn't showing reassuring signs of fear or panic.

Cole, watching them closely, was near certain they were ready to pull out, when a secret fear he had been quietly suppressing became a reality. Cathy, who had been watching from her wagon, could see the men standing together but couldn't hear the conversation. She learned little from the few expressions and gestures she could make out. As minutes passed her curiosity increased. Finally she jumped down and started toward the parley. Hattie, sitting out in the open, had a feeling Cathy's appearing at that moment was a mistake. She should have stayed out of sight, just as Chloe, at Hattie's insistence, was made to do. But it was too late to wave her back, she was already nearing the group and the two men facing the campsite had spotted her. Most settlers' wives, plain or coarsened by hardships and overwork, were not females likely to cause a stir, but Cathy's figure and her swaying walk had the two visitors glancing at each other. Cole thought he saw a silent communication pass between them.

"Sure yuh won't sell us some horses?" remarked the thin one, but now showing no interest in an answer.

Cole simply shook his head.

"Could be you be sorry," grinned the fat one, pulling his horse about. "When we 'uns come asking a favor . . . smart folks usually grant it right handy."

The three men watched the two visitors ride off. "Glad the ugly varmints is gone," said Cheatem.

Cole, now noticing Cathy had been standing in full view behind him, looked at Troy and shook his head. "No, they're not gone," he muttered. He looked up at the sky that was now beginning to darken. "They'll be back, count on it."

As night fell Cole, in spite of the need for warmth and a desire for hot food, was reluctant to light a fire. A thin cover of cloud was making the moon a pale mask, a featureless disc, its vague light defused and lost in the depths of the prairie night. Rising tension made the campsite seem weird, everyone whispering to allow sounds coming from the darkness beyond to remain clear and easily identified. Cheatem was the only one arguing for movement, wanting to travel in the hopes they could lose this menacing gang during the night. But Cole and Troy both knew that was asking for an ambush. No, they'd have to stay put until morning. They knew this ground and while it wasn't ideal it had a few boulders that would help a defense.

Since it was agreed that the others were hovering somewhere close by, Sam and Skeeter wanted to crawl out and find what direction they were likely to attack from. But Cole insisted they all stay together. If shooting began in the dark he wanted a common field of fire. He had been in a few wild gun fights. Fighting did strange things to the mind; once people got excited they often ended up shooting friends as well as enemies. Only Sam wasn't convinced. There was a lone tree twenty-five yards from the edge of the campsite. He explained to Cole a man in that tree would be a thorny problem for anyone attacking the camp.

Cole didn't disagree but he also foresaw a man in that tree could be dead long before one behind a boulder or a wagon. Troy, studying the dark plain around them, finally spoke up. "I think we've got to figure out what they ain't expecting. If we just squat down here and fight we're sure gonna pay a price."

Earlier Cole had posted Dennis on the far side of the camp, beyond the lumber wagon, stopping only to ask Ben if he could handle a gun. "He cain't see rightly enough to shoot," declared Hattie, staring Ben into silence as he fought to say, "Wat you mean? Ah cain't shoot?"

"Which is it?" demanded Cole.

Hattie sighed. "Give dat fool a gun if you a mind to," she lifted her eyes to throw a supplicating glance to heaven. "Great sassafras! You'd think ole Hattie didn't have enough to worry her bones!"

Hours later, when fatigue began numbing the stabs of anxiety taxing their minds, they heard a horse galloping up to stop a hundred feet from the wagons. A voice came out of the darkness. Cole was sure it was the thin man's. "You over there! You sure enough listening?"

"Just who we listening to?" responded Cole.

"Don't make no never mind . . . just do like I say and you folks will maybe get out of here alive!"

Like Cole they were all peering out into the darkness, trying to make out the speaker's face, but it evaded them. His words however did not. "We'll take three horses, two good guns, and a spell with that woman you got along." There was a suspenseful silence in which the muscles around Cole's heart tightened, and Cathy's hand came up to grip her throat. Then another horse could be heard coming up. Low words were heard being exchanged. The rasping voice punctured the night again. "Leave them horses, guns, and that gal right here and git on your way, otherwise buzzards aplenty will be picking your bones clean come dawn."

Troy and then a breathless Dennis were suddenly beside Cole. "Let's go after that bastard and kill him!" rasped Dennis.

"Believe we can still catch him!" added Troy excitedly.

"Don't worry. We're going to get our chance," answered Cole, his voice suddenly thick with swelling rage.

Another figure came hustling up. "Got us figured for a pack of hog-lickin' dirt farmers," said Cheatem, holding a shotgun and strapping on a second pistol. "I ain't looking for trouble, but if swine like that aims to buffalo Silas Cheatem out of his goods, they got a few surprises coming."

Troy, who resented Cheatem, and felt he dodged every risk, realized when outraged enough even Cheatem was willing to fight.

Cathy, aware now allowing herself to be seen was a mistake, remained silent, waiting for Cole to come back to their wagon. She heard the remarks coming from the darkness, shocking her with the realization that the evil she had thought only befell others was suddenly claiming her. Cole found her hefting Troy's pistol in her hand. "Don't believe you're going to need that," he said, his voice sounding too calm to be believed. "Best you get under the wagon."

She leaned up to him, her face inches from his in the darkness. "Cole, we gonna get out of this?"

"We got six . . . maybe seven guns. Should be able to hold 'em off."

She reached up and hugged him. "Cole, I'm afraid we're all going to be killed! . . . murdered!"

He hugged her back. "I know . . . but when it comes to fighting best let the other side do the worrying."

Skeeter, light-footed as a puma, came up behind him. "Where d'you want me?" he whispered.

Cole turned to him with a start, then, pausing to study him in the darkness, was aware something was missing. "Where's Sam?" he asked.

"Don't know."

Cole gazed into the darkness. "Is he up that damn tree?"

"Might be, Mistah Cole, dat Sam ain't got a lick of sense."

Cole went to the edge of the campsite nearest the tree. "Sam!" he called several times, but got no answer. Troy was beside him again. "We better be getting ready, we may not have much time."

Cole sent Dennis back to the other side of the lumber wagon, suggesting Troy join Cathy at their wagon and urging Cheatem back to his rig. He kept himself free to reinforce whatever side was hit first. There was little more he could do. The hardest part of the fight now had to be endured; waiting for the other side to strike.

Dennis, crouching under the lumber wagon, clutching his gun, soon realized Chloe was lying hardly three feet away. Beyond her he could see Hattie's larger bulk, but as the tense minutes slipped by, and the night noises filled the plain around them, he sensed Chloe was slowly getting closer to him. Finally he looked down to discover she was less than a foot away. In spite of the tension Dennis felt excitement starting in his loins. An impulse, unbidden and seeming beyond control, started his hand towards her. He touched the fabric of her dress and, pressing down, felt the flesh beneath, telling him he was gripping the back of her thigh. She didn't move as his hand slipped up over her rump and onto her back. They lay like that until some nocturnal animal scrambled through the grass before the wagon and distracted everyone. But as the night settled down again he felt Chloe slowly turning until she was partially resting on her back, by then his hand had slipped around her body and was cupping her breast. The excitement in Dennis now had his heart racing, and a desire to pull her to him near beyond containing, when a low rumble of hooves, thundering across the prairie, broke into his consciousness and he whipped his hand back to grasp a firmer grip on his gun.

Traveling alone Lame Fox moved far more rapidly than the wagon train. He had no trouble following it that first night, for the trail led directly west without a split off until the Topeka settlement. He arrived there shortly after dawn. He could not risk going in among the shacks and pitch tents but slipped around the outskirts until he picked up the heavy wagon tracks again, heading west along the river.

Now, with daylight, he was slowed by the need to slip into the nearby brush at the sight of even a lone rider. With his life at stake he dared not be seen until far enough away to greatly reduce the chance of being recognized. In spite of appearances Lame Fox, careworn and approaching fifty, old for an Indian, had not always been a shadowy figure on the fringe of the white world. As little more than a boy he had fought in Kentucky against the Cherokees and the tribes to the south, he had taken scalps and seen his enemies burnt at the stake. While still a youth he had listened to inspiring tales about his great tribesman, Tecumseh. If since then he suffered from years of poor food and worse whiskey, the redman's palliative for dangerous or degrading work, he refused to surrender completely to civilization's corrupting of his body and spirit. He still dreamed of days when he was a fighting warrior, prominent among his people. Though now embittered, watching the cruel isolation forced upon pathetic remnants of the once powerful Shawnees, he held tightly to his earlier dreams and fought to hold his tribal beliefs. If that proud and adventurous world bequeathed to him was gone, and his kinsmen a collection of beggars, drunkards, and vagrants, Lame Fox remained at heart a Shawnee warrior, with a warrior's pride in his ability to suffer and survive.

He was not sorry to be heading west. There were tribes out there still masters of their own fate, still proud and defiant, still able to honor bravery and loyalty at their council fires and meet other tribesmen with dignity.

Contrary to popular belief more than a few eastern Indians had managed to join western tribes, their superior knowledge of the whites increasing their value as fighters, many not only quickly gaining acceptance but renown. Lame Fox had a talisman, a small medicine bundle containing a hawk's claw and some mysterious bones. He touched it now, feeling it was strong medicine. It made him feel good, confident, favored by the spirits.

Though he was pressing forward it was the latter part of the afternoon before he spotted the little wagon train, drawn up in a triangle on the plain little more than a mile away. He was glad. He wanted to join them, show them Quarles's note and hear them agree to let him stay. He had been running like a furtive animal long enough.

Suddenly, picking up an annoying sight, he slipped from his horse again and retreated into the brush. A large body of riders was gathered a short distance from the wagons. He could not make out their dress or equipment but he dared not let them see him. He would have to wait until they moved on before getting any closer. Resigned to another delay, he worked his way further into the brush and settled down.

Cole heard the thunder of hooves approaching, just giving him time to shout, "Don't shoot 'less you see something . . . they'll be aiming at the flash of your guns!"

He was almost right. The riders had noisily circled the wagons, firing blindly into them, hitting sideboards and canvas, but very few slugs struck the ground beneath.

Only Skeeter and Cole got off any shots and these were against riders who had dismounted to approach the wagons on foot. Dark as it was eyes adjusted to the night could make out forms suddenly growing larger with powder flashes marking their way.

But it was a futile attack; the wagon defenders could never be rooted out by such means. The raiders only succeeded in stampeding the horses, which broke away from the rope corral and, spooked by noise, thrashed about wildly until, finding themselves free, they fled across the prairie in a dozen directions.

"We'll fetch 'em later," the thin man was shouting as he called off the sweating, swearing riders. Another way to overwhelm these wagons had to be found if they were to get what they wanted. Since she had been seen, gruff male asides had aroused fantasies, making Cathy more voluptuous and desirable with every remark.

"Gonna have to crawl up and shoot under them wagons," the thin man was wildly bawling. "Buggers are squattin' under 'em . . . don't figure to come out . . . gonna have to smoke 'em."

But dissension was secretly beginning. Two were already wounded, others were reluctant to crawl through the grass against ready guns. "We got the horses, why don't we clear out?" shouted one.

"Those bastards are dead set on fighting . . . got to be easier pickings somewheres else," squealed another.

"Now don't get to talkin' rabbitty," growled the fat man, leaning back to ease his stomach around his saddlehorn. "Quick as we wing one or two of 'em, they bound to quit, like whipped pups."

But no one answered and tension salted the air as they moved into a nearby grove of trees. "Leave your horses here," ordered the thin man. "Won't take us long to finish this."

The fat man dismounted but left his rifle in its saddle scabbard. "Don't 'speck I could do much good crawlin' through that grass . . . me being a little heavy and all," he muttered aloud. "Best I keep an eye out here."

Some of the men looked at him, a glint of resentment in their eyes. Nothing was said but there was reason for their rancor. This foul-smelling saddle tramp had joined them but three days ago. To their suspicious and wary eyes it was clear he had something on the thin man, something that gave this porcine figure power over their leader. Glances were exchanged but only muted grumbling could be heard as the men slipped back to the wagons, spreading out to attack from all sides. Some of them were chafing that their boss, lusting over a woman, was putting them in a dangerous fix. The little wagon train was proving itself gutsy and capable of making work for the undertaker. What rankled most was if that woman were taken, the fat man's hold on their leader would surely make her his first.

Sullenly they flattened to the ground and moved up toward the wagons. Here and there shots rang out. At first they were single, isolated ones with a tenuous silence in between. But then two shots started sounding in rapid procession, with one of the men yelping in pain every second or third time. The attackers quickly realized someone besides the wagon defenders was firing on them, but from which direction they couldn't tell. They kept straining cautiously to peer around, but while hugging the ground for safety none of them thought to look up.

When the raiders first attacked and circled the wagons at a distance, Sam was sure he had made a mistake. Surrounded by the tree's foliage he could neither see about him nor follow a single raider long enough to get a decent bead. But with this second attack he had only to wait for the muzzle flash of a gun and then fire at a spot two or three feet behind it. He was missing more times than not and couldn't aim at vital points, but he was hitting enough of them to raise a few cries of pain.

The thin man, cursing to himself, realized this attack had to succeed quickly or it was doomed. He wondered if he could get these men, who were now grunting profane epithets that smacked of defiance and even desertion, to charge forward and take these wagons by storm. While swinging his head about he caught the faint glow of a powder flash dying out above him and realized at once the gun bedeviling them was in the tree. He

shouted to his men and a dozen rifle barrels turned
upward.

Lame Fox had suffered a maddening day of frustration
and doubt. That annoying gathering of men refused to
leave, removing any chance of approaching the wagons.
He had decided to wait until dark and then sneak
around them. It looked like a simple task, but with
darkness a startling event took place. Those faceless
riders began to attack the wagons, with Lame Fox
looking on in shock and dismay. They were trying to
destroy his hope of protection and survival.

Shaken and appalled at the sight, he abandoned
caution, picketing his horse in the brush and racing
forward on foot. If possible he was going to slip into that
triangle of wagons and help defend them. They were his
passage to another chance at life. But suddenly, adding
to his quandary, the shooting stopped. Coming much
closer now, he was able to vaguely make out a line of
horsemen disappearing into the dark shadows of a
cluster of trees. Boldly he kept moving forward until he
was near enough to hear voices. He sensed the men had
dismounted and by holding himself in studied stillness
was just able to hear a husky voice issuing commands.

Under the embattled wagons the party's expressions
ran from frantic fear to smoldering rage. Hattie, though
continually sitting up and praying in loud whispers, still
managed to badger a curious Chloe and an excited Ben
into staying down. Skeeter, not taking his eyes off the
swirling figures around him, had to reach over and grab
the back of her dress, pulling Hattie, flat between them
and out of his line of sight. "Stay dere!" he commanded.
"Ah needs to see every whichaway."

Dennis had moved behind a wheel and, following
Cole's warnings, was waiting for a target. Two bullets
striking the lumber overhead made him glance around
to look for Chloe. He saw her lying on the ground, her
body posture hinting her eyes were on him.

Under the Sadler wagon Cole's suppressed fury and
gnawing fear for his wife kept leading to desperate

moves that had Cathy holding her breath. Troy kept
cautioning his brother. "Let 'em come to us, a little
straight shootin' gets 'em thinking quits every time!"

But Cole kept wanting to charge out into the night,
getting his gun sights on that thin man and his fat
companion. Ignoring his own warning, he had been
leaning out from under the wagon, praying to catch sight
of one or the other. But it was not to be. After he had
fired at some figures riding too close to the wagons, he
was stunned by the realization that their horses were
being stampeded, their snorting and rearing forms
breaking free and disappearing into the night. There was
nothing he could do, but in his furor he thrust his hands
forward and started to leave the protection of the wagon.
Troy, grabbing his gun belt from behind, pulled him
back. "We can live without them goddamned horses," he
shouted. "Right now we need that gun of yours a damn
sight more!"

Cathy, seizing his arm and desperately hoping the
outlaws would take the horses and go, could only keep
breathing in his ear, "Cole, please! Don't leave me!"
Suddenly the shooting stopped and they sat for a tense
spell in silence until Cole, raising himself on one knee,
peered into the darkness and turned to gasp, "By Jesus,
now they're crawling through the grass!" He lifted his
voice to reach the other wagons. "Get ready! They're
fixin' to rush us!"

Lame Fox, moving like a wraith through the darkness,
suddenly realized what he had stumbled upon. The men
had left their horses in this grove to attack the wagons on
foot. Desperate and searching for a way to rescue the
ones who an hour before he expected to rescue him, he
immediately thought of stampeding these horses, forcing
these figures to stop attacking the wagons and recover
their mounts. But could he manage that many horses?
He saw they were lightly hitched around the grove, some
simply standing with their reins hanging down, but
others were tied tightly enough to keep them from
pulling away on their own. These he would have to free.
Slipping his knife out he began to circle the grove,

cutting loose those he found tied, but it wasn't until
he had nearly completed the circle that he realized he
wasn't alone. His ears picked up a wheezing that he
recognized as heavy breathing a dozen feet away. Freezing in his tracks, he knew he had unwittingly given his
presence away and that someone, left to guard these
horses, had heard him moving about. The click of a gun,
followed by a high, coarse voice, proved him right. "You
move erry an inch and you git blown to hell!"

Lame Fox couldn't stop to think; there was no hope if
he was taken here. Only the darkness of the grove, which
kept his features obscure, saved him. An Indian found
cutting loose white men's horses would be shot out of
hand. But that was coming, death was only a closer look
away. With the knife he used cutting still in his hand he
dove to the ground, causing the gun before him to roar
and spit its orange tongue over his head. Like a heavy cat
he sprang forward and drove the knife into a bulky figure
that grunted loudly as it tried to fend the knife off. But
Lame Fox knew that shot was a death knell if he didn't
get out of that grove. Fortunately the figure he was
grappling with proved so fat the man had trouble using
his limbs. Lame Fox kept plunging the knife into him,
whipping it from hand to hand to cut into other parts of
the body. He heard a labored squealing that was struggling to be a shout and deftly slashed his knife across the
bloated throat to silence him.

Then he was off, knowing the shot fired had already
stampeded many of the horses, but grimly aware he had
just murdered a white man, and now there would never
be a sanctuary for the Shawnee called Lame Fox.

In the grass before the wagons the thin man kept
commanding his men to fire at the sniper hiding in the
tree, and one by one guns were turned upward. Sam,
hearing shots slicing through the leaves about him,
scrambled up the trunk like an agile monkey till he
reached a perch formed by two large branches reaching
outward. This wouldn't save him but would make him
more difficult to hit.

From the wagons Skeeter and then Cole saw the guns being lifted and knew they had spotted Sam. Skeeter, without hesitation, stood up and started firing below the gun flashes; within seconds Cole was doing the same. More cries broke out. The thin man knew they either had to charge these wagons or quit; this kind of fighting was only asking for trouble and flirting with death. It wasn't their game, they had always counted on intimidation and raw fear to get them what they wanted. It was time to call this risky hand. He wanted all of them to rush forward together, and needed quiet to signal a common start. "Stop firing!" he kept shouting until slowly a hush settled over the grassy ground around the wagons. "When I give the signal," he cried, "everybody charges!" Then he stopped and took a deep breath, counting to three, expecting to end with a piercing "Let's go!" But a heartbeat before his voice rose the puzzling crack of a pistol sounded from the grove behind them and men were suddenly turning to glance back anxiously. Was somebody after their horses?

The thin man wanted to start the charge but this threat was too great to ignore. The horses from the wagon train had already disappeared, they couldn't be left afoot. Heavily armed cavalry units were forever using these trails to relieve garrisons in the west. He couldn't risk an encounter with them, not afoot. Without being ordered, two men backed away and left in a run for the grove. As they did horses could be heard galloping out the far side. "Jesus!" cried a voice. "They've spooked our ponies!"

"Let's git over there!" bellowed another. "The hell with these wagons!" A mad rush started for the grove and Cole, still standing, lowered his gun and watched them go. He was too relieved or too spent for speech. When he turned he found Cathy rising beside him. She didn't speak, just took his arm and hugged it. He stayed silent too. It was only from the way he pulled her around and embraced her that she sensed the attack was over. After the embrace she heard Cole and Troy talking but their words meant nothing; she only knew the horror

hanging over her for hours had just been swept away by
some unexplainable shot from the grove. She just hung
there feeling empty.

It was Cheatem coming up with his shotgun who
broke the spell. "Could be somebody lending us a hand,
eh?"

⚔ 18 ⚔

An hour before dawn Lame Fox, moving furtively
through the heavy darkness, came within fifty feet of the
wagons. After the killing he had fled from the grove to
hide in the nearby brush, but his mind was on heading
back to his horse, convinced his only hope was racing
westward and losing himself in the mountains or those
wild river valleys legends of his people said lay beyond
the setting sun. But his heart resisted this; it smacked of
a long, lonely struggle to survive in an alien land. Much
as he had suffered in this white man's world he had also
grown used to its comforting sides. Surely he did not
need coffee, sugar, or even whiskey to survive, but once a
part of life their loss would seem a hardship. Desperation made him gamble, perhaps they would never know
who murdered the man in the grove. Perhaps those in
the wagons wouldn't care. He knew the raiders had
rounded up what horses they could and left. Finding the
body of the fat man had a weird effect upon them,
causing the one with the commanding voice to shout
shrilly, "By Jesus, they've cut him to pieces! Let's get out
of here! Damn if I won't be next!"

After the raiders, many riding double, departed, he
raced back for his own mount and in spite of the
darkness started rounding up what strays he could find.

The draft animals proved easy, several had stopped to munch lush grass within a mile or two of the wagons, others were found drinking along the river. The saddle horses were harder to corral, but without knowing who they belonged to he managed to get three. Now he was approaching the wagons. Now the answer to his desperate hopes was only moments away. Drawing a deep breath he threw his head back and, with one hand over his beating heart, gave two loud hoots of the hunting owl.

Cole, who was standing with Sam and Skeeter, heard the hoots and stared into the darkness, thinking it was a strange time and place for a feeding owl. He was not alone. Both Sam and Skeeter mumbled almost together, "Dat ain't no owl."

By some random association peculiar to the mind, Cole remembered it was owl hoots they listened for the morning Crolly died. It was a signal Lame Fox was to give. But his next thought was almost too ridiculous to express, for he knew this simply couldn't be Lame Fox! Almost simultaneously the three of them dropped to the ground in the hopes of seeing a figure outlined against the sky, but the pitch blackness just preceding dawn had blended heaven and earth.

Skeeter, settling against a wagon wheel, his gun aimed outward, spoke up. "Who dere?"

After a silence a voice croaked uncertainly, "Me friend. Me Lame Fox."

Cole let his breath out. "Lame Fox! I'll be goddamned!"

"Who dis Lame Fox?" muttered Sam warily.

Cole was still dealing with the incredulous. "An Indian guide . . . used to work with Crolly and Quarles's outfit. But what in Christ's name is he doing here?"

Cheatem, coming up, heard Cole's remark. "Maybe he fired that shot a while back . . . it sure took starch out of that thin bastard's pecker . . . could be t'was him."

Cole took a couple of steps forward. "Come in," he half shouted, "but come slowly and don't be pointing any guns." As an afterthought he decided he'd better offer the Indian a little reassurance. "We'll be doing the same."

Lame Fox came out of the gloom, looking like a man gingerly approaching a critical haven he was doubtful would receive him. But without knowing why, every member of the wagon train, watching him approach that murky dawning, was glad to see him.

Three hours later, with four of them searching, they had all but one of their draft horses back and one more saddle horse than they started with. Not having eaten since yesterday noon, Hattie and Cathy prepared a large community breakfast, and Chloe carried everyone a hot tin plate heaped with bacon and cornbread. Troy, standing arms akimbo by the fire, insisted they had done themselves proud and had taught that trail trash a lesson. Cheatem allowed this was true but made possible only by his prudent providing of adequate arms. Cole, shrugging off both comments, muttered they had been mighty damn lucky, and now he understood why wagon trains traveled in such large numbers.

Hattie had finally gotten Skeeter and Sam, along with Chloe and Ben, to bow their heads for a moment while she thanked Lord Jesus for their deliverance. But if Chloe's ears were listening her heart was secretly thanking Dennis, in spite of the fact he sheepishly admitted he hadn't fired a shot that counted. Skeeter, head bowed beside her, was wondering if Hattie's thanking Jesus meant the Savior had fired that shot in the grove. Sam, standing far back and never convinced he was righteous enough for divine favors, figured a sinner didn't rate any safer hiding place in that tree.

In a recovering mood, Cathy sat eating quietly, her thoughts on how this ordeal seemed to have brought them together. There was a budding sense of community in the campsite that morning. Cathy was beginning to sense how danger and sharing common trials had a cohesive effect on humans. Even old Ben, carrying in an armful of wood, gestured to Cheatem for help in piling it by the fire and got it.

Only Lame Fox, hanging back among the wagons and

feeling alone, was still weighing his lot. With relief he had watched Cole and others reading Quarles's note, then nod approvingly in his direction. It was his luck to arrive at a moment when any useful addition to the train was welcome. But his luck extended beyond that. Though he watched carefully not a soul ventured into that grove until just before they left when he, himself, slipped in to find the fat man still lying there, his handgun lying beside him, apparently overlooked in the dark. He scooped it up and turned to go, but that morning he had heard much talk about the thin man and his fat companion, and decided they were truly evil men. His old instincts flashed over him and he decided this fat man deserved the same treatment Shawnees gave their enemies. With a quick motion of his knife he cut a circle on the dead man's head and ripped out a scalp lock of messy red hair. Tucking it under his belt and out of sight, he loped back to join the hurriedly departing wagons.

Henry Quarles had been living through days of mounting tension. Lee had gotten the new escapees safely into Kansas and with time to arrange matters they were now well on their way north. But in spite of a week-long respite he stayed edgy and restless, his thoughts often going to the fugitives he had sent with the Sadlers. Regretfully he had no way of knowing how they were faring, and on occasion when the lonely fate of Lame Fox crossed his mind, he sipped a glass of sherry and put his faith in providence.

But what was slowly dominating his thoughts, and troubling his sleep, was the increasingly calamitous news from the east. South Carolina had seceded, other southern states were joining her. The country was in crisis and verging on civil war. He spent two restive and perplexing weeks waiting for word from his sponsors concerning Ebert Devine's departure. But when it arrived it threw him into even greater confusion.

Please handle this communication with utmost discretion. It must not come to the attention of any but yourself. All efforts at assisting slave liberation are to cease immediately upon receipt of this instruction. Future policies are being examined in view of political crisis. Have been advised of probable visit by government intermediary. Urge your fullest cooperation. Also recommend this letter be read and destroyed.

Quarles studied it with distant alarm, with a feeling that tumultuous events had already taken command and his life was being driven toward crucial changes he couldn't foresee or control. He poured himself another glass of wine and took it to the window, gazing out on a long stretch of trees arching toward the sky until they topped a nearby hill and fell away. It was spring. Even in the distance he could see birds flitting about the foliage, carrying food to their nests, pursuing the great cycle of life. But then he threw down the wine and slammed the glass to the window sill. He didn't like moods that perversely brought his lonely life into focus, raising thoughts of Ellen, his long-lost wife, whom he had recently dreamed was watching him from another shore. Abruptly he turned away from the window. Memories of her and their brief days together made him a stranger to himself. All that was long ago, in another time, another world, one not burdened by inhumanities called slavery or war. The killing of Coyne flashed through his mind, that lost world had been void of Selganys or Charlie Coynes. But a man became part of the world he lived in. Thank God Ellen would never know the cynical, even deadly, man he had become.

A day or so later a gentleman, dressed in civilian clothes, but introducing himself as Major Creel, appeared at his doorstep. Apologizing for this unannounced visit, the man entered, accepted a seat, and pulled out a leather pouch. He politely refused Quarles's offer of a drink.

Eyeing the heavily stamped papers being extracted from the pouch, Quarles remarked, "May I take it this is an official visit?"

"You may regard it as such," replied the major, quietly straightening the papers out. Then gathering his breath for what sounded like a prepared statement, and one that shocked Quarles, he began. "First, I must advise you this conversation is highly confidential, in fact classified. Under the articles of war misuse of any matters discussed between us may be punishable by a military court."

"Articles of war!" exclaimed Quarles. "My God! Are we at war?"

"Unfortunately fighting has broken out . . . the government has taken steps for public safety."

"I see."

"As you can imagine there is considerable confusion at the moment, but the government hopes to acquire the means of obtaining information from certain parts of the country. It would ease their task of resolving possible threats to law and order."

Quarles sat back and crossed his arms. He noticed the major had taken out a pen. "I can see you're here for a purpose, sir, but perhaps you'd be good enough to come to the point. I'm unable to see how I can be of service."

"Very well." The major seemed relieved to be getting to the real reason for the visit. "We're hoping to establish a series of observation points throughout the south, a means by which information can be funneled back to Washington or designated posts. You have an organization set up, your people are experienced and in many cases have gained local acceptance. Of course they will have to be carefully vetted . . . at the moment we are faced with many conflicting . . . perhaps a fairer word would be 'uncertain' loyalties."

Quarles shifted in his chair. "Are you suggesting my people serve as spies?"

"That's too harshly put. We would only want information they could supply without risk to themselves, troop recruitments, amounts and locations of supplies, perhaps some indications of public morale. The government would appreciate it being done on a voluntary basis."

Quarles let his breath out in a long, emphatic sigh. "Major, believe me, I have no experience in that kind of work and I'm sure none of my people do." He shook his head. "With fighting breaking out, to me it sounds extremely dangerous."

The major's brow tightened with a tinge of impatience. "Mr. Quarles, are you a patriot?"

"I'm a loyal citizen, if that's what you mean."

"I'm sure you don't favor slavery or you wouldn't be involved in the work you are. Can't you think of this as just one more way to help the fight against slavery?"

Quarles shook his head again, blankly staring at the major for several long moments. "Sir, no matter how casually you present it, when men start fighting and dying the information you're requesting could amount to life and death for individuals rightly or wrongly defending their beliefs. I repeat, it seems to me extremely dangerous work."

"Well, we can't order you to cooperate but your government would appreciate it."

"So you keep saying, but whatever my own feelings I certainly can't speak for my people on an issue such as this."

The major cleared his throat and tapped the pouch. "We intend to contact them one by one, all will be given a chance to serve the government voluntarily."

"And if they choose not to?"

"We will be prepared for that."

"How?"

"Mr. Quarles, I am not at liberty to discuss government policies with you, my visit here was simply to solicit your personal cooperation." He straightened himself up like a man preparing to rise. "I'm anxious to know if I might have it."

For several awkward moments Quarles stared mutely at his visitor, then, coming slowly forward in his chair, said, "I trust it will not be regarded as lacking in patriotism if I ask for a day or so to consider it?"

"No, that's understandable. Perhaps even preferable. We favor people whose convictions are firm." He took an addressed envelope from his pouch and handed it to Henry. "You will not be contacted this way again. Mail this if you decide to cooperate."

Taking the envelope, Quarles found it empty. "There's nothing in this," he muttered.

"It's its own message . . . just mail it."

"I see."

The major started toward the door. "And, as I've mentioned before, Mr. Quarles, this conversation is highly classified, please bear that in mind."

"I will."

"Good day, Mr. Quarles."

⋈ 19 ⋉

A week had passed before they reached Salina, a raw settlement beyond which lay only open prairie and vast stretches of grasslands rising slowly to join the great western plateau called the northern plains. But it was a week where much happened that affected the party for months to come. In the evenings, when Cole and Troy, often joined by Cheatem, discussed travel plans or when and where they might stake a claim, Hattie would urge her people to sing her favorite songs, mostly simple spirituals learned in crossroads meetings popular among slaves in the south. Sam and Skeeter didn't always join in, preferring to slip off alone to scheme and search for ways to continue north, their quest for freedom becoming a quest for safety and, above all, for work.

Chloe would obediently sing but she was becoming ever more fidgety and moody, drifting off by herself, picking a flower and smelling it by day, or staring up at a lonely moon voyaging across a sea of stars by night. Somehow she kept finding time to be alone, especially when Hattie took to prayer or was busy admonishing Ben for his lack of religious fervor or failure to sing on key. Ben never defended himself and serious arguments never arose, but Chloe was beginning to resent her mother, who seemed forever carping about things or busily directing others. One night an incident took place that focused her resentment and insured its inevitable growth.

How she got to that spot even she couldn't recall but it wasn't by accident. She had been quietly isolating herself from time to time without apparent reason, until, finally standing beyond the wagons, gazing up at the night sky, a tinge of smile softened her mouth as she felt Dennis coming up behind her, his arms appearing and encircling her waist. Somewhere in her mind she thought she should pretend surprise or perhaps a little shock, but her first impulse was to drop her hands and grasp his. They stood like that for long moments drinking in the thrill of each other's touch. Dennis, who for days had been fighting a desire to hold her, to feel the softness of her body and the exciting moisture of her lips, realized that though she was firmly returning his ardor he didn't know what to do next. His desire for Chloe had grown until it dominated his thoughts, making him more and more willing to take steps too bold to imagine but a few days before. But now that this embrace affirmed in both minds the beginning of an intimacy no third party could share, Dennis was too overwhelmed with the ecstasy of their embrace to think of spinning her around and kissing her. Chloe, snuggling back and bracing against him, thought of it, but unfortunately her thought came too late. As she turned into his arms, Hattie appeared, peering through the darkness and screeching, "Wats dat you two doin' over dere?"

When he heard of it Cole shook his head. "Dennis got to realize that kind of funning brings trouble."

Cathy, busy tidying up her wagon, threw him an impatient glance. "Those two youngsters have been lovesick for days. If Hattie was surprised she must be blind."

Only Troy's voice raised disapproval. "Has Dennis forgotten that girl is black?" He turned reproachful eyes on his brother. "Believe you'd best have a talk with him, Cole."

"Why not you?"

"He never listens to me, its not the kind of thing he and I can talk about."

"Whose fault is that?" snapped Cathy. "If you stopped treating him like a child and started treating him like the man he's becoming you wouldn't be begging off from a little manly talk."

Troy looked away as though "manly talks" weren't a subject women should pretend to understand. "Just suggesting someone ought to warn the young fool what he's getting himself into," he muttered. "If Cole isn't willing, guess it has to be me."

"No, best be me," said Cole, looking uncomfortably into the distance, "but I don't believe Dennis gives a damn about her being black. The girl doesn't look like a Negro, she could easily pass for Mexican."

"Maybe you both ought to leave him be," said Cathy, washing her hands in a basin. "If they're not right for each other they'll find it out. Trying to keep that boy away from her is only going to make him want her more."

"Figure you might be right," mused Cole, weighing her remark. "What about Hattie?"

"Hattie is a woman, she understands these things better than men. She's probably still stewing about white men abusing black women in the south. Can't say as I blame her . . . probably has good reasons for her anger."

But Cole finally decided he had to talk to Dennis, he didn't want this trouble turning their trip west into a long, bickering ordeal. It was serious enough to split the party up. But Dennis appeared to have recovered from Hattie's tirade and stood, with one hand on his hip, regarding Cole with the steady eyes of a man taking a stand and intending to hold it.

"I guess you know you've managed to get a hell of a lot of people upset around here," began Cole.

"They'll get over it."

"How far do you figure to take this?"

"Chloe and I ain't hardly had a chance to talk . . . reckon we will after a bit."

"You gonna be careful?"

"What does that mean?"

"You know what it means . . . don't do anything you don't figure you can live with."

"That all you got to say?"

"Dennis, I'm just trying to steer you right. You know that, don't you?"

"Yeah, I know it," he took a step back. "But I've had all the steering I can stomach for a spell, so tell Cathy and Troy I'd be mighty pleased if they didn't come to share any wisdom with me." He looked around as though his mind was being drawn elsewhere. "Now I got me a wagon to drive. Best I get to it."

Cole watched him stride off, knowing Cathy was right; Dennis had reached the full measure of a man. From now on he would follow his own insights to determine friends and enemies, and no "advice" was going to deter him from pursuing or even possessing the woman he wanted.

In the end, to all appearances, the incident simply caused some changes in wagonloads. Hattie refused to ride on the lumber wagon with Dennis anymore and instead sat up front with Cheatem. But she couldn't induce Chloe to move with her. The girl put her head down and refused to budge. Hattie decided to leave Ben, Sam, and Skeeter there to guard against any covert conversations between her daughter and Dennis, an intent she announced loudly enough for Chloe and Dennis to hear.

No one said anything, but when the wagons started moving again old Ben shook his head, resignedly mumbling to himself, "Dat woman!"

Sam and Skeeter had tried to take Chloe to task but she cut them off saying, "Got no business fussing me out!"

Now hush up 'fore I tell dese white folks what you fixin' to do!"

"Lordy, what you talkin' 'bout, you doan know nuthin'!"

"Don't I . . . wait and see."

Actually she knew nothing, but her bluff silenced them and they moved further back in the wagon, Skeeter finally muttering under his breath, "Dat Chloe in heat . . . best we don't fool wid her till she cool down."

"Gonna need a mess of ice houses to cool dat one down," whispered Sam back sourly.

On the fourth day they met an old trapper coming back from the mountains, returning to civilization and regretting he would never see the far country again. His hair was snow white and his body showed the effects of a hard and sometimes hazardous life. But he kept them entertained for a full evening with stories about near fatal encounters with Blackfeet or Crows, yet his easy manner and often chuckling voice made it sound like an adventure he would have hated to miss. No one enjoyed his stories more than Troy, who pressed him for knowledge of the mountain passes and finally quietly questioned him about a mountain man named Salter. Did he know him? The old man scratched his head. "Dang if that name don't stir up some tales."

"What tales?"

"Well I don't rightly remember all of 'em but seems that's the fella who hankered after silver . . . all the time claiming he knew about hidden lodes and sech. Most folks figured he chewed too much loco weed or had wandered by himself in the big lonesome so long it bent his compass. Heard he went east somewheres, got in a gun fight and went under."

"Do you think he really found silver?"

"Don't rightly know. Him being a little tetched . . . hard to say."

Across the fire Sam and Skeeter exchanged glances then shifted about, their eyes fastened to flames climbing around fresh wood Ben had placed on the fire.

But it was Cheatem, leaning forward at this exchange,

who spoke up. "You got something on your mind, Troy? Something you ain't letting on about?"

"Not really," answered Troy, rubbing his hands like a man thinking fast. "Just curious about a few things, that's all."

"Where did you get the name Salter from?" queried Cheatem.

As though he had been planning it for a while, Troy rose and hiked up his heavy gun belt, stamping one foot and pretending his leg had stiffened from long contact with the ground. "It's a long story," he said as he turned away into the night, leaving them, including the old trapper, staring after him.

No one saw Cathy poke Cole in the ribs, though Cole needed no one to cue him on the new problem Troy's wild scheme had just created.

Everyone enjoyed something about this old storyteller. Dennis, who sat closest and stayed up the latest, was interested in the old trapper's reminiscences about his wild youth, when he had rode down the old Santa Fe trail to trade with Mexicans. The trail, which was still there and much rumored about, ran far to the south, crossing the Arkansas and working its way southwest toward Santa Fe. The old man described that sleepy adobe town, where people sang, traded everything, and if Dennis understood the passing twinkle in the old trapper's eye, spent a fair amount of time making love. "Trail ain't bin used much lately," the old timer concluded. "Damn Comanches got to raising too much hell. Gawd, but they a bloody pack of varmints! Bad as them Blackfeet were they couldn't hold a candle to Comanches for deviltry." He looked across at Dennis and Cheatem, and the quietly sitting Sam, who hadn't missed a word. The old man's sudden pain-filled expression lent force to his words. "You folks best keep that in mind. They and them damn Kiowas have been raiding north of the Cimarron lately. Wouldn't get too close to 'em was I you."

"Ain't there a fort out there?" asked Cheatem.

"Forts don't frazzle Comanches . . . never waste their

time attacking forts. Folks settin' up claims though bin catching hell!"

"We'll see," grunted Cheatem.

"Mister, you fool with Comanches and you sure as hell gonna see!"

Henry Quarles worried through a week without a decent night's sleep. Try as he would he couldn't resolve the issue by himself and at last had to call in Lee. Lee listened carefully but the slow spread of dark lines across his face warned Quarles his favorite scout didn't cotton to the government's request. "What do you think?" he finally asked, sitting back and pouring another splash of bourbon in his glass. Lee, who rarely drank, and had yet to touch his drink, gingerly took a sip before he began.

"Doesn't sound like work I would shine at," he said quietly. "They planning to talk to me?"

"You're the one person they don't know about."

"Good, ain't eager to make their acquaintance."

"Well, you know we're finished here. You can't carry on this kind of work with a war going on." His eyes caught Lee staring out the window. "What you planning to do?"

"Been thinking on that a bit . . . maybe try the forts, see if the army needs scouts."

"Likely they do. Heard tell both sides are trying to get the western tribes to help them, mostly by harassing the other."

Lee shook his head. "Probably giving 'em guns and sech as pay . . . they'll be sorry." Lee took a final drink and placed his glass out of reach. "And what you figuring to do?"

"By God, I don't know. But tomorrow morning I'm going to do something." He held the envelope up. "I'm either going to mail this son of a bitch or tear it up."

The following morning he mailed the letter and within a day or two regretted it, for it was the start of several weeks of doubt, confusion, and continual vacillation. Days went by and nothing happened. The great silence that surrounded him bothered him. The region, being filled with proslavers and Free Soilers, was a powder keg. In the war-charged atmosphere most conversations were little more than attempts to smell out your neighbor's sentiments. He had given up coffee houses to avoid troublesome misunderstandings. He had also grown wary of entering bars where talk of the spreading fight was not only inevitable but interminable, causing sympathies and emotions to conflict and spawn violence.

One terrifying scene brought the town doctor to dress wounds caused by a gunfight between soldiers from Leavenworth and some passing southern sympathizers. Quarles knew the doctor, having visited him the previous season for a recurring fever. The doctor had given him some pills and the fever had disappeared. Now the doctor, noticing him standing outside, had approached him with a surprising interest in Quarles's complexion.

"You're looking mighty pale and wrung out, Mr. Quarles," he said solicitously. "Something keeping you from sleeping well?"

Quarles, taken unaware, answered without thinking. "Guess you might say that."

The doctor stopped and looked at him steadily. "Got any pains?"

"Nope."

"That damn fever at you again?"

"Can't say it is."

"Well, why don't you come by in the morning, maybe we can give you something to help you get some rest."

Quarles pondered this encounter for hours but decided to appear the following morning. The doctor examined him, finding nothing wrong but saying he could see Henry was under considerable stress. "You've got to stop worrying about things," advised the doctor. "Could be as bad for you as any damn infection."

Quarles, whose own medical training had already assured him he had no detectable symptoms of serious illness, settled back in his seat, even managing a half smile. "What makes you so damn sure I've been worrying?"

The doctor looked at him meaningfully. "Maybe I've been worrying a little myself."

Slowly and stiffly Quarles came forward again, his hands gripping the arms of his chair. "And what exactly does that mean?"

"It means I made the same decision you did, Henry, let's hope we made the right one."

Henry Quarles left as an active undercover agent, with an assignment that would shortly convince him how wrong his decision had been.

The Smoky Hill was not a large river, measuring not more than sixty or seventy feet across, but where it narrowed the channel ran deep, leaving the flow generous and swift. There were game tracks all along it and a rocky bottom to show where it could be easily forded.

Yet nothing was so noticeable as the gradual disappearance of trees. As they moved westward more and more often they came upon immense sweeps of prairie, covered with thick waves of grass, shorter than the grass found in valleys to the east, but heavier and rolling in undulating waves that reached the horizon. Cheatem kept saying this land would surely take a crop, though Cole thought it looked better for grazing than farming. They also spotted their first buffalo and a herd of wild mustangs. Perhaps more importantly the occasional settler they had sighted along the river disappeared and they found themselves alone with only a low moaning wind to break the silence. It was usually a westerly wind, soft and relentless and seeming part of life in this endless land stretching with hardly a hill from horizon to horizon.

One morning they came upon a promising expanse that drew audible and agreeable grunts from every wagon in the train. Even Cathy, who was secretly wondering at the terrible loneliness of this country, agreed. It was a beautiful stretch of land that the river seemed to have marked out for its own, circling around it almost protectively. Cheatem, after riding about and dismounting several times to pace off and measure the curving south bank, declared he was ready to lay out his claim. Upon inspection the land had a slight roll and a tiny stream running through it, its flow spreading out at its mouth and seeping into the Smoky Hill. "I can dam that up to fetch me some water," he said with confidence.

Cole and Troy, watching him determinedly move about, realized Cheatem had vital equipment, such as that iron plowshare, that they lacked, and decided to pick a site not too far away. By late afternoon they had staked out a claim just above Cheatem's, where the river curved in the opposite direction, giving them, if nothing else, more waterfront than Silas.

It was a busy and burdensome day, but everyone gathered around the fire that evening ready to eat, knowing tomorrow real work would begin. A new mood had gripped the group. Hattie, frying a mess of fish Sam and Skeeter had taken from the river, was still looking sharply at Chloe, who was sullenly attending her mother, but her quick furtive glances were directed at Dennis. Dennis, believing he and Chloe had a silent understanding, was biding his time.

Cole knew the issue was far from settled, but Dennis made it clear it wasn't something to discuss. Sam and Skeeter, deciding they'd best leave Chloe to Hattie, were quietly pondering Troy's curious remarks about silver, or repeating in wide-eyed whispers what the old trapper said about Indians. Still the feeling of having arrived had kindled a suppressed excitement in everyone. Only Troy seemed unmoved by Cole and Dennis's riding about and putting down stakes, marking the borders of their claim, as, almost unnoticed, Lame Fox, whose elusiveness was his main trait, studied the countryside, scouted about, and occasionally stared off into the distance.

Though the wagon train slept soundly that night the following day broke on a disturbing note. It began with an army courier racing westward and pulling up when he saw them camped by the river. For the first time they heard war had broken out, and listened in amazement as he said the southern states were forming a confederacy and battling federal troops in Virginia.

"Jesus! We 'uns just left in a nick of time," rasped Cheatem.

A troubled murmur ran through the group. "Where you headed?" inquired Cole, looking up at the courier.

"To the fort . . . 'bout thirty miles further upriver. They got to be warned. Damn Texans are seizing federal property, even forts. Don't know if the bastards will come this far north but the army ain't taking no chances. You folks planning to squat here?"

"Figured we would," responded Cheatem cautiously.

"Well keep an eye out."

"Is there some danger?" asked Cathy, peeking out from behind Cole.

"Lady, out here there's always danger. There's bin talk of Indian trouble over to Sand Hills, Comanches and Kiowas been palaverin' with Cheyennes and Arapahos . . . likely that spells trouble. Best keep a steady look out!"

"Are you telling us the army can't handle them?" declared Cheatem. "You're talking about a bunch of painted savages."

"The army can't always find 'em to make 'em hold still and behave," the courier shot back. "Injuns don't mess with soldiers if they have folks like you to bedevil. Like I said best keep a sharp look out!"

The courier rode away, leaving them looking at one another with a vague unease. "What do you think?" asked Troy over his shoulder to Cole, a question Cheatem thought was directed at him.

"I say we get to work," Silas replied. "Injun scares come regular as rain out here, most of 'em don't amount to pig shit."

"Lordy!" exclaimed Hattie, "we didn't count on no messin' wid redskins."

Ben leaned toward her. "Hattie, ah think . . ."

"Shush up, Ben." She pushed him aside and turned to Skeeter and Sam. "Wat y'all think?"

Sam looked about the ground as though weighing whether it was worth fighting for. Finally he shrugged his shoulders. "We gots to stop somewheres, dis as good as any."

Cole avoided looking at Cathy, aware of the disapproval already building in her face. "Believe there's some sense in what he says, if we're going to stake a claim this is as good a spot as we're likely to find. The only other choice we got is heading back, but you better remember why we left and now there's a war going on there to boot."

In its own way that settled it.

Within minutes they were pulling shovels and lumber from the wagons and Hattie, Chloe, and Cathy were carrying stones from the stream to set up a place to cook. Still, no one forgot the courier's warning and while everyone was busy with a growing number of tasks, Lame Fox drifted off to explore the country and watch for signs of danger.

Quarles was to discover his first assignment was detecting and reporting activities of southern sympathizers in neighboring Missouri. The Union desperately needed to hold that state, now bitterly divided between its proslavery south and free soil north. Already skirmishes had taken place and the critical fighting was about to begin. He was not surprised to hear almost all of his organization refused to cooperate with the government. They were not people who looked kindly on war in any form.

Only one person, a woman living near Springfield who helped escapees cross the Arkansas border, had volunteered to serve. According to instructions forwarded by army command and conveyed by the doctor, he was to meet her in Sedalia at the end of the week.

Almost at once he longed for Lee. Traveling by himself

through Missouri meant great risks, but in war he knew risks had to be taken; spies, like soldiers, were expendable. Surprisingly he had little trouble, the war had come too quickly for forces in the state to be properly organized. He was stared at in towns he passed through, but strangers always were, even in peacetime. He was stopped only once and that was by a group of citizens, asking if he had seen any armed men in woods he had just passed through. He reported he had not and continued on without ever knowing which side they were on.

In Sedalia he found the eating place he was to take his meals at until contacted. The food was tolerable but the guests were gruff and often raucous, many coming in armed. They were dirt farmers, teamsters, and drifters, indelibly stamped with meager means and recurrent poverty. To Quarles it seemed a place where too many pugnacious rural types gathered, a strange setting for a woman to enter alone. But Saturday night, with a large crowd causing a deafening din, he noticed that his waitress, bending over, placing cheap silverware on his table, was whispering under her breath. "It will be under the last plate."

Astonished, he could only stare at her. She was pretty in a coarse way, clean-looking yet hardly well groomed. A typical back-country girl. He could only grapple with the feeling that a less likely looking figure for dangerous spy work would be hard to imagine. The incessant noise about them enabled her to get in a few words every time she served his table. In this way he discovered a relative owned the eatery and she worked here when in town, helping with weekend crowds.

The last plate was a selection of baked pastries, which he studied for a moment, gently lifting the plate as though wanting a whiff of the contents and moving a single sheet of paper deftly below the table line. Almost immediately she retrieved the plate and, leaving her a healthy tip, he thanked her and left.

He was astonished to find her at his boardinghouse the following day with a glove she pretended he'd left behind. Heavy as her powder and rouge was, it didn't cover the sheen of fear in her eyes. "I thought it might be yours," she said nervously, holding up the glove. Both knew it wasn't his but Quarles realized it was something important.

"Good of you to think of me," he said, glancing about to make sure they were alone. "What is it?"

She followed his eyes and then, assured they were alone, gasped, "You'd best git, quickly. My cousin wanted to know who you were. They might come for you. They think nothing of killing folks they don't trust. Please! git, quickly!"

Within ten minutes Quarles was on his horse and heading for the Kansas border. He had already secreted in his boot the single sheet of paper on which she had scrawled, *They plan tak arsenel at Jeferson City. Dun kilt already for way.*

Two days later he was back in Lawrence, watching the doctor read the note. "Hope the lady's information is better than her spelling," grunted the doctor. He slipped the note into a small packet and sealed it. Then he excused himself. "Be back in a moment. Ought to get this off right away."

Within a minute or two he was back, but the doctor was now looking at him with concern. "Don't make any plans for yourself for a week or two, can't say why but those are instructions I was told to pass on. How you fixed for money?"

"That won't be a problem for a while."

"Good, the government pays, but usually on the day before judgement day." A smile fought with a frown to command his face. "For the record you'll draw a captain's pay."

Quarles, hoping for more talk but sensing long talks were discouraged in this work, rose to go, yet he couldn't resist asking. "Any idea what they have in mind?"

The doctor shrugged helplessly. "No, but likely it could be something big. We'll see."

Two weeks later he read an account of an attempt by southerners to take a small federal arsenal near Jefferson City. The bitterness of a long war had not yet set in. The bulletin reported the attackers were mostly irregulars, armed young men, courageous enough but poorly led. Twenty-three were killed, the number of wounded unknown. The bulletin suggested the death count was high because the government, suspecting an attack, had been heavily reinforced.

That night he had trouble sleeping, the faces of dead young men "courageous but poorly led" peered from every dark corner of the room. Killing Charlie Coyne hadn't bothered him; Charlie Coyne had a chance to kill him in a fair fight. But now he saw again the homespun clothes and crude manners of the rowdy customers in Sedalia. These were rustics, hard-handed men swept up in issues they poorly understood. Proud in spite of their poverty and little or no stake in slavery, they would soon become the core of the South's military prowess. They would fight bravely, die willingly, and leave a legacy of misguided loyalty impossible for outsiders to understand.

Twenty-three dead. The government, suspecting an attack, had been heavily reinforced. Those lines kept running through his head. If he hadn't mailed that letter twenty-three young men might be alive today. But it didn't end there; if the attack had succeeded surely defending soldiers would have died. He didn't like this end of the war. For him enduring battle would be far easier; he understood killing men trying to kill him. He spent a sleepless night thinking, but after twisting and turning for hours he finally left his bed, his last doubt dispelled. He had made his decision.

21

In a few days Cheatem's cabin began to take shape. He planned a large one with three rooms and a short dog run to a storeroom. Not only did he have the advantage of ready lumber but Cheatem knew how to use stone

from the river to lay his foundation and anchor the
corner poles of his dwelling. He even knew how to make
a form of adobe with mud mixed with dried grass. He
was already building a chimney before the Sadlers got
their foundation in. Sam and Skeeter proved to be hard
workers and Ben, if not up to rigorous labor, patiently
plugged holes, corked walls, and pared at joints until
they fit.

The Sadlers had a tougher challenge. Fortunately,
sparse as trees were, there were some in well-watered
spots along the river. Cole and Dennis found small
stands of hackberry, willow, boxelder, and cottonwood,
once even some black walnut and oak but they were rare.
They cut what wood they could and slowly the frame-
work of a cabin appeared. Their dwelling was to have
only two fairly large rooms, although Cathy kept pressing for a third, saying a kitchen would just fit between
the largest room and the spot they had marked off for a
well. Nothing was said but everyone knew Hattie and
her family would have to live in the wagons until they
could manage a shelter of their own. Only Lame Fox
didn't want cover; he preferred to roll up in his robe and
sleep in different spots of his own choosing every night.
But he made a discovery that endeared him to Cathy. In
his ceaseless scouting he had crossed the river and
worked west along the opposite bank. After six miles he
spotted a cabin. Surprised but approaching it stealthily,
he discovered it was abandoned. Someone had tried to
live in this lonely stretch and had given up. Hearing of it
Cole took a wagon across the ford and pulled down the
well-dried wood that had been the walls and ceiling of
this rude dwelling. He was glad he had come alone, with
only Lame Fox to guide him, for it was clear only one
person had used this cabin and some puzzling articles
had been left behind. There was an old shovel, a pair of
patched but usable jeans, and a tea kettle. Items few
people on the frontier would abandon. Lame Fox, grunting from a hundred feet away, signaled him over. Cole
put down his hammer and approached him. Lame Fox
was pointing to something with his toe. Cole was almost

on top of it before he saw it was a human skull, the bone as clean and white as an egg. Lame Fox held up one and then two fingers. "One, two years," he mumbled, indicating how long it had lain exposed to prairie sun and wind.

"Better not mention this," Cole warned the scout. "No point in getting folks upset. After all we don't know what happened. Could have shot himself." Lame Fox looked away, his features tightening in disbelief.

They took the lumber back to their claim and Cathy, seeing it, looked expectantly at Cole. Cole, still worried about the skull and what effect it and maybe more like it would have on her spirits, was now searching for inducements to stay. He smiled at her and nodded at the ground between the unfinished cabin and the well. Not only Cathy, but all watching, knew she was about to get her kitchen.

By now the nights had taken on a different character; people momentarily lost track of each other. Of course it started in daylight when they made endless trips between the two claims. Tools were borrowed and returned. Food was cooked in one place with part of it often going to the other. There were matters to talk about such as planting or starting a garden, smoking meat, or discovering what neighbors lay in either direction. Riders going west and following the river kept bringing news of the war, some of it impossible not to wonder at and discuss. But at night the almost quarter of a mile separating the cabin sites had to be crossed in darkness, often with no one knowing who was coming until they arrived. The days were often exhausting, making most of them seek sleep soon after sundown, particularly the older ones. Cheatem and old Ben would be snoring by the time Hattie bundled herself up and dozed off. Only the younger ones hung about the fire, glad of this relief from adult surveillance if not supervision, eager to express opinions that often met with short shrift during the day. Sam and Skeeter kept speculating on their options once the cabin was built, Sam unable to forget Troy's talk of silver in the mountains and Skeeter wearily repeating a need to find work, the kind of work that drew wages.

But Chloe was secretly the most relieved of all. Instinct told her Dennis still desired her and was biding his time. She sensed the dark area between the two campsites was an ideal spot to meet. They would both claim to be visiting the opposite camp, and something about the way he walked by her that day murmuring "Ah'm waiting" decided her on that evening.

Allowing Sam and Skeeter to get heavily engaged in their nightly talk, she backed away as though she herself had chosen to retire. But once concealed by darkness she hurried down the trail.

Dennis had slowly been grasping how Chloe had to act. He was sure now she wanted him to come close again but was afraid if seen it would make further contact between them impossible. He couldn't believe she would miss the opportunity the nightly solitude of the trail provided. For two days he had been slipping halfway up the trail to stand watch in the darkness. So far she had not appeared but tonight felt different. He had managed to whisper something to her today and the sudden warmth in her eyes was more encouraging than any words.

History has repeatedly proven the instincts of young people mutually attracted are rarely wrong. Chloe slipped up to him in the darkness as though this meeting had been sanctioned by oath. By some magic they were transformed back to the moment they had embraced beyond the wagons. Before saying anything they kissed long and hard, then settled on the ground breathless as though they had run a mile. For Chloe it was her first kiss but it started a strange inner excitement that moved with miraculous speed from her lips to her loins. They couldn't get close enough. They kept sighing and whispering half sounds to each other, as though words were inadequate, as though how they felt could only be expressed by hugging, kissing, touching each other, seeking ways they hoped would express the overpowering need for more. But they were inexperienced and neither could lead. Dennis began to feel her breast and, while she relished the swelling intimacy, when he began to open her dress she didn't know how to respond and pulled away. Still breathless they held each other, both becoming conscious of the storm of protest awaiting in both camps. As though they had been discussing it for an hour Chloe murmured, "What we gonna do?"

Dennis, now aroused and unwilling to release her, pulled her closer. "What we're doing," he muttered tensely into her ear.

"Dennis, we gots to think." She felt his hand on her knee, under the edge of her dress. She put one hand down to restrain him. "Dennis, please, we gots to talk."

He moved inches away and looked at her. "Chloe, you know they ain't going to cotton to us together, but it ain't their choosing."

Chloe's voice seemed weaker. "Dennis, what I do 'bout Hattie?"

He pulled her close again. "Tell her woman to woman you got yourself a man."

Chloe put her hand over his lips, "Do I really . . . sure enough have me a man?"

Dennis's hand firmed on her knee. "I want you Chloe, if you want me we ain't parting. If folks take on too much around here we'll just up and leave."

Her eyes held his in the darkness, a frightened young girl wanting to believe. There was a breathless moment as his hand began to move up her leg and her restraining hand lessened its grip. But with his hand high inside her thigh and a new kind of ecstasy warming and thrilling her flesh she turned to him, helpless with passion, but suddenly a shot rang out beyond the Sadler claim and with a frightened start both knew their tryst was over.

Quarles made his way to Fort Leavenworth. It was a dark, cloudy day and strong gusts of wind swept the great drill ground where troops were learning to march in step, and groups of soldiers were hunched about artillery pieces. In the headquarters building he was received by a boyish lieutenant, who eyed him strangely when he requested to see the colonel.

"Your business, sir?"

"It's with the colonel."

"You'll have to wait, sir, the colonel is busy and no one is allowed in without his permission. Your name, sir?"

"Quarles, Henry Quarles."

The lieutenant left him with an orderly, but was back shortly. "The colonel is finishing a meeting, sir, he'll see you presently. Please be seated."

Quarles sat in a hardback chair that only the army could pretend was comfortable. Noncommissioned officers kept coming in for orders or explanations of those issued. For the first time Quarles saw the inner workings of a military establishment gearing up to fight a war. A certain confusion was obvious, orders were misunderstood, recruits couldn't find their units, requisition papers were a mystery to farm hands who were strangers to paperwork and not always literate. Even officers appeared with little or no military training, being appointed majors or captains by local units they had raised. Every army since Agamemnon's probably suffered from the same chaos but somehow it seemed worse here.

After almost an hour, Quarles was ushered into the colonel's office. The colonel remained standing and Henry knew he was to be allowed very little time. The colonel looked tired, preoccupied. "Yes . . . Mr . . . err."

"Quarles, Henry Quarles."

"What can I do for you?"

"I'd like to be reassigned."

The colonel continued to look harassed, though not necessarily by Quarles. "I don't understand, Mr. Quarles, reassigned to what?"

"To a combat unit, infantry or preferably cavalry."

The colonel, still looking bothered, stared at him. "And what are you being reassignment from, Mr. Quarles?"

"Spy work."

The colonel sat down and let out his breath. "Another one."

"Sorry, sir, but it's not the sort of thing I'd ever be good at. I'd much prefer to fight out in the open."

The colonel shook his head. "Have you been given a rank?"

"I was to draw a captain's pay, sir."

"Your rank is what you get paid," snapped the colonel with a tinge of bitterness. Quarles suspected he was drawing precious little pay for the enormous load he was carrying. Probably the government had still not adjusted wartime conditions to the modest pay scale of its peacetime army. "You'll have to talk to the provost marshal," the colonel continued resignedly. "I'm sure he can arrange something. Right now this office is busy gathering information for some senseless delegation dreamed up by Washington. Damn politicians should be put in the front line for a spell, so they can see what it's all about."

"Then I shall not trouble you further, sir," said Quarles, preparing to leave. "Where will I find the provost marshal?"

The colonel's tone was almost sardonic. "The lieutenant will conduct you to him. I'm sure he'll find time to assist you."

On that peculiar note Quarles left without understanding the colonel's seemingly acid manner until he found the provost marshal was a brigadier. By some quirk of the still-organizing army the man policing the post outranked the man commanding it.

For the next several weeks Quarles was to experience the turmoil, perilous cooking, discomfort, and sheer boredom of life on a military post. He was granted the rank of captain in the cavalry and after two weeks a tailor appeared to make his uniforms. He paid for them himself and was supplied nothing but a horse. He preferred his own mount and used the issue as a spare, which by a new directive was also required. He got a minimum of training in command structure and close-order marching, the second an activity of dubious value to a cavalry man, but one of those endless regulations the army had picked up since colonial times. Training with his cavalry unit was at least practical, but it was mostly quickly changing formations or caring for their mounts. The latter his orderly took care of while Henry retired to the officers' quarters to drink, write letters, or play cards. In time he grew restless and irritable, wondering why they weren't fighting, why they weren't at least traveling closer to where he understood fighting was taking place. But he was to find soldiering was ninety percent standing about and waiting, the remaining ten percent required for latrine and mess hall.

Only after many weeks did his name appear on the bulletin board, ordering him to report to the colonel's office for immediate assignment the following morning.

22

At first Lame Fox thought it was a man but it turned out to be a bear, with its front paws on the high rim of the cabin. He could just see its dim outline against the firelight coming through the empty slats of the cabin. It was surely the biggest bear he had ever seen, and he held his breath as he fired. While aiming a cold stab of fear had started his heart pounding, for just wounding such a bear could be a form of suicide. Luckily the bullet struck behind its shoulder and entered its vital organs, nicking its heart. Even so the great bear roared fiercely and made a wobbly charge of fifty feet toward the Indian before collapsing.

Cole and Troy came rushing up, shouting to Lame Fox in the darkness. "What is it? . . . What did you shoot?"

The Indian came toward them, the gun still in his

hand. "Bear . . . big bear . . . big danger." Cathy, at first hanging back, now came cautiously up with a lantern. Cole took it from her and played its light on the massive body of the bear.

"My God!" gasped Cathy.

"Damn lucky shot," said Cole. He looked quickly about, studying the ground around them and spotting the carcasses of two deer butchered earlier. "We've got to learn to bury our leavings . . . cooking fires will draw 'em bad enough, I'm surprised we haven't had trouble before."

There was several moments of silence as they looked at the whopping body of the prostrate carnivore and their pulses settled from the momentary fright. All were familiar with black bears, common enough back east, but this animal was twice the size of a full-grown black. Troy appeared least puzzled of all. "I've read about these bears," he said. "They call 'em 'grizzlies.' We must be closer to the mountains than we thought. Salter says mountain men consider 'em fair grub."

Cathy turned around at the sound of Dennis rushing up, his face strangely flushed and looking like a thirsty man bent on reaching water. Seeing them standing together and realizing whatever happened was over, he shouted, "What the hell was the shootin' all about?" His tone was almost demanding.

"Lame Fox shot a bear," answered Cathy, a half-amused expression working into her face. "Where you been?"

Dennis didn't answer. Cole, noticing Dennis had come from their end of the trail, stared at him with concern. "Having bears this size around makes that trail mighty dangerous after dark. Best warn the others."

"That's right," added Cathy, her face turning away, concealing a cryptic smile. "Be sure and tell 'em how dangerous that trail can be after dark."

The week before word had swept through the post that the colonel had been promoted to brigadier. It probably explained why Henry found him in a better mood than their first encounter. Nevertheless Captain Quarles's assignment wasn't one the new general enjoyed handing out. Quarles's briefing took the form of a garrulous critique of government policy, which the commandant violently opposed. Washington had become aware the Confederacy was sending commissioners to the western tribes, offering them bribes to harass Union's communications with the southwest and the trails to California, remote but important areas of Union strength and support. Collectively the Indians still represented a considerable force. Civilized tribes, such as the Cherokees, Choctaw, Chickasaw, and Seminoles had already declared for the Confederacy, while the Creeks, Shawnees, and Delawares sided with the Union. But two of the most formidable western tribes, Comanches and Kiowas, had long been in a bloody dispute with Texas and were reluctant to ally themselves with a side that included *tejanos*.

Washington, seizing an opportunity to get these powerful and skillful horse warriors on their side, and aware they held sway over the old Santa Fe Trail, the quickest route to New Mexico and the Southwest, were sending their own commissioners to arrange a treaty, not only with fiery southern plains tribes but with those northern ones that could threaten the Oregon Trail.

The irate general declared a sufficient military force should be dispatched to eliminate all hostiles causing trouble, but the government, with Confederate armies camped a morning's ride from the capital, or poised to seize the now critical Mississippi valley, was husbanding all its military resources, refusing to reduce them for the uncertain loyalties of savages a thousand miles away. At least not if a simple treaty could turn these distant but potentially troublesome nomads into allies.

Captain Quarles heard he was to command a troop of twenty men ordered to escort the commissioners to the warring tribes along the Arkansas and Platte rivers, where details of the treaty could be worked out. At first he was openly nettled; he had joined the army to fight, not escort bureaucrats into the hinterland to keep hostile natives congenial to government bidding. But Henry discovered the army was stone deaf when it came to officers requesting more preferable assignments. He had been foolish to try. Accepting the general's grim assurance that this whole mission was a pointless, even addleheaded venture, carrying little or no prospect of success, he saluted and left.

But in spite of appearances, the new settlers kept discovering it was anything but a peaceful land. Lame Fox found other bones, alongside ashes of wagons and rusting gun barrels. They told their own pathetic story. He warned Cole, who advised his brothers and Cheatem, but spared the women this worrisome news. Finally Sam and Skeeter, hunting late one afternoon, came upon the vulture-stripped remains of a dead horse, saddle and bridle still attached. A short distance away they spotted in disarray the bones of a human skeleton spread over an anthill. This gruesome scene still held some of the terror and agony that must have attended the hapless victim's last moments.

Shocked, but far from panicking, Sam was beginning to understand the strange, watchful mood that had taken the white men lately. He and the cold staring Skeeter soon agreed word of this would only upset Hattie and Chloe, but they also decided they weren't going to be treated like women. When reporting it to Cole, they openly demanded if more evidence of trouble hadn't been found. Cole, realizing if it came to fighting these two young men would be badly needed, kicked himself for not realizing it sooner. "If you want 'em to act like men, treat 'em like men!" was his father's warning when asking Cole to take over the coarse, unschooled, but hard-working youths that labored in the tanning yards. It was a basic lesson he should have learned long ago. Cole, eager to make amends, confided to them what Lame Fox had discovered, and though it heightened the anxiety registering on their faces, neither suggested they leave. Skeeter simply wanted to know if any thought had been given to fortifying the cabins. "How?" asked Cole, not opposed to any suggestions that might contribute to Cathy's safety.

"We gonna give it some studyin'," assured Sam.

"Do that," answered Cole. "And remember if anything happens Cheatem wants you to forget those wagons and run for his cabin."

"We best tell dat to Hattie and Chloe," mumbled Sam.

"Figured you would," responded Cole, "but don't tell 'em any more."

"Wasn't fixin' to."

Cole nodded and Sam and Skeeter nodded back. There was no more to it. Cole had taken them into his confidence, talking and listening to them, as he would have Troy or Cheatem. He was only sorry he hadn't done it sooner, but walking away two former slaves smiled at each other, saying nothing but suddenly feeling the equal of any man.

Fear of rising danger did not keep Dennis and Chloe apart. Twice they had met on the trail, covering the many things the pressure of wanting each other kept bringing up. How big an outburst could they expect when they announced their love? Whatever would Hattie say? What would she do? What would Cole do? Less important, what would Sam and Skeeter do? Strangely enough Dennis felt Cathy might understand and be on his side. He confessed he didn't care what Troy thought. Chloe sensed Ben would take her part, though Hattie would make him suffer for it. She had decided Sam and Skeeter didn't matter. Such talk was endless but other things kept happening. They were used to kissing now and their kisses were increasingly intimate, even narcotic. On this third night tension that had been building for days became energy gone wild, searing like fire across the flesh to their sensual parts. Chloe, swept by sensations that dissolved her will, lay open in his arms. She didn't know what the act of love would be like but she was ready. Dennis found his hand suddenly under her dress again with nothing to restrain it. He reached the soft inside of her thigh and soon was holding her, feeling her, pulling away her light underwear, pressing open her legs. Chloe was in ecstasy, never had she believed such thrilling pulsations were possible. She wanted to scream with delight but had to press her mouth against his ear, able only to moan as he entered her, invaded her, consumed her until a series of deep paroxysms rippled through her body. They came down together with a sigh and held to each other for long moments before Dennis kissed her again and shifted gently away. "We tell them tomorrow," he said quietly.

"Tomorrow?" she whispered. He could still feel her trembling.

"Yes, tomorrow."

They held each other in silence for more long moments before she murmured, "You sure, Dennis?"

"I'm sure," he answered, looking up at the stars as though calling upon them to witness his pledge. "Tomorrow."

They saw few travelers along that isolated river trail, only enough to know the war was progressing badly for the north. Mostly it was army couriers or supply wagons heading towards the fort to the west, but even these were becoming rare. Only occasionally did a settler come by, usually asking questions the answers to which discouraged most from going on. Usually they turned back, but one family, to Cheatem's annoyance, staked a claim two miles further upriver. "Don't look like they gonna be much help," he muttered. It was a young family, with two small children and very little else. Within days the man was over borrowing tools and the woman, besides small quantities of flour and salt, needed help in cooking wild game and dealing with her children's ailments.

The woman was pretty and even amiable, but she got off on the wrong foot with Hattie. They were from the south and for some reason assumed Hattie and Sam and Skeeter were Cheatem's slaves. Cheatem, although quietly riled at their presence, still couldn't resist a clumsy flirtation with the attractive young wife. The woman did not respond to him but perhaps felt his unwanted and even brazen maneuvering gave her grounds for more weighty requests. As he showed her around his cabin, which was nearing completion, she remarked, "Y'all being near finished and settled, maybe you could lend us some of your slaves for a day or two. My Burt could sure use a lick of help."

Overhearing her, Hattie exploded. "We ain't no slaves and we don't go 'round like some folks, beggin' fo help and 'specting others to mend dere worryins'. You folks worse'n a bunch of sick cats, all the time whinin' for sumthin' and no end of pesterin'!"

The woman was taken aback, visibly paling but covering her embarrassment by declaring she had to get home to her children. Cheatem managed a quick frown at Hattie but knew better than to chastise her. Hattie's anger was something everyone in the party had learned to shun.

But Dennis, waking up that morning, knew he couldn't avoid it and resigned himself. He put off confronting her only long enough to talk to Cole. As he expected, his brother again warned him he was making a man's decision and his kinfolk expected him to handle it like a man.

"And what does that mean?" Dennis knew his question was unnecessary, he knew what Cole was getting at, but already he was feeling defensive.

"Well, you marry her," said Cole, "you got to stick with her. Remember she's half black and any children coming along could be a problem. But if you take that young girl for a wife that makes her a Sadler, she'll be family, and this family hangs together. Just be mighty sure it's what you want . . . a lot of people are bound to get hurt if you're wrong."

When she heard it Cathy smiled at Cole and nodded. "I've been expecting this," she said softly. "They're in love and you could hardly expect differently."

Only Troy openly showed antagonism. "Know what you're getting yourself into?" he almost shouted. "Jesus, they're women all over this world dying to get married. Couldn't you pick one of your own kind?"

"Troy, you ain't the one doing the pickin' . . . and when you get around to pickin' yourself a woman I intend to let you be. Goddamn it, Troy! Don't start devilin' me!"

"All right, you crazy young fool. Wait till you see how other folks feel about your marrying a nigger. See how many decent folks want you in their homes, wanna sit beside you in church, show you to their friends. Christ, believe me, you're gonna wake up some day and wish you had listened to old Troy."

Dennis left to see Hattie with his resolve only slightly shaken but acutely aware neither Cole nor Cathy argued with Troy or denied what he said was true. In his pulsing mind he realized he was now truly on his own and for the first time in his life sensed what everyone was talking about when they used that word "man."

23

There was a chill, ominous silence as the still angry Comanche war leader, Black Otter, put aside his pipe, signaling it was time for the Kiowas to speak. He had been storming at the warriors for almost an hour, shouting violently, declaring the *tejanos,* the Texans, were vile and cowardly enemies, craven killers trying to seize by some new trickery more of the Nerm hunting grounds. Only an Indian, half blind or drunk, could think of trusting them again.

It was known Black Otter's family, his mother, wife, and daughters, had been slaughtered by Texas Rangers, the "killer ones," but a year ago, making him an implacable foe. But his revenge to many seemed perverse, for the tribe was suffering many losses avenging his. His women's deaths embittered him. Captured white females were given to the warriors to slake their lust on before being turned over to haglike squaws to be enslaved and beaten until demented or praying silently

for death. Many, even among his own tribe, thought hate
was quietly nudging Black Otter towards insanity. But
they also knew so much blood had soaked into the hard
scrabble of the west Texas frontier that peace between
the two races would be no easy matter.

Many had been quietly studying the *tejanos'* terms,
and while some remained quiet the peace-minded Whistling Elk, a powerful chief with a large following, spoke
of the many presents promised, not only this year but for
many years to come. They had only to block the trails,
denying them to the bluecoats, which in a sense they
were doing already.

Not a few scarred warriors grunted in agreement.
These savage horsemen, with their ethos of unrelenting
raiding and war, still had a great fondness for presents,
particularly those they considered pure tribute.

Walking Bird, a Spanish-speaking Kiowa half-breed
who traded with the Mexicans for rifles, said the trader
Armontez, upon hearing the *tejanos* were asking for a
treaty, said the *tahbay-boh,* northern soldiers, would
soon be wanting one too. The whites were fighting each
other. If both sides offered to reward them for doing the
same thing, they saw little harm in profiting from it.

When Whistling Elk finished speaking, the great gathering knew Black Otter would be coming to his feet
again. Talk of presents had gathered support for the
treaty as Whistling Elk hoped. Many rattled their bows
in the air or pounded rifle stocks into the ground. They
were impatient for a decision. A feast was waiting and a
social dance, traditional at gatherings with the Kiowas
and now popular with the Comanches, was to follow.

Black Otter's tone was never soft. He was a man who
lived his anger. Turning to the warriors, he stamped his
foot several times. "Have not the many deaths of our
people taught us trusting whites is to trust the snake that
hides in the lodge by day so it can strike by night! Can't
you see it is not our friendship they want! It is our deaths
so they can take our land! They fight each other now,
both sides asking us to help them win, but no victory
will be shared with us; listen to me, whoever wins will be
our next enemy."

The warriors heard his words and a few old and gray heads nodded solemnly in agreement, but most were restless, wanting the council to end. Black Otter, sensing it was time to finish, ended with a warning. "The eyes of the whites have long gazed on our lands, they see the buffalo going and their spotted cattle feeding, they see their many dwellings rising where once our spirits roamed free, they see the iron horse roaring across our land and screaming beyond the mountains, they see many things but they see no Indians, no red man belongs in this world their eyes seek. Remember this my brothers, whatever your hopes the hearts of the whites are closed to us, and the words of their treaties are as written on the wind."

Chloe could see Dennis coming up the trail; she knew he was coming to speak to Hattie. Her heart was beating so fast she feared it would stop, yet something told her this scene had to be endured, this crisis lived through. Dennis was right, they could not go on the way they were going; their secret was already suspected and would soon be known. Better they declare it before everyone.

Once she would have shied anyway from any such impending outburst of Hattie's wrath, but this morning, much as she wanted to disappear behind Ben or the farthest wagon, she decided she wanted something more. She wanted Dennis. She wanted this boy-man beside her, she wanted him to publicly claim her and be allowed to share his bed. Why were people always so uncertain about love? Never had she been so sure of anything in her life. She had found her mate and the little girl who all her life had been warned against white males and their vulgar lust was now desperately in love with one.

Coming up the path Dennis felt a strange weakness in his knees but he kept moving in a steady line toward Hattie. She had just set some pots on the cooking grate and was standing up, straightening her bandanna and turning about to catch him approaching. She had stopped speaking to him some time ago and looked surprised to find him clearly coming to address her.

"Hattie, I've got to talk with you."

"You got to talk wid me?" She turned away from him and bent over the fire. "Wal, ah ain't talkin' none wid you!"

"Hattie, you're gonna have to . . . Chloe and I are planning to be together."

Hattie rose slowly and turned back to him. "You wat?"

"Chloe and I want to get married."

Hattie's eyes slowly widened in shock. She took a step back but still had to struggle for breath. "Wats dat?!"

"Hattie, you heard me. Chloe and I want to stay together."

Hattie picked up a fire poker. "Don't come 'round here wid no crazy talk like dat! You and Chloe . . . where is dat child? . . . ah ain't puttin' up with no young jackass pesterin' me wid such tomfool talk." She gestured with the fire poker. "Git away from me, ah gots cookin' to do!"

Chloe appeared at his side. "Mama, he's right. We wanna git married."

Hattie raised both hands, one holding the fire poker high in the air. "Married! Wat you talkin' child, yuh ain't got 'nough sense to peel onions and yuh talkin' marrying!"

"We're fixin' to do it," said Dennis determinedly, aware Ben was coming up. In the background Sam and Skeeter could be seen turning their way.

Ignoring Dennis, Hattie turned her mounting rage on Chloe. "Child, you needs a good whoppin', comin' 'round here, talkin' such foolishness, makin' like dis white boy is fixin' to marry you! Wat you think he wants with you?"

"Says he loves me."

"Lovs yuh! Dis rascal lovs wats under yo' skirt! Marry you? Child, you a nigger, no white boy ain't marryin' no nigger!"

"You're wrong," said Dennis. "And stop calling her a nigger."

"Look white boy, her daddy wuz a miserable piece o'

white trash, but her mother was a nigger—and she a nigger!"

Ben was at her elbow. "Hattie, if dey wants to git married . . ."

"Shut yo face!" screamed Hattie, the force of her voice driving him back a step or two. "Ask me to believe duh devil done got into muh daughter's head, but don't 'spect me to believe dis white boy really gonna marry my Chloe. Soon he gits wat he bin after he be far away."

Chloe, licking her lips, her mouth hardening slightly, stepped closer to her mother. "Mama, you sayin' he jus wants to bed me . . . dat wat you sayin'?"

"Yeah, and when he through you ain't gonna hear no more talk 'bout marryin'!"

Dennis, sensing what was coming, tried to silence Chloe by pulling her to him, but Chloe was fast gripping her sides, fixing her eyes upon and bravely holding to her mother's. "He's already gotten me bedded, and he still cain't wait to git us married."

A palling silence fell over the group. Sam and Skeeter, now close enough to hear, looked at each other and turned away. Their beautiful cousin with her shapely body and bewitching looks had given her virginity to this white boy, who supposedly was in a heat to marry her. This was surely a different world from the one they knew. Ben, looking mildly rattled, just slowly shook his head, watching Hattie, knowing Chloe's statement would deflate her faster than anything he could say. But Hattie had dropped the poker and, lifting her hands to her face, was moaning to herself. For the first time she felt helpless, for the first time she sensed all her efforts had been in vain. Now she could only pray Chloe wouldn't end up as she did, nursing a young one and eating turnip peelings, when another white boy with an itch in his groin, one who used promises instead of physical punishment to open a black girl's legs, was long gone.

Quarles looked at the roster of men he was going to command and, though still disgruntled by what the new general kept calling an inane assignment, he couldn't resist a quick, spontaneous chuckle of delight. Listed under scouts assigned to his small escort force was the name Tom Zacklee. He couldn't believe his luck. He was to have his old partner back. Since civilian scouts had no rank he immediately sent word to Lee to come to his quarters for a drink. It was well that he did; he had a few things to learn about the task before him. Hardly had he expressed his irritation at drawing this assignment when Lee, looking at the general's orders, took an uncharacteristic hefty swallow of whiskey and placed the glass down with emphasis. "They only giving you twenty men?"

"That's what my orders say. Why?"

"You got any idea what it's like along the Arkansas?"

"Of course not, but I was told not to expect any fighting. I think we're carrying a white flag."

"Whoever told you that likely hasn't been there."

"Lee," concern was edging into Quarles's face, "just what you getting at?"

Lee sighed and settled on the edge of Henry's small table. "There's a southern gent, an agent, name is Albert Pike, who has managed to work up treaties with every tribe west of here. He's even got old enemies like Comanches and Arapahos talking to each other. Don't expect to get any warm welcomes out there unless you're ready to offer a heap more than he has. Considering some mistakes the army has made I'm not even sure that will work."

"Come on, Lee, surely the government knows all that."

Lee smiled but his eyes stayed sober. "What the government doesn't know could wake up a churchyard and give the dead hives. Comanches and Kiowas are as treacherous a crowd as you're gonna find this side of hell. Don't go out there with twenty men unless you've got something to give them they'd rather have than your scalp."

Quarles shook his head. "Jesus, I don't know. I doubt if I'm going to have any say in the matter. The general isn't the kind that does a lot of listening."

Lee finished his glass. "Well, that's the army for you. The guy with the most stripes sends somebody else to find out if he's right or wrong. That way it hardly hurts when he's wrong."

Quarles reached for the bottle. "Lee, it's not always that way."

"It's that way often enough. Glad I'm a civilian."

But the arriving commissioners almost put his mind at ease. They were well dressed, though unused to rough travel. They arrived at the fort disheveled and eager for food and drink. Still they exuded confidence and advised him, over a plain but substantial dinner, that they were fully prepared to meet whatever demands the tribesmen might make. It was imperative the trails remain open and contact with the Southwest and California secured.

There were two of them, and Quarles found them a curious contrast, as different in build as it was possible to be. Marren was tall and spindly and Kaster short and fat. Kaster was given to pointing up when he talked and Marren to glancing downward or stroking his beard as a prelude to speech. They would have a day to rest and the following morning they would leave. Quarles decided not to mention Lee's concerns to the general. The general's attitude toward the commissioners was adequate proof it would have had little effect. Though the commandant was meticulously polite, and his remarks to these political appointees from Washington cautious and diplomatic, his eyes said he was entertaining a couple of parasitic bureaucrats and resented it.

They left on a Thursday morning, with Lee explaining they would follow the Kaw River, and its southern tributaries, westward until they reached the fort, then turn south to the Arkansas. While he made no mention of it, Quarles knew Lee still thought it madness for a force this size to be entering hostile country, where thousands of mounted savages with uncertain sentiments stood waiting, especially since there was talk that month of a large party being surrounded and massacred on the Santa Fe Trail. Quarles told himself it only happened because they were civilians; an equal-sized military force would have survived.

Trying this rationale on Lee, he received only a laconic smile. "Yeah, they were civilians all right, but they were also buffalo hunters, carrying sharps rifles. They could have outshot and outfought any equal number of troopers who ever answered chow call."

📯 **24** 📯

A strange mood hung over the two claim sites, one that Cheatem complained was making it hard to get anything done. Hattie had sunk into a bitter silence, mutely going about her chores, mumbling to Ben when she needed help. Sam and Skeeter resigned themselves to the job of planting a small garden, making use of the many seeds Cheatem had prudently brought along. They still talked of slipping back east for work or of learning more about Troy's silver mine. But Skeeter was beginning to fret about leaving Hattie and Ben behind. Cheatem's large cabin was almost finished, their part of the bargain was completed, but leaving Hattie and Ben here, with no choice but to continue serving Cheatem, would hardly be different from slavery.

In contrast, life at the other claim was curiously divided. Dennis and Chloe had taken over the Sadler wagon, the cabin now being finished enough for the others to sleep indoors. But the arrangement failed to bring the hoped-for harmony. Troy would not acknowledge Chloe, and was bothered when Cole and Cathy did. "How long you think that's gonna last?" he spat one day when Cathy upbraided him for being rude to what she now chose to call her sister-in-law.

"I hope a lot longer than it's taking you to learn a little manners." She had been examining an opening that was to become a window, but as she spoke she spun around to confront him. "By the way, just when are you leaving?"

Troy gave her a wiry look. "Don't worry, I'm going. If Cole is fixing to settle here and be a dirt farmer for the rest of his life that's fine by me. But if he had an ounce of sense he'd be fixing to help me find that mine." Troy stopped to glare at her, the big visionary eyes judging her like a flawed piece of art. "The things a woman does to a man's head."

Cathy stared back at him. "Really."

Chloe was both happy and bothered by a secret feeling that all was not well. In spite of their angry dispute, she missed Hattie and Ben, and found herself hoping Sam and Skeeter would still be her friends. She discovered being with Dennis was both strange and wonderful, but already sensed it was going to mean painful adjustments. On the plus side they were at least together, and the excitement of having each other could hardly be contained. They clung together every night and Chloe's appetite for lovemaking grew by leaps and bounds. With confidence Dennis had begun to try different positions, which Chloe always managed to improve on. Sometimes she giggled so much with delight Dennis had to cover her mouth to keep those in the cabin from hearing. He had moved the wagon twice, but there was a limit to how far away they could safely settle. Some nights their passion was such that they got precious little sleep.

On the other side was the open hostility of Troy and the occasional uneasiness of Cole. She could feel Troy's rejection of her because of her breeding, but she sensed Cole was only worried about Dennis. Only Cathy seemed completely at ease with her, and it proved a blessing, for Dennis was busy working all day. Helping Cathy cooking and washing gave Chloe the tiny sense of belonging she dearly needed.

There were still visits between the two claims but it had fallen off dramatically. Now it was mostly Cheatem coming to discuss plans with Cole, telling him he wanted to corral some of the mustangs running wild beyond the river and breed them to his saddle stock. Later, he concluded, when the war let up, they would send east for some blooded stallions and start breeding horses in a businesslike way. But that would have to wait.

Cole listened but had trouble matching Cheatem's energy for enterprise and, above all, his optimism. Repeatedly Cole alluded to the fact that they were dangerously isolated here; the threat of Indian attack at any moment couldn't be discounted. Capturing wild mustangs meant trailing for miles in a day-long effort to drive horses into a makeshift trap. Spaced out as they would have to be made them even more vulnerable, and Cathy would hardly look kindly on being left alone. Cheatem gruffly dismissed these concerns. He didn't come out here to sit around worrying about Indians. If the Sadler boys didn't want to grab this opportunity, he'd make other plans. For a moment Troy almost seemed to sympathize, making an aside, meant only to air his personal irritation at Cole's lack of interest in his own plans. "Nothing ventured, nothing gained," he muttered. But Cole and Dennis, knowing Troy's mind was on silver, shook their heads.

Returning to his cabin, Silas called Sam and Skeeter over to discuss setting up a fence line, and a series of corrals that he decided would be needed. "Dats a lot of fencin'," said Sam. "Wats we holdin in?"

"Horses!" answered Cheatem.

"Must be a powerful parcel o' horses."

"It's gonna be," answered Cheatem. "Better get to that fencing tomorrow, 'cause day after we running a trap." He started away and then, as though a thought hit him, turned back. "Better get Ben started on that garden . . . gonna be his job from now on. You two will have to ride with me." Starting off again, he had one last thought that he shouted back. "Tell Hattie we'll be wanting some grub to take along."

Lame Fox came in long after dark. Usually he was back by sundown, so his absence was noticed and for Cole a matter of mild concern. Dennis and Chloe, already in a heated embrace in their wagon, were startled to hear the two meeting a few yards away in the darkness.

"Why so late?" Cole's voice, heightened by a touch of anxiety, rang out clearly. There had been a heavy thunderstorm that afternoon but the wind had since dropped and the night air was clear as a bell.

"Bad! Bad trouble!" rose the husky voice of the Shawnee. "War party on river."

"What?"

"War party come scout river, maybe come here."

"Jesus!" Cole looked back at the cabin where Cathy was clearing supper dishes. "How close are they?"

Lame Fox shook his head. "Not know . . . they movin' now."

Cole turned back to the cabin. "Come on!" he half shouted. "Got to warn the others!"

Dennis was out of the wagon in a flash, Chloe right behind him. Seizing his rifle, Dennis headed for the cabin; a second later Chloe, pulling down her skirts and straightening them as fast as she could, went racing up the trail toward Hattie. Within a few minutes both camps were standing in the darkness, looking upriver, all lights extinguished and Cole and Cheatem, in hoarse whispers, assigning defensive positions to the others.

No one knew how long they stood there but it was long enough for Cole to ponder abandoning their cabin and retreating to Cheatem's, where their combined firepower might be the difference between life and death. It was disturbing that Lame Fox was unable to report how large the war party was; he had come upon them holding a hurried council by the river, but couldn't be sure he saw them all. Their vigil lasted over an hour and ended with a muffled shriek from some of the women and heavy gasps or whispered oaths from many of the men.

In the distance, but where everyone knew the new couple had settled, a lone finger of flame climbed into the sky. It was shortly joined by others. Even at this distance shots could be heard in the still night, and a chorus of war cries lapped lightly against the ear. It was a terrible sight, for though the screams of the hapless family couldn't be heard, knowing what must be taking place forced grotesque images of savage slaughter upon their minds.

"Can't we help them?" cried Cathy, the first to speak.

"How?" moaned Cole.

Their helplessness brought home again their own jeopardy, further sobering the men and sending an icy if numbing sensation down the spine of the praying Chloe. Cheatem was swearing profanely under his breath, belatedly admitting to himself he had misjudged the hazards of this lonely and treacherous land. "Damn!" he kept saying. "Always something!"

"Wats we gonna do? Jus stand here?" Hattie suddenly challenged him, sounding less frightened than she should have been.

"If dey come y'ere we g'wine to fight!" answered Sam. "No way they gonna burn us out!"

Chloe was quietly shocked but weirdly thrilled by this unexpected spark of defiance, for she herself was choked with fright. She stood closer to her mother and slipped her hand into Hattie's. At first her mother didn't respond, but then her heavy arm closed around Chloe's shoulders and a momentary but meaningful hug took place. It left a smile struggling to inch its way into Chloe's stark, straining face.

In time the distant fire lowered and went out, and for the remainder of the night everyone looked into the endless reach of shadows, trying to make out dusky figures moving toward them in the darkness. But dawn found them still vainly searching and a blazing sun rose over the land with only the muted sound of an early wind and the screech of passing birds, seeking food for their young along the river, to be heard.

With Lee leading the way and the entire party well mounted, they made excellent time riding westward. Unknowingly they were following the trail of Cheatem and the Sadlers. It wasn't until Lee raised his arm to indicate they were approaching yet another lonely claim on the barren banks of the Smoky Hill that Quarles realized where his one-time charges had ended up. The first ones spotted were Skeeter and Sam, out digging holes for fence posts, but a curious air marked the two as they stared with relief at the small column of soldiers coming up.

Skeeter couldn't resist audibly repeating, "Hallelujah," and Sam made a vigorous gesture of clapping his hands. Lee looked at them curiously, seeing they were in the aftermath of some draining ordeal. But he wasn't surprised to hear Indians had been threatening their claims. It was always a mystery to him why settlers didn't expect trouble when squatting on land Indians had claimed for generations.

When Quarles came up he inquired at once about Cole and was directed to a cabin he could see in the distance. "Dey all over dere," said Skeeter. "Dey fixin' to see wats left upriver."

When he reached them Cole and Cheatem were readying a visit to the site of their neighbor's cabin. Lame Fox had reported the cabin burned down and the ground deserted. As close as he dared get, he saw only one body lying near the ashes.

Quarles, after greeting them warmly, insisted Lee and some troopers go with them. Cathy, relieved to see soldiers, now wondered why Cole had to go at all. But Cole simply smiled at her; if Cheatem had the brisket to go he was damn sure he did too. Cheatem unabashedly declared he was really going to see if some tools they had borrowed and never returned might still be lying around.

When they left, Cathy, after being introduced, made Quarles and the startled commissioners some coffee. The tall Marren and the short, fat Kaster were mumbling to each other, disturbed to find they were finally approaching the Indians they were sent to deal with and finding them hostile. Quarles wondered if the white flag his troop carried would help. Like himself they had been advised there would be no fighting. Was this a harbinger of what was to come?

Both officials, however, were impressed with Cathy, Marren in particular, smiling at her continually, and

Kaster trying to compensate for his less imposing stance by continually gesturing upward as though he had hopes of growing taller.

But Quarles well remembered her and was once again impressed by her unpretentious ways and the frankness with which she dealt with her fears. "I'd make a poor heroine even in a story about outlaw mice," she said, discussing her scare. "I sure hope you folks have come to stay!" she added more soberly while serving coffee.

"We're hoping to arrange for a reliable peace," said Marren, his tone implying the transactions would prosper under his hand. Kaster pointed to the almost-finished roof overhead. "You needn't concern yourself, madam, that roof should be all the protection you will require shortly."

Quarles, remembering Lee's warning, had begun to wonder at their prospects, but saw no reason to add to the trace of alarm he had suddenly detected about these cabins.

Sometime later, alone with Cathy, he saw Chloe and Dennis walking together, his arm about her. "Am I seeing something in progress?" he asked, his tone light and delicate as though afraid of saying the wrong thing.

Cathy gave him a reassuring smile. "They're going to be married," she said simply. "Let's hope love conquers all."

Quarles was a bit more shocked than he looked. On the face of it there was nothing wrong with their marrying but all he could manage to say was, "She's very pretty."

"That she is. No woman could complain about having her looks. I certainly wouldn't."

Quarles almost said, "You have something far more than looks," but caught himself at the last moment. Such a remark might seem too forward, too suggestive of qualities only a woman's husband should be concerned with.

Cathy gave him an amiable but slightly challenging look. "I take it you're not one for marriage yourself."

"On the contrary, I emphatically approve of it." There

was a moment of strange silence, as Cathy knew he hadn't finished. "Unfortunately my wife died some years ago. I'm afraid it has cast me into a different life . . . one I'm afraid she'd hardly have approved of."

"I'm so sorry."

He shrugged. "It's God's will they tell me, though I confess I have found that rather little comfort."

Cathy suddenly had a queer feeling Henry Quarles was saying this for a reason. He wanted her to hear it, he wanted it to play some part in her estimation of him. As she looked at his strong features and deeply searching eyes she had to admit it did. Dressed in his uniform, he no longer looked the unknowable power behind a vast, shadowy slave operation, used to the tensions and risks of grim and often mortal struggles every day for people's freedom. Now he seemed just one more decent man caught up in a tragic war and without much fanfare quietly trying to do his best.

"Perhaps I'm beginning to bore you," she heard him saying a trifle uncertainly.

She came over and took his arm. "One is never bored when one discovers how faulty quick impressions can be."

Henry's smile was almost internal, almost as though some distant anxiety, flickering on the rim of consciousness, had been put to rest.

In spite of their pleasant hour or two the report from the scouting party threw a pall over them all. The body Lame Fox had spotted turned out to be the woman. She had been stripped, raped, scalped, and her left hand had been chopped off. "Probably for rings they couldn't work off," muttered Lee. The man had been tied inside the cabin before it was torched and had been cremated by the intense heat. The children had disappeared.

In the brush nearby Cheatem found a two-handled saw and a file, but his spare ax was gone. Cole looked a little pale, but added self-consciously they had buried the woman and said a few prayers over her grave. Somehow it didn't lessen the shock. Somehow the de-

scription of this death scene hung in their minds,
reminding them of the price this land might demand, of
painted faces stealthily crossing horizons in the night,
of a silence broken only by the wind, of the imminence
of death.

Black Otter knew of the two cabins further down the
river, but he also knew flames rising from the one
destroyed denied his warriors any element of surprise.
Unlike the isolated cabin, so easily taken, these intruders
were more numerous, well armed, his scouts spotting
three empty wagons nearby. All signs said they had
entered buffalo country with the many things whites
used to change the land. He would watch them for a day
or two; settlers grew careless with time.

He had mounted this raid to prove to the tribes the
tahbay-boh were coming in larger and larger numbers to
seize their land and must be driven back. But his boast
of a powerful war party and its promise of many coups
failed to draw important men like Whistling Elk. Only a
handful of young warriors lusting after plunder joined.
In his heart he was hoping to return with many scalps
and reports of whites overrunning the land, driving off
the game. With such evidence he could rise in council
and move the people, but so far only two scalps had been
taken.

Attacking the lonely cabin had been ridiculously easy,
the frantic man getting off only one shot, slightly wounding a Kiowa youth, Standing Bear. When seized the man
screamed so loudly they cut out his tongue, tied him
inside the cabin, and set it afire. The warriors then

stripped the woman and used her several times before scalping her for her long blonde hair. But that might have been a mistake. They should have taken her back for the squaws to torment and enslave; it was a way to humiliate these whites and diminish the fear of them Black Otter suspected lay in his people. The children, a girl of four and a boy of five, were to be carried back and raised as Comanches. Pale as death and too paralyzed with fear to even cry, they were tied on the single captured horse and led away.

But the cabin had yielded little else, a few trinkets, some pots and metal utensils, and one gun with less than twenty rounds. Had they never been attacked these whites could not have lasted a season. Black Otter shook his head. Did these foolish ones think taking a piece of earth and building a flimsy shelter on it would keep them alive in the land of the mighty Nerm and their wily Kiowa allies?

Those other cabins, with their many men, promised far more, but the attack must be well planned. Large losses hurt a war chief's standing. His scouts had managed to determine where the newcomers were located, even that some of them were black. It was now known a man and a young squaw lived in a wagon near one of the cabins. He did not believe, as did some, there was an Indian scout with this party, for only a fleeting glimpse of him had been reported near the ruins of the burnt-out cabin.

But he was shocked when late the following day a column of soldiers, the mounted *tahbay-bohs,* rode up to these claims. This had caused his warriors to pull back. They hadn't come to fight soldiers. But, eyeing the white flag, Black Otter wondered why these bluecoats were here. Why had they come? Were these the ones offering the white man's goods for peace?

Black Otter was determined to find out.

When the peace commissioners left a pall hung over the still bare and sparsely furnished cabins. Cole and Cheatem's repeated assurances of a promised treaty to pacify these murdering tribesmen didn't dispel it. Cathy kept her questioning eyes on Cole, and Chloe, noticing the sun sinking, suddenly began to fear the oncoming night. Only Hattie sounded more irritated than distressed. "Jus mo' misery for ole Hattie, das wat!" she exclaimed, ordering Ben to fetch her more wood.

They had been cutting their wood from a little grove a half mile down the river, not a long distance but far enough to take Ben away from whatever safety the cabins offered. He was slow getting started, fussing with his carrying sack and mumbling aloud he needed a gun.

"You cain't carry a parcel of wood if you tottin' a gun," declared Hattie. "Now scat while we still gots daylight."

Ben left, but as he passed Sam and Skeeter, digging at the fence line, they hailed him. "Where you headin'?"

"Hattie want mo' wood."

Sam stood up and wiped the sweat from his brow. "You can't traipse down dere alone." Skeeter nodded agreement.

Ben looked back to where he had left Hattie. "What I gonna do? She bound she wants wood."

"You jus wait," said Sam. "Ah'm gonna fetch a horse and some rope. We bring back 'nough wood to fix dat Hattie for a spell."

When Sam returned he looked keyed up and more than a little edgy, but he was carrying a rifle and together they led the horse with a heavy coil of rope to the little grove.

It wasn't until they were ready to return that Sam saw a flash of color at the far end of the grove. Luckily Ben's slow movements, cutting and gathering pieces of wood one at a time, made Sam so anxious that by the time the old man was finished Sam was as tense and wary as a plunging hawk. It proved to be his salvation, for had he been a split second slower he would have been dead. Instinctively he pulled back and fired as a whistling arrow smashed into the pack of wood only inches from his head.

Shocked but quickly lifting the frail figure of Ben, and throwing him across the horse's withers before the wood,

Sam grabbed the halter and began running back toward the cabin.

The shot, though not loud, was heard like thunder at the Cheatem claim and within moments Skeeter, Cheatem, and even Hattie were standing armed, watching Sam racing toward them, the heavily loaded horse trotting behind. Their appearance surely kept Sam from being pursued but old Ben came in so shaken he couldn't talk.

For a moment it seemed to be over but the shot had reached the other claim too. Cole and Dennis had been asking Troy if he would help cultivate some land if they borrowed Cheatem's plow, and Troy was pointing out, with rising irritation, he had his own plans and had never promised to farm to begin with. Then that solitary shot rang out in the distance.

The men stopped and peered in that direction, and Cathy appeared at the door, a hand across her throat. But Chloe, trying to rest in the wagon, suddenly feared her mother might be in danger. She jumped from the wagon and went bounding up the trail. Dennis broke away from his brothers and started calling after her. But by the time he had pulled his gun from the wagon he could see Cheatem and Skeeter standing out in the open and Sam coming up with a horse. No more shots were fired and it appeared the threat was over. He stood looking up the trail, deciding she'd soon be back. Chloe never stayed away long, particularly when it was getting dark.

Chloe finally reached her mother, whom she found clutching Cheatem's shotgun and telling Ben to stop shaking so he could drink the water Skeeter brought him. Sam was standing, arms akimbo, confronting her like a headmaster calling a delinquent student to account. "Why you send him down dere by he'self?"

"He gots to do somethin'!"

"He's an old man and ain't so spry no mo'. From now on ah'll git duh wood!"

Cheatem turned to him, ignoring this exchange. "What in hell were you shootin' at anyhow?"

"A face . . . face wid mess o' red stripes."

"You sure?"

"How sure is ah suppose to be. Dat arrow hangin' out of dat pack of wood is sure 'nough for me!"

By now Chloe was hugging her mother, Hattie resignedly opening her arms and hugging her back. "What you doin' here, child?"

"I was frightened . . . worried 'bout you."

"Ah'se fine."

It was several minutes before everyone was quieted down and Ben was settled on the tailgate of the lumber wagon to watch Sam and Skeeter untying the wood, piling it up by the fire. No one wanted to say the incident proved the Indians were still close by, waiting, watching, perhaps planning an attack that very night. To the west the horizon was slipping from lavender to blue and darkness was almost upon them.

It was Chloe, noticing she could no longer see her wagon clearly in the gathering dusk, who suddenly turned toward the trail, anxious to hurry back. Hattie, walking her to where the land sloped away, promised to see her the following morning. They were still holding each other, whispering back and forth, Hattie putting one arm around her daughter, Cheatem's shotgun dangling from the other, as Dennis could be heard shouting in the distance, "Chloe! Chloe!"

"I'm coming!" she shouted, and, kissing her mother good night, headed down the track. Chloe was a slim but well-built girl and could run like a deer. She was speedily making her way along the path when suddenly a form started taking shape on the trail before her. At first she thought it might be Dennis or one of the men coming for her, but in a flash she knew the rough outline was wrong. It was too large, too gross; in the dim light she made out a horned headdress and something long and black held high in the air. With a shriek she spun around and scrambled to retrace her steps. With the sound of feet behind her spreading panic in her brain she filled her lungs to scream "Help," but it came out in labored gasps seeming too weak to penetrate the night. The footsteps behind were fast closing on her and a heavy breathing kept rising, threatening to drown out her own. Her last recollection of this terror that had engulfed her was Hattie's form looming up before her as she crumbled at her mother's feet, her face striking the earth as the blast of a shotgun roared overhead.

She came to in Cheatem's cabin where all of them, including Ben, were standing around armed. Her head was in Hattie's lap and her mother was soothing her, telling her she was safe. After a time she saw Dennis bending over her, his hand shaking a little, the dampness of perspiration on his brow.

"What happened?" she murmured weakly, clutching Dennis's sleeve with one hand and Hattie's arm with the other.

Dennis patted her hand. "Some Injun was trying to seize you," he explained, his voice so soft it was almost a whisper.

"Seize me?" Chloe struggled to sit up. "Tried to seize me . . . where did he go?"

"Where he ain't never comin' back," mumbled Hattie. "Ah done killed him!"

Black Otter had offered a reward to the warrior who captured one of these whites. He had only eleven braves now that a second had been wounded, this one seriously; hardly enough to attack these cabins with three or four armed men in each. But he was intent on learning why those bluecoats had come under a white flag; surely these settlers, whom the bluecoats had visited, would know. Any captive taken could tell him what he wanted. Reluctance would soon vanish under torture.

Unfortunately both his wounded braves were Kiowas and, suspecting his medicine was weak, were headed back to their camp on the Arkansas, the slightly wounded helping the other along. Black Otter didn't think the badly injured brave would live, but that was a warrior's lot, trained for years to bring death to others, they stoically accepted that one day it would come to them. This fatally injured brave had been hit trying to sneak up on two men gathering wood in a little grove down the river. It was a remarkable shot and might have discouraged many, but his nephew, the daring Iron Fox, almost immediately slipped away in the lowering darkness to stalk the trail between the claims, saying he had seen individuals pass along it after dark. That day he had been making *puha,* secret medicine, to win Black Otter's reward.

Watching from a distance, it was hard to pinpoint exactly when and where it started, but suddenly violent screaming broke out, and what sounded like fierce pursuit of a frantic and desperately fleeing female kept swelling in vehemence until it ended abruptly in a shotgun blast that echoed across the land. Black Otter could only grumble to himself. He could see little in the darkness and was able to surmise less. Only the very obvious was left. Whatever encounter took place beyond his sight, it had ended with a shotgun blast, and although the Nerm had acquired a few such guns from the Comancheros, no one could recall Iron Fox carrying a shotgun when he left.

26

The reception Captain Quarles and the peace commissioners received at the fort fell far short of cordial. A major welcomed them in such a proficient manner and address that his words were drained of warmth, and though he did all the proper things a veiled irritation in his manner had Henry wondering if anybody in this army was satisfied with his lot. That evening over a brandy it became clear the major felt himself marooned on this frontier, while opportunities for promotion on eastern battlefields were occurring daily. A man couldn't prove his mettle or talents for high command chasing painted nomads.

While the others sipped their drinks the major paced the floor and puffed fretfully on his pipe. He regretted the country was at war but for a career soldier it presented one of the few quick ways to reach high rank. As a military school graduate he was appalled to hear politically connected civilians, who didn't know a "flint-lock from a frying pan," were being commissioned colonels or even generals at induction, immediately outranking him and drawing higher pay.

Had the major settled down that evening might have proved informative for the visitors, but his complaints seemed endless. Quarles began to suspect the major's frustrations arose from more than an indifferent army command. Chance comments, after his second or third brandy, began to hint he was having little or no luck subduing the Kiowas and an ever-increasing number of Comanches, who were killing settlers, raiding trade routes, and rampaging at will over his territory. When finally questioned about local conditions the major explained his evident failure by an awkward treatise on military science, declaring the issue was purely tactical, a question of greater mobility. Mounted war parties struck with such deadly swiftness, killing and looting and disappearing before even his experienced cavalry units could muster, reach the devastated area, and commence what was sure to be another futile chase.

Quarles and the commissioners, satisfied with one glass, were suspecting by now the major was addicted to drinking and exercising his woes. His slightly inflamed face began showing the strain of speaking clearly as liquor stiffened his tongue and put visible effort into his delivery. Ominously he grew more resentful with each additional complaint. Like the general at Leavenworth, he was firmly against making peace with marauding Indians, and didn't believe in treaties that were bribes in all but name. The commissioners, becoming restless, shifted forward in their seats, paling as he resorted to profanity to express his contempt for these "heathen bastards" who should be hounded to extinction.

With some effort Marren cleared his throat. "Major, I must tell you frankly I heartily disagree with such sentiments and am considerably shocked to hear them expressed here."

For a moment the major looked as though he realized he had stumbled onto dangerous ground and wisdom called for retreat, but either the brandy had worked too deep, or he decided it was too late to recoup, for his response was "Don't be, you'll find everyone out here but greenhorns from the east agrees with me."

Kaster was coming to his feet, one finger raised like a prophet reminding mortals of divine retribution. "Surely you must know differences between peoples, between us and these misguided natives, can never be resolved with such attitudes," he proclaimed.

"Differences between us and them will only be resolved when we send the last of 'em to hell!"

Quarles, seeing matters now dangerously out of hand, pointedly interrupted by pleading a need for sleep, then ceremoniously rising and excusing himself. The commissioners, grasping this opportunity to escape, quickly added how long a day it had been and that they had also best retire. The major, not so drunk that he didn't notice the abruptness of their departures, made a little ungracious bow as they left. Quarles, looking back, could see him sitting down again, staring at the floor, faintly bewildered and appearing lonely beside his brandy bottle and three empty chairs. . . .

As the commissioners' rooms were next to his, Quarles noticed they stopped for a moment and whispered to each other before going in. Marren kept gesturing back to the room they had just left and Kaster, looking pious, waved his finger in summary judgement. Quarles was learning something about the army and its peculiar ties to Washington. He suspected that poor major would remain a major for a very long, long time.

* * *

The patrol that captured Standing Bear did not realize they had set in motion a process that would bring peace to the plains. At the fort the major turned him over to Marren and Kaster, saying here was a Kiowa who would take a message to their chiefs, an approach preferable to running down their leaders, a task Quarles suspected he wouldn't have relished.

Lee, who was surprisingly adept at sign language, questioned the captive, learning from the brave, who had an open flesh wound, that he had left a hunting party with a badly wounded companion and was making his way to the Arkansas. His companion had died and he was taking word of it to his people.

Lee suspected the Kiowa was with a war party, likely the one that killed Sadler's neighbor, but the young warrior would prove handy in making contact with the hostiles before any shooting started. Lee still believed they had underestimated the dangers of riding boldly into this country.

Trying to decide how best to proceed while at the fort, Quarles confided to Lee some of the major's demonstrations the night before. The scout simply shook his head. "They all git like that out here. These forts are nothing but godforsaken sinkholes, freezing in the winter and broiling in the summer. Officers are allowed wives but no woman in her right mind stays. There's not a goddamn thing to do out here but booze up and wish you were somewheres else. If they could whip these Indians it might help, but Washington can't make up its mind what it wants to do, adopt these tribes, hoping they can learn to follow a plow, or just wipe 'em out."

"Maybe they should just prohibit liquor on the post."

Lee guffawed. "Suicide rate would soar. It's plenty high enough already."

Quarles opened the top buttons of his tunic. The noon heat had begun to feel like a weight on his body. "How long do you figure before we'll hear from them?"

"Not long. It's their season for hunting, trading, or raiding. Either way they're likely to be craving action."

* * *

Hattie's killing of the Comanche brave had a strange effect upon everyone. Cheatem was treating her with more respect, and if Sam and Skeeter were saying little they had started looking upon Cheatem's orders as suggestions open to amendment. At first it had Silas glaring back at them, but he was coming to realize the cabin was finished; they were free to leave. They had already proved they could deal with Indians as well as any whites, but secretly his mind had been ranging well beyond even that crucial disclosure. Silas Cheatem was built to look ahead. His claim could never become the ranch he dreamt about without help. One glance at the barren stretches surrounding them told him no other help was in the offing. His growing quandary soon had him stewing in silence for hours.

Even old Ben started carrying himself differently, for Hattie, realizing she had almost caused his death, was finally offering grunts of approval over his garden. But Chloe, still wary, came only on mornings Dennis could accompany her, though there had been no sign of Indians since that night. But Chloe, whom many thought was prettier than ever, looked healthy and happy, and Hattie, noticing Dennis never let her out of sight, was beginning to believe Chloe had gotten herself a man who truly loved her, and was not the cagey racist lecher she feared. But secretly she was watching Chloe's figure. From the little her daughter told her, for they still shared confidences, she gathered they made love every night and it was clear from Chloe's dancing eyes that wasn't likely to stop.

While Cheatem could hide his nettlesome worries about former slaves, who were suddenly not only free but now near indispensable, dissension in the nearby Sadler camp was harder to conceal. Troy, spending days preparing to leave, was still pointedly cool to Chloe, and several incidents had taken place which had Dennis inwardly seething. Cole and Cathy, indicating both bluntly and obliquely that they sided with Dennis and were ashamed of Troy's behavior, had little effect. One morning Troy, irritated at their admonitions and angrily pretending to let the matter drop, ranted, "He's made his bed, goddamn it, let him lie in it!" His hand swung down in a deprecating gesture at their wagon.

Dennis, outside chinking a corner but close enough to overhear, came charging in until their faces were only inches apart. "There ain't room in that bed you're talking about for you or your filthy mouth . . . one of these days somebody figures to help you button it up!"

Cole was between them, Cathy hurrying over to pull Dennis away. "If you two can't get along, stay the hell away from each other," ordered Cole. "We got problems enough without this fool nonsense."

Dennis, because of Chloe, stubbornly refused to leave the claim but Troy, to get away from this environ soured by strife, decided to stroll over to visit Cheatem. Much as he disliked, even despised, Silas, a man he considered a braggart and bully, he respected his ability to foresee and prepare for problems others had to stumble into to realize existed. Losing Cole meant he had to explore the dangerous mountain country on his own and secretly it bothered him. Like all dreamers who've experienced the perils of unfettered fantasies he wisely sought another's anchor to reality. He had always counted on Cole's firmness of mind, steadfast disposition, and courage in the face of uncertainty. Now as he approached Cheatem he couldn't deny he was seeking for something similar, guidance perhaps disguised as curiosity, from this crude operator whose ability to foresee many pitfalls in life smacked of clairvoyance.

"You've read a heap about conditions out here," he began casually enough. "What might you figure to be the best way to go about a little exploring in them mountains yonder?"

Cheatem, settling down and turning to Troy, looked as though he was ready to smile but thought better of it. "Exploring? And just what might yuh be exploring for?"

"Could be a lot of things."

Now Cheatem did smile. "Could be something you ain't figuring to let on about, eh?"

Troy already had a feeling he was being trapped. "Could be," he muttered.

Cheatem sat back like a man not given to fencing, preferring plain talk. "Now I happened to hear you mentioning silver the night the old trapper came by . . . is that what's got you traipsing into the mountains?"

Troy glanced at Hattie, who was coming back from the river with a bucket of water. "All I'm asking is how you figure a man should be setting up if he wanted to poke around up there for a spell?"

Cheatem gripped his chin. "To start with, a hell of a lot more luck than the law allows." His eyes drifted to Hattie settling the bucket of water near the fire, but his hand rose to rub his forehead. He seemed to be rapidly arranging things in his mind. "Troy, you go into those mountains alone and you ain't never coming out!"

"How do you figure?"

"Can't be looking for pay dirt and keeping a sharp lookout all t'once."

Troy shrugged. "You talking about Indians?"

"Yeah, but there's a few whites interested in that stuff too. Gits around what you're huntin' for you're likely to have some mighty rough-looking company." Cheatem's hand, starting at his forehead, had slipped down to where one finger was tapping his lips. "You got some notion where to look?"

"Maybe." Troy was now well aware of what was happening but, hauling back on the balls of his feet, tensely studying Cheatem's face, he wasn't sure he wanted to stop it. He needed help. He was a long ways from finding any silver mines. He had nothing but a sketchy map and the word of a dead man who when alive had people suspecting the moon was full. Last of all he didn't relish going into those mountains alone. What had seemed alluring, exciting, even romantic from a distance, had become a chancy venture with frightful risks up close. When measured against its unpromising prospects even questions of sanity arose. Yet Troy wasn't ready to give the idea up either, even if the thought of another's sharing the risks and possible costs was slowly beginning to appeal to him. "Well, do you have any suggestions?" he said, as though wanting to suggest Cheatem's remarks had so far produced little of interest.

"Tell you what," said Cheatem, straightening himself up and rubbing his hands. "Give me a day or two to chump on it, could be I'll have me some ideas that kin save you a heap of misery."

"I'd be right grateful."

The two shook hands and Troy, waving at Hattie, started back. For the next hour both felt the other had unknowingly given them something valuable. Troy strode away strangely relieved and somehow feeling the mountains had become far less threatening, while Cheatem, once Troy was out of earshot, emitted a deep chortle of satisfaction. Whatever his troubles, his ambitious, acquisitive heart was whispering he might have just put his front paw on the opportunity of a lifetime.

27

Black Otter watched the stately array of Kiowa and Comanche chiefs settling in the grove where the two white peace talkers waited with interpreters and a handful of bluecoats. An uncertain tension in the air appeared misplaced on this beautiful day, with light breezes rippling through tall prairie grasses and wedges of geese drifting northward overhead. The heavily decorated Kiowas were there in force but it was hardly an auspicious showing for Comanches. Many important chiefs of the Nerm were missing and some whole tribes, like the Antelopes of the Llano Estacado, declined to appear at all.

Black Otter, sitting to the rear, listened to the blandishments and many promises of the white peace talkers. To him the spindly tall and comically short figures didn't look like warriors. It had him grunting to himself, for he felt only warriors could make peace, only fighting men could agree to end fighting. It would have been far more convincing had it been a soldier chief, with a thousand armed bluecoats at his back, calling for brotherhood between red and white. As it was his anger and suspicions only increased. He gripped the string holding his medicine bag about his neck between his teeth and scowled at the cobalt sky. This treaty would be one of those written on the wind.

The Kiowa and attending Comanche chiefs nodded when told of the generous annuity the government was offering for peace and a promise of safe passage on the trails west. But Black Otter backed away as popular leaders such as Red Elk went forward to touch the pen, consenting to the terms of a treaty, solemnly translated by stony-faced interpreters as Marren read it slowly, line for line, from a white man's paper.

Quarles was impressed with how quickly the terms were accepted, it could only mean the Indians were also anxious for peace. But Lee's smile had a cynical edge to it as he listened to Quarles's impression. "That's a mighty big annuity . . . worth more than any loot they could come by in a season . . . maybe they ain't had no schoolin' but they ain't stupid."

The commissioners had arranged for a large feast and a formal ceremony to celebrate the treaty signing. Presents of hats and studded military belts were presented to every chief who signed. The Indians, not to be outdone, responded with a great dance, over two hundred warriors whirling about and stamping the ground as a frightening array of drums rocked the air and squaws screamed shrilly as their braves, reciting their brave deeds, pranced by. If Marren or Kaster noticed many of the warriors, dancing and chanting to the wildly beating drums, were carrying scalp sticks adorned by blonde, silky black, and even red hair, they didn't comment.

The next day the peace delegation turned north. They still had to secure the vital Oregon Trail; they had to meet those legendary scourges of the northern plains, the powerfully mounted Cheyennes and Arapahos, two tribes backed by the surly and now restless Sioux. Only Lee was surprised to find the Kiowas, as a demonstration of friendship, were sending two scouts along to help the peace commissioners make contact with these truculent tribes. Only he was struck by the calm way the warlike southerners heard their legendary northern foes were also going to enjoy the white man's largesse. "They've bin enemies since Adam was a pup, if they're squattin' together now to smoke, this child doesn't like it."

Quarles looked at him quizzically. "Lee, what's the matter with you? You never seem to trust Indians, why?"

Lee glanced around him like a man too sure he was right to quibble. "Got my heart set on a long life, that's why!"

Cheatem was trying to plan the building of a horse trap but his mind kept gravitating to silver. It left him quietly irritated at the choices he would soon have to make. If he went ahead with the brush trap, and started corralling wild mustangs, he couldn't leave with Troy. If he left with Troy the building of the ranch would be set back for months. Another problem kept peppering his mind. Those mountains were reputed to be dangerous. Hopefully Quarles's party would succeed in arranging peace with the warring tribes and reduce the risk of traveling west, but Troy was ready and anxious to leave at once. Silas knew the type. Impulsive dreamers, quick to enlist others in their dreams but capable of striking out alone if rebuffed. No matter how he turned the facts over one thing was certain. If Troy managed to come up with a silver mine, only those who were there helping him find it would have any legitimate claim to the lode. Silas Cheatem wasn't about to have a slice of silver mine slip through his fingers. But his quandary remained. Only a decision would dispel it, a decision upon which so much depended that being hurried into it was upsetting.

The sight of Troy coming up the trail warned him time

was running out. He had promised Troy some help, help which he secretly hoped would make Silas Cheatem a partner in the venture. But the critical moment was approaching. He had always thought he read people well, even considered it the reason for his business success. He had already calculated Troy was as innocent of skillful manipulating and the subtleties of sharp bargaining as a child. His instincts whispered he had only to think of something that would dissolve Troy's buck fever, those self-doubts that assail visionary types facing the maw of reality. He was about to kick himself for failing to find a prudent solution to his quandary when his eyes fell upon Sam and Skeeter, dutifully measuring off and digging post holes along the marked fence line.

Troy Sadler was well aware he had allowed Cheatem to glimpse his long-concealed scheme for striking it rich. Though he hadn't planned such a seeming misstep, he knew in some deep way it was partly deliberate. He wanted something from Silas and had to offer something in return. By appearing uncertain or vaguely groping for help he attracted, as he hoped he would, Cheatem's nose for easy profit. Silas was going to suggest ways to make his efforts succeed, but what Troy really wanted to hear was Cheatem's judgement on the whole project, its chances for success. There was no denying this man's business acumen, his knack for spotting bargains, his adeptness at perceiving problems in advance and preparing accordingly. All those qualities that Troy sorely felt he lacked were bunched in this coarse figure, whose enterprising ability he envied and at the moment wanted to use. In short, Troy was counting on Cheatem's avarice to determine the promise and even soundness of his plan.

After they settled down he was to find Cheatem's advice was preceded by some chance remarks, a few of which had Troy suddenly measuring his responses.

Cheatem's expression suggested he was assuming Troy's answer. "So you know where to dig, eh?"

Troy nodded lightly. "Got some notions."

Cheatem's smile implied he found something faintly

humorous in Troy's reply. "Troy, a gent tackling a mountain range needs more than a shovel and a notion."

"Let's say I have me a map of sorts."

"A map . . . of sorts?"

"Yeah, but there's a fair piece of description with it."

"You figure it's enough, eh?"

"Reckon."

Cheatem looked as though he were summoning up a military campaign with too many doubtful issues for comfort. "Well, best face it, a man by hisself is going to be a mighty risky proposition . . . if you was to break an arm or a leg, catch fever or come down with snake bite, you be licked! Best you take along a second gun, someone to keep an eye on you, on your back trail . . . some handy galoot to be there if'n you hit trouble."

Troy would have gambled that Cheatem was going to volunteer himself, and he moved quickly to squelch that possibility. "Really don't think we'd hit it off, Silas," he stated firmly, as though it was a truth both should recognize.

But he was wrong, Cheatem was shaking his head in agreement. "No, I figure the same, I was thinking maybe Sam or Skeeter should trail along, just so someone be there if needed."

Troy pulled back in surprise. "What makes you think they'd even want to go?"

"They will when they hear I'm fixing to pay 'em a dollar a day."

"A dollar a day? For what?"

"For representing me."

Now Troy pushed back his chair and put weight on the balls of his feet, preparing to rise. "Somehow I get the feeling you're trying to work yourself into this deal."

Cheatem raised a cautioning and at the same time a placating hand. "Why not! Even if you find silver it's gonna take money and plenty of savvy to mine it . . . turn it into cash. You couldn't have a better man holding a small interest than Silas Cheatem. What do you say?"

Troy brought his hands together before him and rubbed them slowly. "Think I'll try it alone."

Cheatem looked at him for a long moment, then sighed audibly. "Guess I'll just have to be satisfied with what I make on that bet with Cole."

Troy was half out of his seat, his eyes skeptical. "What bet is that?"

"The bet I'm going to make that you ain't ever coming back!"

Chloe used the mornings to tidy up the wagon and repair their few well-worn clothes. It was a pleasant time, for she would often bury her head in a pillow, giggling to herself about their lovemaking the night before. But there were also moments when she wished for pretty dresses, some means to keep Dennis proud of her. She knew he and Troy had argued over her and was worried there might be others, for she was slowly beginning to grasp that having a half-black wife created problems for a husband living in a white world. Of late even that word husband was beginning to concern her, for they weren't officially married. Dennis swore nightly they would be by the first preacher that came by. Now she found herself praying that faceless cleric would hurry. But above all her newly vibrant body captured her thoughts. As Dennis explored it nightly she too began to uncover things about herself. She enjoyed responding to his lovemaking and had learned to give herself in ways that pleased him and increased his passion. There were moments when their love for each other swelled to such unbearable heights that she heard herself sobbing with delight as he climaxed and released his male urge to possess her. They were clearly well mated. Shy at first, Chloe was slowly becoming increasingly involved, finding new ways to intensify their intimacy, becoming on some nights near insatiable. Last night for the first time she clawed his back and chewed his earlobe as he grasped her, suddenly making her join him as he writhed in ecstasy. After each exhilarating and exhausting session a deep restoring sleep seemed to magically claim them.

Her daydreams, if fanciful, were exciting, for she saw herself as a young girl becoming a young woman, a process worked upon girls by boys. Boys, she had decided, were wonderfully strange and fascinating creatures. They saw you, wanted you, married you, made love to you, and turned you into a woman. Of course, girls and women did some things too but to the outside world it appeared as though men did it all. She liked that. Still, it faintly worried her to recall that it was she who had first flirted with Dennis, she who allowed his caresses because she was fantasizing about being possessed by him, and now she was boldly adding as much heat to their coupling as he. Maybe she was one of those rarely mentioned women people whispered about, women who were overfond of men, women who didn't wait for marriage, women who gave themselves to men they didn't know for money. She would have to ask Hattie, she would have to find out more about those women. She shut her eyes and held her breath. Mercy! Could she be one of them? Suddenly she bit her lip and moved back in the wagon. In the distance she could see Troy coming down the trail. No matter what her thoughts, they scattered at the sight of this man she often found staring at her, looking as though her living with Dennis was either a crime or a sin. She didn't like him. She waited until he strode past her, then, knowing she couldn't be seen, stuck her tongue out at him.

She was glad he was going away.

Cheatem didn't often ask them in for coffee, so when Sam and Skeeter were told by Ben that Silas was inviting them they exchanged glances and, looking puzzled, put their spades aside and trooped to the cabin.

"Come in, fellows. One of you get that pot, should be enough left to go around." Cheatem was savoring a cup he had poured earlier. "Hattie sure makes dandy coffee."

Sam and Skeeter filled the wooden mugs Hattie used to serve them and settled down on a bench that served one side of the table. "You fellas are probably wondering what I got in mind," he began, "but we all got to work together here, it's what's gonna make us prosper."

Ben was standing at the door, Hattie behind him.

Cheatem waved them in. "Come on, we don't have no secrets or sech around here, we do things together, only way to succeed."

Sam was eyeing Skeeter and Hattie was waving Ben down beside her on a box just brought from Cheatem's wagon. This "together" talk was a new note; it had them listening warily.

Cheatem gestured toward the Sadler claim with his cup. "Fact is neighbor Troy has got hisself a notion where a heap of silver might be sitting in the ground a'waiting to be discovered. Naturally, he's bin visiting . . . wanting some help. Seems to me t'wouldn't be neighborly not to lend a hand, would it? So I figure one of us ought to go along, kind of see he has a little help gitting there and back."

There was a long silence before Skeeter asked delicately, "Where is 'there'?"

"Oh, in some mountains just west of here, t'wouldn't be nothing to speak of for a young sprightly fella."

There was another silence. "You goin'?" asked Sam.

"Damn if I wasn't just a'sittin' here wishing to hell I could! Truth is I got to git on with this here ranch, season is passing, some things got to be done right pertly."

Hattie finally spoke up. "What yuh gittin' at?"

Cheatem leaned forward, his eyes slipping to Sam and Skeeter, his tone faintly fatherly. "Thought maybe one of you fellas would like to make some money, and give a neighbor a hand whilst doing it."

"Money?" said Sam, looking up.

"Yeah, we share here," roared Cheatem. "We don't expect a fella to take on more than others less he git a little extry."

"How much?" intruded Hattie.

"A dollar a day for every day it takes. Course we got to hold it to a month."

"Das a lotta money," said Hattie. "Something you not tellin' us? . . . Ah suspect dem mountains mighty dangerous."

Cheatem shrugged. "Just like here . . . probably a few natives around . . . nothing to take on about."

Sam was on his feet, taking a few steps closer to Cheatem. "Wat if he find dat mine, wat happens?"

Cheatem looked as though the picture was obvious. "Shoot, Troy will be taking that silver out, gitting rich."

"Ah mean what happens to us? . . . you?"

"Well, naturally I'll have a small share in it, after all I'm paying to help find it."

"How small dat share?"

"Does it matter . . . anyway it's all bin arranged."

Skeeter was suddenly standing beside Sam. "How small dat share?" he repeated.

Cheatem looked like he might not answer but realized sooner or later they'd have to know. "I figure to git one third," he said blandly, as though that were nothing more than a nomimal return on his investment. The silence this time was shorter. "Wat happens to us?"

Cheatem slapped his knee. "Oh, I see, you fellas figure there ought to be a reward for success. By God, I believe you're right! Tell you what, if whoever goes gits back here with a real proof of a silver mine, there's gonna be a fifty-dollar bonus waiting. Now, by Jesus, you can't beat that for fairness!"

A light rain was pelting the skin-covered lodge the Cheyennes had set up to meet the white men. They stood in their regalia, their buffalo headdresses seeming stark and menacing among the colorful feathered bonnets of the Arapahos. Both tribesmen appeared taller than Comanches or even Kiowas, and Quarles noticed their lordly manner, especially among Cheyennes, hinting at traditional power, a people proud and secure behind a formidable reputation. It was known other tribes, like the powerful Sioux, had tested Cheyenne arms on the high plains and had chosen to seek an alliance. At any rate here the Cheyennes did most of the talking, and in their deep, sonorous tongue made it clear they weren't supinely accepting the white man's terms. If the *veho,* the spider, their name for the whites, wanted peace, they would have to stay on the holy road, the Oregon Trail, and not stop to settle the land or kill the buffalo. A small group in red blankets, sitting with dour expressions in the rear, puzzled Quarles until Lee nodded at them and whispered, "Those mean-looking hombres squatting yonder are Sioux. Likely they here to see what their friends are agreeing to. As a rule they don't agree to anything except being left alone. Damn ornery bastards when riled up."

"I don't remember their being invited," Henry whispered back.

"Sioux don't need no invite, they reckon you the visitor. I'll sleep better when we get shut of this place."

Quarles smiled and shook his head. Lee's years as a mountain man had soured him on all Indians. Strange, since Henry had heard some mountain men married into tribes and willingly adapted to their way of life. "Squaw men," Lee had once called them. "Critters likely to eat their own kin. Can't never tell about folks. Had a neighbor once back in Tennessee who lived with his hogs . . . must have started to smell a little like slop, for damn if one night they didn't up and eat him."

Again Quarles heard big annuities being promised, again he saw chiefs coming up to touch the pen. It all seems so simple; why was there ever trouble with these tribes? Surely forty or fifty thousand dollars in trade goods was a cheap way for the nation to pacify its frontiers, save lives, and open trails to the West. It wasn't until they started back that he heard something which started him wondering. It was Marren explaining to him that these were treaties, not requests for annuities, that they were taking back to Washington. Treaties were covenants between nations, in this case the United

States government and several Indian nations. Like all treaties they had to be ratified by Congress. Quarles, noticing a vague web of lines appearing about Marren's eyes, couldn't resist a question. "Going to be any trouble?"

Marren stroked his beard and glanced at the eastern horizon. "Hopefully not, but with a war going badly on their minds one never knows."

Sam was pacing up and down the river bank, Skeeter was hunched down beside Ben, and Hattie had settled herself on a large boulder along the water's edge. There was tension in the air, for everyone except Sam thought Cheatem's proposal was typical of him; the work, the risks were going to be theirs, the rewards his. Hattie didn't like it, Ben just shook his head. Skeeter was undecided but Sam was all for seizing this opportunity to learn something about tracking down a silver mine.

"You sho dere is a silver mine?" said Hattie. "Huntin' ain't finding!"

"Dat Cheatem ain't spending no dollars on silver mines wat ain't dere!" insisted Sam. "Ah'm going!"

"Likely you catching yo'self a mess of trouble jus to make that rascal rich!" answered Hattie.

"Das wat he thinks," grunted Sam.

Skeeter turned to him slowly, staring for a moment, looking concerned. "Wat you conjurin' up, little brother?" Skeeter always used "little" when not sure he could control Sam.

"Got me some notions."

"Don't you start no fool thing dats gonna fetch us trouble!" cautioned Hattie.

Ben was trying to rub stiffness out of his right arm. "Yeah, things gittin' kind of good now," he muttered. "Ain't no point to spoil it."

"You call dis good!" Sam was slapping his thighs. "We sweatin' here jus to git dis fat pharaoh a mighty fine ranch. Soon it gotta be makin' mess of money. And wat we gittin', we workin' for beans and beddin', like we wuz doin' down south. Ah say we gots to git out of here . . . start buildin' sumthin' for us'selves."

"How we gonna do dat?" mumbled Ben.

"We gonna start duh way dat Cheatem start . . . we gonna study 'ways ahead."

The sight of empty supply wagons returning from the fort caught Troy's eye while starting up the trail to visit Cheatem a final time. The drivers, pulling up their teams and stopping for coffee, relayed the news that peace treaties had been signed and travel should be safer from now on.

Troy immediately saw this as a bargaining chip with Silas, yet he knew, no matter what advantages he started with, when it came to negotiating Silas always seemed to have the high cards.

"There's less to worry about now," Troy argued. "One third doesn't hardly seem fair anymore."

"Shit! You still got plenty to worry about," countered Cheatem. "Say you find silver, what then?"

"I'll be rich."

"Not till you get that stuff out of the ground."

"For Christ's sake! I know that!"

"Then maybe you know it won't come out by itself. It's gonna take money, equipment, maybe even a sizeable crew to dig up and haul that stuff where it can be turned into cash. You reckon you can handle all that?"

"Silas, I'll stake a claim, borrow some money. Plenty of people have done it before."

"Yeah, and plenty of people have found some galoot, who had more money and savvy, digging only a hoop and a holler away and ending up stealing their mine. Let me tell you something Troy, prospecting and making a tricky business shine calls for different breeds of cat. If you think you can handle the whole shebang by yourself I ain't aiming to stop you. This a free country. A fella can kick horse sense in the belly and piss on good advice all he wants."

Troy began to look irritated but also on the verge of decision. "Silas, best tell you straight out you ain't a man easy to trust. You do mighty handsome by yourself, but most folks wonder if it's all luck. But, by Jesus, if you're so damn handy with answers, maybe you could come up with one more for me."

"Certainly! Shoot!"

"Why can't I carry enough away from that mine to get me started? Seems to me plenty of folks have done that before."

"Christ! You're thinking of gold, man! A fella can carry off enough gold to make it count, but this is silver. You'll need maybe half a ton of ore to smelt down before you can even figure what you've got. Hell's fires, if you don't know that much about it you best go buy a Bible."

Troy, settling back in his chair, looked long and hard at Silas, but Cheatem knew he had won, even if a tense and excruciatingly long minute had to pass before Troy reluctantly extended a hand and gave him a reluctant shake.

That morning Cole had staked out a section in the north corner of their claim and was harnessing a team to Cheatem's plowshare to plow it. Dennis was outside the cabin, marking off a space to dig a well. Both were conscious Troy was preparing to leave and, if neither commented, both had reasons for wanting him gone. Dennis because of Chloe and Cole to remove the guilt Troy kept making him feel for not joining him. Cathy Jo couldn't resist joking about Troy's suddenly running up to visit Cheatem. "He's latching onto Silas cause he wouldn't know what to do with a silver mine if he found one. Believe me, Silas is just the gent to put him in a fix, one he ain't gonna dream his way out of."

Once when Troy had disappeared up the trail, Cole, busy stamping into his boots but appearing unconcerned, asked, "What do you figure they're talking about?"

Cathy sighed. "Well, I'm no prophet but if I said they was buying a cow for Troy to feed and Silas to milk, likely I'd be close."

But it came as a shocking surprise when they heard Sam was going. Cole whistled to himself and stood looking toward Cheatem's cabin as though it housed some crafty wizard whose magic blazed forth in weird and unexpected ways. "That Cheatem!" he mumbled to himself, for no one needed to tell the Sadlers that Sam was some sort of legal extension of Cheatem, or that their neighbor's grandiose plans for his claim would surely flower if any silver were found.

Troy, set to leave at dawn the following morning, had Cole and Cathy up to see him off. Sam stood outside in the semidarkness, watching these white folks taking leave of each other. Hattie, Skeeter, and Ben had hugged him an hour before sunrise, Hattie giving her inevitable advice. "Don't you git yo'self hurt chasin' round dem mountains. Remember, de Lord look after duh righteous!" Sam wished she hadn't added the last, but Skeeter knocked thoughts of it out of his head by warning him that southern guerrillas were still running loose in parts of Kansas, and army teamsters told of travelers killed by them in northern Texas. "Watch yo' butt, brother, hate to see 'em git you so you can cheat duh devil." But the light banter was to conceal a deep, gnawing fear. Skeeter was hugging him extra hard, a hug that said, *I'm going to be lonely without you, take care of yourself . . . don't leave me alone in this world.*

Somehow Sam noticed these white folks didn't embrace the same way, and seemed to have trouble thinking of fitting things to say. He wasn't surprised. He always felt whites didn't live with the pain and anguished feelings blacks did, or that he himself was experiencing at that very moment, standing off in the dark. Blacks finding themselves alone were lonely, they needed each other to believe in a future, they needed each other for that very need made them feel wanted. Slaves had few possessions, companionship was their real wealth.

Suddenly in the half light Sam saw Chloe peeking at him from the wagon, and immediately it saddened him. He knew Chloe had fretted about Troy to Hattie, he suspected Chloe thought Troy's leaving would ease her hurt at his rejection. Poor Chloe, seeing her searching the darkness burdened him with a premonition he wouldn't shake for hours. His beautiful cousin, she with the bewitching body, was searching for a happiness she could only glimpse in that white world, for she would find only those born to that world were allowed its bounty. Coming from the black world she would find that human birthright, a sense of belonging, was denied to any caught in between.

Summer was in full bloom when Quarles led his troop back along the valley of the Platte. Talk of peace was spreading across the frontier, only to be overshadowed by reports of bloody battles and shattering Union losses in the east. The northern armies, with men and materials on their side, lacked both the leadership and the rugged farmers and mountain men that flocked to the Confederate standard. Robert E. Lee, the best military mind of his time, by opting for the South and declining command of Union forces, plunged his country into the most devastating war in its history. Many thought his genius, coupled with the resources of the North, would have ended the struggle in months.

But other forces were at work.

At Leavenworth Quarles soon realized two conditions had arisen to speed the ever-growing migration west. One was the knowledge that peace with the tribes had finally been achieved, and, two, the resolve of many families, in this final favorable season, to get as far away from the ravages of war as possible.

Quarles, fully expecting to be sent to Ohio to join in the fight against rebel forces in the Mississippi valley, as usual was wrong. Typically the general had other plans for him. He and Lee bade Marren and Kaster goodbye and good luck, and Henry endured Lee's cynical looks as the peacemakers left for Washington. Back in his room they pulled off their boots and outer clothes to lessen the heat. "In a few months, I imagine those annuities will be arriving," Henry remarked, pouring two glasses of beer from a bottle his orderly provided. "Unless I miss my guess, the general is figuring on us to see they get to where they belong."

"Right pert of him."

Henry sighed and settled in a chair. "When do you suppose we're gonna get to do some fighting?"

Lee yawned and raised his glass. "Henry, never go looking for a fight, 'cause there's always some galoot out there looking too, and the damn critter might just be a mite bigger than you."

There were still many heavily wooded areas along the Arkansas, and the frequent breaks were filled with wild game and nourishing berries. One who knew the land well could survive there without great effort for years. Black Otter was not truly a renegade, many of his tribe agreed with him. No lasting peace with *tejanos* or the *tahbay-boh* was possible until the whites vacated their land and promised not to encroach on it again. Foolishly Whistling Elk and others assumed this was part of the present treaty. Didn't they realize this was part of every treaty ever signed, yet every season more and more of the squat, smoky cabins of the whites dotted the land? Couldn't Whistling Elk, and those so greedy for the white man's goods, see the buffalo disappearing, the deer and antelope becoming restless and too wild for the bow?

Black Otter still had ten followers; he would have to be careful, the tribe would not forgive losing the tribute they now expected from the whites. But whatever the peace-talking whites expected from their glib talk and degrading bribes, he had something else in store for them.

29

By evening of the third day the horizon, clearing after a brief summer storm, revealed the mountains, the setting sun etching out jagged peaks lying low on the rim of the earth. Although it was June snow still clung to the distant summits, and a breeze that had played along the skin all day suddenly stiffened and gusted in chilly waves that washed against the face.

Sam couldn't help feeling there was something menacing about those mountains. At first glance its peaks appeared like watchtowers on massive ramparts, behind which mystery dwelt and danger lurked in cloistered valleys hidden from view. As they made camp he kept glancing toward them until dusk and a spray of stars left them indistinct in the night.

While he could, Troy quietly studied the distant range, aware his map gave only vague instructions on where to enter its sheer slopes. The trouble was old Salter kept using landmarks only one familiar with that high and torturous terrain would readily recognize. As many times as he had pored over the dead mountain man's map he suddenly wanted to scrutinize it again. But he found it too difficult to make out the crude markings and Salter's scrawled notes by firelight. It would have to wait until morning. Reluctantly he joined Sam who had made coffee and put out some biscuits with beef gravy which Hattie had sent along.

For two men alone in an awesome wilderness, there was precious little talk. Keeping to their own thoughts and cautiously watching the terrain, Troy had kept riding doggedly ahead with Sam following silently behind. Peace treaties or no peace treaties a lonely land, vacant from horizon to horizon, worries the mind. Occasionally Troy would stop and point to a herd of pronghorns or a string of buffalo feeding in the distance. It was comforting to know game was tranquilly grazing nearby, but even then no words arose. Sam didn't care, he was busy remembering the ground they were crossing, and once they left the river this grew more and more difficult.

Though revealing it to no one, Sam was secretly bent on remembering the way to this mine, it fitted into a vague plan he was concocting. For the moment he wasn't concerned about tracking, one had only to keep riding west into the setting sun to reach these mountains. It was once inside that towering range that he visualized mazes of valleys, steep curving slopes, and endlessly twisting trails, making it near impossible for a man to recall the way taken. It wasn't until he was in his blanket that night that he thought of how he and Skeeter kept track of goods, secretly gathered and cached deep in the southern woods, articles needed to make escape possible, that he decided the little trick he and Skeeter used to find their carefully buried goods in the meager light of dawn would surely work here.

Chloe was glad she didn't have to watch Troy moving about anymore, except she realized one day he'd be back. She kept telling herself he would find that silver mine and be rich, and rich men didn't stay in raw country with no way to spend money. He would go back east and be out of her life. But an incident took place that had Chloe wondering if it was really Troy that bothered her or was it something else, something less definable than a rude, arrogant man, something not visible yet ubiquitous, something with no discernible logic to weigh or physical form to fight. It happened when a heavy wagonload of settlers came up the river trail. Chloe had been picking flowers a few yards from Skeeter's fence line, and they had hailed her first. She smiled shyly and answered some of their questions about game in that area. They seemed to be pleased peace treaties had been signed and they could now make their claim without worrying about Indians. There were two men, brothers, two women, and a young girl almost Chloe's age. They seemed hardworking and sun-darkened like Dennis and Cole. Their name was Hunt. The oldest girl, sensing in Chloe a female near enough her age to share secrets with, sneaked a bashful but expectant glance at her. Almost unnoticed they grinned at each other.

One of the women, the one she heard the men calling Flora, commented on how pretty Chloe was, insisting she take some rock candy. Clearly they wanted to make friends.

Skeeter had gone back to fill his water jug, but seeing the strangers stopping to talk with Chloe, came back to join her. Hattie, who rarely took her eyes off her daughter, came along. How it happened Chloe was never sure, but some slight reference to Hattie being her mother brought a subtle change in the Hunts. It wasn't something she could point to, but it started a weird sensation in her breast that grew as she walked back down the trail, finally imploding into a shocking realization that the Hunts had thought she was white, and suddenly felt awkward and somehow deceived at the sight of Hattie's ebony black face.

Was this the fear Hattie continually fretted about? Was what Chloe had thought was only a wicked streak in Troy really a malady, pandemic in a world she was about to join? It left her pensive, troubled, depressed, and strangely listless by nightfall when Dennis tried to embrace her. Puzzled, he first asked and then suddenly demanded to know what had thrown her into such a mood. Reluctantly she related the scene with the Hunts, adding only that she didn't understand their shifts in tone and expression. Almost afraid to hold to his eyes, she clutched his hand and held it to her breast. Could he or would he tell her the why of it?

Dennis shrugged. "Likely they southern slop farmers," he said consolingly. "Got no breedin', no learnin', what can yuh expect?"

"They fixin' to be neighbors," said Chloe quietly. "They squattin' down where them other folks got burned out."

"Well, you don't need to pay 'em no heed. Trash mostly cottons up to trash, not folks like us." He pulled her to him, lifting her chin and guiding her lips to his. "Besides you ain't hardly kissed me yet."

But the coming days weighed heavily on Chloe for she discovered the Hunts were not southern slop farmers, they were from Maine. From Cathy she learned one of the women was a schoolteacher, the other had led Bible classes. The young girl was accomplished at reading and writing and one of the men read passages from the classics or the Bible every night. Like Cheatem they had come well equipped to maintain themselves, but while the men came to talk to Cole, though only rarely to Dennis, Chloe saw little of the women, or that young girl whom Cathy said was called Alice.

Dennis deliberately avoided mentioning the Hunts and nothing more was said about Chloe's troubled meeting with them. But Chloe never quite recovered. The strange hurt that started that afternoon hung on. It lingered somewhere in the far reaches of her mind, back where she sensed loneliness dwelt and something akin to bleak exile loomed. If neither she nor Dennis mentioned it both were aware that whatever lay behind the Hunt's disconcerting behavior, sheer ignorance or the prejudices of southern dirt farmers didn't explain it.

Chloe's lingering dejection didn't go unnoticed by Cathy, who saw at once the Hunts were uneasy around Negroes. Why she could only guess. But they were conspicuously religious people, and in time Cathy surmised it had something to do with miscegenation clashing with their idea of the soul's smooth ascent to heaven. Flora finally remarked one day, "My, it beats all how a black woman could have that perfectly adorable child . . . it's what comes from straying too far from gospel teaching."

Cathy's eyes held hers firmly. "It comes from being raped by a white ruffian who was doing all the straying. Hattie, by my sights, is rightly religious . . . could be gospel teaching means different things to different folks."

"Mercy, I hope not! My dear sis-in-law, Charity, says His light shines the same for all of us. But, as I say, it sure beats all . . . pity. She seems such a nice girl."

"She *is* a nice girl."

"That's what I say, it's a pity."

They were a whole day getting to the swift-rising foothills that fronted the mountains. As the peaks drew nearer they looked steeper and more foreboding. That evening, after a difficult climb, they reached the first valley floor and Troy, consulting his map, nodded affirmably to a right fork of the valley, which split to surround a low but sharp almost coral-colored peak. Sam found himself breathing heavily and wondering if they couldn't start camp and fry a few strips of bacon to eat with the remaining biscuits. It was getting dark and the air, more rarefied at this height, had them breathing like sluggish bellows. Troy consented, helping with the fire but then settling down with his map and notes to study them one more time. Sam began to get the feeling his companion's only preparation for this venture was prayer. Although they had blankets, the icy stab of wind coming down from sheets of frost, visibly shining around the peaks, convinced him they should have brought far heavier clothing and even sleeping bags. They had some food but it was mostly jerked beef and dry meal Hattie had scrounged from somewhere. It wouldn't last long, but Troy paid little attention to food; his mind was elsewhere. Sam's warning that grub might soon be a problem evinced only a casual response. "Best shoot a deer then . . . first chance."

Sam quietly chewed his bacon and biscuit, rolled his single blanket around him and, noticing the horses were quietly munching clumps of wild grass nearby, tried to sleep. After only a moment or two the shrill screech of a puma nearby startled him. Not wanting Troy, who hadn't looked up from his map, to see him jumping up scared, he determinedly closed his eyes, turned, and cradling his face in the crook of his arm, tried to sleep. He was dead tired; this trip with its eerie suspense and long stretches of silence was exhausting. And he was slowly growing angry, angry that he was being made to follow this mute figure like a shadow, obediently trailing this man who said nothing, whose real companion, if any existed, was those time-worn papers and map. Only those words and scratchings, left by a man rotting in his grave, existed for Troy, while Sam, only fifteen feet away, was forgotten for hours, only reluctantly remembered when the search halted for food or rest.

As they pushed on in the morning the terrain grew ever harsher but the landscape was now becoming breathtaking. As they climbed higher they found fast-

flowing streams that sparkled in the sun, and park lands
nestled below magnificent peaks, where game could be
seen at great distances, moving dreamlike through shadows cast by surrounding rock steeples. Sam couldn't
help feeling this country brought a man closer to the
walls of heaven, closer to whatever judgement awaited
for a life of sin. Moments arose when he forgot about
Troy, who kept forging ahead satisfied the map was
proving true, and his mind turned to Hattie, knowing if
she were there she would be constantly praying, likely
making him pray too. Sam wondered why he didn't get
the same comfort from prayer everyone else did, but the
things he had prayed for in life never came. He knew he
shouldn't be thinking this way. He had been warned high
invisible people didn't like that kind of notion, but he
was slowly reaching a conviction that many of the things
he prayed for and never got were things he suspected
silver could buy.

Except for the wind the mountains seemed quiet,
serene, sun-bathed, and peaceful. It was hard not to
think of them as nature's upraised sanctuary, a lofty
garden of Eden. It was surely not a place where violent
passions belonged. The grandeur of one lordly vista after
the other kept a man aware of powers beyond his own, of
massive creative forces carving out unspeakable beauty
the heart could only struggle to encompass. The warlike
Comanches and Kiowas seemed far away, and indeed
they were, but the legacy of their bitter, bloodstained
history was not. Whites were not the only enemies those
feral horsemen of the southern plains had brought upon
themselves. Within their own race, tribes lived in fear
and hatred of them, a few formidable enough to redress
old scores and contest their suzerainty of these eastern
mountains. As Troy and Sam made their way through
the great valleys and along the granite slopes, a sense of
isolation seized them, a feeling they were alone making
their way between earth and sky, crossing terrain unseen
and probably unknown by human eyes. For long spells
they felt only they and these majestic mountains existed.

But they were wrong.

The terrain they were laboring over was well known,

and was even now being approached by a powerful and, in view of its mission, deadly force. Running Bear of the Utes had brought his many warriors to avenge the death of two sons, killed by Comanches the year before. The painted braves were sworn to adorn his belt with twenty Comanche scalps to comfort this old war chief, bereft of sons in the twilight of his life. They had stopped for their last war dance, after today they would be too close to Comancheria for anything but stealth and the swift savage strike of vengeance Running Bear had planned. Yet his scouts were shortly to mount a rocky knoll, their eyes glinting like plunging eagles and falling upon an unexpected but enticing sight. The spirits had delivered them two strange-looking figures, intruders already surprisingly high in their mountains and helplessly alone.

The scouts nodded to each other.

Ah, gifts from the mountain spirits! Running Bear's medicine was strong!

30

The Hunts were only the first of a fast-rising wave of settlers seeking land and new lives on the windswept plains of western Kansas. Almost every day wagons came by, most stopping to chat, asking the age-old questions settlers asked. How was the soil? The water supply? The availability of game to tide them over until crops ripened? Some came with livestock herded by children lagging behind the wagons, or with crates of chickens or pigs roped to tailgates. For the first time people appeared across the river, and Cole and Cheatem went over to welcome them and get a verbal agreement on boundary lines down the center of the stream. There

were lots of questions about the legality of many of the
larger claims, but the government's policy was to allow
heads of families or other responsible citizens to stake
out a hundred and sixty acres, which if lived on and
somehow improved over a five-year period settlers could
claim as their own. Often in surrounding areas un-
claimed land could be bought for as little as a dollar and
a quarter an acre.

Yet Silas Cheatem still found plenty of space to build
his horse traps. He and Skeeter had already corralled
over twenty head. But capturing wild mustangs was only
the first and in some ways the simplest step. So far he
had only gotten one stallion, a wicked-tempered brute
that resisted breaking and had thrown Skeeter every
time he mounted. Along with that stallion he had
captured two mares with reasonably good lines and three
yearlings that showed promise, but the rest of the herd
were culls that would have to be released or destroyed.
Skeeter found the work backbreaking and Cheatem was
often in a foul mood when the traps failed to hold prime-
looking stock driven toward them. They discovered
much depended on the dominant stallion. These pack
leaders, incredibly cagey and crafty, would often rear up
and change directions at the last moment, avoiding the
carefully concealed traps, while a powerful few, even
after being driven hard for a fair piece, still managed to
find and break through weak spots in the hastily built
brush corrals, escaping with an entire band galloping
after them.

But pained as Skeeter was with the work, his mind was
rarely off Sam. As the days went by he had visions of his
brother high in the mountains, probably sharing with
Troy the excitement of tracking down a silver mine, or
perhaps consoling him after realizing they had been
pursuing a dream that vanished on some barren mountain slope, the pall of defeat slowly numbing the heart
and clogging the tongue. Often in the evening he approached Ben, wanting confirmation of his thoughts.
"Know wat? Betcha dat Sam squattin' on a patch of
silver somewheres, jus laughin' his fool head off."

"Likely he dreaming 'bout Hattie's cookin'."

"Oh, das mighty interestin' work, huntin' silver."

Ben stretched out and hugged himself. "Betcha sumthin' else, gardenin' done got it beat to blazes!"

"How you figurin'?"

"Put a mess o' seed in duh ground and you g'wine git food and flowers, stuff dat keeps folks smilin'. Put a mess o' silver in duh ground and you g'wine git trouble, cause you cain't eat silver, you gots to hide it, and folks who cain't find no more in the ground come lookin' for it in yo pockets."

"Dats jus duh way you see it 'cause you an old man."

"Dats duh way it is! Don't be waitin' till you gits old like me 'afore you sees it too!"

Chloe watched many settlers coming up the trail but the sight no longer brought the excitement felt in the past. For her all faces either carried or took on a quality that reminded her of the Hunts, even those simply stopping to rest horses or gaze about, driving on without comment.

Dennis tried to convince her it was all in her head. But Chloe knew better. She had been watching carefully for a peek at young Alice Hunt, and when Alice came with Flora to visit Cathy she waited patiently for the girl to come out of the cabin. When she did Chloe called to her. Alice started toward her but stopped almost thirty feet away, seeming embarrassed and looking furtively back at the cabin. Within moments Flora appeared at the door and, casting a wary glance at her daughter, just perceptively shook her head. Alice raised a limp arm and waved at Chloe, but then circled awkwardly back toward the cabin. When she appeared again she deliberately looked the other way and went to stand alone by the water.

Chloe couldn't explain it, but she felt her senses were failing. The world was now cast in different hues, the blue sky seemed vapidly pale or even grayish, the morning sun rose with a lurid yellow glare that was far from comforting. She couldn't conceal a heaviness in her breast that rose to swell and press tears from her eyes. Hattie, her pillar of faith, could only sigh and hug her.

Hearing about Alice she murmured, "Dats de way dis world is, child . . . you gots to go on livin' and put yo' faith in de Lord."

But Chloe wondered why the Lord allowed such misery to exist to begin with. There were other things troubling her, things she couldn't reveal even to Hattie. Dennis had tried to pretend her fears were groundless, but his lovemaking now said he knew that wasn't so. His ardor had lessened and he was stopping more and more often to ask questions about her responses to his now familiar and intimate handling of her body. Things that had once excited her were simply making her hug him more tightly, each time with more desperation and less fire. But she couldn't help herself. Somehow she knew a rejection of her must one day mean a rejection of Dennis; a man couldn't live in a world apart from his wife. But would that change Dennis? Would it affect their marriage? What marriage? They weren't married yet! As Dennis slid between her legs and entered her, giving her that sense of belonging only a joining of bodies can bring, she pressed her mouth to his, knowing if she lost him life would never be worth the agony she felt engulfing her. But she knew people were already treating Dennis differently than Cole or Cheatem, doubtlessly egged on by their wives to see him as a man using an ex–slave girl as a concubine, ignoring biblical strictures on lust and sin. Lying in her wagon or sitting silently as neighbors passed, she overheard things. Because of her, both she and Dennis had become objects of gossip, of prurient curiosity, of male interest in novel sex. Certainly, in spite of his protests, Dennis was experiencing a subtle ostracizing of his own. Should she allow this man she loved to lose his birthright to belong, to walk forth respected as an equal? The wind was whispering through the wagon canvas as she felt him rise and climax. She held him tenderly, not wanting him to pull away. He didn't and after a spell of lazy kissing they started to make love again. This time she rose and climaxed with him. But when they turned to sleep the painful quandary came flaring back to capture her mind once more. She lay in the darkness wondering if the good

Lord, having allowed this to happen, would help her now with some answers. For Chloe was lost, hopelessly, fearfully lost, and as uncertain of her way as the restless wind, suddenly racing against the canvas from all sides and howling off into the night like a spirit exiled from its tomb.

Strangely enough Lame Fox had become so elusive people forgot he was part of the settlement. Even Cole, who knew he was gone for days at a time, could never account for his whereabouts on any given day. What no one realized was new faces coming into the settlement had the Shawnee worried. From cover he searched them thoroughly, a few he thought he recognized; one occasion, with his heart leaping, he feared one recognized him. But he knew with people moving in from eastern Kansas it was just a matter of time. One night he gathered his few belongings and, leaving his knife at Cole's door, pointing west, quietly slipped away.

As the summer advanced families kept arriving, setting out claims and hurrying to build shelters or get seeds into the ground. Within months they were dotting the countryside, small cabins each with its feather of smoke ascending the evening air. Once three families, all related, came together and settled between the Hunts and the Sadlers, taking up an enormous plot of ground. It was no longer unusual to see wagons on the trail, or riders going to and fro. For the first time Chloe heard the word "community" being used by newcomers who kept talking about what was needed to make this settlement fit for civilized living. Cheatem encouraged them, adding occasionally the inevitability of a town being raised here, a town that should be named after one of its earliest settlers. The stream of new arrivals continued until a fiddler and a banjo player showed up, and finally, raising in Chloe a feverish seizure of hope and fear, a preacher.

When it started she didn't know but suddenly there was talk of a gathering, a spontaneous celebration to mark the first days of September. It would resemble a

community picnic with dancing and games. The three
families that had come together were great organizers.
They invited people to their homes to discuss building a
schoolhouse, a church, and a general store, which all felt
would be needed the following year. Cheatem had
attended many of the meetings, Cole a few, but Cathy
had become quite active. Chloe didn't know when it
started but she would always remember the moment she
heard about it, for she had just come back from visiting
Hattie, just finished telling Hattie her menses was worri-
somely late and that morning a strange tingle had started
in her breasts. She had just mounted her wagon to watch
Dennis approaching with news of the gathering. She
would remember it because it was at that moment she
realized she was pregnant, that moment she realized the
first test of their love was upon them, that moment she
looked into Dennis's eyes and wanted to hope, but with
a heart not knowing what to hope for.

The long climbs were exhausting, and staggering
downhill was now proving as wearying as the struggle
up. Yet Troy kept doggedly onward, a grim look of
achievement relieving the tension on his straining face
each time another guiding feature on the map was
identified and seemed to point the way. Sam trailed
behind him carrying a haunch of deer along with his gun
and blanket. He was not so much sulking as he was
moodily resigned to this ordeal, draining as it was and as
confusing as he found the twists and turns Troy made
among the rocky crevices and cold, windblown slopes.
Bleakly Sam plodded on. It was their third day in the
mountains and the imposing heights of granite peaks no
longer held their eyes. Now the towering walls of rock
were simply near impassable barriers to two small
creatures working their way into a vastness that grew as
they struggled to join it. Without warning they were
buffeted by winds and soaked by rain. Steep rock fac-
ings, caused by rock slides, continually replaced narrow
trails that wound around mountains. There was much
backtracking to find safer passage. Often the horses had

to be led for hours. If Sam could have he would have packed grass under a rocky ledge and slept for a month, for fatigue was dragging him down like a broken limb. It was only with the faintest glint of interest that he saw Troy stopping and looking long and hard at a great jagged cut in a mountainside dead ahead. It looked like some mighty hammer had cracked the mountain open and left it with a deep wound that narrowed to a flat basin at its base. Troy sat looking at it for all of several minutes before he turned to say, "Goddamn it! We've found it! Damn if we haven't!"

Sam came up alongside him. "Wat we found?"

"The mine, goddamn it!"

Sam stared across the deep vaulted chasm separating them from the split mountain. "Where you see dat mine?"

"You can't see it! But by Jesus I do believe we've found it!"

Sam gave another quick look and seeing nothing but what appeared a badly cracked mountain, muttered, "Let's bed down and eat."

"No siree, we can make it across that rift before dark. Ain't no time to be dallying around."

They made it an hour before dark and Troy, jumping down and seizing his small shovel, started to walk around the basin, kicking the ground with his boot and grunting. After a time he settled on a spot that looked to Sam like white sand. Here he dug for five minutes before giving the shovel to Sam and stepping back to catch his breath. Sam dug for a while but suddenly he noticed the sand he was shoveling up was turning blue. That brought a shrill cry from Troy, who grabbed the shovel back and dug furiously for several moments before the sharp snapping twang of a bow string caused skin at the back of Sam's head to tighten, and his eyes to rise to meet a terrifying row of painted faces staring down at them from a rock ledge above. When he glanced down again poor elated and perspiring Troy was on the ground, lying on top of his shovel with a feathered arrow sunk deep in his back.

➤ 31 ➤

The preacher who had reached the settlement was called
Dillby and had a penchant for ready sermonizing. Stopping for water or the health of an ailing settler, he would
spend hours explaining the hazards one's spirit faced
passing through a world where Satan held a beachhead
and temptation was rife. He missed few community
meetings, especially where food was served or punches,
often of a sharp and exhilarating flavor, might be sam-
pled. He seemed particularly welcome at the Hunts and
was soon announced as the man most favored to lead the
group planning a church. He tended to ignore signs that
his denomination, Congregational, didn't sit well with
the Methodists or a few hard-shelled Baptists who also
wanted a house of worship and were concerned about
their piety being properly represented in heaven. He was
wise enough to assuage their feelings by several resound-
ing pronouncements, the most frequent of which was
"We are inspired to build a house in His name, let us
gather there and worship as our hearts dictate."

He was a favorite of Flora and her sister-in-law,
Charity; the three were often seen walking together along
the stream. Apparently the Hunts held prayers every
day, with Preacher Dillby frequently invited to lead
them. Chloe watched all this from a distance, often
wondering what these people talked about. Did they talk
about her? Did they know Dennis was going to approach
Dillby at the gathering to request he marry them? Did
they know she was beside herself with worry, with fears
about what that day might bring? She didn't know what
their prayers were but they surely couldn't have been

more fervent than hers, for she pleaded with God to see her through these agonizing days of doubt, beseeching him to enable her to keep the decision she endured a night of torment to make. If the preacher agreed to marry them, she would tell Dennis about their baby, if he did not she would run away or escape this cross of rejection and despair in the river. A young girl on the verge of womanhood, cringing under the sting of reproachful eyes and now frightened by the bounty her young body promised to bring forth.

Desperate, Chloe sat alone in her wagon, clasping her knees to her chest, peeking out a slit in the canvas, sensing this freedom, so dearly bought, was the freedom of an alien in a land where only natives were allowed the sunlight or hope for salvation.

Preparations for the big gathering went forth at a steady pace. People were anxious to turn their minds from the gloom of a fratricidal war which passing troopers reported was still going badly for the Union. Many families had relatives serving one side or the other, and neither distance nor the demands of settling this raw country dampened partisanship. But if many people still held strong convictions, others began to wonder if the issues causing the war justified the carnage it was causing. Other factors served to avoid trouble. Like all beginning settlements there was great need for unity; opinions too forcefully expressed could cost the cooperation of one's neighbors. Soon the subject became one many deliberately if self-consciously avoided.

But while the one black family in the settlement sensed immediately which new arrivals were from the south, those from the north, if less given to censorious glances, hardly seemed any more accepting of equality. It kept cropping up, even as preparations for the gathering got under way. It was clear many in the settlement expected Cheatem's "servants" to set up tables and gather wood for a fire they were expected to build and maintain. All the manual and menial tasks seemed to fall their way, or at least brought them to mind.

Cheatem, with his new and now pressing need for popularity, was reluctant to refuse these requests, but Hattie, when told she would be cooking for as many as forty or fifty people, exploded. "Ah'se cookin' for me and my folks . . . dats all!" She swung around, confronting Cheatem with her hands on her hips. "Wats wrong with dem other wimens? Dey too busy gossiping or tellin' other folks wat to do to cook?"

"It will only be this one time."

"Dats one time too many . . ."

"Hattie, look, they probably just got to figuring they need a damn good cook."

"Den dey best hire one!"

Cheatem screwed up his mouth and stared at the floor. If this reluctance was to spread to Skeeter and Ben his standing in the community was bound to suffer. "Listen, Hattie, what say I hire you?"

Hattie puckered her lips up. "Suppose ole Hattie asks a question?"

"Sure, why not?"

"Wat dem other wimens fixin' to do while ole Hattie cookin'?"

Cheatem looked away to hide his embarrassment. "Well, best I can figure they plan a little dancing . . . maybe some games . . . don't rightly know, reckon they expect to join right in."

"Dey g'wan to be dancin' and jiggin' round while ole Hattie fussin' wid da frying pan."

"Hattie, I'm gonna pay you well."

"How much dis well?"

"Ten dollars."

"Lordy, you cain't git no fittin' cook fo' no ten dollars!"

"Sure I can."

"Den best go fetch 'em."

Cheatem turned around and kicked a nearby chair. "Hattie, goddamn it, what's got into you? You know we got to get along here . . . make folks think we're doing our share."

"You gots to git along here, dey ain't nobody gittin up mornin's to fix grits for us black folks."

Cheatem sighed and resignedly slapped his sides. "Well, let's have it then, what do yuh want?"

"Twenty dollars."

Cheatem rubbed the back of his neck, his temper contained by the risk of losing Hattie altogether. "Well, all right, but I sure as hell don't want word of this getting to Mrs. Hunt."

"Mrs. Hunt? Wat she gots to do wid it?"

"She's in charge of cooking."

"Das different . . . twenty-five dollars!"

"Hattie, you crazy?!"

Hattie's eyes couldn't conceal a seething fury. "Sorry, but ah don't like dat woman."

"What's wrong with her?"

"If you wuz black you'd know. She walks by us like she smell somethin' bad passin' over her head."

"You imagine things."

"Mebbe, mebbe not . . . twenty-five dollars."

Fear had Sam paralyzed. He stood, his gaze frozen on Troy lying on the ground, the big protruding eyeballs searching for escape from pain that swept all other sensations from the body. Even as he looked he could see surfacing in the tormented features a realization that death was the only anesthesia possible against such pain, an agony that could only end with life itself. He hardly noticed the grotesquely painted figures slipping down to surround him, seizing his gun, pulling his clothes from his body, one kneeling down to scalp Troy as he gave a muffled cry. It could have been the last gasp of some tormented animal as the ill-starred dreamer coughed up blood and died. The horror of it dried Sam's mouth and had his heart beating like a heavy, resonant drum. He was afraid to look up, afraid of what he might read in these cruel faces, afraid of the knives he could see circling his body, cutting the cord that held a small sack of coins about his neck. They finally stripped Troy's body, took the shovel, and, seizing a rope from Troy's horse, tied Sam up, making him realize he was to follow them on foot as they headed east again through the mountains. Only the fall of darkness made them stop to eat his haunch of deer and pull the shoes from his feet. From now on he would have to follow this war party over the rocky terrain, with its sharp pebbles and coarse grasses, barefoot. Running Bear, a war chief who believed in stripping more than goods from prisoners, sat down and put a burning stick to Sam's ear. Sam drew himself up, terror making him struggle back from the burning brand. The chief looked about and shouted something in a weird, choppy tongue. One of the braves came forward. Sam realized this one spoke a few words of English. "Where come?" demanded the brave at some direction from the chief.

"Over dere," cried Sam eagerly, his eyes fixed on the glowing brand, his chin gesturing toward the east. The chief reached forward and felt Sam's skin. It was clear he had not seen Negroes before and the color puzzled him.

"You *koh-mahts?*" continued the warrior, his frightening face reaching into Sam's.

Something told Sam *koh-mahts* was too close to Comanche to risk anything but a denial; the Comanches were supposed to be at peace. If these were not Comanches who were they? Now instinct warned him whoever they were they didn't have a high opinion of Comanches. Sam began to shout, "No, no, no! Not Comanche!" He lurched his body back and forth in an unmistakable gesture of denial.

The warrior looked at the chief who seemed to be cogitating on this queer-looking prisoner who surely didn't look like a Comanche, who, in fact, didn't look like anything yet seen in the western mountains. But he had been found with a white man and Running Bear was no friend of the whites. The chief would sleep on his fate, though it had long been decided this war party's medicine would not hold if any prisoners were taken.

Sam spent that night realizing it might be his last, shivering with the cold and wondering if the quick glimpses he had of the surrounding peaks, as he was dragged in agony up and over the cracked mountain, would enable him to return there again should he live. But the whole matter dimmed in importance as he realized only heaven could help him now, and heaven didn't fuss much with sinners who hid secret thoughts about girls and didn't sing in church. That night seemed endless as Sam watched icy-cold stars above him inching their way eastward until the fateful light of dawn began to approach, and Running Bear came out of a troubled dream, grumbling and reaching for his knife.

Skeeter and Ben were to be paid ten dollars for a long list of chores Cheatem had accepted on their behalf. Neither man knew Hattie had demanded this before she assented to Cheatem's request for her own services. Silas Cheatem, as usual looking ahead, was now obsessed with political opportunities this settlement offered as it grew into a village or even a town. He had finally caught enough quality mustangs to start his breeding ranch and was now waiting to bring some blooded stock from the east. It was this damn war that held everything up that bothered him. Still he was secretly convinced he had arrived here at the right time, was making the right moves, building the right image. Hattie's stubborn refusal to do anything beyond earning her keep, unless paid, was an annoying problem, but knowing he needed her he easily convinced himself the money was really an investment, an investment in a commodity Silas Cheatem understood better than most, power.

The gathering was blessed with a gorgeous day. It was one of those soft spells in early autumn when the amber of the few fields ready for harvest dotted the land and the tang of wild grasses, coming on the west wind, spiced the air. A few hymns were sung and Dillby managed a short benediction, but jokes were increasingly being cracked and women coming up exclaimed loudly about each other's dresses as the merriment everyone came to share could not be contained. The few musicians struck up a tune and the dancing began. Hattie stood over the large fire, heating a skillet and watching Skeeter and Ben pulling rough-hewed benches and food containers about, leading draft and riding horses people arrived on to a picket line, and in general looking like bond servants hanging about to serve. She could only grunt grimly to herself. There was nothing in this gathering to suggest she or her family were really part of this community, which had gathered here to eat, drink, and revel in the knowledge that the first trying months of struggle and toil were over. She knew the money she had demanded from Cheatem was all that separated this setting from those quietly arranged and often scandalously wild "bourbon and crinoline" parties she had labored through, mutely serving arrogant, cotton-rich folks in a South she thought she had left behind.

But her mind couldn't stay long on Skeeter and Ben for her heart was near breaking over Chloe. She knew her daughter was torn about facing this day, desperately hoping her young life could be held together, her marriage become a reality, her approaching motherhood allowed its season of joy. But getting her to come to this gathering turned into an ordeal for Dennis and Cathy. Chloe pleaded she was not up to meeting an endless string of curious, judgmental eyes, and only tearfully agreed to go when Dennis refused to attend without her. She could not be the cause of Dennis becoming more isolated than he was. Whatever her fears Dennis had to stay part of this community; to succeed here he needed its cooperation, an equal share of its promise and above all its respect. The settlement would surely see in the absence of both some measure of shame if not guilt.

Cathy helped her create a pretty dress, one cut and stitched again to give more figure and a slight touch of maturity, reducing some of the girlishness her well-developed but willowy body still held. The final result was stunning. Cathy, who suddenly looked luscious herself in her own gay gingham dress, a startling change from Cole's altered pants and shirt, could only laugh. "Chloe, you'll be the prettiest girl at the gathering, bar none."

"Cathy, please, stop! I'm frightened enough already."

Dennis swung her around and kissed her. "Reckon I'll have trouble hangin' on to you. Best remember you're mine, my girl, yuh hear!"

Both Cathy and Chloe were unknowingly courting a surprise women on the frontier smiled about, for conditions rarely gave them a chance to dress invitingly for their men. Usually when men had a chance to view their chosen females in party dresses, the women experienced a wild and surprisingly sustained bout of lovemaking that night, one they rarely forgot.

32

The gathering was held on a flat piece of ground a quarter of a mile above the Sadler claim. A space had been cleared for dancing and rocks from the stream had been piled in a circle to form a cooking pit. A long table held bowls of cider and fruit punches, along with baked goods, cut to small servings, and a variety of candies made from private recipes but all molasses sweet to the taste. Cuts of venison and buffalo meat were laid out on a large block beside Hattie, and several loaves of home-baked bread lay beside a red-handled bread knife on a table just beyond. Skeeter had already started the fire that had to burn for an hour before the hot bed of ashes was right for cooking meat. Earlier that morning he and Ben had gone out on the prairie for a load of buffalo chips, which burned with a blue flame and produced surprising heat. Hattie stood over the fire watching Dennis and Chloe, followed by Cathy and Cole, walking up to the gathering. Her daughter had never looked more beautiful, and even the shy way she was clutching Dennis's arm could not keep her from seeming a jewel among the plain-faced farmers' daughters that turned to stare at her, a few faintly awed as she slipped by.

Mothers, aware this was the much whispered about Chloe Boggs, were glancing inquiringly at each other, surprised at her near-Caucasian features and light skin.

Within minutes there wasn't a man unaware of her presence, the older ones shaking their heads and looking distantly amused, the younger ones nudging each other and quickly looking away so mothers and sisters wouldn't catch them staring. Cathy and Cole caused far less stir, though not a few of the men took a deep breath as they caught Cathy's figure, walking with that strange seductive sway across the gathering grounds. They were used to seeing her in tucked-in shirts and pants, but her body in a dress was another matter. The crowd was surprisingly large, with sizable groups of young girls on hand. They weren't all shy. The bolder ones were already flirting with farm boys they fancied, and one or two strolled demurely about, eyeing targets of opportunity. But these were exceptions. Most of the young girls were too bashful to look back at young men trying to catch their eye, and kept their eyes timidly down when asked to dance, a few continuing to look down even as some plucky boys took their hands and swung them in step to the music. A few mothers, to their offspring's dismay, nudged daughters forward as boys came through the crowd seeking partners.

The fiddler, standing on a platform supported by barrels, seemed addicted to lively tunes, and the banjo player kept one foot pounding a flat drum as though he were stomping it to death, but the young dancers hopping about loved it.

Excitement seemed to grow by the minute as the crowd continued to swell. People arrived from as far away as Little Creek, twelve miles to the south, to attend. A surprising number came from across the river, some who had staked their claim less than a week before.

Dennis proved hopeless as a dancer but he trudged around the floor with Chloe, who fortunately was graceful enough to keep him from looking like he was wearing snowshoes. But Dennis wasn't concerned about looking awkward. He was secretly anxious, worried. He saw

Dillby standing with the Hunts, watching the dancing and chatting away. From the way their eyes moved about he sensed they were discussing the dancers and at one point their eyes fell upon Chloe and him. Almost at once he caught Flora and then Charity leaning closer to Dillby and whispering while shaking their heads.

Chloe kept her eyes from focusing on anyone. She was sure if she did she would meet a disapproving expression and at the moment she couldn't deal with a single frigid glance. She clung to Dennis, her face buried in his chest, wishing she were in her wagon with a blanket over her head. Dennis's heated and sustained affection the night before only left her near sobbing at what she would be losing if she lost him. Now their bodies seemed to belong together, one part of the other; to separate them would be like cutting away half of life.

It was Cathy who first noticed the men standing far back by the wagons, slapping each other on the back and occasionally roaring with laughter. She needed no more than a glance or two to realize they were slyly passing a jug about, making the slightly exaggerated movements of men feeling drink. She nodded at them impatiently, muttering to Cole, "My God, so early in the day! I hope they don't become a nuisance."

"Likely they won't . . . see some women headed their way looking mighty upset . . . probably put an end to it."

Resting from dancing, Dennis and Chloe settled on a bench and for the first time Chloe peeked about to find people bustling by, some glancing at them with passing curiosity, others hesitating a moment to stare, as though affirming their identity. There was no question they represented something different, for as the morning worked its way into afternoon, and Hattie began to lay the meat on the fire, eyes were caught rapidly swinging from Hattie to her as though trying to reconcile the two. Fighting to keep her mind on something else, she caught sight of Alice Hunt, dressed in bright pink and seeming to have partners vying for her hand at every dance. Alice was only fifteen, but fifteen-year-old girls were candi-

dates for marriage on the frontier. For a moment Chloe
thought of smiling and quietly greeting her, but instinct
warned her Alice was not likely to respond in public, at
least not with Flora and Charity looking on. But Chloe's
greatest dread at the moment was knowing Dennis
would soon leave her to speak to Dillby. He had decided
to do it while food was being served. At first he had
wanted them to approach Dillby together, but Chloe
wouldn't hear of it, she knew she would be so nervous
she would say or do something foolish. So now she had
to seek out Cathy and Cole and cling to them while
Dennis was away.

But Chloe was in for a surprise. Dennis was no sooner
gone than she was approached by a shy-looking young
man and asked to dance. She shook her head but before
she could reach Cathy's side she had been asked twice
more. Breathless, she registered her shock to the two of
them. Cole laughed. "These young bucks know a pretty
girl when they see one. Reckon Dennis better hustle
back, choice goods don't figure to last long in this
market."

Cathy, more observant than most, noticed a woman
turning to admonish one of the young men who had
asked Chloe to dance, and found herself muttering,
"Two-faced bitch!"

Not hearing her clearly, Cole and Chloe turned toward
her. "What was that?" inquired Cole.

"Nothing," responded Cathy. "Just hoping nothing
spoils this beautiful day."

Dennis found Dillby seated with Flora and Charity
Hunt. Flora looked well groomed in a blue dress, her
dark hair swept back and coming down almost to the
outside corner of her eyes. She had large breasts and a
dimple in her cheek that she continually fingered as
though to call attention to it. Charity had stringy blonde
hair and long shapely legs that could be seen outlined
under her free-flowing skirt. Neither woman wore rouge
and Dennis sensed his appearance had slightly tightened
their expressions.

But Dillby didn't hesitate when he heard Dennis wished to speak to him alone; he readily moved to a spot where they were out of earshot. Dennis, hands clasping the front of his shirt, explained his need of Dillby's services and requested the clergyman advise him on how to prepare for the nuptials he wanted performed as soon as possible. As Dennis finished Dillby smiled benignly and took his hand. "Young man, have you thought this matter through?"

"Sure have," responded Dennis. "Done thought it through and want it bad as a fella ever wanted anything."

"Well"—Dillby stroked his chin, his tone turning faintly judicial—"suppose we discuss this at a proper time. I don't feel this a suitable setting for decisions involving the sacraments . . . perhaps you could come by tomorrow?"

"Tomorrow? What's wrong with today?"

"Marriage is not a simple step, my boy, it has many ramifications that must be considered. Surely you can delay your decision until tomorrow."

Dennis looked puzzled. Delay his decision? He had already made his decision. He was beginning to sense a vague resistance in Dillby that suddenly irritated him. "Aren't you suppose to marry folks whenever they take a mind to?"

"Surely, my boy, but a man who serves God also serves as shepherd to his flock. My mission is to guide youths, such as yourself, in righteous ways so that they will come to know the serenity and blessedness found in concord with the Almighty." He stopped, as though admiring this flash of eloquence, and cleared his throat. "Will two o'clock tomorrow be convenient?"

Dennis, kicking the ground and forcing back a sudden surge of temper, grunted tightly. "Reckon."

It was talk about the war that riled Clint Ferris. News of the serious Union defeat at Second Bull Run had just reached the settlement, and being from Alabama and one of the drinkers he wanted to toast the South.

Unfortunately some of his fellow imbibers were from Pennsylvania, bearded stalwarts who warned him to quit crowing, no single battle decided a war. This was not said with any rancor, but it started Clint feeling defensive and led to a silly rivalry that sober minds would have sensibly avoided. Whatever comparisons Clint now mounted to give southern manhood an edge over its northern counterpart were quickly countered by others, soon equally stubborn and ready to argue the reverse. Attitudes slowly soured and the level of conversation descended until it bordered on the vulgar.

It was then that someone saw Chloe making her way through the crowd to reach Cathy and Cole. Grunts of puzzled amusement sounded as they saw Chloe turning down one suitor after the other to dance. "She being mighty fussy," exclaimed one of the bearded giants. "Might be a little drink could loosen her up some."

"Don't need no liquor," snapped Clint. "Trouble with you Yankees, y'all don't know how to handle an uppity nigger wench!"

"Meaning you do?" came the gruff rejoinder.

Clint raised the jug and took another swallow. "Damn right, and got me half a mind to do it!"

"You always talk so big, Ferris, or is you just fouling the air like them Arkansas hogs you keep bleatin' about?"

Several of the men looked at Clint and laughed.

But Clint Ferris was already striding forward. "Keep yer eyes open . . . might learn somethin' you simple bastards just ain't found out yet . . . nigger wenches got to be treated rough or they get to thinkin' they kin sashay around like they wuz white!"

For some reason the half-drunk man moving determinedly through the crowd, swearing at an occasional misstep, went unnoticed until he was almost at Chloe's side. As usual it was Cathy who noticed him first, but not quick enough to head him off. Before anyone had time to react he had grabbed Chloe around the waist and was pulling her toward the dance ground. "C'mon nigger," he croaked with that hoarse breathlessness of drunks. It all happened too quickly. Chloe tried to free herself but terror suddenly filled her eyes and she could only scream, fear draining strength from her limbs. She could smell whiskey on his breath and feel the stubble of beard as he pulled her face up to press against his. It was several seconds before Cole could yank him free and punch him hard enough to send him reeling two or three yards before collapsing.

Cathy, rushing over, was embracing Chloe, while Cole was pulling Ferris to his feet, ready to hit him again. But Clint's drinking companions suddenly appeared, the bearded giant openly trying to placate Cole. "A leetle too much to drink, that's all," he said, looking about, attempting to soothe the situation.

Cole let them take the drunk off his hands but stood eyeball to eyeball with the big newcomer. "If I see him again he's gonna need more than drink to ease his pain!"

People about could now be heard reacting vocally. "Damn shame!" said one man. "It's liquor every time," opined a woman, looking at her husband as though it had special meaning for him. But Chloe heard other things too. "Figured she'd make trouble one way or t'other," came a syrupy southern accent that in the thick surrounding crowd had no discernable origin.

People, though still commenting, were already dispersing when Dennis came rushing up. He was stunned to find Chloe sobbing in Cathy's arms and Cole redfaced with anger. When told what had happened he wanted to go after Ferris again but was assured the man was too drunk to deal with. Had he looked to the edge of the crowd in the direction of the wagons he would have seen a large black woman, standing with a heavy frying pan in her hand, addressing the drinkers carrying Clint off. Unfortunately he was too far away to hear her speaking. "Yuh see dis frying pan is flat and dat bugger's head look mighty round, but if ah ever sees him again dis frying pan gonna be round and dat head of his is sure gonna be flat!" Looking awkward and uncomfortable, they shifted around her and hurried him away.

Chloe sat between Dennis and Cathy, both trying to console her as best they could, but the damage was done. She wanted to get away from there, she refused to look up and would speak only in whispers.

In the wagon that night there was a long silence. Not until long after dark did Dennis embrace her and ask how it had happened. He hadn't seen Clint Ferris seizing Chloe and had only heard curt accounts from a shocked Cathy and a grim-faced Cole. Chloe pulled away from him and buried her face in her hands. After a moment Dennis put his hand on her shoulder and rubbed it gently. "Did he hurt you?" he asked softly.

"Yes," she sobbed, sinking down to conceal her face in their pillows.

He turned her about so that she was lying on her side, looking up at him. "Where did he hurt you?"

"Here," she said, pointing to her heart.

"There?" His eyes seemed troubled, confused, but his voice remained hushed, tender. "How did he hurt you there?"

She turned again, her face sinking deeper in the pillows. He could just hear her as she said in a voice brittle with pain, "He called me 'nigger.'" After a few moments she lifted her head and her eyes locked desperately on his. "He called me 'nigger,'" she repeated. "Dennis, do you want to marry a nigger?"

33

The United States Congress, that fountain of legislative milestones, had known few seasons darker than the summer of 1862. Embroiled in a war that pitted citizen against fellow citizen, both sides bound by fierce cultural convictions that ruled out compromise or defeat, many congressmen had started viewing their chances of preserving the Union with grave doubts and diminishing hopes. Trust in an inexperienced but costly military was eroding. McClelland, Pope, and Hooker proved no match for Lee and Jackson, whose gray-clad troops were poised distressingly close to the capital. Inconclusive victories in the west could not make up for heavy and critical losses in the east. If Lincoln's simple, stirring eloquence and his unfaltering grasp of America's historic mission managed to sustain faith in "One Nation," the steadily mounting war debt, like the death lists now regularly shocking and appalling the public, was daily growing harder to justify or endure.

The consequences roiled across the entire continent.

Marren and Kaster dutifully presented the treaties their diligence had accomplished to the Office of Indian Affairs, a step regarded as a formality in the complex skein of federal bureaucracies. If there was little discussion about the terms it was because there was little intent to carry them out. At a time when graft was rampant, and corruption an accepted part of influence, the Office of Indian Affairs would still have won the palm for abuse of power and pilfering of public funds. Time after time the treasury paid for livestock never delivered, shoddy goods of little use to the tribes, and gewgaws of no use to anyone. The Indians, without voting power and only rare advocates in government, were soon convinced the whites could only deal in bad faith, a charge that would lead to a sense of national guilt and strain relations for half a century.

The agreements, as drawn up, were considered treaties requiring congressional approval. Here in both houses they encountered the rage and resentment of isolated westerners who knew the mendacity of the Indian office was creating perilous conditions on distant and poorly protected borders, but any and all problems connected with the frontier were dwarfed to insignificance by the national crisis brought on by the burgeoning Confederacy. The sixty thousand dollars required for annuities was cursively voted down and the treaties never ratified, less from a belief the fraud charges were true, than a realization that every penny available was desperately needed to arm the nation and save its seat of government from rebel hands.

If imperiled Washington felt it had no choice but to ignore potentially hostile nomads a thousand miles away, scouts patrolling the border and outposts with only skeleton forces did not enjoy that option. By October Comanches and Kiowas were gathering along the Arkansas to receive the promised goods, to the north Cheyennes and Arapahos, joined by a handful of vigilant Sioux, were settling on the Platte, smoking and discussing what the whites would send in return for this long summer of peace and safe passage to the west. In the settlements the ripened crops were harvested by grateful settlers, and hurried preparations for winter were underway. No one doubted spring would bring fresh abundance, and this peace, in which the land would increasingly reward their labors, was here to stay.

Sam didn't know the great screaming bird landing on the dead top of a mighty pine towering above him was the magnificent golden eagle, the largest flying predator on the continent, nor did he know the fierce bird was the sacred war eagle of the Utes, whose war parties, hoping to emulate its far-seeing eyes and striking power, prayed to it when stalking their enemies.

He had been watching Running Bear approaching him, knife in hand, and saw the eyes of the warriors following their chief, urging him on with grunts of approval to dispatch this strange prisoner. Their medicine carried a taboo against taking prisoners; to break it meant losing the medicine's power.

But the chief suddenly hesitated as his eyes shot up to the great bird perching above, extending its enormous wing span as it settled and screamed to the morning sky. It was a moment Sam would later discover when his life hung in the balance, for the old chief could not help but feel the strange appearance of this sacred bird at this particular moment, soaring down from the sky and landing above the prisoner, was a warning of some kind. War eagles were powerful spirits; they glided over mountain tops, built their eyries on inaccessible peaks, and only young braves, seeking them for their magical tail feathers, pursued them. These cherished feathers were rare, and many a Ute had hunted half a lifetime without snaring one of these powerful elusive birds.

The old chief shouted something at the bird and the eagle, giving a final scream and beating its wings furiously, seemed to fly almost straight upward. By now the braves were all standing, looking up, their eyes alive with a combination of fascination and fear. Few had ever seen a war eagle so close up before, and were awed by its majestic appearance. No one knew, least of all Sam, the great bird had spotted a dying marmot, wounded by an earlier encounter with a fox, lying in the wild growth that proliferated on the opposite side of the tree. It had come down for a closer look before plunging, but the sight of figures on the ground upset it and it was screaming in annoyance. As the chief shouted up at it caution sent it aloft; it would watch from on high, the marmot was clearly too weak to seek cover, it could wait. Great hunters can be patient when assured of their prey.

Sam now witnessed a testy dialogue between the chief and his warriors. The appearance of the eagle had brought confusion. Was this a sign the prisoner was to be spared? Some, including the chief, thought so. Others, particularly the older warriors, declared it dangerous to violate the strong medicine they left camp with. A scarred warrior asked for a council and they settled in a circle, the chief producing a pipe and lighting it. But after many exchanges no agreement was reached. Over an hour went by. The sun was climbing the sky and the chief was growing restless. They had come to kill Comanches, they couldn't keep squatting here.

He finally stood and confronted them gravely, declaring he wasn't going to kill the prisoner. If others wished to they could; he held out the knife. A long silence fell over the war party and a few of the younger ones glanced furtively at the sky. Was the medicine bird still up there watching? After several heartbeats of silence the chief approached Sam and instead of killing him cut loose his bonds. If this strange dark man was watched over by the sacred war eagle, he deserved respect. Sam, bewildered but relieved to be given a mount, got his sore feet off the ground and followed the war party down the long descent, leading them to the rolling eastern foothills and the perilous edge of Comancheria.

Dennis had spent the night hugging Chloe and whispering reassuringly he wanted her, and her alone, for a wife. He didn't tell her the Reverend Dillby put him off until tomorrow to discuss their marriage. It was only in the morning when she asked about his meeting at the gathering that she heard he had been asked to visit Dillby that afternoon.

"Why?" she asked, her eyes holding his.

"Who knows . . . don't know too much about preachers and ain't never been married before. Reckon I'll find out." He pulled her close, trying to make her smile, but she hung back, her eyes refusing to release his. "You sure?"

"Honey, you got to stop frettin' about every little thing . . . gonna worry yourself to a frazzle if you don't."

She continued to stare at him. He tried to distract her by pointing to an uncommonly pretty woman going by, a delicate-looking blonde they had noticed at the gathering whose accent revealed she was from the South. Chloe tried to pretend she hadn't seen her, but the woman, noticing Dennis nodding from the wagon, turned toward them and, smiling shyly, approached. "Y'all been here for a spell?" she asked softly.

"Yeah, for a fair piece," answered Dennis.

"My, we just arrived . . . my Tod is a'diggin' post holes and studyin' 'round for a well." She pointed to a basket she had over her arm. "Baked me a mess of cookies for the gatherin' but got too shy to bring 'em. Tod been pesterin' me to do some visitin', says maybe our neighbors might cotton to cookies—even if little ole me baked 'em." She extended a small plate covered with what looked like tiny neat squares of baked bread.

Dennis, too surprised at the offer to decline, accepted it saying, "Thank you, ma'am." Then, jumping down, he extended his hand. "Name's Sadler, Dennis Sadler. This here is Chloe Boggs."

The woman seemed to blush as she said, "My name is Barry, Charlotte Barry." She paused and then appeared to feel she should explain her embarrassment. "I jest became a Barry, Tod and I jest got married. Folks back home ain't heard yet and letters still come writ to Charlotte Akers." Explaining that seemed to leave her a little breathless. She looked down the trail. "Well, I best be going." She turned for one more shy smile at Chloe. "Tell yo' mother my husband allows she's the best cook as ever laid grub on a skillet!"

Chloe, struck by the woman's simple manner, which if nothing else seemed sincere, could only nod in response to this compliment paid Hattie. Dennis, feeling grateful for the woman's amiable manner, was compelled to add to it. "She will sure be proud to hear that," he half shouted as Charlotte Barry stepped daintily away.

They watched her until she was out of earshot. "Charlotte Barry," murmured Chloe, as though tasting the name and liking it. "She sure is a pretty woman."

"Prettiest one about 'cept one," whispered Dennis, slipping a hand around her waist.

Chloe missed the inflection in his voice and turned curiously. "Which one is that?"

"The one I'm gonna marry, silly."

The Reverend Dillby was living in makeshift quarters, thrown up by volunteers, who, lacking wood, carried stones from the stream bed to set up low walls of three or four feet to anchor the large squares of canvas slanted up for cover. He was content for the moment. It was not a large room but it held a table, a few chairs, and a worn couch, donated by cash-poor families wanting Dillby's services. He had hoped to be assisted by religious connections in Massachusetts, but was recently advised all sources of charity, traditionally supporting missionary work, were now being directed to field services for the wounded, the destitute, the many abandoned children and other victims of war. Reflecting his lot, he preached forbearance and abstinence at every opportunity, and, apart from the steady and liberal hospitality he enjoyed at the Hunts and their growing following, made a public show of both virtues.

Dennis found him with his Bible, holding it before him as he strode up and down the room, obviously practicing his sermon for the coming Sabbath. One hand was in the air, occasionally slashing downward, figuratively pounding into the congregation's conscience the price of wickedness and the calamitous sequels of sin.

Though the door was open Dennis knocked as he stood on the threshold. "Come in! Come in, my son," called Dillby, folding his Bible and gesturing to the couch. "Glad you've come. My prayers have been with you since yesterday, though no doubt you've been praying too." Dillby, seeing Dennis settling stiffly on the couch, pulled up a chair and sat within a few feet of him. "Now what is your decision?"

"Decision?" said Dennis, once again confused. "No decision, sir, just wanting for you to marry us, that's all."

"And the bride?"

"Chloe Boggs."

Dillby cleared his throat. "Young man, I was hoping you would think this matter through, and with God's help see clearly the right road ahead."

Both of Dennis's hands reached forward to grasp his knees. "Preacher, you got me baffled, what yuh gittin' at? What road ahead?"

"My boy, marriage is a serious step. It involves one's place in the community, one's commitment before God, and above all it involves children, who should enter the world without the stain of Ishmael condemning them to loneliness in a desert of human bigotry."

Dennis stared at him, his confusion now mixed with distrust. "Reverend, that sounds mighty like Mrs. Hunt."

"Precisely." Dillby rose and stood behind his chair, his gaze fixed on Dennis. "While I must try to understand and help Mrs. Hunt, as with all who come before me seeking salvation, I am not indifferent to her lapses of Christian spirit. But the world is run by the Hunts and they regrettably deny their blessings to all they feel of inferior origins. My concern, my son, is that you have not thought this thing through. Surely you have noticed, even in this raw unsettled community, your living with a Negress has drawn dubious glances, and her presence at the gathering yesterday brought on that shameful incident. Do you wish to face a lifetime of that?"

"Preacher, I don't give a didilly damn what other folks think!"

"Perhaps, but you mustn't pretend Chloe, that poor frightened girl, doesn't."

Dennis's eyes fell to the other's feet for a moment. "You can tell?"

"She came to that gathering scared to look about . . . she would have given her soul for a place to hide. My heart went out to her, but it will not change."

Dennis made a fist with one hand and pounded it into the other. "This war is a'gonna change it! Slaves are going to be as free as you and me!"

Dillby shook his head. "The war may end slavery, my friend, its defenders fall on the field of battle, but bigotry lies in the heart, it's not an enemy to be fought but a spiritual affliction to be cured."

Dennis stared at him blankly, only dimly grasping the harsh truth behind his words. A long, sullen silence hung awkwardly between them before Dennis lifted his head. There was mute anger in his expression, for inwardly he was seething at a sense of helplessness and a first faint questioning of his resolve. "Well, you gonna marry us?"

Dillby's tone grew even more solemn and was edged with warning. "Are you and Chloe prepared to endure a life of denial, begetting children that will be exiled in the land of their birth?"

"Chloe and I can face anything together."

Dillby sighed and rubbed his forehead for a moment like a man troubled by a judgement forced upon him against his will. "Very well, then I shall agree to marry you before you go."

The remark brought a questioning light to Dennis's eyes. "Reverend, we ain't planning to go anywhere."

Dillby sighed again. "I'm afraid you'll soon find you have to."

Dennis rose to his feet and took a step closer to the clergyman. "We will? Mind if I ask why?"

Dillby looked at him with painful eyes. "Because Chloe will never survive the life she must face here."

34

Against a backdrop of brooding peaks on the front range of the Rockies Whistling Elk watched the many Kiowas and Comanches riding into camp, clearly coming in anticipation of the promised goods to be delivered by the whites. That nothing had come yet troubled him; that the major at the fort offered no explanation for the lengthening delay bothered him even more. His people had kept the peace, that is all except Black Otter, who had been raiding south into Texas, angrily stating, as he had when the treaties were signed, only foolish ones put faith in promises of the whites. Whistling Elk was deeply worried. If the supplies did not arrive soon many of the young restless warriors would be joining Black Otter and the peace would be broken. When he consulted other chiefs they greeted him with stoic faces. They had touched the peace pen, it was now up to the whites to prove their tongues spoke true.

Cold weather was coming. They could only wait another moon before they must seek the protective valleys of the south, where the winter would be spent making and repairing weapons, waiting for spring grass to make the ponies strong, and now perhaps plotting revenge for the perfidy of the whites.

Whistling Elk pulled his blanket about him and scowled at the darkening sky. He would not have sat sulking so deep in thought by his lonely fire had he not remembered the terrible dream of his youth, nor been reminded of the ancient Indian adage that "new enemies do not sweep old ones from the prairie." At least the last was prophetic for less than twenty miles away a slow-moving band of Kiowas and Comanches were moving with their women and children, and a long line of horse-drawn travois, toward his camp. All the men in this band and many of the women and children had only a few hours to live, for Ute scouts were already around them and a small canyon ahead had already been selected as the place for their slaughter.

Chloe was hardly surprised only Hattie, Ben, and Skeeter, along with Cole and Cathy Jo, showed up for her wedding. It was a small affair with Cheatem excusing himself by claiming a sudden request for horses required his bargaining skills at his new rail and rope corral. Hattie arranged a little meal afterward and Skeeter turned up a jug of cider to toast the newlyweds. Reverend Dillby, whom Cole cautiously invited, regretted he had another commitment, and Charlotte Barry, though she sent cookies, failed to appear. It was over in an hour or two and Cathy offered them Troy's empty bed for their first nuptial night together. But Chloe wanted nothing connected with Troy. The wagon would serve, as it had in the past, for a night of clinging and lovemaking, and it was that night in the dark of the wagon that Chloe told Dennis of their coming child.

His response was far closer to amazement than shock, he couldn't believe that their lovemaking had already produced a baby. He let out a deep breath. The feeling of coming fatherhood stirred strange emotions in him, a little like walking in a scary part of the woods when he was small. It was a while before he realized Chloe was deliberately clinging to him, watching him for any hint

of his reaction. As though jabbed awake, he suddenly
sensed a deep trembling fear in her and immediately
grabbed her in a firm embrace, kissing her with abandon
and only letting up when he had to stop to express an
emotion that finally forced its way out in the helpless
laughter of joy. Now feeling his hands grasping her,
wanting her, needing her, she hugged him back and
started to laugh too, making the tears of relief running
down her face seem weirdly out of place.

Sam couldn't believe so many days had passed before
the dawning he knew something was afoot. His life with
the Utes wasn't intolerable, but he couldn't help worrying about how it might end. Running Bear seemed
preoccupied with finding Comanches, but often enough
he turned to stare at Sam, his eyes narrow with doubt. It
was almost a relief at last, when just before sunrise, Sam
could hear scouts darting about in the darkness, whispering to Running Bear and leading small parties off in
the meager light.

They had finally found the quarry they wanted and
Sam could tell from the hurried painting of faces and
quiet chanting that in this strange dawning men were
preparing to bring or receive death. Long aware they
intended to attack someone, he had played with the idea
of using that first moment of excitement to escape. But
these were experienced marauders. They had given him
a horse easily winded and not fast enough to corner a
lame buffalo. They also kept him without food or
weapons.

With the sun beginning to spread light over the low-
lying range, Sam followed Running Bear until they were
overlooking a small canyon, made up of two sharp hills
that funneled a just visible trail onto flat land beyond. It
was some time before he noticed something moving at
the west end of the canyon, but within moments he knew
it was a handful of horsemen leading a long caravan of
figures walking or riding, a few leading horses pulling
travois or packed high with goods. It was a peaceful
enough scene but the old chief was glaring down at the

procession with vengeful eyes and Sam could feel the imminence of violence and remorseless death in the air. In fact, with blood suddenly draining from his head, his pounding heart told him he was about to witness a massacre.

No tribe on the continent matched the pride and arrogance of Comanches and their Kiowa allies. Undefeated in many wars, and a long history of conquest and rule, had made them almost indifferent to danger in the heart of their own hunting grounds. It took a brave enemy to invade Comancheria, for even a small party making a swift sneak raid would often be tracked back to its village, even if hundreds of miles distant, and entire camps had been known to be wiped out.

So here, only one day's march from what was becoming a main village, the thought of attack was furthest from their minds. Many were looking forward to the goods the whites would have delivered by now, others to the comforts of the lodge, with smokes and long talks with old friends. Yet just as the rays of the sun penetrated to the canyon floor, a strange thing happened. A horse moving in front reared up and whinnied in pain. This was followed by a ragged series of shots, punctuated by the shrill ear-splitting war cry of the Utes, as from both sides painted figures appeared and closed upon the column, wildly firing their weapons. Comanche and Kiowa braves, both savage fighters, immediately turned to grapple with the Utes, but many had fallen in the first barrage of bullets and arrows and others were overpowered while still struggling to free their weapons, for the wily Utes fought in groups of two or three. Even so there were dead and dying Utes before all the men were dispatched, and women and children fearfully cowering, awaiting their fate. It was not long in coming. Had they been closer to home they would have taken some of the children to raise as Utes, but the need for a hasty and surely perilous trip back through the mountains ruled out such a burden.

Sam had to cover his eyes as the braves with their war clubs murdered the children. But the screaming squaws hardly fared better. All but the very old were stripped and raped, and only two young ones, who could ride as well as men, were taken along. They would prove to be the unluckiest of all, for after physical abuse by any brave that wanted them, they would be given to the Ute squaws of the men killed in the attack to be tormented and enslaved till their will to live was gone.

As the braves collected scalps, buried the three dead Utes, and eyed the gathering of specks, which proved to be vultures circling in the sky, Running Bear chanted a little prayer to his medicine spirit in thanks for a great victory. When his eyes fell upon Sam he almost smiled, for this prisoner, he was sure, had brought the power of the war eagle to his quest. For such a favor he was not ungrateful. Sam would be taken back to his people, adopted by the chief, and made a member of the tribe. The Utes would then have the power of the war eagle with them forever.

If there was a sour note in the chief's rejoicing, it was his brother, Swift Owl, wounded in the fight and cursing the Comanche that stabbed him in the thigh as he delivered his death blow. Swift Owl was younger than the chief but well on the way to becoming a chief himself. He demanded the Comanche's scalp and several items of the loot taken from the bodies and packs of the dead. The chief, clearly irritated, wanted everything worth taking thrown together on the backs of the captured horses so they could be off. There would be time for dividing spoils later when they had put a safe distance between themselves and the inevitable pursuit. The chief did not delude himself. He had a lot of respect for the power and persistence of this enemy. Reprisals for this day were as sure as sunrise, but he wanted to deal with them where the Utes had greater numbers and the land was familiar to them. Sam, seeing the chief gesturing to him, only knew he was going wherever the chief went, but even that seemed preferable to lingering by this scene of carnage where vultures were already landing on the ground and hopping with their awkward gait toward the dead.

* * *

It was stray Kiowa hunters, returning to the main camp and noticing vultures wheeling above the canyon, who discovered the slain party. Before nightfall a powerful force of warriors, their faces painted black, were hot on the trail of the Utes. For two days they worked higher into the mountains, ignoring the growing cold and lowering skies. But on the third day an early fall blizzard struck and without their buffalo robes they sat in their single blankets, deciding in grim council their reprisal raid would have to wait until spring. But that would not lessen their vengeance nor erode their thirst for Ute blood. Many oaths were taken that day and two Ute scalps were sworn to be lifted for every Comanche scalp lost.

All signs now seemed to suggest the Utes were to make it safely home, except for two factors entering the picture, one unknown to the Comanches and the other unnoticed by the Utes. Swift Owl's wound, though for days seeming only slightly inflamed, suddenly turned scarlet with purple streaks rising around it, and his thigh began to swell until it was too painful to ride. Convinced by scouts, watching the terrain to their rear, that they were no longer being pursued, Running Bear slowed the party down to ease Swift Owl's mounting agony, for he had no way of knowing Black Otter's band was also stalking him, and this rebel chief, gambling the Utes were headed for a village on the western slopes, had been hurrying his band through a string of secret valleys, avoiding the cold and difficult heights of the more direct route and desperately hoping to arrive in time to cut them off. But he would never have made it except for Swift Owl's wound, which became so bad the chief ordered a stop to gather medicine weeds and a special bark to make a poultice to draw the spreading poison out. The chief had seen wounds like this before. He had seen whites, when confronted with that whitish flesh, amputate a limb. But a warrior without a limb was not a warrior, and he knew his brother was going to have to suffer excruciating pain for a day or two until death claimed him. To comfort Swift Owl he ordered some of his braves to take a captured drum and beat it, as others danced a medicine dance and sang the healing chant, pretending this might save him.

Running Bear's victory was beginning to turn sour in his mouth. He sat brooding as his restive warriors pulled the young Comanche squaws from their saddles and raped them repeatedly. But a growing number held back, wondering if there was wisdom in this delaying, wondering if it wasn't time to seek the safety and comfort of their village before the weather turned bitter, or their medicine, now ominously forsaking Swift Owl, ran out.

That night these forebodings became reality.

Poor dying Swift Owl, burning with fever and now hallucinating, was the only one awake to see shadows rising from the rock formations surrounding them and rushing forward to fall upon the sleeping Utes. Within moments the quietly slumbering camp was like a scene from bedlam, with Comanches and Kiowas pouring fire and arrows into huddled forms and Utes trying to escape blankets and ward off hatchets awaiting them as they rose and tried to bring their weapons to bear. Ute warriors knew better than to be captured alive by Comanches, so they fought valiantly. But surprise and the quick loss of near half their number gave the attackers too great an advantage. Running Bear died beside his brother, and Sam only survived because he had been forced to sleep as a guard next to the two captive squaws, who kept screaming in Comanche that they were not Utes. Black Otter had the fire built up so that the full camp could be carefully searched. He wanted none left alive, they were too close to Ute territory to delay long or risk word of their presence getting out. Within half an hour all the enemy bodies had been scalped, the loot and the many Comanche scalps retaken, the captured horses herded together, and the whole party rapidly moving eastward before the first light of dawn broke eerily before them.

Sam, his heart in his mouth, rode along stunned by the amount of death he had seen since the pathetic figure of Troy lay dying beside his mine. He knew he was going east again but to what fate he didn't dare guess. He suspected these were Comanches and the Comanches were supposed to be at peace, but he saw nothing peaceful about the countenance of this leader. Sam was to find he had much to learn about Black Otter, most of it leaving him more shaken than those first dark glances of Running Bear.

35

Though Captain Quarles had twice been promised a transfer back east to a regiment drawn up in his home state, the general reversed himself on both occasions. The first because the brigadier truly believed requests for transfers should always be rejected on first try, the army was full of officers who imagined transfers would improve their lot, the reverse often proving the case; the second because word had reached him that the peace treaties had not been ratified and the major at the fort now needed special orders, particularly since his garrison had been stripped of all but a company of men and the major himself, from petulant remarks that inevitably reached the general, hardly seemed the commander to deal with dangers confronting an isolated outpost. Captain Quarles had visited that country out there and had previously dealt with the major. More to the point, Quarles had by now impressed every ranking officer on the post with his powers of organization, his natural bent for leadership, and his general good sense in handling matters of poorly disciplined recruits, and the few cases of summary court-martial that arose. He seemed the ideal man to send into this precarious situation, so the general with his customary curtness ordered him to take a troop of men, and whatever else he needed, and report posthaste with new orders to the fort.

Henry Quarles, aware by now army instructions had no negotiable side, resignedly returned to his quarters and sent for Lee. The half-amused scout only shook his head, his expression declaring there was no sense in pretending surprise, he had yet to see the treaty that wasn't broken by one side or the other. "But sure is gonna be hell to pay," he mused quietly. "Them redskins set a store by free goods . . . to my figuring them settlers need warning a heap more than that damn fort."

Lee's remark about the settlers immediately put Quarles in mind of someone. No one familiar with Henry's inner life would have been surprised to hear it was Cathy Jo Sadler. His fantasy, which had been drifting lately to a desire for a woman in his life, had him visualizing a misty figure approaching, unseen yet bringing a warm, comforting presence. In the beginning it was only for a split second that Cathy's face flashed through his mind, but lately something more lingered on, something marking the pall of loneliness which the death of his wife had visited upon him and which for many years he could not dispel.

Lee, noticing him gazing into space, grunted quietly. "Something got yuh stewin'?"

"Oh, no," responded Quarles, a little startled. "Just trying to keep what's important in mind . . . that's all."

The coming of cold weather cut into the field work being done in the settlement. The result was more meetings to plan community projects and a rising rhythm to their social life, making "teas" given by the Hunts on Thursdays, and "coffees" arranged by Reverend Dillby after Sunday services, two events around which many settlers began to plan their week. With an ultimate church in mind Dillby's quarters had now been expanded from his small room with its low stone walls to a spacious hall that was serving as a meeting place, an arrangement he soon found agreeable as Cheatem, after the sale of some horses, paid for the building of a huge fireplace to keep the hall warm. Silas, repeatedly hinting at the settlement's need for an elected leader, one who

could officially request the government for help, was
finding politics a near taboo subject in this community,
where sharp differences of opinion had to be kept in
check. Tod Barry, a discrete man, but one clearly of
southern sympathies, had the wisdom to turn down
gestures in his direction; he foresaw a contest between
himself and a northerner like Cheatem disrupting the
settlement, and bringing the blight of a torn nation upon
them. His pretty wife, Charlotte, was popular because of
her friendly way of approaching everyone, bringing them
cookies, which some women bit into and cocked their
heads, puzzling at the ingredients. Secretly her prudent
husband warned her against getting too friendly with the
young Sadlers, not because he objected to the marriage
of Dennis and Chloe but because that couple was
increasingly controversial and he had an aversion to
issues that smacked of conflict. It wasn't completely
without reason; though the settlement was mixed, southerners were a definite minority. He had already seen
miscegenation trigger violent emotions, emotions he
suspected were in part behind the calamitous war raging
in Virginia. Could they be kept in check in this raw
western community? Pretty Charlotte Barry truly loved
her husband, and usually accepted his guidance, but
nothing could keep her from visiting Cathy Jo and while
there talking to Chloe, insisting she try some new
cookies just concocted. Dennis, in gratitude for her
friendship, dutifully ate the cookies and, whatever their
taste, his eyes strained to express their succulent flavor.

If Charlotte saw no harm in mingling with Chloe,
Flora Hunt, who oddly never discussed her, did. Invita-
tions to the Hunt "teas" had become something of a
distinction, not everyone was invited. She kept a close
checklist, and while some were on hand every Thursday,
others only appeared on alternate weeks and a few
became only infrequent monthly guests. Dillby,
Cheatem, and even Cathy and Cole had originally been
weekly attendees. But when Dennis and Chloe failed to
make the monthly list Cathy confronted Flora. Mrs.
Hunt, from the icy pinnacle of her dignity, made it clear

her teas were for proper and respectable people, and
coolly flounced away from an issue too explicit for
comment.

After that Cathy, in spite of Cole's reservations, refused to go. But such loyalty did not protect Chloe from
a thousand hurtful incidents, impossible to predict and
hence avoid. When Chloe's pregnancy began to show so
soon after her wedding prurient minds concluded the
child had not been conceived in wedlock. Children,
picking up chance comments from their parents and
babbling them publicly with that youthful unconcern for
compassion, had Chloe choking back tears. Dennis,
infuriated but helpless, kept insisting they could live
without this damned community's blessings, but in his
heart he knew this simply wasn't true. The uncertainties
and challenges of a hinterland made support from one's
neighbors vital, on occasion crucial. But finally an
incident took place at the Sunday church service that
made him realize only one alternative was left to him
and he vowed as he prayed to take it.

The Sabbath saw near everyone in attendance, the
only exceptions being Hattie, Ben, and Skeeter. It wasn't
that they weren't invited; Reverend Dillby told them
they could stand in back of the congregation and join in
the prayers when their spirits so moved them. But Hattie
couldn't follow the staid rituals of Dillby's church, and
the spirituals she liked to sing seemed unknown to the
choir master, a dandified elflike creature whose expressions continually suggested his charges were singing off
key. Finally the three blacks took to praying together by
the river, mostly for Sam, who by now they were
convinced had met trouble. Skeeter wanted to go searching for him, but Hattie and Ben, both having appealed to
Cheatem, repeated his warning that snow would now be
blocking the mountain passes and nothing could be done
until spring. At the end of their praying Hattie led the
singing, especially one song, a spiritual, she had made up
herself about Ishmael wandering the wilderness. It put
her in mind of Lame Fox. Would he ever come back?
Maybe Lame Fox would find Sam for them.

But it was a Sunday in church when the fading hopes Dennis had been clinging to were finally dissolved by an empty half bench, a half bench lying bare in a room where people braced themselves against side walls and squeezed in together in some discomfort on benches before and behind. They had come with Cole and Cathy, and Cole had stepped back to let Chloe and Dennis be seated in the center of the bench, while Cathy settled next to Dennis and Cole sat on the aisle. That left Chloe sitting beside Dennis with half the bench empty on her right. As the church filled up those seats remained empty, and had pig droppings been smeared across that empty half bench it could not have outraged Dennis more. He sat looking at the faces around him, which he could have endured had they been hostile, but they weren't, they were indifferent, remote, apparently determined to keep their eyes directed elsewhere. It wasn't as though he and Chloe were being ignored; it was as though they didn't exist.

The congregation may have been following Dillby's prayers, but Dennis, rigid with fury, was suffering a weird transformation, for accidentally his eyes caught a ray of sunlight breaking upon the small display of flowers arranged on the makeshift altar. A good life was waiting for them somewhere! If this settlement was as petty as its people, at least God's flowers bloomed for everyone everywhere! He and Chloe were going to find a better life, and no matter the price or even the peril, to that end, squeezing Chloe's hand, he bowed his head and fervently swore.

The major decided another drink couldn't hurt. The delegation of angry Kiowas he had just turned away looked anything but satisfied with his promise, a promise he made unaware it couldn't be carried out. Communications with Leavenworth were so miserable he felt abandoned in this thinly manned outpost, where worried scouts continually reported large gatherings of Indians in anticipation of government provisions which were alarmingly overdue. Telegraph lines did not run

west of Leavenworth, and his dependence upon couriers
kept him weeks behind events. He only knew the war
was going badly for the North, and his requests for
transfers continued to be either denied or ignored. He
had just finished a stiff drink, bemoaning his fate, but
was considering stopping for a while, something about
those sullen stares with which the Indians greeted his
words sent a warning vibe deep in his brain and uneasily
he called in his orderly.

"Have the sergeant report to me at once, and see if any
scouts have returned. If they have I want them here on
the double."

The orderly saluted and left.

Five minutes later the sergeant, an old hand on the
frontier, and a half-breed scout called Dice, were sitting
in his office. The sergeant was smiling almost cynically.
"Sir, you needn't ask if trouble is coming . . . to my
reckoning it's a'ready here."

The major stared at him. "You expecting hostilities?"

"Ain't you?"

"Sergeant, you're here to report your opinion, not to
ask mine!"

"Sorry, sir, but if you saw the numbers gathering
you'd sure be convinced them supplies is all that's lying
between peace and the goddamnedest uprising ever hit
this range."

The major turned to Dice. "You got anything to report
. . . any signs of trouble?"

Dice nodded. "Signs very bad. Much talk of white
men's false tongue. Many say one moon only." His hand
made a circle in the air. "Need more soldiers here."

The major shook his head. "The army hasn't got any
soldiers to spare—it's busy fighting a war." He turned to
the sergeant. "Perhaps you'd better start doubling the
guard, 'specially at night."

The sergeant grimaced. "Major, no single company of
men is gonna hold this fort. You got to insist upon more
troops!"

"Sergeant, you've been in the army long enough to
know you don't 'insist' on anything. I've got to believe
Leavenworth knows the situation here. It's a fair bet

we'll be getting reinforcements or at least new orders
before long."

Being curtly dismissed, the sergeant and the scout,
both frowning, left. The major stared for a moment at
the door that closed behind them. Then, sighing as
though their statements had only increased his quandary, he reached for his bottle and poured another drink.
It didn't help but it sure wouldn't hurt either.

Captain Quarles led his wearying platoon along the
river until he caught sight of the settlement. There was a
cold wind blowing in from the mountains, sending deep
ripples over the water and groaning ominously through
the few trees left standing on the banks. Snow would not
be long in coming and he wondered at the prospects for a
settlement facing its first winter with trouble brewing,
trouble which few were aware of.

He found the Sadler household in disarray, with Cole
and Cathy trying to dissuade Dennis and Chloe from
leaving. The young couple had grimly packed and further insulated their wagon, and Dennis was moving
about, his jaw set, his few words harsh and brusque and
of unmistakable intent. He was going!

In spite of the trouble Cathy greeted Henry warmly,
she was surprisingly glad to see him; curiously enough he
represented something decent and even comforting to
her. She had learned how vulnerable he was on his last
visit, and that seemed to bring them closer, perhaps in
the way their vulnerability reassures women about men.
The settlement turned out to treat the soldiers to hot
biscuits and coffee, but it wasn't long before word that
the peace was being threatened started sobering even
herders trying to keep livestock from drifting with the
wind on the settlement's outskirts.

Cheatem was soon confronting Quarles in the Sadler
kitchen. "Just how serious is this? We got a heap of
women and children here . . . ought to be giving us some
protection."

"The government will do what it can. Right now we're
not sure how much trouble we're talking about. Could
blow over."

"Not likely," said Cole. "Injuns are bad enough without feeling cheated and gittin' themselves riled up. Can't the damn government keep its own promises?"

"They're fighting a war . . . suspect it's more than promises they're trying to keep."

People began to appear, seeking the captain in charge of the troop. Tod Barry and the Hunt men showed up, followed by Dillby and some teenagers sent by worried families. Uninvited, they crowded into the Sadler kitchen. "What do you suggest, Captain?" asked Tod Barry. "Ought'n we be preparing one way or t'other?"

Quarles regarded the swelling group with both concern and a reluctance to unduly alarm them. "For the moment you ought to sit tight. My guide, a fellow called Lee, claims they rarely get rambunctious in winter, but come spring you best keep a close watch out."

There was a strange silence in the room. "Is that all?" asked one of the Hunt men.

Quarles heaved a sigh and crossed his arms. "Well, you could always pull back to Salina until this business is settled."

A number of voices rose in dissent. "We can't leave everything we've worked for behind here," cried a hatchet-faced man who had worked his way up to Cheatem. "Silas, you know them red devils are likely to burn everything to the ground if we give 'em half a chance."

Cheatem, shifting his weight from one foot to the other, stared meaningfully at Quarles. "You gonna reinforce that fort?"

"No plans for that."

"There ain't enough soldiers left there now to stop a barroom brawl. What they gonna do if big trouble comes?"

Quarles thought of the orders in his pocket. He had no right to disclose these to the public, but he felt maybe this settlement had a moral right to know. In spite of his reassurances things would work out, that information might one day be the difference between life and death. Besides, having failed to receive orders regarding the settlers, he felt he had a right to use his own discretion.

Not only Cheatem but everyone in that room was waiting for his answer to Silas's question on what the garrison would do in the event of trouble, and more than one blinked back at him when he said without changing his expression, "Evacuate."

36

For the second time since poor Troy lay dying on his mine Sam was sure his brief and largely fugitive life was over. As Black Otter's band hurried him along, he could see his captors more clearly in daylight and caught not only fresh Ute scalps hanging from every warrior's belt, but the dried scalps of whites, strands of blonde and reddish hair, many curled like women's. What they had in store for him he tried to reason out, but judging from looks he was getting, not only from Black Otter but from individual braves, one in particular whom he gathered was some sort of sub-chief, it was far from encouraging. A chilling sensation warned him he was surrounded by inveterate killers; they seemed to be loping along beside him like slavering wolves, prowling the plain by night, dispensing terror and death.

It took two hard, feverish riding days before they came to their camp, partially concealed in a break of woods along a wide river Sam soon discovered was the Arkansas. Here a minor celebration took place. Though there seemed to be few women in the camp those that were there came out screeching with joy at the sight of Ute scalps. They took the two recaptured young squaws, stripped them, and dabbed their bodies with bright paint, making weird designs. Then the women hurriedly set about cooking.

Sam thought for a moment he had been forgotten, but regrettably he wasn't. Within minutes he found himself tied to a stake, while a fat, heavy-featured squaw came up to poke at him with a sharp stick. He had the feeling he was being sized up for a cooking pot, but again he guessed wrong. His shirt had been ripped off, and his chest was showing several cuts from the stick before he gathered this ugly squaw was in some way related to Black Otter, and he was being given to her as a present. She had a venomous glaze in her eyes and Sam was repulsed by the rolls of fat that covered her neck and thickened her body above her skirt. Fortunately she clearly liked to eat and as the meal began she abruptly left him to lug a large bowl over to the nearest steaming pot. She was the only woman allowed to squat and eat beside the men, and even Sam, who was beginning to learn Indian ways, divined she must have some kind of rank. The sub-chief, whom Sam would soon learn to his regret was called Red Hand, kept glaring at him and only seemed distracted when a string of young warriors rode into camp, chanting words that sounded ominous and warlike. For some reason this noisy demonstration made Red Hand smile. Sam could only surmise these were angry young men, coming to Black Otter's camp, furious at some grievance they wanted him to join them in redressing.

Strangely, after the long, noisy meal, he was callously forgotten, for, shaking in a stiff breeze without his shirt, he found he was to be left tied to the stake all night. In the early morn one of the recaptured squaws brought him a bowl of cold soup. He was released so he could drink, but then was led to the fat woman's tipi and pressed down until he was squatting at the entrance flap. Sam by now was so wretched that even the prospect of imminent death hardly seemed frightening, but even so the sight of Red Hand approaching him with a large hatchet had him holding his breath, until he saw this malevolent-looking warrior was only coming to visit the fat lady. Before he left Sam realized this obese female was some sort of medicine woman, and Red Hand had come with a richly decorated hatchet to reward her for strong medicine she had given them when departing to pursue the Utes. The medicine woman, whom Sam was shortly to learn was called Bad Eyes, tested the hatchet's sharpness by pulling up and cutting some of Sam's hair. Then she broke wind, almost in his face, and reentered the tipi where he could hear her chanting and rattling what proved later to be crow bones in a gourd.

But this day was marked early by a rising tension that curiously charged the air. Something big was about to happen here, though Sam, beginning to suffer from the cold, could only rub his limbs and shake. Finally he watched a young wounded warrior approaching and leaving a blanket before Bad Eye's tipi. When the brave disappeared Sam summoned the courage to take the blanket and wrap it around him. That made him less conspicuous, though he kept sensing other things were drawing the camp's attention from him. The people were obviously preparing for an important event. Women were readying food, men were dressing in their finest regalia, and young boys were gathering wood for several fires, particularly a main one in the middle of the camp.

Late that afternoon a long string of Kiowa and Comanche chiefs and war leaders, headed by Whistling Elk, rode into camp, and following them was an endless train of angry faces shouting bitter words or shaking scalp sticks against the sky. Sam didn't know it but he was about to witness a war council that would touch off one of the bloodiest uprisings in the history of the frontier.

When Dennis and Chloe left only Lee had any inkling of where they were headed, and that only because he had been closely questioned by Dennis about trails to the south. Hattie took their leaving hardest. She hugged her daughter and pleaded with her not to go, but in her heart she understood it had to be; this settlement had its own form of bondage, a servitude no law could end, a banishment only the banished could feel. She gave her what money she had, which included Skeeter's and Ben's, and made her promise to pray every Sabbath, if only a little. Chloe hugged her back, secretly dreading the birth of her coming child without Hattie's comforting presence. Skeeter and Ben stood by, looking down. But Dennis simply hugged Cathy and resignedly shook Cole's hand. Then he climbed the wagon, only nodding at the others, for he had made his decision, and this tow-headed boy turned man no longer needed others to steer him through life. His family was now his sole concern, and he was going to search for and claim its birthright, hope and happiness.

It turned out to be a day of memorable departures.

Quarles bid Cathy farewell, she seeming to shake his hand slightly more warmly then usual, while he advised Cole and Cheatem to make some preliminary plans in case of Indian trouble. However, he was careful to assure them they would be warned at the first sign of danger and that experienced hands did not expect any difficulty until spring. Cheatem would subsequently call a few meetings, which he presided over, to get a consensus from the community. Though a few ideas were discussed, in the absence of any immediate threat little action was taken. Most of the settlement, beginning to notice frosty winds and close to freezing rain, turned to packing in wood and buffalo chips to sustain fires needed to keep their families warm for the winter. They were too new to this country to read the dark lowering skies that were beginning to gather in dull bronze over the distant mountains, but with the passage of time, after many rigorous trials that came with this awesome land, they would learn.

At the fort the major could hardly conceal his joy at Quarles's arrival, even as he made a studied attempt to pretend things were in hand and no problems beyond his powers of command existed. A new tack, thought Quarles, remembering the litany of complaints he had heard on his first visit. But when advised that the promised annuities were not coming the major visibly paled and his knuckles started beating a staccato rhythm on the desk top. "Not coming . . . not going to be delivered!" he repeated. "My God! Are you people crazy?"

"*We people* had nothing to do with it," returned

Quarles evenly. "The government simply didn't ratify those treaties . . . suspect they had other problems."

The major gripped both arms of his chair. "Then you've got to reinforce this post. There are thousands of hostile Indians gathering out there, ready to explode. This garrison hasn't got a Chinaman's chance of holding them in check!"

Quarles, rubbing his chin, settled back in his chair. "Major, I was told to advise you there are no units available for reinforcement. All troops capable of duty have been assigned to combat areas."

The major came to his feet. "Combat areas? Combat areas? What the hell do you call this?"

"Right now it seems pretty quiet."

"Quiet? Wait till they discover those treaties were hogwash!" His eyes pinned Henry suspiciously. "You gonna be the one to tell 'em?"

"No, you are."

The major sat down and began slapping the drawers of his desk till he found the one holding his liquor. He pulled out a bottle and poured himself a sizable measure. Downing it he turned and determinedly confronted Quarles. A tiny line of moisture had appeared just above his brow, it didn't quite reach across his forehead. "You'd better say that again, Captain. I've always had trouble making sense of damned foolishness, even when it comes from headquarters."

"Certainly," responded Quarles calmly. "You are to advise the tribes that unfortunately the supplies are not coming as intended, but their needs will be reconsidered next year. If this results in hostilities, you are to evacuate this post and burn it before reporting with your command to Leavenworth. You are also to advise surrounding settlements several days in advance if this final action becomes necessary."

The major, by now breathing heavily, pressed his chair back from the desk. "Jesus! Is all this in writing?"

"Of course." Quarles handed him a sealed packet. "I was only asked to relay these orders to you verbally in case you had questions about their intent."

"I have a hell of a lot of questions . . . but one will do

for a starter. What happens to me when I get to Leavenworth?"

"You know the army, Major. Nobody knows what
they have in mind, but it's a safe bet you won't like it."

The major poured himself another drink and gestured
with the bottle to Quarles. Henry gave him a cautionary
smile. "A little early for me, Major, but be careful, that
stuff can get a man seeing things that aren't there, and
maybe missing a few that are."

The major stuck a half-smoked cigar in his mouth and
bit into it. "Holy Christ! Please don't start preaching to
me!" he half shouted, slamming the bottle down. "I've
been sitting in this goddamned hole so long I'm talking
to myself!"

Henry almost said *Maybe the only audience a drunk
deserves is another drunk,* but thought better of it and,
saluting properly, left.

Dennis was boldly heading south, traveling across
country with a strong wind sweeping wide stretches of
brown grass and rock outcroppings. Occasionally they
spotted sun-whitened buffalo bones or a lonely shrub
oak, or a skeletal cottonwood filled with crows cawing at
them as they passed. Several times he noticed hawks
circling lazily above or caught sight of coyotes watching
them from a distance, often the same animal traveling
behind them for miles. He hadn't told Chloe yet where
they were going because he wasn't sure he could get
there. For Dennis knew very little about the west. Only
one place had stuck in his memory, hanging there as a
town he'd like to see someday. It sounded like a heap
better place than Kansas. He had never forgotten the old
trapper telling of his youth in a place called Santa Fe,
relating how easy life was there, how music filled the
evening hours and people spent a fair amount of time
making love. To Dennis it sounded like a spread the
Hunts would never choose, making it all the more
appealing to him. In quietly sounding Lee out for
directions, he was more than irritated by the scout's
persistent attempts to discourage him. "That's mighty

dangerous country, son, gets worse below the Arkansas.
Might be best you go east."

But Dennis's mind was made up. What he was escaping from couldn't be avoided by going east. What he needed was a different kind of world, a world the old trapper's words seemed to promise. Lee, sensing his determination, reluctantly told him that south of the Arkansas he could pick up the Cimarron and follow it southwest till he struck the Beaver. He'd be on the trail by then, which should be clearly enough marked to follow into New Mexico and through the mountains to Santa Fe.

For days Dennis found it a little sketchy in his mind, but in this season he was still running into occasional hunters or traders, moving between settlements. Many pointed the way, though most did so with warnings. One he kept hearing more and more often was when crossing the Arkansas be sure to cross at a well-marked ford. The river could be deceptively deep and was known to have quicksand. He was also advised to keep careful watch on his horses. Keeping them healthy was a constant problem in the wilds. Dennis had two pulling the wagon and two that could serve as saddle mounts tied behind. But the ground was rough and treacherously pocked with gopher holes. Dennis wisely moved slowly, switching those in harness from time to time, and stopping early enough each afternoon for all to graze. With this measured pace they didn't reach the Arkansas for nearly three days, and once there spent many hours finding a safe ford.

But it was at this clearly marked ford that they met three hunters coming north, who told them there were rumors of Indian trouble along the Cimarron, that Mexican traders had been reluctant to travel, hearing of attacks by renegade Comanches who from the beginning had ignored the peace. Dennis, now heading for the Cimarron, was only glad Chloe was beyond hearing in the wagon, but she saw their expressions and their gesturing to the south, and she hadn't forgotten the furor raised by Quarles's arrival at the settlement. Her hands

gripped his in a silent questioning, as she watched his
eyes to see if, in spite of his assurances, he shared her
fears. But nothing could deter Dennis. He could think of
no other direction to head and turning back, in his
emotional state, clearly would have taxed his sanity.
With the weather turning colder Chloe cuddled next to
him during the night. She needed loving and her need
rose with her feelings of loneliness and despair. Dennis
marveled at her continuing passion, which curiously
ignited his at the first press of her soft, moist lips. He
found it deeply comforting, though often when they
finished, breathless but soothed again and reassured in
their love, her quick drifting to sleep left him lying
awake, listening to a distant wolf or the wind moaning
about the wagon, wondering if he wasn't taking himself
and this girl he loved to their deaths on these desolate
plains. Ah, could it be they were doubly cursed! Risking
a real hell ahead to escape a specter of hell behind? In
the dark of a prairie night a man's heart is truly alone,
yet decisions had to be made, some involving death. He
pondered each, feeling the warmth of Chloe beside him,
finally falling asleep, deciding his decisions were already
made. He was not afraid to fight, but a man had a right
to see what he was fighting against. He would take his
chances on whatever hell lay ahead.

37

The sergeant and the half-breed scout, Dice, entered the
office and sat tensely before the major. They already
knew the sullen rage their commander was in, their
concern now was would it be directed at them? If so,
how? Bringing word of the government's failure to honor

its treaties to thousands of aroused and suspicious tribesmen, belligerent and truculent under the best of conditions, was not a task any sane man would relish, but the order had come down and delegation, that favorite army dodge, had reached its last leg. The sergeant, who had great faith in the major's lack of mettle, was hardly surprised to hear him using the journalistic "we." He knew only too well what it meant. Dice, Cherokee by birth and less attuned to the subtleties of English expression, took several moments longer, but the slow tightening of his mouth indicated he understood.

"We've got a bitch of a problem on our hands and *you* might as well start handling it," the major began. "My own suggestion is you take some men and visit their camps, the sooner the better, let 'em know we're sorry but we'll make up for it next year."

There was a strange silence, ended by the sergeant clearing his throat. "Begging the major's pardon, but don't you think an officer of higher rank should report the government's position to these people? Injuns place a big store on status."

The major shrugged and broke eye contact. "You can say your message is from the great father in Washington, that should give it status enough."

Dice, a poor speaker but now desperate to comment, had to take time to marshal his words. "Major, they Comanches, they Kiowas, they not say 'thank you' for message . . . much trouble come quick."

Another silence ensued before the sergeant muttered, "If we're gonna enter camps for a pow-wow we're gonna need the whole company."

The major looked up, a little startled. "What? And leave the fort undefended?"

The sergeant stared back at him. "Major, inside or out, one company isn't gonna hold this fort. We ought to be thinking about getting the men to safety."

The major's eyes narrowed. "Sergeant, you're getting into my area of responsibility. Please restrict yourself to your own."

The sergeant let out a long whistling breath. "Major,

in case you ain't noticed, most folks would reckon
you've just about deserted your area of responsibility
. . . Dice and I ain't drawing no major's pay, but we'll fill
in as best we can."

All three knew army sergeants get court-martialed for
less offensive remarks than that, but the major was
suddenly on his feet, as though his mind had been
abruptly drawn elsewhere. He rattled a sheaf of papers
and slammed so many desk drawers that Dice, at least,
was convinced he simply hadn't heard the remark. For
surely the major was acting queerly, something must
have flustered him for as they left he failed to notice the
sergeant didn't bother to salute.

Hattie had been adamant. The two rooms built for
her, Ben, and Skeeter were now part of Cheatem's
expanding house. His suggestion that they be built away,
closer to the corral, was shrugged off. "Don't want no
folks thinkin' we got us slave quarters 'round y'here, do
we?"

Cheatem studied her with a pained expression. Truth
was he didn't know what to do with her. She was the best
cook in the settlement, ran his household with an
effortless touch he had to admire, and above all he could
only get Ben and Skeeter to do what she approved of.
Other quirks in her makeup also irritated him, but he
had learned it was dangerous to suggest changes, particularly since her daughter left. Hattie may have spent her
life as a servant but she had the pluck and pugnacious
spirit of a coon-hunting dog. Nor did she show this
community any more respect than it showed her or her
people. At times it put a serious clamp on Cheatem's
subdued but ceaseless ambitions. An attempt to emulate
the Hunt's tea parties had to be dropped when Hattie
heard Flora and Charity were to be guests. "Ah ain't
serving dem wimins no tea in dis house," she said flatly.
Talk was useless. Only Cathy and Cole, and sometimes
Charlotte Barry, were warmly received in his absence,
and only when he was willing to discuss her worries
about Sam and Chloe would she sit and listen atten-
tively. It almost made him laugh at himself. Hattie was

now like a boulder sitting in the roadway of his life. He could work around her but he couldn't move her. But aggravating as she was, even Silas Cheatem had to admire her refusal to be, or allow her people to be, abused, and in spite of many painful public rebuffs her demand for respect never lessened.

The settlement, readying for winter, had started quietly ignoring the blacks, except for Dillby, who began to question the propriety of their holding services on their own. Certain parishioners felt something pagan about it. He visited the Boggs one blowy day, with a crisp scent of snow in the air, and settled before all three with his Bible. "Be assured the matter has been given considerable thought," he began, "but we think it preferable you come to services with the rest of the community. I assure you you'll find it most comforting and I daresay uplifting. Let me remove any doubts you may have about the feelings of others, we are all true Christians here and believe in charity toward all."

Hattie looked at him long and hard. "Preacher, we done give dis a mite of thought us'selves, but we is kind of used to singin' and prayin' on our own. 'Course we Christians jus like you folks, and we gots plenty charity too, if y'all want to come and join us, sure as gospel ain't a soul here gonna say a word."

The council that began with the arrival of the powerful Whistling Elk, and an array of other chiefs, soon dominated Black Otter's camp. But it wasn't a completely harmonious gathering, even on the issue of white false promises. Black Otter's raiding, continued during the agreed peace, was known to many rival chiefs, and more than one suspected it might have caused the failure of goods to be delivered. But it was too late for recriminations. Many of the tribesmen, mistakenly counting on the supplies, had not prepared properly for winter. Though war was on many lips they were not ready for it, and several warrior leaders rose in council to say as much. Red Hand, whom Sam now knew was the main warrior leader of Black Otter's band, stood by the fire and to the astonishment of many demanded that Black

Otter be made head chief, who, because of his skill at marauding, could plan and lead a successful revenge attack upon the whites. Though a host of young braves, angry and chafing for action, cheered this suggestion, other more sober heads cast glances at Whistling Elk, who, until it was known the supplies were not coming, discouraged all talk of war. Now however a chief's thoughts meant little, fury and outrage were steadily mounting among the braves, and even Whistling Elk knew there was no hope for peace.

The great aging headman slowly came to his feet. He was a proud and perceptive man who had been a fearsome warrior in his time. He knew little about the great war the whites were having in the east, but he knew most of the soldiers had been withdrawn from the frontier, and the fort was now being held by only a handful of men. Yet Whistling Elk saw beyond the stresses of the day. Clearly the whites had been weakened by events beyond his knowing, but Whistling Elk had lived long enough to remember the whites being weak before. Somehow they always grew stronger after a few snows, and whole tribes resisting them, or striking them while they were weak, were not only defeated but driven from their hunting grounds and made to live in distant, arid country devoid of pride or even hope. But the ears of this maddened throng were hardly ready for such reflections. Whatever mask was put on it, chiefs who had touched the peace pen had lost face, with Black Otter seeming the only one wise enough to see through white treachery.

But if they must fight they had to fight cleverly, putting the whites where they would be anxious to make peace again. Yet with violent firebrands like Black Otter, driven by hatred of the *tahbay-boh* and drawing great power from their recent shameful betrayal, it wouldn't be easy.

"Listen to me, brothers," Whistling Elk began. "We cannot raise our weapons in war with the frost giant ready to descend from the mountains; soon he will silence the rivers and drive away the game. Listen to what the spirits have taught our fathers, what many wars have taught us will bring victory. Let us live through the snow moons by sending our hunters south to find buffalo or west for the great *wapiti*. Until the grass comes to give our ponies strength again we must sharpen our weapons and seek better ones. When the ponies are strong again, and the great spirit brings back the buffalo, our war cries will be as thunder upon the prairie as we drive these whites from our lands!"

They were good words; they pleased all but Black Otter, who was now standing, his face streaked with ocher and vermillion, across the leaping fire. "We cannot sit before the tipi flap gossiping like old squaws while these whites go on infesting our lands. Are we warriors if we put food and the comforts of the lodge before killing our enemies?"

"Our old and weak ones must eat," answered Whistling Elk stoutly. "It does little good to kill our enemies if hunger and sickness steal spirits from our lodges while we do."

A chorus of assent, particularly from the chiefs, added new lines to Black Otter's already visibly straining face. "And what of the trails?" he shouted. "Are the *tahbayboh* going to travel through our hunting grounds, bringing goods that should have been ours to exchange for Mexican silver?"

There was a long silence. Almost everyone forgot the treaty was really to insure the whites' passage to the west. Now that the treaty had been broken that right was gone. Black Otter had shrewdly tied whites trading with Mexicans for profit to the Indian loss, which, true or not, warriors, enraged at what they thought a brazen deceit, were ready to believe. But Whistling Elk was not one of them. He knew illicit traders from New Mexico also used those trails, traders who were the Plains Indians' only source of guns. Blocking those trails, particularly the one to Santa Fe, would cut them off from a vital supply of weapons, and Black Otter's bloodthirsty band, spreading death along the valley of the Cimarron, was likely to do just that.

There was much talk among the chiefs; supplies of
guns and particularly ammunition were critical matters
when fighting well-armed whites. Though Black Otter
had mustered considerable support, many of the chiefs
began to share Whistling Elk's concern. After much
wrangling Black Otter was advised he could attack the
whites going south to Santa Fe, but Mexicans coming
north must be turned back with only warnings. Whistling Elk cautioned Black Otter, deliberately within the
hearing of all, that violating this tribal ruling would
make his own people his enemies, a dire threat even the
rebellious Black Otter couldn't ignore.

Before sundown Black Otter had left with his band,
swollen by a multitude of new braves with blackened
faces, the color of death, while the remaining chiefs sat
in a somber circle, drawing rude maps on the ground
with pointed sticks, talking of the numbers needed to
overwhelm the fort and raze and destroy every white
settlement between the Arkansas and the Smoky Hill.
The red pipe of war had already been sent to other
camps, for the Kiowas and particularly the Comanches
had bands dwelling hundreds of miles to the south and
west. Distant chiefs would know what that pipe meant.
They would start readying their people, making medicine and putting power into amulets to be sewn into
their young men's hair. War hatchets and scalping knives
would be sharpened and bullets for the rare rifles hidden
away. They had only a few short moons to wait before
the great and bloody war the red pipe promised would
rid their hunting grounds of this pestilence called the
tahbay-boh forever.

Dennis and Chloe had traveled several days below the
Arkansas before striking the dry bed of the Cimarron,
telling them they had almost crossed the *Jornada,* that
stretch of trail that terrified earlier travelers. Warned of
its dryness, they had brought a barrel of water from the
Arkansas, and soon began to see little arrow signs
pointing to small water holes, and even an occasional
dwelling, sitting lonely and brave on the barren prairie.

More and more often they saw wagon ruts in the ground and knew they were keeping to the trail. The dwellings they passed were usually empty but occasionally a single prospector or trapper was holed up in one, not sure of how long he'd stay or be heading next. One lonely-looking old prospector, who couldn't keep his eyes off Chloe, warned that the recent quiet meant nothing; Indians were still a threat. "Won't be sure yer shut of 'em till you reach the Beaver," he cautioned. "There be bones aplenty along this stretch to fill a fair-sized town." His eyes still strangely followed Chloe as they left.

Though many days passed, their journey toward the southwest seemed endless, and they met only one caravan of Mexicans coming north, for it was the worst time of year for travel. Heavy winds from the north and west shook the wagon and brought dust storms that nearly blinded when not choking them, and as they moved further south they were hit by torrential rains that lasted only a few minutes but sent brimming rivulets across the trail, bogging the wagon down in mud. It made for slow going, endless labor, and exasperating delays in reaching the Beaver, proving in the end to be the most taxing part of the trip. But they plodded on, unaware this torturous pace was opening the door to tragedy. For empty as that country seemed many miles to the north Black Otter's band was racing over their tracks, also heading for the Beaver, the very spot he had chosen to cut the trail. Any whites not already south of that stream would soon be in the maw of death.

Dennis and Chloe were still a few miles above the stream when they decided to stop and camp for the night. It had been a difficult day, and Chloe was near tears with fatigue. Her pregnancy was beginning to drain her strength and even heating some coffee and stale biscuits seemed a chore beyond her command. Dennis, as always, carefully tending the horses and clearing away hardened mud from the wagon wheels, was in truth exhausted too, and for once both could hardly wait to roll in the blankets and sleep. It was a strange night with a lowering sky overhead, blacking out the stars and allowing only a faint flush to mark the silent passage of the moon. But sometime past midnight, Dennis and Chloe, a couple already sorely plagued by fate, were to know the most ghastly awakening of their lives.

 **38**

There were snow flurries in the air when Quarles returned to Leavenworth. There he discovered the northern tribes, faced with cold weather, had dispatched a delegation of two chiefs with large followings to demand supplies. A blunt rebuff by the officer of the day, whose orders were to allow no Indians on the post, had already led to hostilities. A bloody attack on the last supply train of the season had effectively cut the trail to Laramie.

The general, looking more irritated than worried, shook his head. His mind was on the Union's attempt to fight its way down the Mississippi Valley, where he should have had a command, instead of holding this post on the edge of nowhere, its lack of importance invidiously suggesting his own. He had no troops to police distant immigrant trails, likely to get themselves snowbound and impossible to support. His one response to inquiries about the safety of settlers was "Tell 'em to evacuate!"

Those pleading that hard-won dwellings and farm fixtures left unprotected were certain to be destroyed by Indians were turned away. "In war we all got to suffer!" he snapped, dismissing even petitioners from the governor's office.

Quarles, uneasy in ways he couldn't express, tried to find comfort in Lee's assurance that real trouble was still a few months away. "But come the thaw and first grass you'd best keep an eye out," the scout quietly opined. "Figure by then all hell is a'gonna be breakin' loose, unless someone smarter than this horse comes up with an answer."

Quarles glanced at him, his mouth faintly rigid with concern. "What about our friends on Smoky Hill?"

Lee started to answer with a smile, but it died aborning. He had no friends on Smoky Hill but he understood what prompted the question. "Henry, I sure ain't no prophet, but chances are if they hit the fort first, should be time for those Sadler folks to make tracks east."

Quarles pulled thoughtfully at an earlobe. "Think that's how it sets up, eh?"

"My thinking don't make it so, but if the fort puts up a fight most settlers should have time to git clear."

Quarles produced a bottle and neither man spoke again until they had downed a stiff drink. "Jesus, it's cold," said Quarles.

Lee swallowed his drink, rubbing his stomach as the warmth reached it. "Better pray it gits colder . . . redskins under buffalo robes ain't very handy with scalpin' knives."

Sam soon realized he was not only a prisoner but a slave. The fat squaw would poke him with her stick and point to where firewood was piled. Without waiting for more painful jabs he would join young boys bringing driftwood from the river or buffalo chips from the plain. She also had him fetching bowls of water to her tipi, and carrying away leftovers from her many meals. He was given no hint of what was in store for him, but from the many scalps he saw around camp, and the row of skulls sitting inside the medicine squaw's tipi, he reckoned life, at best, was a tricky business among these menacing faces.

To his shock he discovered he was not the only captive in camp. He had noticed some females across the circle, trudging back and forth, continually harassed and occasionally struck by a group of wicked-looking old crones.

At first he thought they were simply captured enemy squaws, who, when the braves were through with them, had been turned over to merciless hags who had lost a son or a husband to their tribe. But in spite of the filth in which they lived, he suddenly realized two of the slaving women were white. It took him a day or two to get close enough to talk to them, but once they discovered who he was, they watched whenever he went for water and if possible, seizing any handy container, followed him. After a few muted exchanges he discovered one's name was Sara, she was from Texas and had been taken with her child on the Brazos. The child had been killed and she repeatedly raped before being turned over to these embittered old squaws to torment and enslave. She knew she had been made pregnant but didn't know by whom, though Red Hand had kept her in his lodge, humiliating and abusing her for many days. Appalled as Sam was, her next words shocked him even more. Now she only wanted to die but lacked the courage to take her own life. Would Sam help her?

Sam, aghast at the prospect, urgently whispered to keep her hopes up; help might come. But it was clear his words only drove her into a deeper abyss of despair. She was so disgraced in her own eyes she didn't want to be rescued. Her reflection in the river told her she had aged grotesquely, her skin was caked with dirt and her eyes looked fever racked. Her once well-shaped body was now an obscenity, covered with flesh wounds and draining sores. God forbid her young husband should ever see her again; if he did he would fall to his knees, praying for her death.

Sam came away shocked at the brutality this poor woman had endured. If God allowed this to happen to a poor defenseless woman, what awaited a sinner with evil thoughts who didn't even sing in church?

It was much harder to get to know the second one called Carrie, who was at most sixteen, for on his first approach she seemed too petrified with fright to speak. It was some time before he discovered her family had been killed and she captured on the San Saba. She had been raped many times and incredibly felt it almost a relief to be turned over to these pitiless squaws. He got only hints of the vileness of her earlier handling by a string of brutal and surely sadistic braves, an ordeal that clearly fractured her sanity. He continually caught her staring past him as though seeing terrifying figures in the sky beyond. Often when she rose she stumbled about, having lost her sense of direction. Sam never felt so helpless, never so unfit to be the one turned to by others for help.

But his own suffering was shortly to increase. The obese medicine squaw began to take him into her tipi, where kneeling before her he held skulls as she chanted incantations and filled them with animal blood and strange grasses. When she was not eating she was making magic and treated objects others brought to her for *puha,* power. But the smell of decaying skulls and bones, or animal parts not properly cleaned, combined with the fat squaw's endless and voluminous flatulence, soon had Sam nauseous to the point where he was too dizzy to hold steady the objects being invested with magic.

Misjudging his plight, she assumed he was trying to disrupt her secret rituals and beat him soundly. But his punishment actually saved him for she ended by forcing him to kneel and hold a skull up to the moon for half the night. But this at least got him outside, where his head cleared, his stomach settled, and his mind came back to normal. He knew now the gemstone amulet she wore around her neck was the source of her power, for she rubbed it after every word of magic uttered. Still by dawn the sharp stick was in his side again and she was pointing to a nearby pot that was just beginning to smoke. He took a bowl and filled it with half-cooked meat, which the squaw took into her tipi, deliberately ignoring the approach of the now scowling Red Hand. The war leader had come with a well-decorated robe and some sticks of vermillion. He left them outside the tipi, but not in the way they would have been left had he wanted them endowed with magic. They were a gift, and when he returned later with several horses, Sam, by watching closely, was able to determine what his gifts were for.

* * *

The frantic teamsters of the Mexican mule train, finding themselves surrounded by Comanches, started crossing themselves and calling upon their patron saints. The cruel features of Black Otter were suddenly confronting them. He might have been the devil springing out of the desert, demanding their souls for hell. The caravan boss trembled with fear as Black Otter told him to turn back, the trail was closed. But the man's fear visibly turned to gratitude when the shaking Mexican realized he and his companions weren't to be slaughtered, only deprived of this opportunity for profit. His gratitude, and a desperate hope it wasn't misplaced, led to food and wine being laid out to reward the fierce-looking savages for their unintended clemency, a gesture not without certain risks.

Black Otter did not want to delay but they had come from the Arkansas, a long, exhausting ride, and the warriors were reluctant to pass up such appealing refreshments so easily come by. They dismounted and grabbed the peppered bread and strips of dried beef. They lifted and slugged at the wine from jugs so large it splashed over their faces and hands, which they wolfishly licked clean. It caused a gathering and just enough of a commotion to catch the eye of the lone prospector, who had left his solitary dwelling and was traveling north in the wake of the mule caravan.

From a distance he realized the train that had passed his hut earlier that morning had been stopped by a large war party; amazingly, they seemed to be feasting together. But the prospector's concern was not for the mule train but for himself. He looked at his tracks stretched out behind him. Surely if the warriors came this way they would know he was here and alone. Instinct told him to retreat and watch the direction in which they moved. He was suddenly tense and swearing nervously as he pulled his mount behind a rock outcropping, but he did not wait long. The caravan leader, seeing the warriors slugging more wine, wisely started his men and mules back down the trail. The old prospector, watching in the distance, needed no more. Only one fact fitted here; the trail was closed. If the Mexicans were being spared, made only to turn back, the Americans were in trouble. He mounted and rode as hard as he could to the south.

Sam understood no Comanche but he was getting a feel for sign language and gestures that indicated emotions of anger or joy. The fat squaw was not particularly sociable but he noticed those she deigned to talk to let her do most of the talking. Her name, he had already discovered, was Bad Eyes, a title appropriate enough for one who reduced a man's vision with foul odors. But Red Hand, coming with his horses, had apparently on this occasion decided to do some talking himself.

After a long speech he pointed at the horses and the decorated robe still lying by the tipi flap. He ended by pointing several times at Bad Eyes, herself, who kept staring back at him fiercely. It was a while before Sam decided Red Hand wanted to trade for something that Bad Eyes wasn't willing to part with. A cold shaft of fear suddenly impaled him as he began to suspect it was himself. The war chief had the look of a brutal and merciless master; repulsive as Bad Eyes was, he preferred to take his chances with her.

It took another quarter of an hour, and many rough exchanges, before Sam realized Red Hand wasn't pointing at Bad Eyes but at the amulet around her neck. It was her source of magic or medicine he wanted, and his imperious manner implied he had some claim on it. He finally left, taking his horses and his robe with him, as Bad Eyes, now resentful and deeply angered, reached for her pointed stick and, jabbing Sam in his rump, made him jump toward the parfleche used for water. This she did as she laid on his head a string of invectives he didn't understand but heard her punctuate with a fart.

The storms that piled up over the Rockies as the year ended abruptly started whistling down the eastern slopes, bringing a cataract of icy air that made shoulders hunch and faces turn downwind or burrow into collars. The sheer bite of the wind made all but the heaviest clothing unable to retain the warmth of life. Without proper cover frost petrified hands and feet and all exposed skin waxed blue. For those who had never wintered on the prairie their first exposure was fraught with danger. The cold is unrelenting, the wind drives its icy tongs through the flesh and chills the bones. Blizzards obliterate all landmarks and snowdrifts cut a man off from his well, his woodpile, his neighbor. There is no game, bringing wolves closer to the settlements, howling about barns where straggling livestock, without warmth and often fodder, struggle to hang on to life. Travel is nigh impossible and wandering too far from shelter involves risks few people run twice. In clear spells paths would be dug and people could move about, particularly if they had that rarest of items on the frontier, a horse-drawn sleigh, but most clung to their hearth and prayed for spring. Only a few kept a troubled eye on the passing of winter, quietly suspecting the coming spring might not be the joyous one for which the settlement so fervently prayed.

39

A high wind was driving dark clouds out of the northwest as the old prospector pressed his pony as hard as he dared, keeping to the trail as best he could, but hoping at some point to turn off and conceal himself in stretches of scrub pine or ponderosa appearing on low hills to his right. Only one thing kept him moving southward throughout the day. He could not conceal his tracks, he could only hope the war party would miss them when he turned off. That they would miss them in broad daylight was a risk only greenhorns, unseasoned in these parts, would take, but after dark the odds would favor him, after dark he could dismount and lead his horse over rocky ground, where hoofprints left little sign, easily missed in the darkness. His trail, once lost, would never be found again.

He was a strange man, this prospector, a loner who had taken to the hills to escape a broken life and a failure to make his mark on civilization. He was well built, with the energy and strength that comes from a lifetime of fighting rugged terrain. He had made only a few minor strikes, which curiously satisfied him, knowing by now he was not seeking fortune but something far more elusive, freedom from guilt. There were many like him. The west was vast, much of it still uncharted, fugitives of all stripes soon became faceless, their earlier history dissolved, their persons as anonymous as the barren hills. This particular wanderer was running from the sight of fire consuming his wife and child, a fire started by a oil lamp smashed as he collapsed drunk on a kitchen floor.

At first, desperate for absolution, he had tried to make a fortune in business, hoping to provide a home for orphaned children or women abandoned by husbands as derelict as he. But he lacked the talents for business, his one venture down the Santa Fe Trail was wiped out by rampaging Indians and he hadn't the resources for another. It was then he was struck by word of gold strikes in the west and decided, with God guiding him in his supplicating mission, he would find that fortune in the earth, a fantasy thirty years of effort had not erased.

He had not forgotten Chloe. She had captured his gaze because of the lonely torment in her eyes that reminded him of his long-suffering wife, enduring a fate she could not understand. From the mixed and confused tracks of the wagon he realized the young couple had encountered many delays, often being forced to dig out of mud or escape deep rocky holes washed clean by heavy rains. Surely they had made very poor time. Toward the end of the day, with his horse lathered and himself beginning to tire he realized the wagon tracks were fresher than they should have been if those youngsters had reached and crossed the Beaver days before. There was no question the Comanches saw those same tracks, and with their uncanny skills knew they were overtaking this prey. Perhaps, sensing a capture near, they might even be redoubling their efforts. Suddenly he was perplexed; darkness was settling over the plain, the time to escape was drawing near. His horse could not last much longer. The high wind, harrying clouds all day, had come down to punish the land. Even on the southern plains winter was a time of treacherous weather, freezing sleet and even snow often striking without warning. A deep chill ran through the prospector's body as he rested his horse and studied the land about him. He sat there outlined against the fading sky. A man in a quandary, a man fighting his past, agonizing over his present, and warily glimpsing his future, a future still fettered with guilt. Was there really redemption for him in this world or was he destined to wander forever, thinking the key to salvation lay over the next hill? A solitary wolf appeared on a mound of earth fifty yards ahead. The wolf looked old, worn, abandoned by the pack. The prospector stared at the exhausted animal, sniffing desperately for familiar odors in the wind, and sensed he was looking at himself.

At the fort the grimness of winter was setting in, guard duty had become a frigid ordeal, and supplies, among them liquor, were running low. The sicknesses that bedeviled barrack life in these arctic months began to appear. The post surgeon, watching his rising sick list, appealed to the major. "Sir, we got to have half a dozen medicines we're out of and the men must start getting fresh food. I've got stomach ailments piling up daily and men running high fevers in an infirmary that could pass for an icehouse. Conditions have to improve or I can't take responsibility for the health of the command."

The major answered him dryly. "I can't give you what I haven't got," he responded. "Nothing is coming through from Leavenworth and hunters report game has all but disappeared."

"Well, it's my responsibility to advise you our sick can't be returned to duty if conditions don't improve."

"Will you put that in writing?"

"If you wish." The doctor looked ready to leave but his expression suddenly registered concerns deeper than those expressed. "Are we expected to hold this fort all winter?"

"We're expected to follow orders."

"Might I ask what those orders are?"

The major considered the surgeon for a moment. The doctor wasn't one of his favorites. The man had been pointedly suggesting he stop his drinking. With liquor for the troops in short supply, his frequent overindulgence was affecting morale. Yet he needed the doctor for a plan he had been contemplating, and was slowly working out. "We're to hold this fort as long as we can," he said without emphasis, "in the event of a major uprising we're to burn it and return to Leavenworth."

The surgeon studied the surface of the major's desk for a moment, then lifted his head to fix the other with his stare. "Major, sick men can't be left behind, make sure we evacuate while there's still enough healthy hands to get my hospital cases back to safety. I know the army isn't concerned about lives, but trying to hold this fort with a handful of wretchedly supplied men defies sanity. If anything epidemic breaks out we're finished!"

The major stroked his chin. "As I've said, perhaps you'd be willing to put your professional opinion in writing."

"Believe me, Major, I will!"

The major quietly watched the figure of the doctor rising and briskly stamping out, almost breaking into the smile that had been subtly forming around his eyes. He had spoken earlier to the sergeant of scouts and Dice, their most experienced guide. Both had reported trouble in the making, Dice particularly pointing out that with the first grass a major attack was inevitable.

The major had already decided not to wait for the first grass, but didn't wish to appear to be destroying an army post out of fear. He would need corroboration of the imminent overwhelming threats hanging over them, it must seem he had saved his command from a serious defeat if not annihilation. Only in that light could his career be protected. Now with Dice's reports, carefully worded by himself, and the surgeon's dire prophecies about such a weakly supplied garrison, he was ready to act. That night he dined well and drank heavily, after all they'd soon be where food and liquor would be available for all.

Black Otter was seething with rage. After their long race south to cut the trail, the warriors, sleepy or becoming recalcitrant because of widespread gulping of wine, were beginning to straggle behind. As they overtook the caravan again the chief in his anger smashed every barrel with his hatchet, but this act openly displeased many braves and drew howls of disapproval from a few. It could have been a mistake and he knew it. He was experienced enough to be wary of disgruntled warriors, there was little to keep them from deserting without warning. Indians willingly followed popular leaders but loyalty was often a matter of whim.

It had been another mistake to come without Red Hand, a war leader respected and even feared, but that warrior would not leave camp without his medicine, an amulet taken from a slain Osage chief, one Bad Eyes had seized during the attack and refused to return. Since Bad Eyes was Black Otter's sister, and a formidable medicine woman, Red Hand had not tried to demand it but was offering to barter it back. Bad Eyes, suspicious of having such a powerful source of medicine in another's hands, had rejected every offer. One day that promised to bring grave trouble.

But here Black Otter, his eye on the trail, knew there was a rider only a short distance ahead of them, a rider going south, likely a *tahbay-boh*. They could follow his tracks as long as it was light but with darkness they would disappear. Instinct told the chief this rider knew they were behind him, and was waiting for darkness to make his escape. Also, though at first he had paid little attention, for the ruts seemed too old, too wind-filled to date, he was beginning to notice those wagon tracks were steadily getting fresher as he led his drawn-out war party southward. The wagon had been stalled for long periods, mud and the rough terrain had slowed its progress, and its occupants were not experienced travelers. There were no imprints of planks, dealing with mud, or pivotal stones used to leverage wagons out of holes. Black Otter, looking back at his lagging war party, began to wonder if he couldn't excite them with promises of a few scalps and loot. If he could this prize might soon be theirs.

He would try.

The old prospector, resting his horse, stared into the darkness as the best part of an hour slipped by. Only a sudden flash of lightning on the distant horizon alerted him to the need to move. But there was no helping it. Impulses unlike any he had experienced before were crowding his mind, arresting his thoughts, trapping and reshaping his fear. It was one of those moments when deep, inarticulate emotions cast life in a different mold, when values are found wanting and new visions emerge, when a man realizes a part of himself has awakened and must be heard.

He knew the young couple would follow the trail and even in the darkness could be easily tracked, just as these wily redskins would be doing. Surely by now the wagon couldn't be far from the Beaver and might even have crossed it, but something nagged at him. This couple was ignorant of their peril; if they stopped this side of the stream darkness would hardly save them. The thought of pregnant Chloe falling into Comanche hands suddenly galled him. Here was a woman and a forming child whose fate might easily match that of two who faced a fire still burning in his memory. He had seen what Comanches did to captured women; the thought spawned an anger that clamored for decisions. Perhaps he had been wrong, perhaps it wasn't money he needed but a chance to fight the evils of this sinister, sin-ridden world. Perhaps it wasn't in dreams or even endeavors that his redemption lay, perhaps it lay in simple courage. Perhaps a man saw himself differently when serving something beyond himself, beyond even his own salvation.

Within minutes he was mounted and moving down

the trail. Behind him a storm was coming out of the
north, lightning and a distant roll of thunder occasionally teasing his senses, telling him a storm was slowly
veering his way. A violent thunderstorm might help,
Indians had a strange awe of lightning, but it was foolish
to count on it. On these plains a storm could easily move
off and leave a canopy of stars glittering overhead.
However, a dim moon rising to his left was half masked
with dark tendrils of fast-moving clouds. The old prospector put his money on rain.

Hours later he would have put his money on trouble,
for a mile or two from the Beaver he spotted a wagon
looming in the darkness, his momentary relief brutally
cut short, for at that very moment an owl started
hooting on his right and was answered immediately by a
second closer on his left. In this country owls didn't
answer each other like that. Now was the time for
courage.

40

The sleep that comes from deep exhaustion is not easily
thrown off. The mind sinks to levels well below consciousness and one's awakening must come about in
steps. If it comes too quickly it comes with a shock,
making the sleeper feel he is hurling through fog to
collide with reality. Chloe, always a light sleeper, was
already stirring, enough to faintly hear the rumble of
thunder, husky and horizonal, like distant cannon. She
was not yet ready to wake up; her limbs still ached and
the warmth of the blankets seemed a balm too soothing
to surrender, but she could hear Dennis breathing heavi-

ly, dimly grasping his exhaustion was surely greater than hers. His one hand was still across her stomach, making her draw her legs up to complete a turning maneuver. This effort awakened her a little more, but then suddenly she was peering out through fine slits in her eyelids, trying to see into the darkness beyond, chilled by a premonition something was wrong.

The advancing storm did not bother her but she knew every creak and groan in that wagon, and someone's hand on a sideboard had brought a slight straining noise, rising only to be swept off by the wind. She prayed it was only her imagination but something in her brain sounded an alarm. Raising her head she listened so hard she could hear her own heart pounding. Somewhere owls were hooting and a fresh peal of thunder warned the storm was drawing near. Dennis moved in his sleep and his breathing changed rhythm. Her hands rose to grip her mouth. Should she get up? Awake Dennis? Reach for the gun that lay over their heads? . . . Bury herself under the blankets and die of fright? Now someone was at the tailgate. In turning one of her feet had slipped out from the blanket, and as though the angel of death were reaching for her she felt a hand grabbing her foot and screamed in a screech of terror that brought Dennis up, flaying his arms desperately, attempting to both awaken and pull Chloe to him. A figure could now be seen outlined against the charcoal sky, hissing lowly, "Shush . . . shu . . . shu . . . for God's sake shush!"

There was an eerie moment of silence, while Dennis fought for his bearings and reached back blindly for his gun. "Who the hell are you?"

"You met me up the trail . . . but forget that, you're surrounded here and there ain't no time for talk."

"Surrounded?" gasped Dennis. "By who?"

"Comanches, they've been tracking you for a spell."

Once again owl hoots penetrated the night. Chloe clung to her husband's arm. "Dear Jesus, what are we going to do?"

The prospector's voice had become a hoarse whisper, struggling against a sense of urgency and hazard. "Storm is about to hit, likely they'll wait for it to quit . . . maybe they'll even wait till dawn . . . but you sure as hell can't stay here."

Chloe's fingers were digging into Dennis's arm. "What . . . what are we going to do?"

The old man was silent for a moment. "Soon as this storm breaks saddle two of your horses and get across the Beaver. Keep going till you find good cover . . . don't spend time looking back."

By now Dennis was on his knees, reaching over the tailgate for the old man, seizing his shoulder, pulling him closer. "What about our wagon?"

"They're watching the wagon. I'll take it across . . . know the stream a site better than you."

"All our things," whined Chloe, "all we have is here! We can't lose our wagon."

"Lady, you don't worry about losing anything when you're running for your life."

Dennis was hurrying about now, lowering himself from the wagon, pulling on his boots, when a great bolt of lightning suddenly struck nearby, shaking the ground and filling the surrounding area with its eerie light. The thunder that followed brought a brusque wind that struck the wagon and within moments a sheet of rain came down upon them with a deafening roar.

"Best git going," shouted the prospector, "this ain't gonna last."

Dennis was soon soaked to the skin saddling the horses, but his mind was in a growing turmoil, trying to decide if what he was doing was right. Maybe the old man was wrong, maybe they weren't surrounded, maybe they could fight off whatever was threatening them. But something about the night and the resolute quality in the old man's voice told him their peril was real, and their chance of escape even less than he implied. The loss of the wagon already seemed a certainty. Chloe couldn't help grabbing things she couldn't bring herself to part with, as the old man kept cautioning her to ride light, while helping to tie a blanket around her. "It won't keep you dry," he muttered in her ear, "but it'll help keep some warm in."

Dennis took his gun and pistol and a pocket flint, quickly pulling his old coat about him as he helped Chloe to the saddle. With lightning flashing all about them the horses became fractious and difficult to control. Dennis deliberately kept the reins to Chloe's horse as he mounted, knowing he'd feel better leading her mount than running the risk of losing her in the storm.

The old prospector moved quickly to hitch the other horses to the wagon as they left, Dennis only shaking his hand and Chloe quietly accepting his arm about her shoulders to express their gratitude for saving their lives. But neither, including the old man, were even faintly convinced their lives were saved. They were still in barren country, there was nothing but empty plains in every direction as far as the eye could see. The storm would finally let up, daylight would come, and, once again, the Comanches would be free to stalk this country they knew so well.

Black Otter was still in a testy mood. It had been a tormenting day, with his warriors either sulky or unruly, first because of the wine and then because of its aftereffects. It took continual urging to keep them moving south. At sundown he called a halt to harangue them for not hotly pursuing their enemies and asking for volunteers to race ahead in the darkness and overtake a wagon that was surely not more than an hour's swift ride ahead.

Night was not a popular time for braves to pursue enemies. If death came the spirit, lost in darkness, would wander forever. The chief groaned to himself. Now did he not need Red Hand! The fiery war leader would have raged at these men, making the sign for cowardliness and shaking his stick of scalps contemptuously in their face. Stung by the lash of that scathing tongue they would have roused themselves and continued on, but Black Otter, though a wily and cunning fighter, was not an orator; his plea brought only five braves forward with their horses. Well, so be it. Five might well be enough. When they rode off flashes of lightning were streaking the northern sky and Black Otter was grasping a medicine bundle inside his shirt, for in it lay the teeth of a

puma, wrapped in weasel skin. Savagery and guile were
the powers given to him by the spirits. He now intended
to use them.

By the time they discovered the wagon, the storm had
overtaken them, but they saw the old prospector approaching and Black Otter knew the single tracks, lost in
the early darkness, belonged to this solitary figure. His
warriors had been spread out in the brush to surround
the wagon, planning to attack from all sides, but the
arrival of the old prospector changed the picture. Black
Otter gave two owl hoots, which meant delay the attack.
This newcomer would surely alert occupants of the
wagon, which probably contained two, that would make
three against his six, good but not the kind of odds
Comanches liked. Three alert defenders, getting off even
a single shot, would cut his force in half. Besides the
storm was bearing down upon them, and bad storms
made for treacherous fighting conditions. Lightning
blinded the eye and thunder drowned out the enemy's
movements. Still now they could wait, the clumsy wagon
could never escape them and that lone rider could easily
be picked off when daylight came.

The storm, with a mighty clap of thunder, finally
broke with a vengeance and a curtain of rain descended
to conceal three fearful figures beside a wagon, surrounded by six hideously painted faces, squatting in
heavy brush, stoically waiting in the darkness for this
awesome downpour to end.

With the rain whipping his face and soaking through
his clothes, Dennis slowly made his way forward over
the rough and broken ground that still plagued the trail
approaching the stream. His horse needed strong handling for the frequent flashes of lightning and ear-
splitting cracks of thunder kept it rearing away, trying to
bolt in fear. It was almost as though the horse sensed
death was riding this storm, its deadly flashes balefully
closing in and engulfing it. Chloe's mount, following,
was only slightly calmer. When they reached the stream
Dennis was soaked to the skin but, aided by a wide fork
of lightning, now managed a glimpse at Chloe, whose

hands were clutching the pommel and whose head was buried behind a cuff of blanket. He was glad the storm had just started and the stream was still low. He was across it in no time and soon climbed to high ground. He began to brush against heavy foliage and occasional lightning revealed distant stands of trees. It could be time to look for cover, there was only a few hours left until dawn. He knew he, and surely Chloe, could not get their wagon out of their minds. Even if it were looted there might be things left behind, things important to them. It was his reluctance to lose the wagon that had him pulling up the first time he realized a lessening of the pounding rain told him he was under some trees. As he brought her horse up, Chloe's face found his in the darkness. "Where are we?" her voice trembled and her face looked pale against the night.

"I don't know, but we better wait for a spell."

"Dennis." Chloe's striving to put simple words together was a sign she was in pain. "What we gonna do without our wagon?"

He reached out and gripped her shoulder. "We're gonna do whatever the good Lord has in store for us . . . Chloe, if your mother were here she'd be praying to God. Mebbe we best do too."

They were silent for a moment, Dennis quietly but urgently praying and Chloe looking up at the heavy streaks of lightning and sinking within her blanket, as though to escape the heavier and heavier peals of thunder, but her mind was on her stomach. Her prayers would have shocked him, for she had just felt the first movement of life within her, followed by a strange pain that warned her not to climb to that saddle again.

The old man had a challenging time getting the wagon to the stream. It kept bogging down in pools of mud and once the wheels were locked between protruding rocks and he had to turn the wagon around slowly, backing and twisting away many times to escape. The storm and the constant demands on them made the struggling horses rank but he couldn't afford to rest them. He sensed far too much time was passing and anxiously noticed the rain was lessening and the wind shifting around to the west. Then a hundred yards from the stream he felt the front left wheel sinking into a deep crevice of mud. There had been no warning. Deceiving pools of water lay everywhere, and though the team labored to pull free, the wheel, rocking back and forth, failed to break loose. The old man spent no time swearing at his luck. He had to get across that stream; his desperate plan depended upon it. The crevice had to be filled to give the wheel traction and clay wouldn't work, it would only turn to more mud. He needed gravel and for that he had to hurry to the stream bed. Using his hat he took a load back and dumped it beside the wheel, but clearly he was going to need many such loads to bring the wheel free. Time kept slipping by, the rain stopped, and dark clouds milled about overhead as he nervously watched for a faint flush in the east, warning dawn was coming. The flush had already started when the wagon finally pulled loose and the old man, now near exhaustion, worked his way into the stream and with only one tricky moment where the wagon almost overturned he made it to the opposite shore. There he pulled the wagon up thirty feet from the water, and taking his own horse retreated another fifty yards into some heavy foliage. There he left his gun and hurried his horse back another hundred yards where he concealed it among some dwarf trees. Back at his gun he was finally ready, the moment when his hurried plan would be tested could only be moments away.

Even during the storm the Indians were aware the wagon was moving, but where could it go? Not expecting anyone to leave at the height of the storm they had missed Dennis and Chloe slipping off, but now they were stalking the old man, grunting to each other in the darkness, eagerly awaiting daylight.

Black Otter's mind was on killing these *tahbay-boh*, but he sensed his warriors' minds were also on loot. He didn't care about the contents of the wagon; when fighting the *tejanos* only firearms were taken. Men encountered were slain, women and children abducted, scalps of the dead lifted while their wagons burned. He was a master of striking hard and disappearing quickly, a tactic that made him deadly against unwary settlers. His plan was to kill any of these enemies he could before attacking the wagon. He did not want to return to his band, reporting the death of even one brave who had chosen to follow him.

Still using the darkness and ready thickets of dark foliage to conceal themselves, they watched the wagon crossing the stream, grunting with satisfaction when the first faint light revealed it had stopped on the other side, sitting above the water line, apparently resting the horses after their long ordeal. Black Otter, gazing intently through the paltry light, saw no sign of movement, no figures hurrying about the wagon. He didn't like it. As more light fed in from the east the warriors began to murmur their eagerness to attack; the wagon was as good as taken. But Black Otter wasn't ready. The stream bed made an open space where someone hiding in the foliage beyond could draw a fine bead on riders crossing from this side. He didn't like it. But his warriors were growing impatient, some horses earlier tracked were now missing from the wagon. Surely it meant the enemy had deserted their belongings and ridden off in an attempt to escape. Black Otter shook his head. He wanted two braves to slip upstream and cross over, then work down through the foliage, flushing out any danger there. But the braves looked away, the two who did this would be last to the wagon. They hadn't come this far to give others first chance at the plunder. Besides, anyone could see, for increasing light confirmed it, this wagon had been abandoned, somehow its occupants had realized the danger they were in and raced off.

Black Otter sensed insisting on his cautious approach would only turn some braves surly. But the risk he saw them taking he didn't intend to share. Making the sign for courage, he led them in a low tribal death chant, then raised his arm in the signal to attack.

They needed no urging. It had been a long night, and a

deep irritation was stirring in many of them. These *tahbay-boh* had led them a cruel chase; when taken the whites would suffer the kinds of death that brought grins of satisfaction to Comanche lips. Into the stream they rode, splashing their way across, beginning to sound the war whoop as they closed on the wagon. The first brave there jumped onto the wagon seat, the second landed with his hand on the tailgate. But suddenly with wicked abruptness death struck. A shot rang out and the brave on the wagon seat toppled over, making a failing grab for the whip socket as he fell helplessly to the ground. The one at the tailgate turned toward the spot where the roar of a rifle had come, but in the next moment he was down on one knee, trying to get under the wagon. The other three, still mounted, wheeled their horses about, two returning across the water, the third disappearing in tall brush bordering the stream below.

Black Otter began spitting furiously with rage. He saw the returning braves glaring at him in mute anger. He knew that look. Without a thought to their own impatience they were already blaming him for weak medicine. He glanced about quickly. Day was breaking. He had already lost two braves, but retreating now meant accepting defeat. A chief's power diminished with defeat. Was there not another way? Across the stream he caught sight of the warrior who had ridden into the brush, now dismounted and carefully circling around to get behind the gunman, who must be crouching up the bank beyond the wagon.

He studied the scene with new tension. At least one brave was fighting with some skill. In a covert movement he rubbed his medicine bag. Perhaps the spirits would smile on him yet.

The old prospector's gamble was half won. He had had to wait for an attack to see their numbers. Had they been twenty or thirty he would have slipped back to his mount and vanished, but five howling bucks was a different matter. Any loss he could inflict on them could easily end the fight. Indians refused to take serious losses; warriors weren't made in a day. With the whites seeming inexhaustible the Indians' diminishing man-power was every chief's nightmare. With surprise on his side he had already gotten two, but trying to get a bead on those rushing to recross the stream had caused him to miss the one slipping into brush further down the embankment. Aware one had disappeared, he had no way of knowing that warrior was already circling behind him, seeking a position that would seal his fate. But the prospector, for the moment, couldn't help feeling he was ahead, and so settled to watch daylight slowly filling the valley. For the first time since they disappeared in the storm his mind turned to the couple he had risked his life to save. He hoped by now they were long gone. He hoped by now they were racing toward the Sangre De Cristo mountains, to a long and happy life in Santa Fe. He would never be able to explain it but their salvation was really his, at least that's what he felt—it was enough.

But Dennis and Chloe were not as far away as he had hoped. Chloe's pregnancy was too far advanced to make riding astride a hard saddle over rocky terrain anything but an easy task. The pain convulsing her stomach warned her she might be harming her baby. When settled under their first cover she had shocked him by saying she could ride no further. "God!" she whispered, "if only we had our wagon." Made anxious by the anguish in her voice he cradled her in his arms for the longest time, trying to keep her warm in the damp darkness, listening to rain dripping from surrounding trees, praying and comforting each other until dawn. Dennis knew they had not gotten far. In fact he had heard the Indians' war whoops as the wagon was attacked, and now sat wondering at the silence after two solitary shots. Dennis was slowly looking about, his expression hesitant. What was happening? Chloe opened her eyes and stared back toward the stream. It was a terrible moment, the unknowing was torment. Could the savages be coming? Could the old man have been trapped and, even now, facing his end? Dennis knew from Chloe's increasing grip on him she was afraid he was going to leave, but if the old man was in trouble he deserved help. But if her fears were mounting, for Dennis waiting became unbearable. "I've got to try," he said, his eyes telling her there were imperatives in life decent men simply obeyed.

"Dennis, I'm so . . . so terribly frightened!"

"So am I . . . but that old man tried to save our lives."

She knew he was going; she struggled to smile but then instead pulled him to her and hugged him. "I'll pray," she said, choking on the words. It was a moment they'd both remember, his going could mean an end to their world, an end to their love, an end to a life that mixed the enchantment of young love with those ills of the mind and maladies of the spirit, hatred and bigotry.

Chloe was left muffling her sobs as Dennis, taking his rifle, slipped back through the lessening foliage, using small rock formations to conceal his approach as he neared the stream. When he drew close enough to spot the expanse of the valley through some dwarf trees, he dropped down and went forward, half on his knees.

Actually it was movement that caught his eye, a moving figure crossing his line of sight, apparently staying low enough for concealment, but bobbing up from time to time as though searching for something. It was the single feather held by a headband that told him he was coming up behind an Indian, an Indian who was stalking someone closer to the stream. Surely it was the old man, nothing else seemed possible. Holding his breath he saw the Indian had now stopped and was bending forward on one knee. Biting into his lip Dennis watched the man whipping an arrow from his quiver and setting it into his bow. The act galvanized him into action. He threw his rifle to his shoulder and fired. He was too close to miss and the man pitched forward; the arrow, not fully aimed, broke limply into the air. The single shot echoed through the valley, the prospector glancing back saw the arrow flying in a harmless arc and knew someone had saved his life. Black Otter, from across the stream, saw the warrior pitching forward in the foliage and realized another gun had been leveled against him. It was enough; his medicine was truly bad.

He had better withdraw before more whites came down the trail and he, with only two warriors left, was helpless to attack them.

It was some time before Dennis and the old prospector dared to work themselves together, but after a half hour the old man knew the Indians were gone and came up to where Dennis was still keeping a thicket between himself and the opposite bank. He grasped the young man's hand.

By now daylight was flooding the land and the sun coming up was painting cloud banks, still massed in the west, in the brilliant colors of dawn, crimson and gold, and a strange kind of lavender that together turned the sky into a canopy set for some sacred ritual, like light through the stained glass of a cathedral.

"By golly, I sure owe you plenty son, may you and your good wife git to Santa Fe and be happy as hell."

Dennis returned the shake firmly but a slight confusion was clouding his eyes. "Sir, you don't owe us anything . . . we're the ones who should be . . ."

"No, son, it wasn't you I owed it to, but you sure helped me pay it."

Dennis shook his head, trying to understand. "I still don't know . . ."

"T'ain't necessary, son." The old man looked at the specter in the sky. "Figure it's only important that He knows."

The major had been watching snow mount against the low buildings of the fort, aware drifts were near topping the outer walls and wagons sent for firewood were returning with both men and horses exhausted. He knew now he should have moved sooner but a series of dispatches sent to and from Leavenworth, setting the stage for abandoning the fort, took more time than calculated. Finally a blizzard struck and snow, though abating for hours at a time, continued to drive in from the north and west, blanketing every structure and drifting up with ceaseless winds until it measured fifteen feet on the flagpole and made digging paths, even within the fort, a daily chore. Studying his calendar, where he kept notes on the weather, he realized they hadn't seen the sun for a week.

The tedium of waiting was made worse by querulous discussions which surfaced every day: the surgeon urging the very sick be convoyed east at any break in the weather; the sergeant and Dice declaring decisions about the fort shouldn't be delayed because of harsh weather that might last a month.

"Why burn it?" queried the sergeant, his tone hardly reflecting their difference in rank. "Why don't we just leave it? The redskins will burn it for us."

The major stared at him, his expression conveying the other's inferior access to classified information. "The government doesn't announce everything but Leavenworth informs me it's our new policy. If we allow them to burn it they'll regard it as some kind of victory, if we burn it ourselves it says we didn't need it to hold the country."

Dice, as always, finding it hard to speak, was sitting tensely in his chair. "Major, Injuns maybe not watch. They all in camp now, some way south . . . not move around much bad weather. If you leave and no burn fort . . . weeks maybe . . . maybe more before they know."

"What the hell difference does it make?" the major was pressing back in his chair. "They're bound to find out sooner or later."

"Might make a difference to some settlers," said the sergeant. "Remember they got to be warned . . . they got to decide whether to leave or fort up!"

Settlers had completely slipped the major's mind.

This reminder sobered him and he moved up again to his desk. "Sergeant, you'll consult the post surgeon on how the sick can best be transported. I want the whole command advised that at first break in the weather we're pulling out. Dice, you'll report to me any signs of Indians in our vicinity; make sure you know from which direction they've come. We'll send a troop to warn the settlers tomorrow. Any questions?"

"Just one," replied the sergeant. "Most of our supply sheds are empty and useless. Can we pull them down and use the wood to keep fires going? Every day my men go out they return in worse shape."

The major threw him a judgmental glance. "Why didn't you think of that sooner, Sergeant?"

The sergeant refused to break eye contact, but pointedly ignored the question. "Sir, can we pull them down?"

The major grimaced, rapping the desk with his knuckles but mumbling as he turned away. "Affirmative."

Cole Sadler had his head down, bucking the driving snow as he made his way to Cheatem's. Like the rest of the settlers he made short trips to neighbors to discuss supplies or the condition of livestock weathering their first winter on the plains. Most people were reasonably well stocked. Flour, cornmeal, molasses, and salt had been shipped from Salina until the snow struck, and some pigs, chickens, and a few head of cattle had been butchered for meat. But game had vanished and only once were some deer found yarding up in a shallow valley across the Smoky Hill.

He found Cheatem's place warmed by a low fire and Silas glad to see him. Secretly he suspected the company of Hattie, Ben, and Skeeter was beginning to pall on Cheatem, particularly since Hattie insisted on singing every morning, and had started pestering him to join in. Silas had to listen daily to Hattie's prayers for Sam, Chloe, and occasionally Dennis, with Ben and Skeeter repeating her every word as though emphasis insured heaven's attention.

"When this blow lets up we ought to break some ice

and see if we can't angle a few fish from the river." Cole stamped snow from his boots before settling at the table. Cheatem went to fetch a large coffee pot from the stove.

"Damn if a few trout wouldn't taste mighty good," he said, starting to pour. "Think they'll bite in this weather?"

"They did back home. Got to give it a try anyway."

Suddenly someone was banging at the door. Cheatem, his face puzzling—a visitor, let alone two, was rare in this weather—pulled himself from his chair and went to answer it. It was Tod Barry.

"Howdy," Cheatem half shouted against the low roar of the wind as he opened the door, gesturing the other in. "What you doing traipsing about in this weather?"

Barry, stepping across the threshold, brushed snow from the shoulders of his coat. "Sure ain't doing it by choice, by golly. Some soldiers just came by. Damn if they ain't pulling out, going back to Leavenworth!"

Cole was on his feet. "Back to Leavenworth? Why?"

"Orders. They didn't do no explaining."

Cheatem whistled lowly. "Well, I'll be goddamned! And what are we 'uns suppose to do?"

"That's what I come 'bout. Meeting is a'gonna be held over to Dillby's place in a few hours, figured you best be there."

"Sure thing," answered Cheatem.

Nodding his head Barry, pleading he had others to call upon, turned back into the storm and strode away. Silas, shutting the door firmly behind him, swung slowly to Cole. "Well, what in hell d'yuh make of that?"

Cole took a moment to stare at the fire burning low in the grate before replying, "I think we just got our first whiff of trouble. Price of this land could be a mite higher than we reckoned."

At Leavenworth Quarles, secretly alert to every dispatch from the fort, began to suspect it was about to be abandoned, so he wasn't surprised when withdrawal was made official. But he was worried and Lee's doubtful expressions were doing little to ease his mind.

"What's the general got to say?" Lee was looking through Henry's single window, watching a handful of recruits tramping through the snow to their barracks.

"Claims the fort couldn't be held in any case, keeping it supplied didn't make sense."

"And the settlers?"

"Says he's sorry but the Union is got to be preserved first."

Lee shook his head. "Ought to evacuate them women and young 'uns . . . get 'em back to Salina while there's time."

"Imagine they've thought of that."

Lee grunted, his expression turning skeptical. "Show me a settler who thinks of anything but holding to his claim and I'll show you a settler who's already halfway home."

Both remained silent for a moment. Then Henry rose, joining Lee at the window. "Damn it all, I'm worried."

Lee patted him on the shoulder. "Don't be, she'll be all right."

"Who?"

"That Sadler gal."

Quarles stiffened up. "What in hell makes you think I'm worried about her?"

"Henry, when a man worries about anything else he's fussin', when he worries about a woman he's scared. You just look a mite paler to me."

The real blessing was getting their wagon back. Between spells of sitting bundled up beside him, Chloe lay in back and rested. What's more they started encountering others, traders or trappers heading north for the season but swinging over to the Colorado Trail upon hearing the Cimarron cutoff was closed. They also drew Dennis west, advising him he could follow the western trail down through Taos to Santa Fe. He was told with any luck he should be in Santa Fe in a week.

But travel now was a different matter. As they drew near Taos the beauty of the country began to strike them, patches of greenery separating golden mesas stretching

to the horizon, their outlines looking sharp and clear in
the morning air but turning misty in the afternoon.
Chloe had a sense of dreaming her way through this
landscape. They saw Indians but these were peaceful
bands coming to Taos or Santa Fe to trade, some
traveling with whites or mestizos and often dressed in
beaded cloth or colored shirts over baggy pants. Some
had headbands but a few wore sombreros or even
skincaps. Many were colorfully tattooed, others sported
bright feathers. It was good preparation for entering the
polyglot population they would encounter in Santa Fe,
for that fabled town, long the trading crossroads of the
southwest, had inhabitants from Coahuila, Chihuahua,
Sonora, California, and many states east of the Mississippi. These varied denizens mixed daily with half-wild
tribesmen from uncharted regions whose only wealth
was pelts and decorated crockery which they brought to
barter for the fruits of civilization. It was an exciting
day. When the wagon topped a rise and Santa Fe, its
white adobe walls shining like blocks of snow in the
distance, was first sighted, Dennis could only pull the
wagon to a stop and hug Chloe for joy.

They found so many wagons and people milling about
the outskirts that they entered the town almost unnoticed, and had wandered through its great plaza and
nearby sprawling marketplace for an hour before their
minds turned to a place to live. After many inquiries,
answered by smiling merchants in broken English, they
ended up in an old part of the city. Here they found two
small rooms in the rear of a building, looking out on a
tiny garden. The landlord was a scowling Mexican but
their neighbors seemed humble people of every description. Chloe, noticing their skins, found they went from
white to reddish bronze to coal black, their dress from
shirts and skirts with frills to simple wrapped-around
sheets and loincloths. The predominant tongue was
Spanish but the twang of mountain English or the clip of
strange-sounding Indian dialects kept popping up. Before sundown Dennis had carried everything from the
wagon and Chloe had settled their few belongings about
the two rooms as best she could. Both knew they needed

chairs, a table, and a few decorative things to do away with the bareness of the place, but couldn't help sneaking glances at the little garden in back, smiling at each other, conscious it was their first home.

That night they heard music a short distance away, it drew them through two lightly crowded streets to a small plaza. Here they found a swirl of people dancing, laughing, flirting, and adding to the music that rose from several guitars by clapping their hands, tapping their heels, and keeping rhythm with little instruments young girls concealed in their hands. They would discover these were called castanets.

Without asking they were offered drinks from jugs of wine being passed freely from hand to hand, but they smilingly declined. They only wanted to look on and savor this sight of people enjoying themselves, away from fear, away from the pall of ancient biases and prejudices that passed for pride. When they returned to their rooms they lay in the dark, giggling, hugging each other, suddenly breaking into laughter in a sort of manic relief. The humiliating days of the settlement and that nightmarish journey through the sinister Cimarron country were behind them. Now life as it was supposed to be lived could begin. Hallelujah! Praise God! They were safe at last—safe and free to enjoy their love in Santa Fe!

Deep in the foothills of the Rockies a small band of Omaha Indians had prepared a shelter for winter. They were farmers, corn Indians, driven from their mud and thatch homes by raiding Sioux, their historic and near fatal enemy. Earlier that year they had suffered such a devastating attack from the Sioux and their Cheyenne allies that it crushed their tribal spirit. Many of their men had been killed; most of the women, particularly young ones, taken. With the coming of cold weather the numerous orphans were turning sick, even dying for lack of care. To remain another season, holding to their few patches of fertile earth, was inviting oblivion. They had retreated into the mountains, though not too far, they had no desire to encounter the bloodthirsty Utes. To date they had avoided detection but were finally spotted by a pair of eyes also searching for a sanctuary. Lame Fox had spent months looking for an Indian camp he might approach as his only alternative to a settlement that now contained its own threat. But the Comanche and Kiowa camps he scouted were clearly war camps. Instinct told him matters between the whites and these plains Indians had seriously deteriorated. Even the air about their many councils was charged with anger. Grimly he considered his possible reception. They would know he was from the east, from the white settlements. They might think him a spy. No, it was too risky. He hadn't come all this way to be tortured to death by warriors smoldering with rage easily turned upon himself. He had almost decided to winter alone, a dire and even dangerous decision, when he saw a lone hunter stalking some deer. It was an Indian, armed with only a bow and arrow. The man was patient enough but tried his shot from too great a distance. Had he studied the direction the deer were drifting and circled downwind to get in their path he would have had a surer shot. Having lost the deer the man seemed discouraged and weary of hunting; he began trudging up the sloping valley. On a hunch Lame Fox followed him. After an arduous hour of climbing upwards they came to a cleft in the bottom rampart of a towering mountain. There among some heavy foliage surrounded by quaking aspens the man disappeared. It took another hour of spying for Lame Fox to spot several other figures moving about in a well-concealed enclosure, disguised as an overgrown thicket, packed with decaying leaves.

Within minutes he decided this group looked harmless, perhaps even in need of help. Yet approaching them had to be studied. He didn't want them wary or secretly hostile. It was the man looking so disheartened at missing the deer that made him think they might be hungry. Clearly these were not skilled hunters. Game was easier to find in the foothills than in the mountains but in this season it took skill to bring them down. Suddenly, hefting his rifle, he hit upon an idea.

Later that day he was back at the shelter with a young doe tied to his back. He came up slowly, placing the carcass on the ground and leaning back to yawn loudly. Several heartbeats later a head appeared above the thicket. Lame Fox smiled, rubbing his stomach and pointing to the deer. Using the sign for hunger seemed to have an effect upon the head, for it bobbed twice and then others appeared beside it. Lame Fox stood there smiling, then slowly bending over took his knife and started butchering the doe. Half an hour later chunks of venison were being held over an open fire and Lame Fox had been accepted into this little band of desperate Indians. Here he would pass the winter and get to know the mountains. Here he would experience the bitter cold and welcome the first Chinooks coming to melt the snow. Here he would see the many mountain streams break up in a great spring thaw that would send life-giving water to the plains, raising fresh grass to nourish the mighty herds of buffalo and the war horses of Kiowa and Comanche warriors. Lame Fox would live here in peace for a time, but ultimately he would learn the soldiers had left, and after the great thaw he would spot Comanche and Kiowa hunting bands slowly coming together, meeting on the southern slopes where the grass came first. He would be appalled at their numbers, at the loom of their great council fires that blushed in the night sky until dawn. The season of war was coming, but he could only sit and smoke with the Omahas, his troubled heart telling him the settlement he had left behind was sitting in the shadow of death.

42

"Dis country jus swallow folks up," complained Hattie, brooding over Chloe, but mindful that Sam, Troy, and even Lame Fox had not been heard of for months.

"Dey best git back here right soon," muttered Ben. "Deys trouble comin', ah feel it in muh bones."

Skeeter was mending some of Cheatem's saddle gear, the few horses not sold survived the winter on dead foliage dug out of the snow. The animals had become thin and listless but fresh grass was appearing on all sides, a week or two would see them fit again. "Cain't wait no longer." Skeeter's eyes rose and fixed on Hattie. "Ah got to start huntin' fo' Sam."

Hattie stared back at him. "Where you fixin' to hunt? . . . no tellin' where he done got to . . . likely you git lost too."

"Still ah gots to go . . . he my kin."

"Likely he in a mess o' trouble."

Skeeter looked away. "Dats why ah gots to go."

"Dat fool head of yours make you think you kin find him?"

"Figure when ah find trouble ah'll find Sam."

Ben shook his head slowly. Like Hattie he sensed the hopelessness of seeking someone in this vast country, with its many threats, its poorly marked trails, its sinister horizons. Yet he respected Skeeter's devotion to Sam. He patted him on the shoulder, saying softly, "If Sam is where dere's trouble, son, den no need to go lookin'. Trouble comin' here, betcha . . . trouble sure comin' . . . mighty soon."

No one in the settlement suffered more stress than Dillby, who had to listen to the fears and anxieties of husbands for their wives, mothers for their children, and everyone for their claim, often all a family possessed. Grasping his Bible, he listened dutifully, but put more faith in prayer than sat well with men like Cheatem and Cole. Aided by Tod Barry they pushed for a strategy of defense, but could not find a plan that satisfied all. They could either fortify a central point and retreat to it, which left abandoned homes open to pillage and likely burnt to ashes, or each settler could try holding his claim as best he could. The latter, a prescription for massacre, only proved the dread of losing all they possessed and a year's labor to boot made some folks desperate.

Cole figured the real trouble was lack of leadership. The war had polarized the settlement and now, though fear was finally forcing them together, the chance for true unity had been lost. To avoid one side being dominated by the other a committee was formed and as with most committees talk drained away time and energy required for action. But warnings were beginning to pile up. Trappers coming east from the mountains reported talk of a great war with the whites reaching the Crows and other friendly tribes. The few scouts they sent out, often it was Cole or Tod, reported the land seemed curiously empty and ominously quiet. Cathy was amazed that so few people chose to return to Salina. In the end only three women, taking most of the young children, departed. It said something about the breed that brought their fate to the frontier.

The Hunt men, if stern, were also devout. No fate, however odious, was to be seen as anything but the Lord's will. However, though it was known they wanted Flora and Charity to leave, the women refused to go. The wives spent a great deal of time with Dillby and even sat in the back of the big hall when the committee was meeting. Cathy nodded at them when passing but unlike Charlotte Barry, whom she had come to like, would not share a table with them. She herself thought briefly of returning to Salina but there was nothing for her there and Cole made it clear he wasn't leaving. "Start running and you ain't never gonna stop" was one of his favorite sayings. She was worried but not disheartened. With Troy and Dennis gone she had Cole all to herself, and a few nights, for there was plenty of time for rest in this season, he left her moaning with sensual pleasure, the blood pounding through her limbs until, surrendering to the warmth that joined their bodies, she fell asleep.

The alarm first sounded at Leavenworth. An early spring party of couriers was attacked just east of Fort Laramie and a detachment trying to come to its aid nearly wiped out. Then Laramie itself was attacked.

Large parties of Sioux, Cheyenne, and Arapahos had descended upon the Oregon Trail, closing it and slaughtering all travelers caught unaware. A relief column was momentarily considered by the general but troops sufficient to put down such a force of hostiles did not exist. "Laramie will hold out," he assured his officers, "but there can be no offensive until we're reinforced."

Some of the officers offered to try and get through with what troops were available but the general was adamant. "I don't intend to report a string of dead heroes, the fort can take care of itself and the settlers have been adequately warned. There's a war on, you know, we've been losing more men in one battle than all the settlers and troops west of here." He stood up. "Gentlemen, they'll be no further discussion until a force equal to the task is available. You are dismissed!"

Quarles quickly grasped, with the northern tribes already raiding and killing, western Kansas would be next. Lee nodded in mute agreement but the general's words were still ringing in their ears. There would be no troops sent west until reinforcements arrived. With great battles shaping up in the Mississippi valley that surely wouldn't be soon. A brooding Henry Quarles stood and watched clouds roiling overhead in a windswept spring sky, wondering what fate had in store for a small isolated settlement lying on the Smoky Hill many miles to the west.

Sam, weary of drums and the dancing of shrieking warriors, was also brooding, for by now he knew a mass attack upon the settlement was at hand. It had been a fearsome winter for him. His one attempt to escape had led to severe beatings and days of starvation, until the old squaw got so many requests for strong medicine from warriors preparing for war she needed his services again. But he had to witness terrible scenes. Sara finally mustered the courage to end her life and hung herself, her body hanging in the frosty air as young children, pulling the few rags from her body, left her nude, her pregnancy showing. Young Carrie finally lost her faltering grip on sanity and had started laughing or crying in uncontrollable fits. It did not help her lot; the squaws no longer wanted her around. In the end she was led away by some hunters and never returned.

Sam understood enough Comanche by now to know that issues of command were still being debated over endless council fires. Black Otter was popular and he and Red Hand made many speeches that had the warriors raising weapons and shouting war cries. But Sam noticed several of the old chiefs, seated about Whistling Elk, often sucked their pipes in silence until the din had quieted down. It was not hard to recognize, however much they supported an attack on the whites, some of these venerable faces had questions about Black Otter commanding it.

Bad Eyes, though still keeping him busy, had stopped using the pointed stick, and had even given him a mouthful of honey some applicant had left with a newly strung bow. Sam gathered from the many preparations she was making, and the number of things he had to pack and attach to her saddle, that she was going with the war party, but not until the very dawning they left was he to know that he was going too. Pointing to an old badly spavined horse she must have secretly traded for overnight, she made the sign to him to follow her, and Sam, trying to hide his surprise, mounted grimly, knowing this pathetic animal was to rule out any possibility of escape. But he could not believe he was traveling with a war party about to attack his own people. Looking at the numbers of warriors appearing on all sides his heart told him the settlement could never survive a determined attack. Finding himself near sick with dread, he watched the war party moving ahead, approaching ever closer to the Smoky Hill, intent on bringing death to the few human beings who ever loved him and whom he loved in return. Struggling as hard as he could he still failed to keep tears of misery and suppressed rage from clouding his eyes. Thoughts of more captive women suffering the fate of Sara and Carrie ran through his head like flashes from a nightmare one prayed would never return.

Just before evening on the following day, scouts began coming in with rifles or bows raised over their heads.

Sam gripped his lower lip with his teeth, trying to relieve a new unbearable tension by biting into it. In spite of appearances his heart was secretly pounding, for he could easily read such signs now. The little unwary settlement, containing his only kin, had been sighted; its date with destiny would come at dawn.

There were several attempts to pull the nearly forty men in the settlement together. But there were always a few who rose to argue the plan put forward left them or their family too much risk. Hope for agreement was fast waning. Some even began thinking no attack was coming, for not one sign of hostile Indians had been reported to justify their alarm. Men, kicking irritably at the earth, began talking about planting and women stewed quietly about some schooling for their young ones.

In vain did Cole point out that to his knowledge Indian attacks came without warning, and that while no Indians had been sighted, that fact alone might well raise suspicions. Though Cheatem and Tod Barry backed him up, arguments continued to be raised and finally it was decided one last scout should be made before any actions were taken. The Hunt men, whose claims were farthest to the west, offered to do the scouting, but Tod Barry was reluctant to leave this vital assignment to individuals who regarded every misfortune befalling them as God's will.

He hugged Charlotte that night and told her he would probably be gone when she awoke the following morning. Charlotte hugged him back, saying nothing but knowing she had to rise with him. She had no intentions of lying asleep while her husband was in danger. She had watched the sun set that evening, noticing streamers of vermillion and orange streaking into the lavender sky like lines flowing from the blazon center of a warrior's shield. Charlotte was uneasy, even when Tod made love to her that night. Sleep came quickly to her husband but Charlotte lay peering into the darkness until she felt Tod rising and slipped out of bed with him before dawn, wanting to feel his arms about her one more time.

⚔ 43 ⚔

It was a heavy gray darkness that Charlotte saw her husband's mount carry him into as he moved along a silent strip of bare prairie on their side of the settlement. The sudden rush of some nocturnal animal beneath their cabin startled her and she was still trying to catch her breath when through the mist she thought she saw Tod stopping or turning, as though he had met or was being joined by others. But it was the roar of his gun that brought panic to her brain and without thinking started her running toward him. A heart-stopping shrieking broke out from a distant household and a pounding of hooves shaking the earth was suddenly rising from every side. Single rifle shots started echoing across the settlement, and the screams of women and children, joining that of warriors, quickly turned this still eerie mist-laden half night into a string of hellish outbursts as dwelling after dwelling awoke to violence and death. Only those with tentative plans could put up any kind of defense. Cole and Cathy, at the sound of Tod's desperate warning shot, sprang from bed and, grabbing their guns, raced to Cheatem's door. They just made it. Ben let them in, pointing to the far windows where Skeeter and Cheatem were already firing at warriors coming along the river. Hattie was loading the shotgun and Ben was hurrying about supplying ammunition to the fighters. A handful of people had made it to the big hall, but more than one died trying. On the outskirts whole families were killed and scalped, though some women and children were spared only to become captives. Charlotte Barry was the first woman seized, a young warrior tying her to his horse and pulling combs from her long blonde hair. She could only sob, having run screaming until reaching and sprawling across Tod's dead body. Hysteria kept her from realizing strange hands were on her and a rope was binding her arms to her sides. Elsewhere men, trying to protect their families, were dying, women and children were being taken, and on the far western end of the settlement a torch raised its ominous yellow eye into the dying night. The Hunts were up and fighting desperately but their homes were among the first to be set ablaze. There was little time for talk; the men wanted the women to try for the big hall, an almost impossible task, while the women, their lips mouthing prayers, could not bring themselves to leave without their men.

Finally the flames eliminated decisions. Abandoning the house and backing toward Dillby's in this bloody dawning the men tried hard to keep the charging warriors off, but, hopelessly outnumbered, their wounds began to mount until they could no longer keep death blows from gun stocks and hatchets from ending their pathetic stand. Flora and Charity in a panic tried to run toward the distant hall but were easily overtaken. They found themselves bound and tied together, the shock of this ghastly awakening and the hideous faces surrounding them robbed them of even the power to scream. Alice, who had run furthest before being taken, had her night shift ripped off and was pulled naked up behind a burly warrior, who in the melee thought he had seized a child.

Anguished cries and the intermittent crack of rifle fire continued for near half an hour before the warriors pulled back to study the few remaining structures resisting them. Black Otter knew he had just won a great victory, but he wanted it complete. No *tahbay-boh* were to be left to brag they survived his wrath. Whistling Elk, aware it had been a ridiculously easy fight, was puzzled. Were these whites, with so much time to prepare, so blind to their peril? But the large ranch and the big hall were still being defended by determined marksmen; they alone had inflicted the few casualties suffered. Unless a brave could get close enough to set them afire, reducing them might not be worth the price.

While the many terrified captives were hurried back to the pitch camp, and all homes left standing were looted, the chiefs settled on the ground for a quick council of war. The rim of the sun, sending pennants of scarlet before it, was about to breach the eastern horizon. In the returning silence little birds began springing up, chirping and flicking their way through the now gruesome landscape, pocked with dead bodies in macabre settings, that was once an aspiring and, to many trusting hearts, a promising settlement.

Cathy stared out of the window facing west, the strain of viewing the calamity before her leaving only a petrified expression of horror etched on her face. The fingers of fire leaping up, the screams of women and children, growing more and more frantic as they watched their men dying and saw murderous eyes approaching, had her shrinking back with little screams of her own, finding it impossible not to identify with their plight. Cole, his face grayish under a belief their end had come, had managed to bring enough warriors to earth to stop them galloping between the river and the ranch. But Skeeter's screaming "Look!" turned all eyes on the nearby Sadler home which was already sending up streamers of smoke, quickly followed by leaping flames as their hard-earned shelter and all their earthly possessions went up in smoke.

Cathy was too traumatized to cry; she just clung to Cole, her breathing becoming a moan, almost inaudible, a mutely murmured agony too grievous for expression.

Hattie, sighing at Skeeter and Ben, was reloading her shotgun. Cheatem, noticeably shaken, was circling about, deciding, after peering through several windows, the attack had let up. "They must be pow-wowing," he muttered, rubbing his face, "but damn if I believe they finished." He sat down breathing heavily; it took effort to break the shock of that furious attack. "Jesus, what a mess!"

Cole looked at him over Cathy's head. "How many of us do you reckon are left?"

Cheatem gave a particularly heavy sigh. "Not many. Likely some got to the hall, there was heavy fire over thataway for a spell."

Hattie struck her rifle stock against the floor. "Is we gonna pray?"

"Pray away," groaned Cheatem. "If prayer can bring a regiment of soldiers or even a corporal's guard Silas Cheatem will pray all night!"

Hattie, raising her voice with a verve that surprised the others, reeled out a prayer that seemed mawkish in this gory, nightmarish setting. Yet it reminded Cathy that all lives, no matter how spent, were temporary and this woman's simple faith was diminishing her fear of death. She pulled herself back from Cole and joined Hattie in saying "Amen."

Cheatem had found a pair of field glasses and was studying blackened remains of houses some distance away. Mutely he swung them back and forth. After a few moments Cole couldn't resist asking. "See anything?"

"Reckon I do."

"Anything moving?"

"No."

Cathy stepped away from the window. "What do you see?"

"You don't want to know."

Cole snapped a quick look at Hattie, who was standing with Skeeter and Ben. "Is it that bad?" he asked cautiously.

"'Fraid so. 'Fraid if and when them painted polecats leave we got us a heap of diggin' to do."

"You not talking about building again?" murmured Cathy.

"No, just buryin'." His voice seemed to break. "That's all, just a'buryin' . . ."

Sam knew the dreaded attack was on. The distant snap of rifle fire and the intermittent sound of warriors screaming was proof of violence in this gray dawning, and it told his heart the sleeping settlement had been struck. He had no hopes it would survive. Over two hundred warriors had left camp, painted for war and heavily armed. In the gloom he saw the squaws now gathered in the camp center, eagerly awaiting any loot or captives their braves might bring, but for the moment they could only whisper among themselves, suppressing their excitement, occasionally hushing children or dogs, complaining in their own way of hunger. There was to be a great victory feast that had to wait for the warriors to return, for the spoils of war to be distributed, the fresh scalps of the vanquished to be danced about a victory fire.

It was not until light began to spread through the camp that a young boy signaled someone was coming. Sam saw a few warriors riding into camp. Behind them came a line of captives, women and children walking in a dazed way, grasping each other, some mumbling incoherently, shock rendering them incapable of discernment, their eyes vacant or frozen with horror. Many had seen members of their family killed and scalped, others had to leave wounded loved ones engulfed in flames. Dread seemed to have paralyzed them; the women didn't weep, the children didn't cry. Sam felt a lump in his chest, he wanted to run to them, comfort them, do something to dispel the deathly pall that seemed to have embraced them. But such a move could only have made things worse. The squaws were already cackling to themselves. They were only waiting to discover to whom the captives belonged before they plundered them of whatever clothing or trinkets caught their fancy. In time the captured women would be given to them to torment and enslave, but not until the warriors were through with them.

But Sam knew that was coming.

With the terrible reality of it forcing him to cover his face with his hands and stare through his fingers, he saw Charlotte Barry being led into the center of the camp. Her arms were tied to her sides though she seemed unaware of it. Shortly behind her came Flora and

Charity Hunt, tied together and looking deathly pale and appalled at the now screeching squaws. Young Alice arrived, trying to hide her nudity among some other children, but it was evident her body was already rounding. Sam knew she would not be with the children for long. Indian girls younger than Alice were commonly taken as wives.

When the captives were all herded together, dropping to the ground in the middle of the camp, the braves that brought them shouted some words to the squaws, then rode off in the direction of the settlement. By then the sun was up and fires were being started, but a great silence hung over the prisoners until a young baby, finally catching the menacing expressions of faces around them, started to cry.

Cole didn't believe the Indians would simply besiege the house or the big hall, for with their numbers they could easily overwhelm both. But as time passed the attack was not resumed, and the few fire arrows shot by warriors dashing madly by proved the wood, dampened by the heavy mist, was still too green to easily ignite. Once they heard firing from the direction of the hall but it lasted only seconds and must have been another failed attempt to use fire. Cheatem thought of signaling the hall but there was no point in the house from which a makeshift flag could be seen. Their only hope was to get to a little rise back from the river where the distant hall came into view.

Less and less was said as they watched from different windows, expecting any moment to see the warriors charging toward them in numbers too great to repulse, but the morning became full and the sun, burning away the mist, lit the stark remains of the settlement, where only birds and rivulets of smoke rose from the warming ground. Cheatem, becoming restless, kicked at an old chest by his window. "Damn! What they fixin' to do?"

Cole, knowing the futility of trying to guess what was coming, grunted as he peered at the river which had risen overnight. "We'll know when they do it. Water has risen, don't reckon it means much anymore."

"It mean de Lord goin' about His business," declared Hattie. "Folks need water, he sendin' it. Means He watchin' too!"

Ben shook his head, looking wistfully at Hattie. "If He watching . . . reckon he saw 'nough for a spell."

"We need a heap more than water," said Skeeter, licking his bottom lip and trying to swallow away the dryness from his mouth. "Ah ain't ready to die, Hattie . . . think He know dat?"

"Righteous livin' folks . . . only ones ready fo' dying."

Cheatem scraped the floor with his boot. "Reckon that leaves me out."

Ben and Skeeter looked at him, curiously the only time they ever did with empathy.

It was late in the day before the tension broke and they realized what fate had in store for them, but by then much had happened, and in the pitch camp the last horrors of the attack had been carried out.

44

The council lasted several hours, the carnage about them hardly drawing more than a vengeful glance or a satisfied grunt. Wandering livestock were still being gathered up and scalps taken but the warriors were anxious for the victory dance and a great feast they knew was coming.

Black Otter argued there were other settlements to raid and a victory here did not drive the *tahbay-boh* from their lands. He wanted them to stay on the war path, drive down this valley to the east, leaving a trail of enemy dead that would settle for all time who ruled this land.

Whistling Elk, rising in his turn, argued this attack

would surely bring the whites to them. Bluecoats would come here to attack Indian villages, and be easily defeated by the great army of braves still moving toward the Arkansas. The whites would finally come seeking peace, for the trails to the west so needed by them were closed. They would come with open hands agreeing at last these lands were the hunting grounds of the Comanche, the Kiowa. The bloodstained remains of this settlement would teach them the price of speaking with false tongues.

Had the braves not been anxious to share the loot, dance the victory dance, and start the great feast, Black Otter might have carried the day. Some who had done little fighting, or had taken neither loot nor prisoners, were ready to follow him. But too many were anxious to savor this victory, all combat did not end in such triumph and who knew what tomorrow might bring. Plains Indians, with their ethos of war, had to live for the day. A warrior's life was a string of battles, one of which he knew would end it.

After much talk they decided to besiege these two stubborn points, cutting them off from water, food, or aid. They could not last long, there were no armed whites within a hundred miles to save them. A frontal assault would be costly and, in the minds of many chiefs, foolhardy; braves weren't made in a day. Whistling Elk wrapped his robe about him and, smiling at Black Otter, mounted his horse. Then chanting the returning warrior's thanks to his spirits for victory, he led the way back to the pitch camp.

The victory dance, with their braves whirling by, sent the squaws into a moaning then an almost shrieking ecstasy, as the young coming up, imitating the warriors, shuffled to the drums along the sidelines. But the very sight of this wild, fierce dancing terrified the captives. Warriors with their buffalo or great mountain elk headpieces pounded the ground with their feet and gyrated around as they shouted acts of bravery in destroying the settlement. Scalp sticks, arrayed with fresh scalps, were shaken before the captives, making the children, who only dimly understood the ghastly sight, cower behind the women who themselves had to avert their eyes.

Sam knew these women would be treated the same as Ute women, or those of any enemy tribe. Women he had discovered were regarded by these nomads as the spoils of war. He didn't know if any of these wretched figures recognized him, or even noticed him squatting behind a shield stand. His mind had been racked with worry that he would see Chloe or Hattie among the prisoners, but his momentary relief at their absence turned into anguish when he heard warriors shouting that all but a handful in the settlement were dead.

The dance lasted till late afternoon, but by then the cooking pots were steaming and the aroma of cooked meat filled the campsite. Sam realized the claiming of prisoners and loot was about to begin. He watched the children being taken away and the women pushed to the center of the camp. The first woman, obviously a mother whose eyes kept looking back to her children, was claimed by Red Hand. Two squaws who shared his tipi came forward to strip the woman of her clothes, the poor frail figure stood there exhausted, her head hanging in shame until the squaws led her roughly away. Soon Charlotte Barry was brought forth, the young brave who had seized her untying her and declaring she belonged to him. This brave's mother and sisters soon had Charlotte's nightgown and underwear off, but Charlotte stood there, uncaring, making Sam look shyly away even as he saw her body was as beautiful as her face. Red Hand, coming up, pointed to Charlotte and then to some nearby horses, but the young warrior determinedly shook his head, and his family led the captive away. Flora and Charity were almost the last to be brought forward, but they came surrounded by a group of warriors, who all claimed a hand in capturing them. This time, the men being bachelors, no women appeared. The men roughly pulled off the Hunt women's clothes, throwing them to nearby squaws who scrambled for them. There was much jesting among the braves until the two women were standing stripped and shaking in the cool air. Unlike Charlotte, their bodies were not appealing. Flora's breasts were long and pendulous, Charity's stomach appearing too large and white, revealing only a thin wisp of pubic hair. But the warriors, still jesting, hustled them off to the nearby woods, where Sam, attuned to the direction taken, cringed at hearing their distant screaming, knowing what it meant.

The burly warrior now brought up Alice, whose nudity had been covered by a blanket, and after a few loud, half-laughing pronouncements, Sam, who had seen the warrior many times at Bad Eye's tipi, watched his many wives leading Alice off. Red Hand, his eyes following Alice, could be seen talking to the burly brave, but the big warrior waved him off and still laughing strode away.

The loot was distributed next and the children parceled out until their fate could be decided, but many of the hapless women were to face that night what every Indian female knew awaited her when taken prisoner by enemy braves.

It was approaching dark when Cheatem and Cole finally determined, after receiving only sniper fire for hours, they were under siege. It did little to improve their spirits; the pall of a long tension-ridden day didn't lift simply because the threat of immediate attack had lessened. "We got nary a ways to turn," cursed Cheatem. "Salina is a good eighty miles."

"And Leavenworth damn near twice that beyond," added Cole. "Still . . . you know . . ." his eyes leveled on Cheatem's, ". . . someone's got to try."

Skeeter looked up. "Dats a long ways to run . . . don't believe deys a horse left hereabouts."

Cheatem was staring through the window that faced the little rise. "We got to contact the hall, maybe they've figured something out."

Cole stood up. "Gonna be dark soon . . . I'll give it a try."

Cathy grasped his hand. "Cole, be careful, they might be expecting us to do just that."

"Likely," added Cheatem. "No tellin' what them devils is up to."

Skeeter was standing with his hand on Ben's shoulder. "Dey ain't gonna see me come dark."

Ben stared up at him. "Me neither."

Skeeter looked at Hattie for support. "Ah figured dat out first!"

Ben rose to stand beside him. "But you can use a gun . . . fight. Ah cain't. Best you stay here."

Hattie was trying to start a small fire in the stove. If they were going to last the night, they had to eat. "Mebbe dey send somebody here," she muttered. "Dey in no better fix."

"If we wait till it's real late," said Cole, holding Cathy as though he were addressing only her, "chances ought to be pretty fair. Injuns don't care much for moseying about in the dark."

Stiffening, Cathy stared back at him. "You're telling me you're going, aren't you?"

"Reckon it's best, we can't hold out here for long."

Skeeter was suddenly beside them. "Ah'll go wid you."

Cheatem, as though annoyed, looked up. "No point in both of yuh riskin' it . . . we few enough a'ready . . . ought to choose."

Cole and Skeeter studied each other for a moment, Cole remembering Skeeter and Sam demanding to be treated like men. He finally looked away, muttering to Cheatem, "You got a coin?"

Cheatem dug in his pocket. "Silver dollar do?"

"Fine, toss it. Skeeter is gonna call. Loser goes."

Cheatem flipped the coin in the air as Skeeter called, "Tails!"

The coin fell with three set of eyes following it down. "It's heads," announced Cheatem. "Reckon you go, Skeeter."

"Reckon we ought to be prayin' sum," gasped Hattie. She looked around to make sure all were included. "Best you shuck yo' minds of any sinful thoughts, we sure gots to ask de Lord for a mess of help today."

It was near midnight when Skeeter finally saw the hall looming before him. There was no light, but a moon that dodged through a lightly clouded sky occasionally left a faint sheen a few yards from the door. Skeeter reckoned it was a window. He picked up a few pebbles and one by one pitched them against the glass. He had to repeat this twice before he saw the long black barrel of a rifle coming through a slat in the window and leveled in his direction.

"Don't shoot!" he called out in a hoarse whisper. "It's me, Skeeter."

There was a long silence until he heard Dillby's barely audible voice. "Who's there?"

"Me . . . Skeeter."

He heard the door creaking open a few yards away and slipping toward it suddenly felt hands coming out to pull him in. The door was quickly shut and bolted behind him, and he was steered to where he could see figures huddled around a candle being shielded by a blanket. Only then did he realize Dillby had taken his arm and was standing beside him. "We heard your people shooting," the clergyman said, desperation tightening his voice. "Thank God you're still with us."

"How many are you?" said another voice.

Skeeter told them and following Cole's and Cheatem's instructions asked if any knew how to get word to Salina. Apparently they had thought of that and of the nine men and one woman in the hall, not one knew where to secure a horse.

"They've left us helpless," lamented Dillby. "We saw them leading away women and children. What have we done to deserve the Lord's wrath?"

"Someone is got to try it on foot," said a voice that Skeeter recognized as the fiddler's. "Better they leave from Cheatem's place than here. We plum in the center of everything, be hard to slip away, Cheatem's is over by the river, should make it easier."

His eyes adjusted to the strange, almost eerie light in the hall. Skeeter now saw Dillby sitting and hurriedly scratching out a note for him to take back to Cole and Cheatem. He had the feeling that during that long and suspenseful day, it had been remembered, perhaps even remarked, that had the settlement listened to those two it would not be in the fix it was now. Luckily in the darkness he didn't really see the faces around him or have to deal with their expressions, but their silence, occasionally broken by a sob, smacked of a day of horror in which loved ones and dear friends, some within their sight, were slain. One man kept pounding a fist into an open hand and cursing under his breath. The lone woman kept whispering to him, attempting to comfort him, but to no avail.

Out again in the darkness Skeeter began to retrace his steps to the ranch. The trip on his return somehow seemed shorter, but not until he was a hundred feet from the ranch door did he have to drop down, knowing something, coming across the nearby stream, had mounted the bank and was moving between him and the sanctuary of the house. He wanted to cry out to those inside, for he had no gun and the figure, which he could see now was mounted, had moved into the pale light of the moon, and its outline told his faltering heart it was an armed Indian.

Inside the house all eyes were watching for Skeeter. Hattie had laid out some bread and preserves but no one felt right eating until he returned. It was hand-wringing Cathy who first heard a sound she recognized as a horse shaking water from its sides and prancing about for better purchase on wet soil. "Shush!" she whispered as loud as she dared. "I'd swear a horse just crossed the stream." Cole moved to where he could see a dim outline of the bank running east on their side. "Don't see anything."

Ben was studying the land toward the rise. "Where dat boy git to? Best ah go fetch him."

Soundlessly Hattie moved toward him. "Hush yo' fool face. Enough of us in trouble a'ready."

It was Cathy who, straining her ears and suppressing her voice, kept whispering cautiously, "He's too close and too alone to make an attack . . ." Her head turned to Cole in the dark. ". . . What do you think, should we call out to him?"

Cheatem was approaching the door, passing Hattie on the way and hissing, "Gimme that shotgun."

"Easy," murmured Cole coming after him. "Remember Skeeter's still out there."

Cole opened the door a crack and Cheatem stuck the muzzle of the shotgun through it. "Who's there?" he near shouted.

After a moment's silence Skeeter could be heard answering, "It's me . . . but ah'se not alone."

"Not alone? Who the hell else is out there?"

"Cain't hardly believe it—but it Lame Fox."

Before dawn Lame Fox led his horse quietly down the bank, mounted, and sped off to the east. It had been a difficult night for him, he had passed the pitch camp the evening before and knew the settlement had been attacked. But the desolation he discovered where the settlement had stood convinced him he'd arrived too late. It was only because he saw Cheatem's ranch still standing that he watched from undercover until realizing Indians had it under siege. It was hours before he decided his best chance to reach those inside would be to cross the stream in darkness from a point directly opposite, which would bring him almost to their door. At the last moment he had his gun leveled at a shadowy figure he saw crouching near the house, fearing it was a Comanche but relieved to find Skeeter's eyes staring up at him in startled recognition.

Told at once he had to race to Salina for help, and that word had to be gotten to Leavenworth, he sunk down in visible dismay. The very name Leavenworth brought the shaken Shawnee's breath up short. Had they forgotten why he fled west? At Skeeter's description of things in the hall, they had draped some blankets over nearby windows and lit a candle. In this meager light Cole read Dillby's note, halting and looking distressed at the mention of captured women and children. "We got to get help as soon as possible," he muttered, passing the note to Cheatem.

"My God, those poor poor people," gasped Cathy.

"Ah'se ready to leave," chimed Skeeter. "We gots us a horse now."

"You jus gonna git yo' fool self lost," responded Hattie.

"No, it better be me," remarked Cole soberly. "Word *has* to get through, it's our only chance."

"Then it best be Lame Fox," said Cheatem, finishing the note. "I ain't never seen him lost and he the only one with enough savvy to ditch 'em if he gits followed. No white galoot shines next to Injuns at plum disappearin'."

"That's right," added Cathy, with no one knowing whether she agreed with Silas or didn't want Cole to go.

In the silence that followed, Hattie placed some food in front of Lame Fox and after a troubled glance at those around him he began to eat. Cheatem, bringing out some paper, settled down to write a second note. "We got to make it clear we can't hold out for long, and leaving folks in Injun hands for a spell, 'specially women, ain't rightly Christian. I'll say we reckon there be over a hundred redskins, likely more to be dealt with." He stopped and his breath wheezed in and out for a moment. "Any of you got anything to add?"

"Tell 'em how many of us is left," said Cole, eyeing Cathy. "Skeeter says there's nine over yonder. The six of us here makes just fifteen. Reckon they ought to know where we are—just in case."

The night began to work toward dawn, and though most ate something, no one ate much. Lame Fox, restive and staring at his medicine bag, could feel they wanted him hurrying on his way, desperate eyes catching his pleaded every moment counted. He finally resigned himself to going but wrapped the floor lightly with his rifle butt and declared in broken English, backed up by signs, he would go no further than Salina. The road to Leavenworth he refused to face, that was for whites who enjoyed protection from the law.

For a moment the room was silent as a tomb, there wasn't a word of dissent; word to Salina they were sure would certainly reach Leavenworth. Hattie gave him some additional food and Cheatem loaded his belt with ammunition, but Lame Fox was still wondering at his lot in life as he quietly led his horse a distance away and mounted.

Behind him the house remained in silence and darkness for several minutes until Hattie began to pray, her prayers filling the night and, echoed loudly by Skeeter and Ben, must have been heard on the walls of heaven, for Lame Fox raced by a dozing warrior, who sprung up too late to head him off, and by the time others were aroused the Shawnee had alertly recrossed the stream and disappeared.

The misery of the captives was growing impossible to ignore. Sam, running about serving Bad Eyes, saw children wailing for their mothers, and women wretchedly trying to cover their nudity with anything thrown to them, often thin, badly stained blankets or threadbare clothes. The mornings were still cold but the natives, not feeling it, showed little concern for captives who did.

There was no mistaking what had taken place during the night. Charlotte Barry's hair was messed and her eyes sunken but she sat staring out as though what happened to her no longer mattered. Tod was dead, she was still caught in the nightmare of crumbling in despair over his body. Had the young brave's sisters not wrapped a blanket around her she would have sat naked, indifferent to all about her. Sam saw other women searching about for their children, occasionally crying out or weeping as they tried to cover themselves in the rags thrown to them. Sam finally saw Flora and Charity, huddled beneath the same torn blanket, their faces pale, etched with the terror that had filled their night, their heads hanging together, avoiding each other's eyes. Sam wanted to console them, but Bad Eyes was busy that morning and Red Hand had been by to put her in a foul mood.

It was only from a distance that he spotted Alice. She was sitting outside the burly warrior's tipi, her eyes down, fixed on a bowl before her. He couldn't see her face clearly but even at this distance it seemed different. An hour later he went by and discovered someone had dabbed spots of red paint on her forehead and cheeks. She looked pretty by Indian standards but something in her eyes hinted she was older in ways women who decorate their bodies always seem to be.

By now Sam knew that settlers in the settlement were still holding out, and warriors who had helped in the siege were returning and complaining about the hall and the big house by the river, both leaving several warriors wounded in the stalled attack. One brave with a flesh wound, coming to Bad Eyes for healing medicine, angrily denounced a fellow warrior who had dozed and allowed a rider to escape, even though everyone thought the settlers were without horses. It was later realized the rider had come from the outside, from the west, crossing the river by the big house then recrossing it before disappearing. Black Otter, hearing this, swore the rider was too good at covering his tracks to be white. But now they knew a messenger was racing east, it was time to strike down these stubborn enemies, for before long others would be coming to rescue them. On this he got ready agreement. Large bodies started returning to the settlement, but the big feast and the night of revelry had sapped many warriors' thirst for combat. Some brave attempts were made to rush the hall but were repeatedly beaten off and slowly the stalemate that Black Otter feared began. Thwarted, he threw his war hatchet to the ground in fury. "Why did we not finish this when the fever of war was upon us! It is talk from false leaders like Whistling Elk that deprives us of our victories, victories we need to drive the *tahbay-boh* from our hunting grounds."

This was strong talk, talk that would reach Whistling Elk. But Black Otter, frustrated and bitter at events, was suddenly caught up in his own rage. "I will charge these enemies and smash their doors with my hatchet! I will slay them with my spear! I will fight until they are dead, their scalps taken! Who here will follow me?"

An awesome silence fell over the mass of braves. A sudden crisis had sprung from nowhere, men whose bravery could not be questioned were being challenged, warriors who could not publicly back down from any danger were being called upon to openly assault the hall. Some young ones in back stood up, but most eyes traveled to the sprawled bodies of a few braves who had led a courageous but futile attack but minutes before. With Black Otter glaring at them the tension became unbearable, mounting until an old warrior, his face grim with resolve, finally rose to break it. "The buffalo bull does not gore the ground and run against a sharpened stake that will impale itself," he said gravely. "Black Otter, there is no victory in death, show us a road with some promise of life, life in the warmth of the lodge, and we will bravely follow you."

Many of the older warriors grunted agreement, and others, feeling the threat to their honor was now diminished, turned restless, hoping Black Buffalo would say no more. But the damage was done, chiefs did not talk that way about each other without a reckoning. The ire of Whistling Elk would have to be faced. Many returned to the pitch camp with their heads down.

Lame Fox had to husband his horse's strength. Luckily he had a big palouse, traded for his mustang and some knives from Shoshones who, hoping to trade for guns, had brought it across the mountains from the Nez Perce. The small Shoshone band, plagued by the Utes, were as pathetic to behold as the Omahas. Sam had discovered there were Indians with more to fear from Indian enemies than any whites. Lame Fox considered it a good trade. But two full days of hard travel, with little time for grazing, was a test for any horse. It wasn't until high noon on the third day that he reached Salina, and though at once regarded with suspicion, his note brought a flood of excitement and the presence of a heavily armed character who claimed to be the local law. Lame Fox didn't care what happened next; he had served his friends as best he could, now he needed rest and a place to hide. The crowd was growing quickly and faces started crying for a courier to be dispatched to Leavenworth at once. There was some confusion but within the hour a young settler was pressing his powerful stallion to the east, Cheatem's note buttoned in his pocket and the urgency of his mission stamped on his face.

Behind him the crowd, remembering Lame Fox and seeking him for further questioning, was soon baffled. Surely he was somewhere in the large settlement. He looked too exhausted to have gone further. But they were wrong. Lame Fox had vanished, and though some sharp eyes in the crowd had already recalled him from eastern Kansas, few would ever chance to lay eyes on him again.

After that second day the tension began to wear off. Not that they were out of danger. A few steps from the house and well-aimed shots whined by, some perilously close, chipping the wood around one's head. But Cole was convinced one last try would be made to overwhelm them. Unhappily, replacing the tension was the sickening scene of vultures, coyotes, and even wolves being drawn by the dead bodies still strewn about. At night they heard vicious battles as the scavengers, a great bear amongst them, could be heard fighting for the gory feast. Hattie kept her praying up and, strangely enough, that and her singing somehow helped others keep a hold on normalcy. Cheatem, to his surprise, realized if he listened to her singing he no longer grew nettled and annoyed. For the first time he sat quietly, following her words.

> *Ole Pharaoh, he a sinful man*
> *Moses leading folks to da promise land*
> *Moses watched de water open wide*
> *And leave ole Pharaoh on de udder side.*

When she noticed he was listening she sang another verse.

> *Man git rich wid money done stole*
> *Satan jump up and grab he soul*
> *Man don't mess wid evil things*
> *Angels gonna fetch him dem shinny wings.*

Cheatem grimaced, that woman knew a thousand ways to goad him. If he ever got out of this fix, somehow he had to get shut of her. He stopped listening but caught her eyeing him, her expression putting him in mind of a mother suppressing a smile at having slyly twisted the ear of an errant child.

Sam did not need to be told the fate of captives depended upon the whims of captors; his own predicament was proof enough. Bad Eyes, abusing him callously in the beginning, now occasionally gave him presents, such as old but still warm furs or bites of foods left at her tipi by visitors seeking magic. In truth it was no longer a difficult life, though he still had to help make medicine, enduring her odors which seemed to grow worse whenever Red Hand came by to harass her about the amulet. But his secret concern now was for the other captives.

Strangely he could not overcome the shock of seeing whites, particularly white women, ravaged and mistreated with such disdain and indifference to consequences. But these redmen, he discovered, had no fear of whites. Something about their deep belief in a spirit world, an outlook tainted by fatalism, did not allow their love of life to be used against them. Freedom to them was as natural and unstoppable as the wind. Pain and even death were their accepted lot, those trying to force servitude upon them met warriors with death chants on their lips.

Charlotte and Alice, both registering the psychic trauma that comes from intimacy forced against a woman's will, did not look physically abused. Sam could tell the young warrior who had captured Charlotte was watchful and even protective of her. She still sat looking out into space, with no one allowed to approach her except women of his family. They had dressed her in Indian garb and made attempts to feed her. Sam was waiting for an opportunity to whisper something to her, but that might be long in coming from the looks of things.

Young Alice presented a different picture. The burly brave who owned her seemed somehow amused by her. He had several wives who clearly had been sternly admonished or Alice would have been a mass of bruises and welts. Instead she was sitting quietly before his tipi, seeming lost in thought, saddened in ways Sam couldn't read, looking out on the world with eyes too vacant for bitterness, stunned by events her knowledge of life was helpless to explain. He went by her twice, gesturing with his hands, trying to convey sympathy, but she failed to notice.

Many other women, still showing signs of outrages they had suffered, lay in torn clothes, covered with grime and dirt, sobbing off and on but making no attempt to cover their bodies or conceal ugly marks of violence. But even this momentary outlet for their misery was soon denied them. Braves tiring of them were turning them over to the waiting squaws, who came with switches, driving them to their feet and work. Flora and Charity were among the latter. After a night of indescribable agony, neither able to count the many times they were violated, smirking squaws came to whip them from their sobbing prayers, cackling as they reviled them in language they couldn't understand and forcing them to gather wood and buffalo chips with bare and sorely scraped hands. Their limbs and faces were filthy, their soft bodies, heavily scratched and bruised, barely able to function.

Sam, watching from a distance, wondered how long they would last. It took something to survive such captivity, it took a tenacious animal-like hold on existence, though it no longer surprised him that many finally felt surrendering life or sanity a better choice.

⫸ 46 ⫷

A heavy spring rain was deluging the earth the day word arrived at Leavenworth. Reports were still coming in about the great struggle at Shiloh. Across from the gate a long line of wagons stretched beyond the barrack area. Several newly formed infantry units were leaving for the nearby railhead, destined for Grant's embattled command.

The general glanced hurriedly at Cheatem's unfolded note and rose from his chair with an oath. "Damn!" he growled. "Why in hell didn't they get out . . . pull back to Salina. Christ, they've had enough warning!"

His adjutant stared at him patiently, then cleared his throat. "Sir, we have to wire Washington, since the trouble at Laramie they've asked to be kept advised."

"Wire them? What are we supposed to say . . . we've only got one company of cavalry left and I just can't strip the fort!"

The adjutant, gripping his lapel with one hand and placing the other behind his back, replied quietly. "Wiring them could make it their decision, sir, that might be useful later."

The general mused over the adjutant's point for a moment, then, his mouth set, replied, "Very well, wire the note in full and report to me as soon as it's answered." He continued muttering to himself for a moment, as though something wouldn't settle in his mind. "Damn fools, what did they expect?"

Quarles, hearing the contents of the report, almost ran to the general's office. "General, we should dispatch a force at once. God knows what's happening out there by now!"

"What force? We have one company of cavalry left, perhaps a handful of civilian volunteers . . ." His tone sharpened. "You'll be advised when a decision is made." He rustled some papers and glanced at Quarles under his brow. "Captain, we have several problems here. I prefer my officers not to enter this office unless sent for."

Lee watched him pacing his room; two drinks had been poured but sat ignored. The rain sounded like buckshot sprayed against the window and the wind whined like an angry cat as its velocity varied. There was nothing to fill the silence except what had been said a dozen times. "He's got to do something!" Quarles kept repeating.

"He is . . . he's wiring Washington."

"What the hell can Washington do? Jesus, they're a thousand miles away!"

Lee stared at him for a moment, then scratched his chin. "They can tell a general what to do and you can't."

Quarles clapped his hands and slumped in a chair. "With this damn war going on how much thought do you figure they'll give an outpost nobody knows about?"

"Maybe more than you think."

"An attack on a small settlement?"

Lee studied him for a moment, then turned to the window with a faraway but insightful look in his eyes. "My guess is the loss of a settlement ain't gonna ruffle those easterners much, they're mighty strange people, but a white woman in red hands is likely to peeve 'em plenty. Let's wait and see."

The uneasiness of the braves returning to the pitch camp soon alerted Sam to the trouble rising about him. There was much gathering in small groups and pipes lit to be silently passed about. Still it was hours before he grasped how grave the trouble was. Black Otter and Whistling Elk had come to the reckoning that had for so long simmered beneath the surface of things in this war camp. On the face of it the division seemed simple; Whistling Elk, half Kiowa, would be backed by these tribesmen, and Black Otter, a full Comanche, backed by his. But it was far from that simple. There were young Kiowas who favored Black Otter's fiery temperament and fervor to destroy their enemies, just as there were seasoned Comanche warriors, even minor chiefs, who saw Whistling Elk as one who could fight wars with his mind on peace, and Black Otter as one given to dark broodings and dangerous incendiary passions. The tribes needed wisdom, for as the moons turned in the sky and the snows mounted it could one day prove more important than courage.

Whistling Elk was right, the *tahbay-boh* would not leave because a small settlement was wiped out, much fighting lay ahead. The great council called that night, with Whistling Elk and Black Otter grimly facing each other, approached a difficult and dangerous task. There must be no show of violence here, but these two chiefs could not rule together. A question of honor had arisen between proud men and could not be easily laid to rest.

The pipe moved slowly around the circle where war leaders, chiefs, and many renowned warriors waited for the two adversaries to speak. In the background the squaws watched, mumbling to themselves, for they sensed momentous happenings were about to take place. Bad Eyes, sitting behind Black Otter, had beckoned to Sam to slip up beside her, a gesture that surprised him but before long he was to regret. In the shadows that lay between the tall tipis dim figures could be seen holding to each other and looking on. These were the captives, wondering if this somber council was deciding their fate. Their silent, fearful thoughts were prophetic, for in a way, not evident that night, it was.

The young reporter had dropped by the War Office looking for a story. His brother, who had a minor job there, frequently tipped him on developments before being publicly released. It gave him the edge he needed to fight big Washington papers with more clout. He was hoping for a scoop on Lincoln's latest choice for command of the Union armies, a northern general who could provide victories was proving hard to find. But his brother had nothing of interest to report, there were only the growing casualty lists, too depressing to print. It was not a very auspicious day.

The reporter looked disappointed, to turn his readers' minds from the war he needed a story that would catch their interest, offer experiences beyond their reach, describe dire events that would enlist their emotions but remained well removed from their own lives. He was on the verge of leaving when he heard his brother's superior roughly hailing him. "Get over here Gus, there's a report in about some settlement under attack in western Kansas. Must have been damn near overrun . . . says women and children taken prisoner." He paused to shove loose specs back on his nose. "See that copies are gotten to the right offices and be quick about it!"

The young reporter stood watching his brother disappear, his mind repeating the boss's words. Slowly a smile started tugging at a corner of his mouth. He would have a copy of that report within an hour. *Women and children taken prisoner.* Could any reader's heart not want to know more? Ah, yes, helpless American females in the hands of . . . er . . . savages. The story began to form in his mind, he could see outraged Americans clamoring for action. Of course he would have to supply a few details to make this tragedy more vivid, graphic. He recalled a particularly bloody picture of Indians massacring settlers in New England a hundred years before. Perhaps they could even run that with his article. After all his job was to sell newspapers.

If many easterners felt fighting Plains Indians was hardly different from fighting Confederates, people on the border knew better. The governor of Kansas immediately demanded the government, without waiting for peace talks, start negotiating to ransom back the captives. The governor's outcry drew attention to the reporter's article, appearing in a Baltimore paper, and soon people throughout the north were calling on Washington to take action.

Yet what action could be taken was another story.

Leavenworth waited three rain-filled days for a reply to their dispatch, but if long in coming it was clear in its intent.

> *All available troops to be committed at once to relieving settlement. Attempts at negotiating release of prisoners to be initiated at first possible opportunity. Government guarantees all concessions made to that end. No measures to be spared in carrying out the above.*
>   *Report promptly on progress.*
>
>   *Secretary of War,*
>   *Edwin M. Stanton*

The general greeted his adjutant with a vinegary smile. "Guess you were right. Better make a copy of that dispatch for me, stripping the fort is now Washington's responsibility." The general studied the rain still pounding the windows, then blew out a long stream of air. "All right, let's get to it. Tell Captain Quarles to report at once." He glanced at a large map of Kansas hung on his far wall. "Sending a single company of men out there might be the silliest mistake this command ever made . . . I don't mind telling you I'm relieved it won't be my mistake."

The council of reckoning was long and increasingly bitter, ominous signs began to mount. Black Otter would not back down on his rash words about Whistling Elk's will to fight. Whistling Elk would not consent to Black Otter's demand that he now lead the fight against the *tahbay-boh*. "You are like a mad wolf who forgets the power of the grizzly and rushes in to a foolish death."

"Those are squaw words, not the words of a warrior," taunted Black Otter. "It is because of you that those in the settlement still fight, because of you that our victory is not complete. Only a fighting heart deserves to lead when the land that was our mother is threatened."

Older warriors began to shift about nervously. This was edging toward a lethal ending; the honor of one chief might be preserved in these exchanges but not two. Finally one of the accompanying chiefs rose to stand tall and grim by the fire. He wasn't a man of many trophies or ready boasts but he had seen much warfare and proved himself in battle and had the wisdom not to take sides.

"We are a great people," he began, "and a great people need many leaders. The season of war stretches out before us but our enemies are many and the needs of our old and weak ones must never be forgotten. Let Whistling Elk, who wishes time to think through messages our spirits send us before blood stains the war hatchet, let him return to the Arkansas where our people are still gathering, where soon many warriors will cover the plains. Let him return there and prepare our people for the many moons of struggle lying ahead. And let Black Otter, whose heart is in victory over these whites stubbornly hanging on to life, remain here until their scalps adorn his war belt and his spirit is at peace."

Murmurs of assent rose all around the council circle, and even the young standing far back sensed a crisis had been averted. Both chiefs could leave now in honor with honorable roles to fulfill, though many felt Black Otter was far from satisfied. Yet even he knew support for him would fall away if he forced the council back into the impasse that for too long threatened.

But bad blood had been started. It led to a watchfulness between factions that revealed the hazardous issue was not over. A scowling Red Hand followed Black Otter into a tipi where it was known spirit water, the white man's whiskey, plundered from some settler's cabin, was kept. Sam rolled in his new blanket, his old one already slipped to the captives, and wondered what the morrow would bring. It seemed strange to be so near the settlement he left so long ago, not knowing if the few souls he ever loved survived. Like all human beings he hoped they had but couldn't keep his mind from scheming to uncover the truth.

Captain Quarles led his slicker-covered company of cavalry into the rain-swept valley of the Kaw, heading west into the storm. Some twenty-odd civilian volunteers followed them, a supplemental force that would grow until they left Salina. It would be days before they reached the settlement, and Quarles knew it might well be too late. Lee, who stayed well ahead of the guidon, warned him even approaching a besieged area with this small a force could be risky; major uprisings often meant hundreds of warriors to be dealt with. It took the widely suspected dangers of this mission to keep the troopers minds off the weather, a continual downpour that made it impossible to keep formations and caused an endless regrouping that tired the horses. It was late the second day before the rain, tapering off and leaving an overcast sky, led to some relief and allowed a faster pace, but it was Topeka before they saw the sun.

Henry tried to keep a clear head, in combat a troubled mind makes for uncertain leadership, but he couldn't keep the image of Cathy Sadler in Indian hands off his mind. He sensed from Stanton's note the American public, much as they dreaded them, could deal with battlefield casualties better than they could indignities heaped upon helpless women in crude heathenish hands. He had seen white women returned from Indian captivity and the thought of it made him force his attention on a fleeting glimpse of Lee riding far ahead. His old friend was worried about him, worried about what he might find at the destroyed settlement. It was a bad sign. Lee's instincts were rarely wrong.

By the time they reached Salina he had resigned himself to the fact that near two weeks had passed since the attack struck, no remnant of the settlement could have held out this long against the odds their desperate plea implied. He pressed ahead, his heart telling him the woman who had strangely entered his life may have already left it, victim of a horrifying massacre or perhaps, as often happened when outposts were overrun, gone without even a trace.

⚐ 47 ⚐

It was far too quiet.

There had been no movement, no sign of figures darting behind distant cover, even more puzzling, no shots fired since dawn. Cole couldn't believe the Indians had left, but the quietude couldn't be denied. "They do funny things, still it don't hardly make sense."

Cheatem, rising on his toes at a window to peer in the distance, grumbled to himself. "Bastards could be up to tricks. Don't figure they got to play cat and mouse with the likes of us but a fellow never knows."

"We best just wait," cautioned Cathy.

But an hour slipped by and the silence continued.

In a way the sight of wild game wandering through the charred remains of the settlement was reassuring. Two deer drifted by in the distance and Cheatem, with his glasses, caught several coyotes loping beyond. Here and there vultures were still circling and flopping to the ground to feed.

As it approached noon, Cole opened the door and, stepping outside, looked about. To the east a flight of crows were squabbling raucously in trees along the river, to the south a hawk drifted on a high wind, seeming fixed in the sky. "Mighty quiet," he said to Cheatem, who had moved out to join him.

"Like a churchyard," muttered Silas.

Hattie appeared at the door. "Reckon dey gone?"

"Could be," answered Cole.

Suddenly Cheatem was pointing. "Looky yonder!"

On the rise they could see two men waving at them. "Must be from the hall," remarked Cole, as Cathy came out followed by Skeeter and Ben. "Must be figuring the attack is over."

"Reckon," sighed Cheatem in relief. One of the men on the rise beckoned to them and Silas and Cole exchanged glances.

"Don't go up there without a gun," warned Cheatem. "We'uns will cover you."

Cole nodded. Holding his rifle, with Cathy's pistol shoved into his belt, he made his way to the rim of the rise. Two excited settlers, both heavily armed, watched him approach. "We haven't seen a thing since dawn," cried one. "Figurin' maybe they gone."

Cole stared at them, then from this vantage point studied the stretch of desolation around him. "Someone ought to scout a bit before we leave cover . . . never can tell."

The other man, sounding a tad too decisive, like a man anxious to believe his own words, said, "They gone sure 'nough. We can see in t'other direction. Ain't a whiff of redskins nowheres."

Cole grunted to himself.

The first man looked toward the nearest burnt-out homestead. "Dillby wants us to start a'buryin' those poor folks, says it ain't Christian leaving 'em lying about. Figured you people might lend a hand."

Cole kept looking around. "We'll do our share . . . but we ain't starting yet."

The first man shook his head. "Can't wait much longer, over to the hall smells is gittin' to some folks."

The second nodded, adding quickly, "Dillby also says you 'uns ought to come over and join us, 'special them women . . . figures we ought to be doing some prayin' for gitting delivered and all."

A blue jay scolded in the brush and long strings of geese could be heard passing overhead. "We'll give it some thought," said Cole, preparing to return to the ranch. He couldn't stop glancing about, speaking to but not looking at the others. "We'll be in touch after dark, if we can we'll work a little scout before then." He was several yards down from the rise before turning to add,

"You folks better pray with your heads up and eyes open, hear Indians are pretty good at hiding, sometimes even where angels can't see 'em."

Sam was gaining a strange confidence. Not that he still wasn't scared, anxious, sickened at the abuse of captives or depressed by a growing fear that his people were dead, but the utter helplessness of his earlier days was passing, and for a single reason. He now understood the language well enough to follow what was going on. He saw the great breach between the chiefs, and knew many of the warriors were leaving. It was evident Bad Eyes, related to Black Otter, was staying, as were many of the braves who held captives. He discovered to his advantage, few in camp were aware he understood them and many spoke unguardedly in his presence. In such a way did he find out the burly warrior was not taking Alice for a wife, although at times he made her sit nude beside him. He was giving her to his three grown sons, one of which wanted to marry her, but since among Comanches brothers shared wives Alice would soon be at the disposal of all three. Unfortunately his sons were doltish and ill favored, lacking their father's courage or physique, either of which might have attracted females from their tribe. In a similar way he discovered Charlotte Barry's young brave was stoutly refusing Red Hand's offers to buy her, even though the war leader had started backing up his offers with threats.

He did not need anyone to tell him what was happening to the other women, including the Hunts, who now trudged around as filthy and lice ridden as the hags they served. They carried out the foulest jobs in the camp. Too unsightly to attract even the lewdest braves, they were no longer raped or openly ravished as they were in the beginning, but their agony was endless, their despair leaving them only able to moan broken prayers throughout the night. The children were being studied for adoption, some already chosen, others were proving too troublesome for the squaws to long endure. Sam, fearing for their safety, took every opportunity to warn them to behave, but most of the young ones believed Sam, himself, was some strange kind of Indian and shied away from him.

But the most important knowledge he gleaned with his new ability was the uneasy situation developing between Black Otter and Red Hand. He had heard the war leader, that perilous night he and Black Otter gulped the settler's whiskey, going by muttering about becoming a chief. At the time it meant nothing, for many war leaders carried illusions about being chiefs, but since then he had heard other things. With Whistling Elk gone and many of his supporters, Black Otter wanted to storm the ranch and the big hall and put an end to these stubborn figures who denied him complete victory. But Red Hand cautioned him against a tactic that had already cost them the support of many valuable braves, not to mention the edge it had given Whistling Elk in the test of leadership. "Pull back," argued Red Hand in a small council held just beyond Bad Eyes's tipi. "Make them think we have left. They will grow careless, they will go about burying the bones of their dead ones, they will wander from cover and seek food. When fear has left them and they are rejoicing to find themselves alive, we will strike!"

"But have they not sent for help?"

"Help is many sleeps away, no strong rescuing hand can come to grasp theirs before halfway to the next moon. Runners are reporting our brothers to the north, Cheyennes, Arapahos, and their friends the Sioux, are scoring great victories at little cost. We must do the same."

Black Otter grunted sullenly but sensed Red Hand was right. But Red Hand was secretly convinced he was more than just right, for too often he had seen Black Otter charging into combat, paying too high a price for victories that could have been won more cheaply with a little forethought and guile. It was a thing about Black Otter that increasingly disturbed him, the thing that had caught the eye of Whistling Elk and others. The man tended to fight like a mad dog instead of a cunning wolf. But Black Otter was a dangerous chief to oppose. He could not be openly differed with in his own band. Only death would yield that head seat at the council fire to another.

Cole stood in the darkness outside the hall and peered around him. The dead still lay out there, giving the shaft of moonlight working through the clouds an eerie cast and raising questions death curiously poses in the minds of men. What was it like lying there, having your body pecked at by vultures, devoured by animals? His mouth tightened as he forced away the thought. Did it matter anymore or was all care, all worldly fears vanished? Life was after all a fragile thing, once it flickered out all the wisdom man has acquired since the dawn of time couldn't bring it back. Starker questions arose. Why were they lying out there and not he, not Cathy, not the desperate crews of the hall, the ranch? Was there any logic to fate? Perhaps that single preparation, racing for the ranch at the first shot, made the difference, for the two of them could never have held their home, surely perishing in its flames. He thought of carefully approaching the site during the day, hoping the fire had spared something, but he and Cheatem resolved no one was to stray from cover until nightfall. If all was quiet by morning they would help with the burying, but now he had slipped over to respond to Dillby's request that his party, or at least the women, come to the hall.

They greeted him with handshakes and remarks that left little doubt they believed their salvation came not only from their redoubtable stand but from the sheltering hand of the Lord. Cole had to admit it made some sense for them to feel the danger was over . . . that is if something didn't keep nagging at him. Why would the Indians withdraw when with their numbers a determined attack could have wiped out both positions?

"Trouble is you're thinking like a white man," said one of the settlers. "Injuns don't fight the way we do. They ain't got the brisket when it comes to scrapping in close, same as they scared to fight come night."

Cole nodded. Perhaps he was being too cautious, but he pointed out if the danger was over the women might

just as well stay where they were. Dillby came to him
with both hands raised. "Cole, they should be joining us
in prayer. As Christians we must start renewing and
restoring our spiritual strength to deal with this tragedy.
Tomorrow will be a difficult day for us all, we will need
the consolation of divine comfort and guidance. Pray,
have them come, I'm sure they'll find it as uplifting as we
have."

Cole nodded. "I'll sure tell them that."

Dillby wrinkled his brow as though an oversight had
struck him. "Oh, yes, and tell those Negroes they are
also welcome."

Cole resisted a faint smile. "I will," he said softly and,
nodding to the others, left.

Quarles left Salina knowing he had more than two
days' travel to reach the settlement. Over forty civilian
volunteers had joined him, bringing his command to
almost two hundred men. It seemed a sizable force but
Lee kept studying the terrain ahead for likely places of
ambush. He knew with every step they were drawing
closer to country the Indians knew well and had likely
fought over before. On occasion his precautions slowed
the column up, angering Quarles and leading to testy
exchanges. "Lee, we've got to keep moving!" he exploded at the guide. "We'll never get there at this pace!"

"Keep rushing ahead like a blind steer smelling water
and you might never get there at all!" Lee could not be
easily swayed, he knew Henry's concerns were not all
military, and he didn't think a few hours could matter
much now. He wondered what Captain Quarles would
do if confronted with a decaying corpse instead of the
shapely and arousing female he appeared infatuated
with. The frontier was a harsh place; it sucked the
softness out of people, hardened them to a basic law of
survival in the wilderness, kill or be killed. Lee had
accepted this grim truth a long time ago. He saw animals
killing each other to survive, insects doing the same. If
man had illusions about himself it was misleading, he
was still part of a world where killing went with surviving. He held no brief for Indians, he knew their notions

of life were too far removed from any white's to allow a lasting peace, but they weren't wrong, unchecked whites flooding their lands was their death knell, to destroy these intruders, difficult as that was beginning to prove, was their only hope.

Some of the civilians, frontier types used to vying with Indians, came up to help. Lee kept the point and sent them to the flanks to keep every side covered. By the second day the tension had mounted to where the entire column was watching the horizon, and every sudden flight of birds or the distant sight of a wolf or deer changing directions caused comment. By sundown, though Quarles looked fretful and wanted to press on, Lee insisted that the horses needed rest and, having spotted a safe place to bivouac, led them to a vamp in the valley that could be easily defended and offered fresh grass for the mounts. They would reach the settlement late tomorrow morning, and the long wait, a mixture of hope, despair, and attempts at resigning one's self to the Lord's will would be over. But for many of those awaiting word of their loved ones, the agony would have just begun.

Sam knew something strange was afoot. Red Hand had talked to Black Otter and Black Otter had come to his sister, Bad Eyes, for strong medicine. He could hear them standing just inside the tipi.

"You fight in darkness?" Bad Eyes gasped, surprise in her voice. "A warrior's spirit may not find its way by night."

"It is as Red Hand says a time when whites are not watching, believing we attack only at dawn. They have not seen us for two days now, tonight they will stand in their last sunset. Come, say the medicine words over my weapons, the spirits must soon be guarding me in battle."

There was a long silence as Sam heard Bad Eyes mumbling and shaking powders or crushed herbs from the skulls. When she finished there was another silence before she whispered lowly, "Beware of Red Hand, my brother, he has an itch for power in his palm, he would have me trade away my medicine."

Black Otter sounded startled. "He is a war leader and a great warrior."

"He is like the snake who sleeps in heavy grass, awaiting its moment to strike."

"Sister, those are strong words."

"What is in my heart cannot rise with weak ones! He is a man who craves all things for himself. It is not our way. He would make a poor chief."

"Chief? He is not one who thinks of being chief!"

"My brother, the hearts of many war leaders think of being chief, some wait for the fruits of wisdom or their long striving for the people to bring them that honor, others find quicker ways." Sam could hear her drawing in her breath. "The largest snake cannot be seen in heavy grass. Please, brother, beware."

With the camp more and more preoccupied with warriors painting and making secret chants to ward off death in battle, Sam found brief chances to approach the captives. He discovered many were still gripped with despondency and talked only with reluctance. Charlotte still seemed in a partial daze, although she knew now this brave, young as he was, owned her and had made her his wife. Her depression, however, hung on and she lived in an emotional fugue that had her looking without seeing, and listening without understanding. But he thought she understood his telling her not to lose hope, for she sat looking at her hands, mumbling almost incoherently. "Tod is dead . . . I belong to a painted savage . . . What is there to hope for?"

Alice, thinking she was going to escape the torment and debauchery visited upon other women, including her mother, was only dimly aware she was slated to marry her captor's son, a squat, homely brave, whose pock-marked face grinned at her at every passing. Sam didn't have the heart to tell her she would have three equally ugly males sharing her robe when that event took place. Still he urged her to take heart and sneaked her some of the tidbits now routinely falling his way from Bad Eyes's bounty.

Though all the women were wretched, Flora seemed

the worst of all. Charity was beginning to show signs of escaping reality, offering him at times that glazed look, as though apparitions were dancing in the sky over his shoulder. But Flora was grimly sane and painfully conscious of her deplorable state. Her hair was a rank cluster of dirt and muck from the tasks she was driven to. Her face was badly scratched, breaking out in running sores and splotched with swollen bruises. She was being struck repeatedly, her breasts and body showing red welts left by heavy switches. The shredded blanket she kept around herself did not completely cover her, and Sam gave her an old shirt, which she tied into a loincloth, unlike distraught Charity, who often seemed unaware her private parts were exposed.

Strangely enough, in spite of her misery and shameful condition Flora seemed determined to stay alive. She saw Alice with the burly warrior but Sam assured her the girl had not been raped. He didn't mention the coming marriage. Fortunately she didn't press him, but her eyes held his with every word he spoke. He had a feeling she would see through any lies he tried. Whether it was her religious faith or some rugged strain in her Yankee heritage, Flora Hunt ate the garbage thrown at her, suffered the indignities heaped upon her, and stared at her tormenters with a mute resignation that Sam sensed pain was finding it harder and harder to penetrate.

The evening the warriors slipped away, Sam saw her walking from an angry squaw who had been whipping her with a leather strap, silently but resolutely lugging a heavy bowl for water.

He would remember that night for both Charlotte's brave and the burly warrior had gone with Red Hand and Black Otter, and everyone in camp knew the hour to strike down the last defenders of the settlement had come. Bad Eyes, mumbling to herself and looking deeply concerned, went off to a nearby wood, collecting herbs for special medicines. Sam realized how distracted his stout owner must have been when he found she had left him her entire dinner of boiled rabbit and buffalo ribs to eat.

◄ 48 ►

It had been a peculiar day. Dillby came forth with a shovel, saying the burying could no longer be delayed. The grisly job filled a long, wretched morning but by noon Cole was slipping through the outskirts, finding everything quiet. At the most western point he settled for a few minutes, but nothing in the actions of game suggested the presence of others. Coming near his old homestead he couldn't help noticing that the stove and some metal pots had survived the fire and that the well pump was still intact. A closer look would probably reveal other items such as tools or precious nails that could be recovered. He would have to take a look before sundown but for the moment hot food was being prepared at the hall and Hattie and Cathy had gone over to help.

They prayed before eating and Cole noticed the other settlers quietly settling at the table alongside Skeeter and Ben. The horror of swollen mutilated bodies, some with empty eye sockets filled with vermin, all hurriedly covered over with quick shovels of earth, had seemingly shifted values. Hattie, who was cooking, glanced stoically at him and Cathy but appeared unmoved by the change.

Dillby, having heard that Lame Fox was sent for help many days before, now felt their hour of rescue was close at hand. Cheatem, openly restless at the table, kept insisting they weren't rescued yet and that guards should be posted until help definitely arrived. Cole supported him and two settlers agreed to stand watch for the rest of the day. One would be posted where the Hunt houses once stood and the other to the southeast, where the land dropped sharply as it approached the river. Everyone would stay armed, including the women.

By late afternoon a feeling spread that a reprieve from the threat of annihilation, answering their prayers, had been granted. Yet there wasn't a whisper of exhilaration, the pall of the disaster still hung over them, the shattered lives of many could be seen in eyes too gaunt to register pain piercing the heart. Some knew the settlement could never recover from this calamity. Time would only reduce its horrors, paving them off with happier events that hopefully would follow. The years might dim the hurt but not the memory of family members awakened by their murderers that ghastly morning.

By sunset Cole decided to return to the ashes of his home and bring back whatever could be salvaged, particularly that stove, for he could think of no way to replace it. He knew it would be heavy and did not object when Skeeter and Ben offered to go along to help. Cheatem watched them go, wondering when Cathy and Hattie would return from the hall. He had left them up there with the other woman, planning what cooking could be arranged for the next few days, and cutting bandages for the few wounds that still needed tending. Luckily none were serious; serious wounds rarely stayed a problem for long on the frontier.

It was only when he saw it was getting dark that Cheatem peered in the direction of the men and was just able to make them out wrestling with the stove. Somehow feeling safer he lit a candle and sat the coffee pot on to heat. There was still some food in the larder; the women would fix something for him when they returned. Suddenly a strange sense of urgency had him staring up toward the rise but the women were nowhere in sight. Then curiously the settlement seemed unnaturally quiet, the last chirps of birds and the buzz of insects that usually ushered in the night were missing. He glanced around him; it was too dark now to make out forms. Unaccountably he got an eerie feeling things were not right. He moved back slowly in the flickering candle-light, groping for and seizing his rifle. He had decided to fire a shot and alert the others when suddenly he was rocked by shrill war cries rising on all sides, and a cold impale of fear, freezing the gun in his hand, told him it was too late!

At the hall the coming of night had been greeted with relief. Indians were known not to favor hostilities at night and dim figures could be seen slipping out to enjoy the fresh west breeze or relieve themselves. Two candles were burning and Cathy and Hattie, delayed by Dillby's many instructions and insistence that all available food be brought to the hall, were preparing to leave. Cathy, remembering Cole had mentioned trying to recover items from their ruined home, was suddenly anxious to return, a nervous tension started by the attack had not completely left her. She stood on the narrow step before the hall and glanced at the darkness before her. Hattie was busy arranging some things in her arms, ready to follow her. Staring ahead, Cathy caught vague figures approaching the steps and assumed they were those who had slipped out for one reason or another and were now returning. But the figures were suddenly coming too fast and as they entered the feeble candlelight, painted faces beneath great buffalo headdresses formed before her eyes. With deafening war cries exploding against her ears she hurled herself backward, carrying Hattie with her as in desperation she reached for and slammed the door shut.

Gunshots were ringing out from the ranch, the Sadler claim and now, as shock jolted the hall, people threw themselves to the floor beside shattered windows, trying to level gun barrels into the night. The hall that a moment before was savoring a moment of peace was now a shadowy cavern of hysteria and panic. A man caught outside was already dead and two more inside had taken their death wounds, including the woman who had done so much to comfort others. Cathy with her pistol and Hattie with her shotgun were doing their best to fight back, shouting to Dillby to get down, as he took a bullet in his thigh and had to grasp the table's edge as he reached and blew out the candles.

Without warning the shooting suddenly stopped, leav-

ing everyone dazed in the darkness. A minute then two
went by, then Cathy saw a light approaching. Within
seconds she could see it was a torch. "They're going to
burn us out!" she screamed.

For Hattie the shooting hadn't stopped, her ears were
attuned to shots echoing in the distance. Ben and
Skeeter were out there; if her people were going to die
she wanted to die with them. It wasn't a lot to ask from
the Lord. Around her she heard voices gasping bits of
prayer, some managing a word or two but then choking
or repeating themselves or simply giving up in anguish.

She saw a man hurrying to a window next to the door,
shouting behind him that they had to kill the figure
carrying the torch. Someone fired a gun, then a panicking voice yelled, "It's on the roof, it's too late!"

Hattie struggled to her feet. This devil-infested land
that murdered or swallowed people up, had had its way
long enough. If she, Skeeter, and Ben, were destined to
join Chloe and Sam, she wanted them to do it together.

As shots rang out all three abandoned the stove and
scrambled for their guns, but bullets were already whining over and around them and only Skeeter wasn't hit.
Ben took a slug in the back and Cole was doubled over as
a lead ball tore into his ribs. They started toward the
ranch, Skeeter trying to help Ben forward, but only by
stopping could they fire back. Cole had to fire from his
knees and Ben couldn't hold his gun steady enough to
aim. Only the darkness kept them from being overrun,
and only the sound of Cheatem's gun enabled them to
struggle toward the ranch. Cole, seeing the odds against
them, urged Skeeter to run. Someone had to stay alive
for Cathy's sake. But Skeeter only had breath enough to
grunt as he helped both of them forward, stopping every
few steps to fire wildly into the night. It was flames
leaping across the broad roof of the hall that pulled the
attackers' eyes from the near helpless trio. Screaming
warriors sensing victory started racing toward the conflagration where they knew the greatest number of scalps
waited to be taken.

Cheatem, his instincts having allowed him a heartbeat

or two of warning, had fired at the first figures he saw leaping toward him in the darkness. Two warriors lay dead some thirty feet from his side door. But now others were trying to enter the house through the open front door or one of the broken windows, but standing in the middle of the large room he was able to fire in three directions, and raised enough yelps from the wounded to make the others hang back. Red Hand was there, shouting not to throw their lives away, this white was already good as dead.

From intermittent shots sounding in their direction Cheatem knew the three men were trying to reach him. There was nothing he could do to help them but he kept shifting to that side, hoping to catch their attackers in a crossfire. In his heart he knew they were finished. There was no way out of this trap; they were outnumbered and too scattered for any hope of defense. His eye caught the sky brightening beyond the rise. Jesus! The hall was on fire—his ranch would be next!

Had it not been for Red Hand carefully watching Black Otter the fight at the ranch would have been quickly over and the whites dead. But Black Otter, at the first sign of the burning hall, started in that direction. That's where the most whites remained, that's where the biggest coups would be scored, that's where there were still women, and this time Red Hand would take the captives. This time Red Hand wanted a female for himself.

Had he left alone it wouldn't have mattered but to cover his own scheming he signaled some braves to join him, leaving only a handful to take the ranch. It should still have been enough but by now the three had been struggling close enough to bring two sides of the house under fire, and though Cole had to fight from his knees his head had cleared and his aim was returning. Ben had given up trying to fight and had gave his loaded gun to Cole. Skeeter, mumbling prayers to himself, kept shooting, but was watching for every opportunity to work them closer to the house. It was probably the distraction of a wounded brave, lying near the embankment, chant-

ing to his medicine not to let him die in this darkness
that made it possible, for the other braves hearing him
allowed a lull in the fighting when Skeeter with one last
breathless effort managed to get them before the side
door. Cheatem reached out to help them in, but as
exhausted as Cole was he clung to Cheatem's arm,
gasping, "Where's Cathy?"

Cheatem settled him on the floor, feeling his blood-
soaked shirt and seeing Ben collapsing beyond. There
was no way the truth could be concealed. "She's at the
hall," he said, his voice a hoarse whisper, "and damn if
the place isn't on fire."

There was no way the hall could be saved. Their only
hope was the unfinished walls of Dillby's single room,
made partly of rock taken from the stream bed.
Wounded though he was Dillby and another man pulled
the few pieces of iron railing, meant for the altar, across
to that corner. Nothing could be done for the two
wounded and Cathy screamed as she saw the burning
roof falling on them. Hattie, pushing her before her until
she was down behind the low wall, kept saying, "Dey
wid Jesus now . . . dey wid Jesus."

There were only six settlers left with Dillby, and they
quickly filled the small space that had only been a single
room. The smoke and heat were a mounting threat that
Dillby broke their only window to lessen. It started a
draft that sucked the smoke out but heightened the heat
as wooden benches began to smolder and burn. Luckily
the hall was empty and with the wooden roof collapsing
there were only benches and thin walls to burn. Even so
the heat was suffocating and Cathy began to fear she was
passing out. "Stay down! Don't forget them Injuns!"
shouted one of the men. Dillby, who tried to block the
fire until his clothes began to smoke, had to be restrained
by the men until the wind, now coming through the
window, brought the screams of warriors outside. With
that Dillby began to pray to God to take them in his
infinite mercy, allow them to suffer His will and find
peace in the beyond. Hattie heard the mumbled

"Amens" but she was praying for her people, praying she be allowed to reach them, suffer with them, die with them.

As the fire quickly peaked and died down the darkness crept back. The Indians at first were puzzled at what happened. They had expected the whites to be driven from the hall by fire, and if not burnt corpses would be left to mark their victory. But with the wood gone the low stone walls appeared, and while the burnt area was still too hot to enter, somehow some cowering figures had lived through the flames, and though they couldn't be made out in the darkness, sharp-eyed braves began murmuring there were rifle barrels sticking up beyond the low-cut walls. But such walls could never save them; almost immediately a hail of bullets and whirling arrows hit them, one man taking a slug through the head and slumping down without a word, another groaning in agony as an arrow tore open his shoulder. Their feeble returning fire would have been pointless had not the Indians been bunched together so that every shot fired struck some brave. At a command from Red Hand they backed away. There was no need to rush things, these scalps were as good as taken.

Except for the dying crackle of fire and the moans of the wounded once again silence settled over this weird scene and shots from down near the ranch could be heard. Red Hand stood in the darkness with Black Otter. "They are as gophers trapped in a den by hungry badgers," he said. "We will kill them one by one at dawn."

Black Otter turned to stare in the direction of the ranch, his face paint distorting but not erasing his scowl. "Why do those *tahbay-boh* still live?"

"It is a small matter, many are already wounded, in less than half a smoke they will all be dead."

Black Otter snorted. "You are too cautious, Red Hand, a warrior finishes wounded enemies with his war club. Now you say we must await dawn." He looked about him, his fierce visage studying the night. "Black Otter will show you how brave hearts bring victories . . . how the Nerm sheds the blood of enemies, leaving their bones to whiten on the prairie, warning others our hunting grounds are sacred."

Uneasily Red Hand watched him stomping off into the darkness, headed for the ranch. The war leader knew in his chief's eyes he had failed; this was not the victory he had promised. The chief, now angry and frustrated, was going to storm the ranch. By ignoring his losses he would surely take it, and this fight, already won, would then be his victory. Red Hand settled his buffalo headdress more firmly on his head. The road to being chief was more perilous than he thought. Black Otter was acting strangely of late, as though something were preying on his mind. An unwary premonition turned Red Hand's thoughts to seeking stronger medicine, yet the very thought of medicine brought Bad Eyes to mind . . . Bad Eyes? Why did she come to mind with such a jolt? He stopped to look back toward the ranch and then something he had foolishly overlooked struck him—Black Otter was Bad Eyes's brother!

A cold suspicion entered the outskirts of his mind and wandered inward until suddenly meeting fear. Was it only his hope to be chief . . . or was it far more than that at stake here this night?

49

It was the stark silence Hattie couldn't stand. No more shots rang out from the direction of the ranch, and the night about them was as heavy and impenetrable as it was rank with the odor of burnt flesh and charred wood. She struggled toward the door end of the room until Dillby reached out to keep her from going further.

Hattie tightened the strap holding a few remaining

shotgun shells about her waist and rubbed tear-streaked patches of ash from around her eyes. "Ah gots to go!" she whispered firmly.

"Woman, are you mad? You'll be killed!"

"Gots to git to my folks."

"You wouldn't last five minutes," muttered one of the men.

Hattie rubbed grime from her lips. "How long you think us gonna last here?"

Dillby now had a restraining hand on her shoulder. "Hattie, they are no longer fighting down there . . . it could be too late."

Cathy moved closer to her. "Hattie, please, you can't make it alone, wait, if it stays quiet I'll go with you."

Hattie shrugged away. "Ah cain't wait."

Dillby sounded drained, too weak to persist. "Hattie, they're savages, they'll kill you."

Hattie glanced around her. "Y'all think ah 'fraid to die? Righteous souls ain't never 'fraid to die!"

The man with the torn shoulder half whispered, "I am." Darkness covered his futile efforts to smile at Hattie, adding, "You got pluck, lady, kill one of those bastards for me if erry you git the chance."

Hattie shifted over to kiss Cathy, then left on all fours, moving across the still heated ground, making her way to where the door had burned out. Everywhere she raised small flights of ash and crawling outside she had to keep the shotgun at her side where it dragged over scorched ground that lay between the hall and the slope. Once on the slope she sensed she was sharing this darkness with others. By lying still she could make out dim figures moving against the night sky, unable to see their features but some with white paint on their faces could be briefly spotted glancing her way. Most noticeable of all were those menacing silhouettes of horned headgear, making them seem monsters in the night, making her realize even if her black skin made her near invisible, her outline, if accidentally caught, would surely give her away. Slowly she crept forward hugging the ground. It was a long crawl to the ranch, its iron silence rising like an icy tentacle reaching for her heart.

But living or dead she wanted to be with those she had mothered and prayed for for so long, being Hattie she could do no other.

Inside the ranch house it was also silent, except when Ben moaned and begged for water. Cole was mute, propped up in a corner but helplessly slumping to one side as he failed to hang on to a frail fitful consciousness. He was badly hurt and knew it. The bullet was deep in him and a fever was rising, robbing his senses of their edge and making him drift off in hallucinatory spells that reality jerked him back from every few minutes.

Cheatem and Skeeter were squatting back to back to keep four sides covered. Ben's anguished cries for water had to be ignored, for both his and Cole's wounds were internal and Cheatem wouldn't run the risk of giving them water. Cole understood, but Ben lay in agony, tormented as much by their seeming indifference as thirst. "Ah'se dyin' . . . gots to give me water . . . just little sip 'o water."

"They'll be hitting us at dawn," said Cheatem, trying to pretend he didn't hear Ben. "Gonna be mighty tough keeping 'em all off."

"You 'magine folks still at duh hall?"

Cheatem's tone belied his answer's faint flicker of hope. "Hard to tell . . . ain't heard shooting for a spell . . . could mean anything . . . maybe . . . maybe not."

Cole's head turned toward them. "Cathy? Is that you, Cathy?"

"It's me, Silas."

Cole's voice, labored, near lacking the breath to sustain it, filled the night with his pain. "Tell Cathy to come."

"I will," said Cheatem, his voice curiously thick, "directly I'm able . . . best try to sleep."

Outside Black Otter stood forty feet from the ranch door. Two attempts to set this stubborn structure on fire had failed, but he didn't care. He was going back to his favorite way of dealing with the *tahbay-boh,* strike at dawn and keep fighting and scalping until there were

none left to slay. The angles of intermittent shots told
him there were only two defenders left. They would
attack from all sides, he himself charging through the
open front door, others climbing through smashed windows or the side door. There were now several braves
about him, it was time to show Red Hand what a chief
must do. Ah, Red Hand, was there not something new
and strange in this war leader's ways, did he not bring to
mind the young wolf eyeing the aging leader of the pack?
Black Otter looked into the heavy darkness. He could see
nothing, but flashing before his mind's eye was his sister,
Bad Eyes, rage lining her voice, harshly whispering
"Beware." Black Otter mused darkly for a moment, then
suddenly ordered some of the braves standing close to
fall back to the river bank. Here he signaled them to
squat down and, as the false dawn slipped into the
eastern sky, he muttered words that made them shift
nervously, reach for their medicine bags, and moan
secret incantations to the spirits.

Hattie was near exhausted. She had spent several
hours crawling and desperately flattening herself against
the earth whenever she heard the tread or grunts of
Indians nearby. The ordeal seemed endless but she knew
she was getting close. At moments she could hear the low
murmur of the river beyond. If she could get into the
house some spiritual craving in her would be satisfied. If
Ben and Skeeter were dead she would accept death
beside them, if they were still alive they could spend
their last moments together. Hattie was too resolved in
spirit to indulge foolish hopes, but now she could see the
ranch wasn't burnt down, that said something. With her
heart beginning to thump within her, she crawled ahead,
keeping her head low but pulling back sharply when she
realized she had crawled onto a dead body, her hands,
feeling the cold flesh, brought a nauseous clutch to her
throat. It was one of the warriors Cheatem had killed
with his first shots. The brave lay sprawled before her
and she backed away to squirm around him, but at that
moment her eye caught a thin spear of light breaking the
gloom in the east. Heavens! It was getting light! She

would have to make a run for it, but now she realized the
door was only thirty or forty yards away. She pressed
herself to her knees only to freeze again as she caught
sight of gray figures materializing out of the dark and
coming forward, forming a circle around the emerging
bulk of the house. There were at least three between her
and the door. In panic she clasped her hands over her
mouth to keep from screaming. There was no way left
for her to enter the ranch or, with dawn coming, even
crawl backwards and escape. Every second brought
death closer, made it more certain. Bewildered, she
dropped down again, her hands still clutching the shotgun but feeling it jar against the head of the corpse. The
sound could have undone her, but though trembling she
realized it hadn't hit the head but the buffalo-horned
helmet the brave was wearing. In a flash born of desperation, she wrenched the headpiece from the dead warrior's head and fixed it to her own. It was madness but
only madness could now promise what common sense
couldn't. It was still dark enough for her to be taken for a
brave, and if it gave her a few more moments to try for
that door Hattie wanted them.

Black Otter was ready; the moment to strike had
come. The hate he carried for the *tahbay-boh* had put
new strength in his arms and brought fresh keenness to
his eyes. With their deaths he would return to the great
camp on the Arkansas, their scalps hanging from his
horse's bridle or decorating its mane. He would be
received as a great leader, one who brought the people
victories. The squaws would see this, cover their mouths
in awe, and turn their faces away from Whistling Elk.
His warriors were around and behind him, he had told
them to watch him, as he rushed toward the open door
they were to attack from all sides. He held a lance in one
hand, a war club in the other; the true Comanche
warrior going into battle. With the charcoal sky in the
east turning a lighter gray the moment had come. He
began to quicken his pace, filling his lungs for the
opening war cry, but then, incredibly, a brave was
running beside him, trying to pass him. Was another

daring to seek the honor of opening this fight?! Black Otter reached out, grabbing the rushing figure by the shoulder, swinging it about as they came to the door. His war club was poised as he found himself face to face with white eyes in a strangely dark countenance. In another instant his war club would have crushed life out of this alien figure were it not for the cold muzzle of a shotgun pressed against his chest, and a deafening roar his ears only partially recorded, leaving him in darkness and plunging him into oblivion.

The shock was near seismic on both sides. The warriors couldn't believe one of their own had slain their chief. They dropped to the ground, leaderless for the moment, only a few thinking to fire at the house. But the attack was stalled and Cheatem and Skeeter, almost killing Hattie who, staggering through the door, was almost taken for a charging warrior, but saved when they recognized her voice and started shooting at dim figures they could see crouching about the house. Yet neither side could really grasp what happened, the warriors howling about bad medicine now started slipping away for cover, as Cheatem and Skeeter, unable to believe Hattie was there, kept glancing at her between shots, wondering if their eyes were deceiving them. The confusion was too great to sustain a fight, the shooting tapered off and quiet once again settled over the ranch. But it was a silence in which Hattie ran to Ben and, sensing he was dying, began to cry. "Lord, oh lordy, don't take this miserable sinner away," she moaned through her tears. Ben, realizing she was there, opened his eyes. "Hattie, you done come back . . . whyn't yuh come sooner . . . ah'se dying."

Hattie was suddenly turning him on his stomach and ripping his shirt to get at the wound in his back. She felt it for a moment, then crept over to the stove. "What you doing?" cried Cheatem, angling up to finally bar the door. "You can't build a fire now."

"Ah needs heat."

Silas was too frayed with nervous exhaustion to argue. He watched Hattie crawling over to Cole, looking at his wound and feeling around it. She seemed to be holding her breath, in the end letting it out with a troubled sigh. "Dats bad," she half whispered. "Dats fearsome bad."

Skeeter came over to hug her but no one spoke and only Cole could be heard mumbling in his delirium for near a hour. Dawn was flooding the plain and no shots rang out from the direction of the hall, but neither brought comment. Everyone knew the next move was up to savages skulking just beyond.

Red Hand was ready to attack and pick off those pathetic whites, cringing behind the low walls, when a brave came rushing up. Black Otter had been killed, the great chief was no more. Bad medicine, hissed the warrior, was plaguing their war party. Did Red Hand have words to lift the warriors' hearts and rekindle their will to fight?

Red Hand, turning about, looked toward the ranch, both doubt and relief in his eyes. A curious sensation was rippling through his body. Was this the moment he had been waiting for? Would these warriors now follow him if he claimed the role of chief? Surely he must move quickly, making it a thing granted while they felt the need for strong hands to guide them, a proven warrior to carry the pipe in battle and bring wisdom to their council fires. He sent the brave back, telling him to have all the warriors at the ranch meet him at the rise; he would draw the braves around him so that they could all council together. Once their hearts were joined their courage would return and the scalps of these whites would be easily lifted.

Inside the dark, lonely walls, Cathy heard shots rising from the direction of the ranch. She couldn't keep a sob from catching in her throat. She should have gone with Hattie; God alone knew what had happened to Cole. No one there expected to survive sunrise. Their position was too exposed, their will to fight beginning to fade, their capacity for prayer exhausted by Dillby during the night.

Only the wounded man seemed inclined to speak, and

he only to keep his mind off his pain. "Wonder what happened to that Hattie gal . . . ain't seen a female with that much brisket for a spell."

"I only hope to God she made it," said Cathy, biting her lip to keep it from trembling.

"Perhaps we should pray for her again," said Dillby, his voice sounding plaintive after his ceaseless pleas for faith during the night.

"Don't figure praying is going to help a bit," muttered the wounded man. "By now she's either down yonder or dead."

"As good Christians," said Dillby, "we should still pray."

The wounded man swore under his breath as he turned to put his weight on the other side of his body. "We can't all be such goddamned good Christians," he snorted, "seeing as how that Hattie gal plum refused to die with us!"

Twelve miles to the east Captain Quarles, forcing his troop to rise at four that morning and get under way, was listening to his scout tell him they were drawing near the settlement and a more defensive formation should be ordered. Quarles argued they could not take time spreading out and advancing on a broad front; he insisted on getting to the settlement as soon as possible, he was not going to defend himself against an enemy he couldn't see.

Lee tried to explain it was because they couldn't see this enemy or what they might be riding into that a safer formation should be considered.

Henry was adamant. Lee finally had to order some of the volunteers to ride not only on their flanks but actually a hundred yards or so ahead of them. Two hundred men was a risky proposition coming to tame what might be a nation of Plains Indians.

For over an hour they moved up silently, only the clink of canteens striking gun metal or the groan of leather saddles as troopers rose in the stirrups to peer ahead and settle again, was to be heard. It was the second hour before Quarles finally saw Lee's hand in the air, signaling a stop. One of the volunteers was racing back. He had struck the first claim. In a moment Lee was pulling back and riding up beside him. "Well?" said Henry.

"The place has been burned to the ground. There's a fresh grave nearby. No other signs of life."

Henry stared at him. "None at all?"

"None."

The warriors gathering on the rise were no longer shaken, concerned about bad medicine, or even anxious for strong hands to guide them. Those whom Black Otter had spoken to before the attack approached Red Hand with the cold eyes of distrust, the hidden ire of defeated loyalists gazing at a usurper. There was still confusion about how Black Otter was killed. It happened so fast, so unexpectedly, some braves thinking another warrior had done it and mysteriously disappeared. None dared believe a Comanche would take refuge in the ranch. The chagrin, if muted, was apparent and suspicion overt, Red Hand catching it in their stolid faces and sober glances.

The whites in the ranch and behind the low walls were momentarily forgotten. Graver matters than scalps, already considered taken, weighed upon the warriors' minds. Leadership was a tenuous matter among Plains Indians. A chief's power lay largely in the respect granted him by his followers, braves didn't take oaths of allegiance to chiefs. Faith and trust were the only holds a leader had on his band. But faith and trust were missing from the countenances of warriors silently studying Red

Hand that morning. It was not without cause. Beyond all the tension and unsettling thoughts, a traditional fear loomed. Dissension in a war party was an ancient taboo. It angered the spirits, turned braves against one another, led to bitter and often hostile acts that split tribes or plagued them for years. The mood of the moment made the older braves uneasy. They frowned and shook their heads as Red Hand's words only made the crowd more restive, the hot bloods visibly straining to remain silent. One could almost feel a vague pressure of resentment building, and wise heads realized unchecked it would sooner or later explode in rash words that could only mean woeful trouble.

An old scarred warrior finally struggled to his feet. He confronted Red Hand with the confidence of one who has proved himself many times in battle. "Red Hand," he began quietly, "we are not children who need to be told our people need leaders, nor are we frightened men who must grab at the nearest stick to defend ourselves against a threat dealt with since birth. Let us return to our camp where we can hold a proper council, speak of our troubles with dignity, share a pipe at the fire until wisdom dissolves our doubts and courage our fears. These whites no longer matter, the Comanche must move as a great people move, as one. The sun is moving across the sky, giving us light before it leaves us in darkness. Let us use this light to bring us together, before the spirits anger and we stand divided in darkness."

Murmurs of assent broke out from the surrounding warriors and Red Hand knew his bid for power was failing. But his cause was not hopeless. The air around this settlement smacked too much of foiled desires. Even their triumph now seemed distantly tarnished, their victory tainted with defeat by a handful of dogged whites. This was not the setting he needed. He would go back to the pitch camp, arrange for a council fire and stand before the people with his many war trophies. The old warrior was right, these whites no longer mattered, Black Otter was dead, their band must have a leader and who could they choose? When the choice came could the camp point to any but the clever and cagey war leader, Red Hand?

Only a brief quarter of an hour separated the retiring Indians from the arrival of Lee and the anguished face of Henry Quarles. Everywhere Henry saw ashes and grim evidence of a settlement overrun and destroyed with a vengeance. Here and there a crude cross marked the grave of a murdered settler, ironically giving hope to the arriving force, as surely Indians didn't bury victims, certainly not under crosses. Yet it was several minutes before those crouching behind the walls spotted blue uniforms and realized they were saved. Dillby stood up and moved toward the horsemen riding toward him. Cathy with the others stumbled after him. Somehow she couldn't believe they were rescued. Couldn't believe it when she heard commands being given in English, couldn't believe it as she rushed into Quarles's arms and felt herself hugged with a fervor that kept her breathless. Her face was still smeared with ash but she felt Quarles's lips on her forehead and his arms around her. In the excitement and euphoric relief of deliverance she let herself be hugged and near collapsed in his arms.

But shouts from the direction of the ranch brought Cole immediately to mind and she pulled away to start trying to make her way down the rise. Quarles, with one arm around her to support her, moved with her. They could see Cheatem and Skeeter coming out and waving to them, everywhere soldiers and volunteers were riding about, some pointing to evidence that the Indians had just left. Lee was following their tracks to the outskirts of the settlement, stopping there to stare grimly about him. He told two volunteers accompanying him to report to Quarles he was going to make a short scout. Then with no more than a departing gesture he galloped off.

For the first hour Henry struggled to get the bullet out of Ben's back. Hattie, with her hot poultices, had kept the wound clean and infection from spreading. With luck he had a reasonable chance of recovering. Cole was another matter. Almost at once Quarles realized the bullet was deep in him and couldn't be reached. Sepsis would soon set in and death was inevitable. Cathy, remembering his handling of Troy's wound and watching him struggling over Ben, refused to believe it. "You know so much about doctoring, you must save him!"

"Cathy, I'm not a surgeon. The bullet is in his internal organs, taking it out might itself kill him."

"You must help him!"

"Cathy, try to understand, there's a limit to what I can do. Even a surgeon might hesitate here . . . a doctor has moral responsibilities." He took her by the arms, staring into her eyes. "You can go on trying to keep his fever down. I'll try to find something for his pain . . . but Cathy, don't ask me to do something I have neither the instruments nor the skills for . . . it isn't fair."

She bit into her lip and sunk down beside Cole. The cold rags she kept placing on his body seemed such a futile effort. It only appeared to help him stay conscious longer, but she could see the painful crimp in his eyes slowly fading, when he spoke his words were weak, distracted, vague of intent. At times he seemed to wander in some shadowy world, shared by life and death, where all emotion vaporized and crystallized at once to pain. She watched Quarles going off to treat the shoulder of the man at the hall, knowing he was all she could turn to, feeling a strange anger at the kind of man he was, knowing somehow she could not let Cole die, sensing his death would be partly hers. She buried her face in her hands, a pounding in her heart assuring her life without Cole would be an abyss of anguish and loneliness, a darkness no spark of human warmth would penetrate again. Death was taking her man and she was helpless, helpless; and yet, being Cathy, the woman in her had to resist, had to deny death with every means possible, had to fight.

The pitch camp, like all war camps, was becoming fouled with human and animal waste. Scalps, stretched out to dry, and a few impaled heads were still sitting about, waiting for the squaws to gather them, strike the tipis, form them into light travois, and move on to fresh ground. But the warriors returning from the ravaged settlement came with weightier things on their minds. Young boys were ordered to build a council fire and some of the older braves began settling on the ground without removing their war paint or giving their sacred shields to squaws to be placed on protective racks.

Red Hand, appearing in a robe adorned with many dyed scalps, and displaying his prized weapons taken in battle, was clearly preparing to speak again. Sam, watching him from within Bad Eyes's tipi, and now aware of Black Otter's death and Red Hand's bidding for power, silently prayed he would fail. He could see Bad Eyes, sitting beyond the council fire, her expression tinged with dread and resentment, barely concealing her repressed rage. The whole camp was now focused on the ornate figure of Red Hand offering the pipe to a warrior to be lit, and shifting himself about as though seeking the stance of a chief.

But Red Hand's passage to power was not to be that easily granted, there were warriors there, suffering from uneasy feelings and pondering questions which, in the presence of the pipe, they wanted answered. But now they sat patiently through Red Hand's hastily prepared harangue about his many coups, acts of bravery and days when his courage or guile brought victory. The people listened, the warriors studied his features as he talked, but when finished Red Hand sat down in silence.

The burly warrior, Alice's captor, was first to his feet. "Tell us, Red Hand, what mad warrior or evil spirit killed our chief, Black Otter?"

"I was not there, I could not know!"

Another warrior rose, his expression uncertain, cryptic, impossible to read. "Does a warrior whisper of bad medicine just before battle, when his braves stand around him and strong medicine protects him?"

Red Hand looked puzzled. "I do not know what others whisper before battle, my words have always been of victory." He was beginning to feel uncomfortable, irritated, disturbed by such senseless questions; why weren't they asking about his record in combat? On impulse he stood up again, allowing a flash of anger to tighten his mouth and send his fingers digging into his robe. "These are meaningless words. What Comanche warrior would whisper fear of bad medicine before battle?"

His answer was an even deeper silence, with many warriors turning to stare at him. After two or three heartbeats a voice rose from their midst. "Black Otter," it said, and the cruel silence droned on.

Red Hand could only stand there, his face puzzled and suddenly creased with concern. This was dangerous ground. He daren't speak again until this threat without a face had at least a name. Above all he needed time. Thankfully the old warrior holding the pipe, which had been lit but momentarily forgotten, now raised it and, taking a puff, passed it to the left. Red Hand slowly sat down, drawing a deep breath. This council, with its strange insinuation that had sent his pulse racing, was far from over.

Lee first spotted it through the trees but fell to his knees to approach with caution. He knew at once it was a war camp, with many fighting men about and likely on their guard. As he crept around, studying it through his field glasses, he was surprised, but then gratified; it was not as big as he feared. He judged not more than a hundred some odd were in camp. Quarles's force had them outnumbered. But what was to be done? Surely there was a major force of Indians somewhere. How close was the question. His knuckles came against his mouth in thought.

Then suddenly he saw something that galvanized him into action. His glasses picked up a flash of blonde hair. Zeroing in on it he managed to glimpse Charlotte Barry's figure standing before a tipi. Captives! There were white captives in this camp! His heart began to beat more rapidly. This could be a tremendous stroke of luck but he realized speed had suddenly become critical. This opportunity might disappear in the snap of one's fingers. Camps like this could strike their tipis and vanish in a matter of minutes.

Backing away he led his horse well out of earshot, then

jumping to the saddle and using his quirt sped off in a dead run.

Quarles had just finished bandaging the shoulder torn open by the flint tip of an arrow, glad the man, a salty type who said the devil wouldn't have him and with no other prospects he was just naturally spared, assured Henry a little whiskey to dull the pain would now suffice.

He was already on his way back to Cathy, whom he couldn't get off his mind, when Lee came thundering up, jumping down and almost shouting he had found the raiders' camp and had seen white captives there. If they struck quickly they might well rescue them.

Quarles for a moment looked confused, but Lee's words had electrified the camp. Volunteers standing close began to cry out, one at Henry's elbow. "Let's go, them devils is got to pay for this!"

A tall pale man with a heavy beard came striding over. "If we don't punish them red bastards and put the fear of Christ in 'em, they'll figure to do this again. If they got captives, they sure as hell is guilty!" He stopped and allowed his eyes to lock on Quarles's. "Captain, is you going to go after 'em or is we 'uns gonna do it alone?"

Quarles began to sense there really wasn't a choice. Even some of the soldiers, appalled at what they now clearly visualized was the fate of the hapless settlers, were already glancing impatiently in his direction. But his written orders were not to attack Indians but relieve the settlement and barter for captives. Something told him this could be a tragic mistake, leading to the death of all captives in Indian hands. But his faith in Lee proved greater than his fear of ignoring orders. "You're sure this is the right move?"

"If you want those captives back it is."

Henry took his arm and pressed it hard. "Lee, what if we're wrong? They're savages. They're likely to do anything."

"The only time you're wrong about Indians is when you do nothing about that savagery. Take a look at this graveyard we're standing in, let this bunch go and in a few months I'll show you one twice as big."

Cheatem and Skeeter appeared, wanting to borrow horses.

Henry looked at them for a moment, then waved to a nearby sergeant, saying at the same time, "You two coming along?"

"Sure as Satan gets coal wholesale," spat Silas. "Those sons of bitches ruined me, put Ben in a bad way, and likely killed Cole. Skeeter 'n me figure we owe 'em something."

Lee waited until they turned away with the sergeant then moved his mouth within inches of Quarles's ear. "Henry, we got enough men to surround them, but, remember, we ain't coming to talk. We've got to hit 'em so hard they won't be able to make a stand. It's the only chance those captives have."

Quarles shook his head. "Lee, I still don't know."

"Well, by God, I do. And we better get moving . . . the Almighty may not keep this gate open all day."

⊰ 51 ⊱

The pipe council, meant to bring unity to the tribesmen, was unavailing, even disconcerting, unknowingly leading to their undoing. In spite of Red Hand's fitful attempts to remove it, the shadow of suspicion remained. Warriors listening to his words stared at the fire, restive, secretly clawed by doubt. This painful spectacle held the camp's attention, with no one alert or looking elsewhere, all knowing what was at stake at the council fire. In time the struggling Red Hand caught Bad Eyes staring coldly at him and an earlier fear gained purchase in his mind. He would have to settle with that fat cow of a squaw when the next chance arose. He must get that amulet. He could not have one who could make powerful medicine conniving at his back.

What really kept the distressful council going was a lack of choice. If Whistling Elk had been there it might not have been held at all, but Red Hand was right, there were no strong figures to stand against him. And yet the braves were reluctant to accord him any power, many hinting they would leave the band if he were chosen. It was a serious impasse, and the camp watched, held by a drama upon which, for a people whose way of life was raiding and keeping enemies at bay, much depended. Only two captives, who, unlike Sam, could not understand the language or follow what was happening, and were hanging back glancing around, caught a glint of metal in the heavy growth lying east of the campsite. Startled, one started exclaiming to the other. Immediately an old squaw grabbed a switch and beat her into silence. But Sam, hearing the switch striking and looking about, was suddenly seized with a curious feeling that all was not well. There was something in the air that reminded him of the stillness just before a deafening crack of thunder unleashes a summer storm. Instinctively he searched for birds that continually hovered over the refuse and scraps of carrion forever fouling the camp, but there wasn't a single one in sight.

Quarles watched his men picketing their horses and moving into positions Lee pointed to for the attack. He couldn't help noticing many troopers, while hurrying forward, were glancing at the sky. Wasn't it strange he thought, men feeling the presence of death invariably look at the sky. Or was it? He was glad he had Lee along. Lee's eyes were pinned to his field glasses and, when not, he was slipping about like a hunter making sure of his prey.

Lee might have made a good staff officer. He had a natural gift for the tactics required for this kind of fighting. The noon sun was pouring down as Quarles drew his saber, having already told his troopers they were surrounding this camp, while the volunteers, some taking their horses, were joining the side where Indians were most likely to try escaping. He warned the troops their first objective was to capture as many as possible. If the Indians insisted on fighting, males over twelve could be shot but women and children were to be spared. He listened in respectful silence to Lee's curt but in a way more critical counsel. Be careful of shooting white captives, don't let Indian garb fool you. And don't enter the camp thinking Indian squaws or even their grown children are noncombatants; families of fighting warriors rarely surrendered, even while dying they were known to have killed a goodly number of unsuspecting whites. Finally, don't rush into tipis thinking they're empty, it's an old redskin trick. Warriors, figuring they're beaten, often hide inside, with weapons at the ready, wanting only to take one more enemy with them.

But now the talking was over, the troops were in place. As the last squirmed into position the tension and excitement, already long building, threatened to create a stir, especially among the volunteers, some of whom had relatives murdered in the settlement. Lee, with a final glance at the camp through his glasses, amazed to find warriors still sitting in council, knew he could delay no longer. He drew his gun and, as arranged with Quarles, fired the shot that was their signal for attack.

Sam's guts began to tighten in him. He knew his instincts were right; something was moving around the camp. Because of this crisis, this imminent clash simmering in the troubled council like water coming to boil, no one remembered to stay alert to other threats ever present in this war-stricken land. Though there was always the chance it was a Ute or Osage war party, stalking the camp, he knew in his heart it was whites. In some way, and without any warning, retribution for the bloody destruction of that once promising settlement had come.

Yet the attack struck like the crack of doom. No roaring command could have changed the scene more drastically or matched the awesome impact of that first single shot. Warriors who had kept their weapons rose from the council, already charging toward their squaws and tipis. Everywhere hands reached for guns or bows and a screeching and screaming broke out that had troopers believing they were attacking a madhouse in hell. But almost at once people began to die. The soldiers as ordered shouted surrender, but since their ancient ancestors left the taiga of Asia to journey to the new world, surrender had never been an option for warriors of the plains. Like the animals around them they fought to the death and, when necessary, consumed each other to survive.

The advantage was all on the side of the attackers. Before a minute had gone by the ground was littered with bodies, even though wounded and dying braves were everywhere trying to fight back. Squaws with skinning knives were rushing at troopers only to die as nervous troops fired into them point blank. Where the wounded kept fighting no quarter was given. The most savage slaughter took place where the volunteers, unchecked, were venting their fury on what they regarded as murdering hellions, with no right to mercy or even fair play. They fired at women and children they saw running before them. It was they who rescued the first captives, taking four women, Flora and Charity Hunt among them.

It was only around the howling Red Hand that anything resembling a stand was being made, he and the burly warrior had broken through the ring with a few others and formed a ragged line behind which squaws and captives huddled and a few warriors, still up and fighting, began working toward. Lee saw it happening, saw the young warrior whose family lay slain, pulling Charlotte behind him, trying to reach this desperate redoubt. Lee tried to get a bead on him but the risk of hitting Charlotte was too great. By running, and risking being hit by bullets crisscrossing the campsite like hornets escaping a jarred nest, he managed to overtake them, but the young warrior turned and came at him with a knife. It was Quarles, searching for him, that saved his life, for the young warrior was strong and fiercely determined not to lose the near-hysterical Charlotte. Henry, who had stayed mounted, swept by and knocked the brave down with his saber. Then a strange thing happened. The young brave stood up and gave a great war cry, lunged at Lee who by now had his side arm out and, though he fired twice, the raging brave still strove toward him. It was a bullet from nowhere that struck the young warrior's painted face, smashing his cheekbone and leaving an eye socket empty, that swiftly ended his life. He swung to Charlotte and with an antic gesture collapsed at her feet. She screamed, turned away, and sank to the ground. Lee, stooping to pull her up, quickly started rushing her to safety.

Lying on the ground, clutching himself, as a hail of bullets swept around and over him, Sam knew he was lucky to be alive. Slugs had torn Bad Eyes's tipi to shreds. He didn't know where to turn, he only hoped these soldiers knew there were no black Indians. Where the council had been he saw Bad Eyes trying to move her heavy legs fast enough to leave the exposed ground, hoping to find something to shield herself from gunfire exploding all around her. Without knowing why he went forward to help her; in some strange way he didn't want that stout squaw to die. But Bad Eyes couldn't move fast enough and presented too large a target. Before he could get to her she was hit and sinking to her knees. Kneeling beside her he could only hold her up, hearing a gurgling sound in her throat followed by a small vomit of blood. It didn't disgust him; he knew she was dying. Her mouth struggled to form some words. He pressed his ear against it, to hear her mumbling in Comanche words which she now knew he understood. "Take the amulet, it is strong medicine."

He felt her great weight going slack in his arms and with some effort lowered her to the earth. It was too exposed a spot for him to remain; besides he saw a white man on horseback approaching him. After a moment's thought, he reached down and slipped the stone amulet from around Bad Eyes's neck, and hung it about his own. If ever he needed strong medicine, he needed it now.

* * *

Skeeter and Cheatem were with the troops who were trying to overrun Red Hand's position, but the wily war chief kept retreating into heavier brush, shouting to his handful of braves to move back after every shot. Before them, hunched over but staggering forward, were three grim knife-wielding squaws and one terrified captive. It was Alice. Lee, returning to the campsite, saw the volunteers beginning to circle around some of their own badly wounded or the few dead. For some reason they were allowing a small group of warriors to race around them, reach the soldiers, who were trying to gun down the braves firing from the brush, and in the confusion get by them. Swearing, he moved toward the encounter, noticing everywhere the shooting was dying down and the campsite was dotted with what looked like heaps of rags, but were really the bodies of humans who had but minutes before made up a community that lived, watched the seasons pass, and like the rest of mankind struggled to hope. Lee was not a sentimental man, at least not where Indians were concerned, but the scene left him grimacing that such tragedies had to be.

If Red Hand did nothing else, he, joined by warriors just escaping from the volunteers, had managed a temporary stalemate. Lee, coming up, wanted to rush these holdouts before they had time to dig in, but at the last minute someone spotted Alice and shouted there was a captive among them. Quarles, coming up and hearing a captive was in jeopardy, ordered his men to surround the heavy brush, trapping the fugitive band, but to cease firing. The ensuing silence was almost as big a shock as the first uproar had been.

Everyone began to turn their attention to the cornered braves, who could now be heard chanting their death songs and calling to the spirits. Even the greenest recruit on hand knew he was listening to brave men preparing to die. Quarles, appalled at the number of dead lying about, was determined to put an end to the fighting. The Indians had paid a frightful price for their transgression, those left could take word to their fellow tribesmen that attacks on helpless white settlements would be fiercely punished and avenged. He shouted for anyone who could speak Comanche. Sam, who had been following him, his identity established and advised to stay close, raised his hand. This caused two simultaneous outbursts. One from volunteers coming up, homespun figures convinced only Comanches, or those siding with them, understood Comanche, and the other from Skeeter, who, recognizing his brother, started shouting and racing toward him. The two hugged each other, both unable to speak but near crying for joy, until Quarles reached down and took Sam by the shoulder. "You sure you speak their lingo, fellow?"

Breathlessly, not releasing Skeeter, Sam assured him, "Ah kin make it out. Folks who gots to set here a spell ain't got no choice."

Quarles stared at the heavy brush concealing the now hidden Indians. "Tell them to come out without weapons and they won't be killed," he urged Sam.

Sam looked up at him nervously. "Sir, deys Comanches . . . dey not surrender."

"Tell them anyway."

Sam took a deep breath and spit out a cacophony of sounds that had Skeeter backing off and looking at him in awe. A long minute passed before they had an answer. Red Hand left no one in doubt, they weren't coming out! If the whites weren't cowardly dogs they would try coming in.

When his words were translated, Quarles looked at Lee, his eyes asking the question, was there another approach?

Lee took a few steps closer to Sam. "Tell them to let the captive go and we'll let a few of them escape."

This only brought ridicule from Red Hand. "The *tahbay-boh* like to talk better than they like to fight."

Quarles slapped his saddle horn in annoyance, but Lee stood stroking his chin. He had a faint suspicion this Indian was afraid the whites were setting a trap. Surely, in spite of his arrogant tone, this redskin had to know he was dealing from weakness. There was no way they could fight their way out of their position, it was either deal or die. On the strength of his long-standing conviction that all men, however brave, prefer to live, he gripped Sam firmly by the arm and said quietly, "Tell them to release the captive and we'll let them all go."

Now an even longer wait had to be endured but Sam, his face faintly resisting a smile, reported other braves were differing with Red Hand. Some of them were in favor of the exchange.

When Red Hand's answer came, it was typical of a Comanche leader whose search for power and suspicion of all around him seemed to go hand in hand. He would stay with the captive until the other braves and squaws were safely away, if treachery was in this exchange the captive would die. Then he, now alone, would release this captive in exchange for another. This one had to be a male, this one would accompany him until his freedom was assured.

Quarles dismounted and came over to talk privately with Lee. "Do we have a choice?"

"Not if you want that girl back."

"You think they'll kill her?"

Lee nodded. "And she won't make a pretty corpse."

To the dismay of many of the volunteers, Quarles gave the order and the troops pulled back to allow the Indians, except Red Hand and Alice, to slip off into a distant stretch of timber beyond.

But now it was time to select a hostage to replace Alice. Quarles asked for volunteers, but the ranks remained silent. No one wanted to be alone with that desperate warrior who had already sounded his death chant. Quarles was about to go himself, but Lee raised his hand. "Henry, don't be a damn fool, you're in command here, if that crazy bastard gets you alone he'll kill you and claim the biggest coup of the day. This ain't an honorable exchange of prisoners, it's all hanging on the word of a painted savage who's probably never heard of fair play."

Quarles stared coolly back at him. "What then?"

Lee looked around him and sighed uneasily. "Guess it better be me." He dropped his rifle and started to release his side arm, saying, "If we wait too long that bastard is liable to get suspicious and do something to the girl."

There was a moment of silence, then everyone turned

to Sam, who glanced at the heavy brush and quietly muttered, "Ah'll go."

Skeeter, swinging about and seizing him, almost cried, "You jus got loose from dem devils, what for you goin'?"

"Ah know him . . . he know me . . . mebbe we talk some . . . dese funny peoples . . . ole Sam gots an idea."

Quarles looked at him soberly. "You figure that man can be trusted?"

"No, ah figure he cain't, but deys odder ways. Ah gots to have me a small gun."

Quarles and Lee studied him with concern, but Sam looked strangely resolute and appeared confident. Warily they began asking about, until one of the volunteers offered a pocket derringer, which Sam looked at then slipped inside his loincloth.

"We'll be praying for you," whispered Quarles as Sam, calling out some words in Comanche, started walking toward the heavy brush.

52

Silas Cheatem, a man of compulsive interest in the sensuality of women, found the very sight of these captives he was helping to safety made him turn away and wince, not wanting them to see the revulsion in his face. It was some moments before he recognized Flora and Charity, but then he couldn't resist swearing under his breath. Proud, once primly groomed Flora was crouched over, her body filthy, her skin caked with dirt, her arms scratched and bruised, red welts lining her back. Beside her Charity seemed to walk in a daze, a ragged gown hanging about her, a tear in the middle, swaying open at every step, exposing her body from navel to thigh. The other women were in equally bad shape. Foul body odors, some nauseating, struck him as they passed close. There were only two children left, one having been killed in the onslaught, the others already carried away. A hundred yards from the camp the women sunk to the ground, some weeping, some looking about with haunted faces, unspeakable wounds inflicted on their spirits. They were no longer women with pride in their secret bodies, cherished as objects of love, desired by men. They had been used and abused by brutes whose skin was smeared with rancid grease and hair dressed with fresh dung. They had become pitiful obscenities; emerging from bouts of depravity, sanity was struggling to survive.

One woman clung to Cheatem's leg, moaning over and over again, "They did us sinful . . . they did us terrible sinful!" Silas tried to pat her shoulder, but could think of no words that might reach or relieve her agony. All he could do was keep muttering to himself, "Damn shame, goddamn shame." He caught Flora looking at him, her eyes fixed in a dead vacant stare like one who has abandoned faith in God. It gave him a cold chill for he had always thought of Flora as a soul of devotion. Charity simply whimpered and stared at the ground before her. Cheatem, hearing a commotion over where some surrounded braves were still fighting, glanced in that direction, wishing he was there or with the volunteers or anywhere but here.

Sam had entered the thicket to find Red Hand holding Alice, the barrel of a rifle in her side. The girl was almost nude, with only a strip of cloth around her middle. She was trembling and far too scared to speak. Red Hand snarled when he saw Sam, he had hoped for a white captive, preferably a soldier, one of rank. He wanted a man because he feared if he had to travel very far in a hurry the girl could not keep up. But he wasn't sure this black man, who had been a groveling captive, toadying to the fat Bad Eyes, was much protection. Desperation had made the trapped war leader increasingly suspicious and, convinced the whites were dealing in bad faith, ever more cagey. Sam didn't come armed, he carried no rifle, but there were always concealed weapons and Red Hand was taking no chances. He kept him at a distance, and when Sam tried to get closer he was ordered back. Sam, hoping to get beside him where he could use the derringer, was convinced if he left with this desperate, vengeful man he would be killed as Red Hand escaped in one final gesture of defiance. He knew something about Red Hand, this man would relish taking his scalp back to show he could still kill enemies, even in the maw of defeat. It would enhance his reputation with the Nerm, at the moment surely soured on all followers of Black Otter.

But Red Hand had been busily studying the best way to leave the thicket with Sam, reaching that distant grove where escape could be swift and sure. He summed up the risks of treachery from the whites or misjudgements on his own part. He did not leave out the spirits. It was time to pray for strong medicine. That thought pulled his eyes to something he had glimpsed quickly but in the tension of the moment hadn't recognized for what it was. Now his eyes shot back to it. Bad Eyes's amulet was hanging about Sam's neck. His face broke out in a smile of triumph. At last that great source of magic was his!

He took a step toward Sam. "Give me that amulet," he snapped in Comanche.

Sam placed his hand over it. "It's mine, I can't give it up."

Red Hand's face turned menacing. "It's mine, I have given Bad Eyes many presents for it."

"Bad Eyes never took your presents . . . it's mine!"

Red Hand, visibly rising to anger, started moving closer to Sam, clearly intent on snatching the amulet from his neck. Sam stood stark still, he knew the war leader could not be stopped, but he saw the Indian keeping one hand on his rifle, forcing him to use the other to grab the amulet. It was the moment he was waiting for.

Red Hand's anger was beginning to border on rage. He wanted that amulet, its power might save his life. This miserable one had stolen it from Bad Eyes but the spirits had brought it here, knowing it belonged to him. He took a last stride toward Sam and reached for the amulet. Surprisingly Sam didn't try to stop him, instead his hand groped at his waist and a small gun with a large mouth rose to press against the war leader's chest. There was an explosion which Red Hand only dimly heard, for his heart had been shattered by a red-hot slug tearing through it. Had he forgotten the stone couldn't be taken by force?

There were only a handful of prisoners, eighteen or twenty squaws and a few young ones, but several lay wounded. Not all the rest had died, both the troops and volunteers reported here and there individuals had managed to slip through the surround and race away. But the pall of many dead hung over the campsite, and Quarles wanted to move out. Stoically he watched them bringing in the Indian horse herd and turned to find and hail Lee. The scout was walking with Sam and Skeeter, leading Alice to the other rescued whites. Someone had given her a blanket to cover herself with, and though she looked in shock didn't appeared bruised or battered as did so many of the others. He also noticed Charlotte Barry, because she was the only one standing in the group. She looked shaken and distraught but otherwise unmarked. He wondered how different the stories of these women must be.

Lee came up, pointing to the prisoners and shaking his head. "You don't want those squaws, let 'em go."

Quarles looked concerned, even confused. "You sure about that?"

"Henry, you'll have to doctor 'em and feed 'em, they'll be going into mourning soon, they'll be more trouble than they're worth." He waved a dismissive hand. "They figure to slip away anyhow, first chance."

"What about the wounded?"

"Fix 'em up as best you can . . . give 'em some of them ponies, they'll build travois and tote 'em along." He turned serious eyes on Quarles. "We'll need a wagon to handle the few we got shot up."

More than ever Quarles wanted to get away from that

spot. "All right, send for one." He rubbed his hands to bring more life into them, an unconscious gesture he took to whenever faced with doctoring.

Normally there'd be an army surgeon along with this company he was given to command, but with the war they were all assigned to battlefield duty, and even there they were woefully short of numbers required. For every soldier immediate medical care saved, two died from lack of it. When it came to doctoring he always felt strange filling in, especially for anything serious. Never having completed his training he was always fearful some inept move on his part would end in tragedy. However, the thought of army surgeons swept the plight of Cathy and Cole back into his mind. That bitter scene, that distasteful picture of a man dying, was doing strange, disturbing things to his emotions. Yet in truth, he was only being honest. The bullet was deeply seated, the problem beyond his skills, perhaps beyond anyone's skills but God's. Yet questions bored into his brain. How long could Cole last? And what would Cathy do when her husband died? Secretly ashamed of such questions he forced his mind back to problems at hand, but the thought of Cathy being free again had worked its way into the keep of his mind and there, for reasons his conscience now skirted, it was to remain.

It took a few hours before the wounded were given what treatment was possible, and the dead of the camp gathered and buried in a single large grave. A reconstructed wagon from the despoiled settlement had taken away the white wounded and the squaws, finding they were free, built travois for ponies offered them and, refusing to let the whites hear their keening for the dead, made their way sullenly along with their injured to the far timber. For Quarles there was no shaking the grim look of that empty camp. There were still one or two scalps drying on bent sticks and at least one head under a layer of flies decomposing in the sun. The smell of the place was near asphyxiating and the many vile stains on the ground were drawing carpets of insects. To Quarles the place stank of refuse and evil. Although many tipis and other items belonging to the dead were left around, very few troopers seemed interested in souvenirs. Most wanted shut of that place and wished no reminders of the deaths and human misery that had taken place there. But Sam left with a souvenir he had almost forgotten about, approaching the settlement he reached for and felt Bad Eyes's amulet still hanging about his neck.

It was late afternoon before any order was brought to receiving the captives at the settlement. There were nine women and two children. Quarles wrote down their names and the names of others they remembered having been taken by Whistling Elk's band to the Arkansas. This together with a brief report of his attack on the camp he sent to Salina, requesting it be forwarded posthaste to Leavenworth. The courier left in a gallop.

Cathy and Hattie were the only two women in the settlement, and clearly what had to be done for the captives could not be done by men. Hattie came up to them, her nose involuntarily wrinkling, her eyes widening in shock at their condition. "Uh un, Lordy, we gots to git some soap 'n water, gots to burn dem clothes, git some hot food." Taking one by the hand she began to lead them toward the ranch. Cathy was coming up toward them; Quarles, catching sight of her, had to look twice as she appeared so different from the morning. She had washed and fixed her hair. Instead of men's clothes she wore a green and white dress that sat neatly on her figure. He couldn't resist approaching her, his opening remark easy enough for it belonged. "How is your husband?"

Noticing his eyes on her person and becoming aware he was puzzled, she answered with a sigh. "He's been in and out. It's terrible, watching him lying there, knowing the spirit is going out of him. Mercy, I just don't what to do. It's so dark and morbid in there, I thought if I spruce up a bit it might help. He's been conscious for a while now, when he first saw me sitting next to him he smiled."

"I'm sorry, wish I could do more."

Oddly she didn't press him, but turned to join Hattie,

going with the captive women down to the ranch. It was some time before Quarles realized much had happened, that because of his official duties he remained unaware. But Ben was said to be recovering, the sight of Sam being a tonic far more effective than any medicine. Sam had already told Cathy Troy was dead, but she chose not to tell Cole, whose spirits she had been struggling to raise. As much as she feared that bullet poisoning his body she feared Cole losing his will to live even more. Cathy was determined to fight, but, listening to her heart's rapid beat as she held her husband's hand, only she knew how.

The Reverend Dillby arrived at the ranch, his hands folded before him. The sight of the battered women, though washed and dressed in Hattie's and Cathy's old but clean clothes, still managed to stun him. Hattie was preparing turpentine and water to wash lice out of their hair when they saw him enter. Flora looked at him as she might have a rabid dog sidling to get behind her. Without waiting for a greeting he raised his hand in a way that established solemnity. "I've come to lead a prayer for your deliverance," he pronounced softly. "May I ask you all to kneel."

Flora lifted her head, her eyes the only things alive in her death mask of a face. "We've been on our knees and backs with animals fouling our flesh for too long," she croaked. "There is no God, make your prayers to the devil."

Dillby took a step backward. The consternation that warped his face altered his appearance. He resembled a man suddenly fighting back flames. "Surely you can't mean that!" His eyes, searching for succor, landed on Charity. "Charity, tell us you have not lost faith."

Charity stared at him dumbly, until one of the other women cried shrilly, "She's been stripped and put upon by so many stinking savages she too daft to speak. Leave her alone!"

Dillby, in desperation, looked to Hattie and Cathy, but Hattie simply shook her head. "We sure to git to praying later, preacher man, right now ah gots to fetch lice and set out a mite of hot food."

Cathy just looked at him, one hand holding a cold rag meant for Cole. "Try later," she half whispered. "We all have things to pray for. In time I'm sure they'll find theirs."

⚔ 53 ⚔

It was an unseasonably mild evening. A soft west wind was blowing, harbingers of spring could be heard in the melody of birds arriving from the south and the lone mating calls of coyotes coming to sniff at fresh prairie trails visible in the twilight. With their home gone Cathy and Cole had been using one of the rooms built for Hattie, Ben, and Skeeter. Cheatem was glad to have them for he was still hopeful of finding a way to move Hattie and her family elsewhere. But with Cole seriously wounded in the fighting Cheatem, for safety's sake, placed him on a straw mattress in the connecting area, bolstering his head with pillows and warning everyone to tiptoe by him when he seemed asleep. Cathy had spent the day squatting next to him and other than helping Hattie with the rescued women, had worked to keep him comfortable and cool. His fever still seemed to come and go, but his complexion was turning jaundiced, and with no appetite lack of food was leaving him ever weaker. At moments his eyes shone weirdly like one glimpsing death.

One advantage of his position was a view, through a far window, of the rise before the remains of the meeting hall. There was a small tent with a guidon before it erected by the soldiers. It was serving Quarles as a command post and other stretches of canvas had been placed between two solitary trees, as the soldiers pulled together a temporary shelter for the women. But with the coming of darkness the troopers were already building fires, cooking, and in general stretching out after a demanding day. On the other side the volunteers had set up their own camp. They had apparently found whiskey somewhere and noise emanating from their direction was slowly testifying to its effect.

It was almost too dark to see when Cathy, who was watching, saw Quarles stepping out of the tent, saying something to a sentry posted outside and then, shouting some words to Lee who followed him out, quickly turn and start in her direction. She stood up and straightened her dress. She remembered how he had greeted her when he had first ridden in. She bit into her bottom lip and took a deep breath. She was ready.

Quarles had lived through a frustrating afternoon. The attack on the Indian camp still bothered him. His orders had been to negotiate for captives, not trigger a major war. He knew now that many of the warriors had left under a chief called Whistling Elk, taking some captive women and most of the children with them. Surely those that escaped today would take word to the Arkansas and in a few days his whole command could be in jeopardy. Lee assured him it would be more than a few days, though sooner or later they would come. Lee had spent a lot of time talking with Sam and now thought maybe sending a delegation to the big camp to the south ought to be considered. "They're not all as hot for war as this bunch we just tussled with, might be worth the chance."

Quarles scratched his chin, weighing the thought. "Who would we send?"

"Few as possible. We just want to pow-wow, most times they'll hold still for that." He looked aside and seemed to be summing up the prospects. "I'll go," he finally added.

Quarles looked at him hopefully, those last two words meant Lee thought the idea might work. Strong endorsement, but still they had to look ahead. "Suppose it doesn't work?"

Lee sighed. "You say your orders are to negotiate for

captives, it's the only way I figure you could start. If it doesn't work at least you're following orders."

"But if it doesn't work it's likely to go hard on the captives they're holding."

Lee grunted. "Believe me, Henry, it's going hard on them anyhow. Look at these poor wretches . . . 'nough to make a man puke."

Quarles drew back, looking out the tent flap, viewing the shelter he could see set between two trees. "You know, a couple of them look in fair shape, wonder how they managed it."

"Injuns take a shine to women just like you and me. That Barry gal apparently had a young buck with a real fix on her. Goddamn pretty woman . . . sonofabitch had good taste!"

Quarles smiled in spite of himself. Lee rarely commented on women. "Did he get away?"

"No, I killed him . . . or somebody did just as I was fixin' to."

Quarles shook his head. "That young girl back with her mother?"

"Alice Hunt? Yeah, they're together but something is wrong, they're not talking."

"Probably still in shock."

"Could be."

Quarles would have liked to ask Lee if he noticed Cathy that day, how she was dressed and how her body seemed to sway and roll smoothly under the faintly clinging fabric, but he didn't dare start this very astute man thinking along those lines. He was not quite sure what to make of her appearance himself. He was too honest not to admit her attractiveness, his desire to be closer to her, and it was not just lust, she had a deep femininity about her that would arouse any man. From what he had heard apparently in the past it had aroused plenty. He couldn't wait for the duties of a commanding field officer to be over so he could see her again. He had the safe excuse of inquiring about Cole to explain his interest, but in a deeper sense he just wanted to be near her again, wanted to see her move, speak, share a few moments of this coming night with her. He wanted to know if that dress was a subtle message, a message dangerously close to igniting his fantasies, he wanted to know if Henry Quarles was making a damn fool of himself.

As he left the tent and said good night to Lee he felt like a gawky schoolboy approaching the minister's forbidden daughter, rather than an officer responsible for an armed but still endangered camp. Around him rose the many noises that soldiers, beginning to receive shots of whiskey from the volunteers, make when celebrating the blessing of being alive after a fight. He wouldn't interfere. They deserved it.

Cathy met him at the door. He tipped his hat and stood back as she stepped into the near dark and looked about. "I just have to get some air," she said fretfully. "It's surprisingly warm in there."

"Of course, perhaps you'll get a little breeze over by the water."

They moved closer to the river and stood on the bank. Almost together they looked up at the sky to see stars beginning to stud the Nubian blue canopy above. Both seemed to be waiting for the other to speak. Cathy's tone implied her mind was really elsewhere. "Those poor women," she said. "Whatever will they do now?"

"Several of them have relatives back east, I'm sure someone will come for them. Still pretty tragic though."

Neither one really had their mind on the women but the noise from the camp was beginning to be noticeable, even faintly annoying. "Can we move down a ways, that clamor will likely give me a headache." They started downstream until they reached the edge of the camp, but surprisingly Cathy kept walking. Quarles beside her could feel her presence as a deeper darkness began to enfold them. His heart started to beat more rapidly, he couldn't see her walking but in his mind's eye he could visualize the motion of her hips as they occasionally collided lightly with his, and once when they struck uneven ground she turned into his arms to steady herself. They had reached the remains of the grove where firewood was once cut and Quarles was finding it

hard not to mention they were getting dangerously far
from the camp. But now Cathy seemed ready to stop,
though she was standing awfully, awfully close. Henry
without moving found his arms about her, and she,
looking up, had their mouths only inches apart. But
though the silence droned on, something else roared in
Henry's ears. This woman wanted him, this stirring
female was offering herself! He was too sensitive and
worldly a man not to know it wasn't love. He was too
inured to the ignominy and pathos of life not to know
what she wanted, not to know she was doing this to
compromise him into trying to save her husband's life.
In spite of that he could feel himself growing flush with
desire, even as he forced himself to say, "Cathy, I want
you . . . I want you but not this way. You know I'd try to
save him if I thought there was a chance."

She came closer to him, he could smell her skin as
ripples of excitement worked along his spine. He could
feel her breasts pressing against him. *"You are* his only
chance," she breathed in his ear.

Suddenly her lips were brushing his, he wanted to kiss
her deeply, consume her, but tense as he was he managed to force more words into the night. "Cathy, I'm
only being honest, I can't do what my conscience says is
wrong."

She started the kissing, knowing, as he did not, what
kind of man he was. If she stopped now he would tell her
tomorrow in the name of honesty it couldn't be done,
that he had no right trying. He would sit on the high
moral ground and Cole would die. She had to bind him
in some deeper way and she knew only one. Instinct told
her he was that kind of man, he had revealed enough of
himself to assure her her intuition was right.

Together they sank to the earth. Cathy had committed
herself to not making it a farce, she was not going to
pretend, she would enter into it with all the passion her
sensuous body could mount. She kissed him back heat-
edly and helped him uncover her breasts. After many
deep and sensuous embraces his hand found its way
down the soft curves of her body and under her dress.
Somewhere the haunting mating call of a wolf mounted

the wind and came like a mournful lament over the darkened land. Neither heard it, neither cared.

Over a single candle the three of them sat in the dark, Ben now sitting up, and Sam and Skeeter squatting on low boxes around him. Hattie watched them from across the room, warning them to speak in whispers as Cole seemed asleep.

But excitement kept edging into Sam's voice as he told them about his adventures since leaving on that faraway day with Troy. When he came to the scene of Troy finding his silver mine both gasped and reached to take hold of his shirt, wanting to know if he could find it again. Sam swallowed hard but reckoned he could, leastways he would recognize the site if ever he got near it again. Some of this was said excitedly enough for Hattie to hear and she had to shush them again, adding under her breath, "Y'all hear wat happened to dat ole Troy when he found it . . . place likely cursed."

"Silver, Hattie, we rich!" whispered Ben.

"Don't talk foolish . . . silver in de ground far 'way. How you 'spect to git it out?"

"We got to figure a way," murmured Skeeter. "Got to be one."

Cole began to stir. They heard him moving the tin cup that sat beside him. After a few moments, his voice rose, raspy, uncertain, near breaking. "Where's Cathy?"

Hattie rose to look out into the night, thinking to herself that was a good question. She had last seen Cathy standing by the door with that army captain. Where they went to she had no idea, except that Cathy was very strangely dressed for a soot- and debris-ladened camp, where old worthless patched clothes made more sense. She stared down the river and put her hand over her mouth in thought. "She jus step 'way for a spell . . . ought to be back directly," she called to Cole, and her brow knitting in puzzlement sat down again.

Lee had been by the women's shelter twice. Once to bring them some soup the men who survived the hall fire had made for them and the other to see Charlotte Barry.

She recognized him as the one who rescued her and managed to smile when he came by. One of the captives was the wife of the man with the shoulder wound, but their reunion was spoiled by her inability to stop crying and his feeling she needed a dozen more baths to get clean. He could still smell the turpentine in her hair and in some perverse way did not want to hear her repeating over and over again what had been done to her.

Lee found himself delaying longer than he intended, but Charlotte was so withdrawn, not offering the mildest complaint, just sitting back keeping so quiet that he felt a need to stay. She didn't look mistreated so he chanced a probing remark. "Did they treat you rightly enough?"

A faint smile tried to survive on her lips but failed. "I only belonged to one of them."

"The one that tried to stop us?"

"Yes."

Lee felt something tightening in his chest. "Did he do anything to you?"

Charlotte looked down at her hands resting in her lap. "He was very young," she said softly.

Lee hated himself for asking such questions. They were clearly painful, even unfair, but this Charlotte was truly a soft, compassionate woman. She had no bad words, even for her abductor, who had surely made her share his bed.

Across the way he noticed Alice sitting staring at her mother. Flora was wrapped in a large blanket and sat with one hand on Charity's knee. "No," she said to her daughter. "Tell Dillby I do not wish to see him, Charity does not wish to see him. We do not want his prayers, nor his company."

"Mother, he's a man of God, he means well. I cannot give him such a message."

"Do as you're told or stay out of my sight."

"Mother we've just been rescued, can't you show a little gratitude?" Alice got up and moved to the flap to leave.

"Where are you going?"

"To find Sam and thank him. He's the one who rescued me."

Flora turned away and buried her head in her hands. "There is no rescue from what's happened to us . . . you know there isn't. Your father and uncle are dead, Charity and I are alone in the world, there is nothing for us now but disgrace." She stopped for a moment to choke back a sob before starting again. "Am I also to be cursed with a disobedient daughter?"

"No, mother."

"Good, then be back as soon as you can, you must help me with Charity . . . she seems to be lost . . . terribly lost."

It was almost an hour later when Cathy appeared at the ranch door. She came in too quickly for Hattie to get a good look at her. Going immediately to Cole she sank down beside him and found he had fallen off to sleep again.

Hattie stared at her. "He was askin' for you, morn 'n once."

"I'm sorry," said Cathy.

"Don't 'pologize to me, 'spect he know you love him."

Cathy stood up and gripped her sides as though needing to feel she was there. She would try to sleep tonight, knowing it would never make sense to another, but in that deep mysterious calculus of life where humanity finds contradictions in every lasting truth, she had made love to one man tonight to preserve the life and love of another.

Lee could sense something was wrong with Captain Henry Quarles, but as well as he knew his friend there were things in the air that baffled him. Henry looked as though he hadn't slept during the night and his request for a blacksmith that morning only added to the puzzle. It was only after some thought, and his recalling Henry heading for the ranch the evening before, that he began to suspect the trouble lay there. Lee did not consider himself a sage, but Henry's infatuation with that Sadler woman was too overt to miss. Not that he blamed him; she was a damn fetching female, and Lee had not missed her dress the day before. But Lee also knew her husband was slowly dying and Henry helpless to save him. Yet now he heard Henry asking for whiskey, at this hour of the morning, and a blacksmith to boot. Lee gripped his chin with one hand and rubbed it. "Damn funny."

Had he been around before dawn he would have seen Cathy coming to the command post with a handful of small items she had garnered from the back drawers of the ranch. There were darning needles, spools of thread, and an old pair of long thin scissors. Henry, his face strained and damp with cold sweat, had taken them mutely, his mind struggling against a feeling of futility that at times threatened to paralyze him. What was he attempting? He tried as hard as he could to remember the few rules of basic surgery he had learned, or more likely simply heard about, during his few years of training. It seemed pathetically if not tragically little. But that night, whatever Henry Quarles knew about surgery, he had learned something more about himself. This woman, who gave herself to him, not reluctantly but with the fullness of her fabulous body, had in some peculiar way made it impossible for him to deny her an effort to save the husband she had betrayed. It was not that he had forgotten the moral reservations that bound him the night before, but moved by what she had offered in exchange, it was not in Henry Quarles to refuse.

Paradoxically the crazy emotions that ran through both of them only brought them closer together. He, astounded by the experience, could only imagine what love she must have for Cole. Could he find a woman who would love Henry Quarles that much? She, worrying that she had misjudged, that he might reject rather than find himself committed to her, could only watch his eyes, but they remained clear and when meeting hers grew a tinge warmer. Their lovemaking, once started, had been intense and good, both would have openly admitted it. Incredibly they both came out of it with more respect for each other rather than less. It was not a wanton act, it was a woman, ignoring her pride, fighting for her man's life, a woman battling another man's conscience, becoming that other man's woman in the only way she knew to control him. Cathy spent the rest of that night with a strange sensation she had won an invisible battle that only her heart would ever know about, but whatever the outcome she wasn't sorry. She had to try, she did.

But now the great task lay before them, with success only an ephemeral hope that Cathy clung to and Henry dare not mention. The blacksmith, a dubious look on his face, brought back the thin scissors, the end of each blade flattened, forming a crude forceps. Lee brought in a pint of whiskey he had traded from one of the volunteers, and, not trying to hide his curiosity, gave it to Quarles with a questioning look. "Little early for the blood of the lamb, isn't it?"

"T'ain't for me."

"You got a friend with a big dry?"

Henry sighed and looked toward the ranch. "I got a man with a bullet in him. I got to try and take it out. He'll have to be dead drunk to stand it. If he struggles too much he'll bleed to death or I'll kill him."

"Jesus, you mean it?"

"Yes, and I'll need you and a few others to hold him down, whiskey or not this kind of pain is more than flesh and blood can stand. Be best if this stuff knocked him out cold."

Lee whistled under his breath. "Does he know?"

"His wife does."

Lee watched him quietly for a moment but all he said was "I see."

At the ranch Cathy mixed the first whiskey with water. Cole was awake but his eyes were dim and for a moment it seemed he would not be able to swallow it. When it finally worked down his throat he started holding his stomach and Cathy was sure he was going to throw up. But to his murmured complaints she kept telling him they were going to take the bullet out and make him well, the whiskey was just to lessen the pain while it was done. He opened one eye and fixed her in silence. Quarles felt the man, sick as he was, knew it was no use. He decided this act was not something Cathy should see, one mistake and her husband could writhe to death in a hideous and blood-soaked scene. He asked her to leave. She stared at him, but understanding the frantic fears already mounting in her breast might make her cry out, distracting him from this perilous task, she left. At a nod from Henry, Hattie moved in, motioning Sam and Skeeter to join Lee around Cole, as they turned the wounded man on his side, exposing a wound where the blood had congealed and, other than the inflamed flesh around it, looked relatively harmless. Hattie, noticing Cole had kept down the earlier drinks, now gave him a tumbler, half whiskey half water. By now, feeling the relaxing effect of his previous swallows, Cole, understanding what they were trying to do, tried feebly to cooperate. Slowly he emptied the glass.

Quarles, examining the wound which he knew had to be opened again, tried to remember the steps he had to take. Beside him was a small pile of rags, one way or the other there would be a heavy flow of blood. Speed would be essential. The quicker he could work the less trauma Cole would experience, as though this man hadn't suffered enough already. A glance at Cole's torso at least assured him this was a strong and probably vigorous man, there wasn't an ounce of fat on him. Normally he would be a better than average surgical risk, but there was nothing average about this setting, and the surgeon was a rank amateur. He looked at his hands, rubbing them, testing the long darning needle he would have to use as a probe. Seeing Cole's head beginning to loll as the whiskey started numbing his motor system, he spread his hand around the wound and placed the tip of the needle on it. The last thought flickering through his mind before pressing it in was this was the husband of the woman he had made love to last night.

Cathy, taking herself along the river, had gone only a short distance, but she could go no further, even though she began to hear loud moans and muffled screams which she knew was Cole in agony. Ignoring everyone who came near her she prayed audibly, turning and looking back in dread at every painful cry that rose and measured the torment the blind probing was causing. She didn't see Quarles's sweat-soaked figure, also praying under his breath, nor the faces of those holding Cole down, their features screwed up in sympathy with the figure squirming beneath them. She didn't see Hattie soaking up the blood the opened wound now released, but she could visualize the frantic efforts of these souls desperately trying to hold back the death that hovered over them, the death not only of her man but in a way that froze her spirit all that mattered to her in life.

Quarles finally found the bullet; as near as he could judge it was near the spleen. There was no rejoicing in his heart when he finally managed to fix the slug in his forceps and draw it out. It emerged covered with a yellow ooze that he knew was infection. The wound would have to be kept open to drain; he could think of no more he could do. His limited knowledge of medicine did not lighten his conviction that Cole was going to die of blood poisoning if nothing else. Cole seemed to have lost consciousness. Though his heart was still steady Henry found his pulse weak and realized the loss of blood had become another threat. Hattie helped him place the bandage so the wound could drain but the others began drifting away; Quarles's pessimism had been picked up by Lee and the brothers though no one put it into words. Cathy, coming to the door, searched Quarles's face, a desperate hope in her eyes, but try as he did to smile Quarles could only mutter, "It's over."

"The bullet is out?"

"Yes."

"Will he live?"

"Like the rest of us, he'll live till God calls him."

Cathy was so drained she almost collapsed, but she managed to whisper, "Thank you."

Now he did just manage to smile but for reasons she could never have guessed.

Lee's idea of sending a delegation to the Arkansas did not find widespread support, particularly among the volunteers. But Quarles was convinced any hostile move against a large assembly of tribesmen would result in disaster for his command. It was a dilemma, complicated by the fact that several local and state officials, coming in belatedly from Salina, had appeared and insisted on having a voice in his council of war. Lee urged him to disregard them. "They'll start trouble they won't hang around to finish. And we're wasting time. Henry, this will only work if we make the first move. If they come after us it will be too late."

Quarles, still exhausted from the morning, tried to clear his mind. A critical decision had to be made. He tried to consider what steps should be taken. "We'll need an interpreter," he started.

"What about Sam?"

"Will he do?"

"We'll make him do."

Quarles rubbed his forehead and breathed quietly for a moment. "All right then, make up a party, keep it small, as you say they're always willing to parlay. Tell them we're authorized to make full retribution for the goods that weren't delivered last fall, tell them we want peace. Make sure you stress all this depends on our getting the captives back as soon as possible. Tell them the big chief in Washington will be very angry if the captives are mistreated."

Lee grimaced at this last. "Henry, they've already been mistreated. Don't give this Whistling Elk something to worry about when there's no helping it."

Quarles, losing patience, slapped his thigh. "Well, damn it, just get them back!"

Quarles knew Lee resented the irritation in his tone when the scout pointedly answered, "Yes, sir."

The visiting public officials, though assuming an unexpected degree of power, were strangely hesitant about arranging for the care and custody of the rescued women. Some women had no family left, nowhere to go and down to the ill-fitting clothes offered them to cover their nakedness. Their treatment while captives was now common knowledge and for the first time they caught a glimpse of what lay ahead from their own kind. The men looked at them, aware they had been the playthings of filthy brutes, experiencing every humiliation possible, and no one could be sure just how befouled they were. Comanches were notorious for raiding and raping deep in the sordid, squalid villages of impoverished Mexico, carrying north venereal diseases with no known cure. At first the men stood around embarrassed until Quarles almost shouted the government was responsible for assisting these destitute people. Deciding now a little money could resolve this issue and thereby spare them any personal involvement had them all speaking at once, promising to take quick action the moment they returned to Salina.

Some of the women, sensing the estrangement, sat dejected. But not all. Flora wanted her relatives in Maine informed and asked that the death of her husband and brother-in-law be reported. She drew her blanket around her and standing in front of Charity declared her sister-in-law badly needed medical attention. When could she expect it?

A portly man with sideburns assured her a doctor would be along in a day or two; the medical man had been wounded in the war but was coming in a rig driven by his son. This stout gentleman solicitously inquired into the nature of Charity's ailment, and was advised that was something only a physician could determine.

Bowing self-consciously, the officials withdrew. Someone had heard that Captain Quarles had taken action without consulting them, an obvious lapse of discretion on his part. They assembled in reasonable order outside his tent, the man with the sideburns becoming their spokesman.

Quarles, fatigue still dragging him down and, in spite of an effort to be civil, in a testy mood, came out to greet them. "Gentlemen?"

"We've heard," began their spokesman, "you're planning to negotiate with these savages. We consider that ill advised. Those devils will only behave if they are punished and punished severely."

Henry measured his words. "We believe it to be a large camp, several hundred warriors . . . perhaps more. How do you propose we punish them?"

"Surely that is a matter for the army to decide."

"What you see here is all the army can spare."

"Well, perhaps you can muster more volunteers. You'll find our people quite ready to avenge this outrage."

Quarles recalled the fierce way the volunteers fired into the surprised camp. "That is surely true. Your suggestion is well taken. Would you gentlemen like to join us? We can provide you with arms, perhaps you can help plan or even lead an attack."

There was an immediate shuffling of feet as some of the men moved behind their spokesman. But the bewhiskered face had not lost its commanding tone. "Naturally that would be our first choice, unfortunately we are not at liberty to do so on this occasion. Many of us have important duties that can't be left unattended. However we will make your interest in additional recruits known the moment we return to Salina."

"And when is that?"

"Regrettably we will have to leave today. The governor will want a report. Can we have a list of your casualties and any other data that might be of interest to him. I suspect he'll be in touch with Leavenworth."

Quarles nodded. He searched for something other than the profane remarks that almost leaped from his tongue. "I hope you gentlemen found your visit here worthwhile."

"We certainly did. As servants of the people we deem

it our duty to be wherever there's trouble . . . to be in the thick of things so to speak."

"I'm sure the people are grateful."

"Of course, Captain, that's to be expected."

Within days word of the surprise attack destroying Black Otter's band flew in the mouths of those who escaped to the ears of Whistling Elk. It gave him only grim satisfaction, though many of his warriors immediately demanded a vengeance strike, perhaps even Salina itself, lifting the scalps of as many whites as possible and putting that whole village to the torch. As his warriors now numbered near a thousand such a victory was not out of reach.

For two days the warriors danced, many with war hatchets in one hand, rifles in the other, boasting of the blood-letting they would bring to the *tahbay-boh.* Through the night medicine men beat their lonely drums and made medicine for the war leaders. During the day squaws pounded pemmican for the braves to carry in their war belts, removing any need to seek food on the trail.

A lust for scalps by the braves and the spoils of war by the squaws was rising to a fever pitch. An important shaman, Vermillion Paw, shook a rattle and a multitude of screams arose in a fearful chorus as the people cried to Whistling Elk to take the warpath and bring them victories.

A less opportune moment for a runner to race into camp, crying that the *tahbay-boh* were coming carrying a white flag, could hardly have been possible. Whistling

Elk drew himself up and scowled at the runner. Was this a time for talking? Did the whites think to share a pipe when they had just stained the earth with Nerm blood? A murmur of fury ran through the camp, with urgent whispers to seize them and put them to the many-fingers-of-fire death. But Whistling Elk, hesitating for only a moment, reluctantly raised a cautioning hand, a request for parlay was an ancient and sacred rite of war; there might come a day when the Indian had need of it. He heard there were only four in this party, surely they could do little to alter the will of this powerful camp.

The four waiting apprehensively in a nearby meadow were Sam, Lee, and two troopers, who had volunteered and were already sorry they had. The camp was immense, articles of war were everywhere. Within minutes painted warriors rushed out to glare at them, surround them, push them toward the camp center. Lee kept telling Sam to say they had come in peace to report many presents the big chief in Washington planned to send his red children.

Sam's voice was quavering. "Dey still waitin' fo' dem presents suppose to come las' year. Dey look powerful mad."

When first approached Sam had refused outright to go. He looked at Lee as he might have a serpent with a Comanche face coming out of the ground. "Had 'nough o' dem rascals, dey done deviled ole Sam fo' da last time." Had it not been for Hattie telling him, "We gots to do everythin' dem white folk do . . . cause folks bound to 'member dis later," he might have been safely back at the settlement, dreaming about rediscovering and dancing on top of Troy's mine.

They found themselves hurried forward until they were standing before a chief in full war regalia, who Sam recognized as Whistling Elk. He made the sign for peace and uttered in broken Comanche, "We come tell big chief, Whistling Elk, great father in Washington want send many presents . . . more presents than promised many moons ago."

Whistling Elk sneered and pounded the earth with the end of his spear. "White men lie!"

"These men different from the liars."

Whistling Elk could not miss the big amulet around Sam's neck; it was a well-known talisman. He pointed to it with his spear. "Where you get?"

Sam swallowed a lump that was threatening to throttle his voice. "Bad Eyes gave it to me, I was with her when she died."

Whistling Elk studied Sam for a moment. His curiosity about Black Otter's band hadn't been satisfied by those who escaped. They only knew the attack had come during a bitter debate; perhaps this strange dark face could tell him. "Black Otter dies and his warriors no longer sit as brothers. Why?"

"They not sure who killed him."

This made Whistling Elk draw himself up and rest his weight upon the spear. Treachery? His eyes drew smaller as his mind ran to Red Hand. He had never liked that war leader. Ambition and jealousy of his chief's power stained that one's eyes like a touch of madness. It was time to discover where that questionable figure had gone. "Where Red Hand?"

"Dead."

"Your eyes know this to be true?"

Sam held his breath. "I killed him."

Whistling Elk studied Sam for a moment then looked away to the horizon. His dream again swept through his mind. Was it the black cloud they were fighting? Had Black Otter been right to fiercely follow his savage hatred of these *tahbay-boh*? Both dissension and death had overtaken his band. And those same whites were now here before him, talking of presents, valuable things the red men could not make for themselves, perhaps hoping their blandishments, if not their numbers, would prevail in the end. He had seen them fought for years, but many defeats failed to lessen their persistent coming, settling, claiming, and changing the land. It wrung his heart for he knew his people could not and would not accept this. In spite of his anger he was a far-seeing man, rare for chiefs embroiled in the long mortal struggle between red and white. He knew it was not only the land they were losing, with it would go all that made up their life. The spirits, the graves of their fathers, the sacred sites where dreaming brought powerful medicine and great warriors were made, would all vanish, trampled under by the oncoming feet of these noisome whites. Should the tribes go on trying to hurl back this tide forever mounting and menacing from the east, or reach for the hand of these strangers who came constant as the wind and as impossible to stop?

Looking about him wisdom whispered that his people, choked with rage and thirsting for revenge, wanted no talk of peace. It didn't help that in his heart he felt one day it might be their only hope. His brow was furrowed and his eyes like aging embers. In these years of ceaseless war and dark forebodings it wasn't easy being chief.

In the settlement the days spent awaiting the results of the peace delegation were filled with efforts to build a few structures to house the miscellany of people showing up. The lame doctor, driven by his son, arrived one day later than expected. He had been shot in the leg and walked with a pronounced limp. To him went the difficult job of dealing with the rescued women. The few still suffering enough to allow him to examine them kept him shaking his head and muttering to himself. He saw from the condition of their breasts and their genital areas they had endured cruel, even inhuman treatment, but other than the passage of time he had no cure. The real and perhaps lasting damage was to their minds. After examining Charity he drew Flora aside. "Regrettably there is no known medicine for her affliction, perhaps a long rest and gentle handling will help."

"You're saying she's demented."

"I'm saying she's not normal. There is a new field of medicine that would diagnose it as psychic trauma. Regrettably its effects on behavior are unpredictable. Sorry."

He found two women showing the results of extended exposure to the elements. He listened to heavy congestion in their chests and knew one would be dead in a month, the other probably afflicted for life. He was about to finish up and make his report to Quarles when Cathy appeared before him. "Please," she said, "you must look at my husband. He's very ill. He's been shot and we just managed to get the bullet out two days ago. He's running a high fever and looks terrible. Please, won't you come quickly."

Dutifully he limped behind her to the ranch. He settled on the floor and started to examine Cole, but his eye kept returning to the open wound and its drain. "What surgeon did that?"

"He's not a surgeon, he's only had a year or two of medical training."

The doctor, seeing the makeshift forceps and darning needles lying beyond, grunted in admiration. "Lady, if he's not a doctor he should be. There's not a thing more I can do." He looked at her with the grim eyes of a professional who knows when prospects are dark the truth is best. "That your husband is still alive is the only encouragement I can offer you. Most of us would not have survived such radical surgery." He sighed to himself, like a man summoning up his feelings. "Try to keep his fever down with those cold compresses. If you can feed him soups, broths, anything easy to swallow that will help keep up his strength. Other than that he's in the hands of the Lord."

"Doctor, please, is there *nothing* you can do?" The doctor noticed she was trembling. "I'm so helpless, he seems in such pain . . . it's terrible at night . . . Jesus, please, help me."

He pulled himself up and took her by the arm. "I can give you something to ease his pain, it might even help to break his fever and allow him to sleep." Then he squeezed her arm meaningfully. "I'm giving you a small amount too, you best get some sleep or I'll have another patient on my hands."

His report to Quarles was prefaced by a compliment on the captain's treatment of Cole. "You did very well. Should have stayed in the profession, we could use more like you."

"Don't be so generous, Doctor, I'm not sure I had a moral right to even try. Would you venture a prognosis?"

The doctor shook his head. "I'm afraid mine would be pretty negative. By the grace of God he's still with us, but he's badly jaundiced, his liver or kidneys must be infected. However, there is so much we still don't know about the human body and what it can endure. You never know. I had a boy at Wilson's Creek with a bullet lodged against his brain and he went home two weeks later to get married. Best we wait and see." He shifted his limp foot and glanced back at the ranch. "That wife of his seems quite a gal."

"Yes, she is," responded Quarles, looking away.

The doctor's report on the women expressed in medical terms the effects of successive rape and sustained physical abuse, with the doctor stressing that time would prove their mental problems to be the more intractable ones. He recommended observation and prolonged care for at least three, among them Charity. Both he and Quarles signed it, and prepared it for transfer back to Leavenworth, where both knew it would join the thousands of other reports the government routinely demanded and then ignored.

In a strange way Hattie proved a boon to the rescued women. She cooked every day, urging those who could to stop sitting about in depressed or even morbid states and help out. She, like many others, had witnessed a tragic aftermath of their terrible ordeal. The soldiers and especially the volunteers continued to nod at them going by, but some invisible barrier kept them from coming close, exchanging remarks or even pleasantries in a natural way. The women were now almost all without mates, but on a frontier where women were needed and prized not one had attracted the eyes of a host of virile and often lonely men. The stigma of the violated female hung over them, the secretive charms of their bodies had been destroyed by crude loutish men. The magic magnet, the mystique of femininity, had been torn away, and all of Dillby's heartfelt prayers couldn't bring it back.

If there was an exception to this insidious ostracism it

was Charlotte Barry, and she only because Lee visited her before leaving and tried to heighten her spirits by jesting, "In this country when a fellow wins himself a woman in a fight, she naturally belongs to him. Only sensible notion Injuns ever had." But still Charlotte's only response was a faint smile.

But the most poignant incidents took place around Hattie. She, Skeeter, and Ben, who was now able to hobble around again, spent most of their time seeing after the women and the two children. In a strange way they formed a society apart from the camp, and of all those helping Hattie, Alice was by far the most useful. She was at Hattie's beck and call and seemed glad to be learning about cooking and keeping her mind off other things.

The need for soap grew as many of the women took to washing themselves over and over again. Alice willingly helped make the soap, preparing the iron rain barrel in which a fire had to be kept going for two days before there was enough ash to count. While the ash was soaking in water she went about collecting animal fat from game being brought into camp. The fat had to be melted down to be mixed with the water being drained from the ashes, bringing with it the lye that made the soap. When this mixture hardened it became the only cleanser available on the long frontier.

One of the women continually and now compulsively washing was Flora. For a time it seemed she was trying to wash away all trace of her sordid captivity. She scrubbed to get the grime from her face and body, she scrubbed long after it was gone and the harsh homemade soap reddened and roughened her skin. Concealing herself in a corner she scrubbed her private parts and used pail after pail of water to rinse. Skeeter, who was carrying water from the river, realized an uncommon amount of it disappeared around Flora, finally mentioning it to Hattie. "Dat woman sure needs a mess o' water . . . ought to move her closer to duh river."

"Stop yo' fussin', fetching water ain't nothing 'sides wat dem po' wimen bin through."

"It's jus dat bitch, duh one who always sashayed by us like we was hog leavings too long in duh sun."

Hattie turned and rapped the stove sharply with her skillet. "Where you learn dat kind o' talk?"

"It's true!"

"Ah knows wats true 'n wat ain't! Wats true is trashy talk like dat makes you no better 'n her!"

"Why ah got to be better 'n her?"

"Cause dat woman she deviled by pride, she gots to think she better'n us. We don't gots to lissen to her, we jus got to be damn sure she ain't!"

But relations between Alice and her mother began to strain under constant tension and more and more hasty, biting exchanges. Alice readily admitted, though she hadn't been raped, she had been stripped and manhandled by the burly brave, while Flora, who had been brutally forced to submit countless times, refused to allow any mention of it at all. Talk from the other women, who for the most part sat weeping or trying to steel themselves for a future of estrangement from all they had known, made her turn away. Even when Charity, crying out in her sleep phrases that revealed in some nightmare she was still being raped, Flora flatly refused to listen and slapped her awake.

But most peculiar of all was her growing resentment of Alice, which arose in unpredictable steps. "Must you chase after that Negress like you were beholden to her?"

"Mother, I am, you are, we all are! No one else pays any attention to us. Young men used to look at me when I walked by, now they look the other way."

"Don't shout at me. Soon we'll be going back to Maine. The doctor says Charity, poor dear, will have to be confined. It will probably be Boston. It's terrible, but we simply can't have her about reminding people. We must put this terrible place and these dreadful days behind us."

"Mother, they are behind us, but they happened. Stop pretending they didn't. It's shameful the way you treat Reverend Dillby."

"We can't remain acquainted with any aware of this unspeakably degrading humiliation. When you're older you'll understand."

"Mother, I understand these people are trying to help, we can at least treat them decently."

"You're an arrogant young girl, you'll do anything but respect your mother's wishes. Listen to me. You must never say again you were stripped and handled by those animals, do you hear?"

"Mother, I hear, but shouldn't we be grateful we were saved?"

"After such a degrading mortifying experience how could anyone be grateful, let alone consider themselves saved."

"Mother, can I at least be grateful I wasn't raped."

Flora was going to glare her daughter down, but a small flame of defiance was sputtering to life in Alice's eyes. Without warning Flora slapped her in the face. "Perhaps it would have been better if you had been!"

56

Lee wasn't surprised they were herded to the edge of camp and kept under guard. It was hardly more than they could expect from tribesmen who greeted them with rancor and surrounded them with warriors armed and painted for war. But it was then they discovered Whistling Elk knew a few words of English, for he pointed to an distant isolated spot and grunted, "You wait! Not talk now!"

Lee shrugged, hardly seeing it as cause for alarm. Indians rarely did anything in a hurry. But Sam was afraid they'd never see freedom again, and Lee's assurances that Plains Indians held the rules of war sacred didn't help. It was bad medicine, the scout maintained, to go against customs built up over ages and counted on by tribes who looked upon war as a way of life. "They might trail us, even try to ambush us, but to start with they gotta let us go."

The two troopers, settled in the back of the tipi, stared at each other, their expressions indicating Lee's words offered cold comfort.

A grim tension hung over the camp but they could hear voices rising and falling in a large tipi the chief had vanished into, each time the noises tended to end on wilder or more angry notes. "The old boy is having trouble getting the council to agree," muttered Lee.

"Wat dey councilin' 'bout?" whispered Sam.

"Whether they want those presents more than they want our scalps."

"What presents?" asked one of the troopers.

"Presents the government promised to supply," said Lee quietly. The trooper shook his head. "Holy sassafras! We got to hang on a government promise? Nigh unto two years ago it promised I was only to serve three months."

A long silence ensued.

Lee had not missed the sight of captives watching them from a distance, women looking as bad if not worse than those rescued from Black Otter's band. But surprisingly he found a few healthy-looking white children, especially young boys, apparently adopted and already trained to ride Indian style. One or two went racing by on slick ponies, shouting a few words in an Indian tongue, apparently quite content with their new exciting life. People on the frontier were well aware such youngsters were often hard to coax back to the confinements and endless drudgery of settlement life. Indian children, no matter how long held or well treated, rarely stayed with whites, but to the consternation of many settlers the reverse was not always true.

It was hours later and growing dark when they were

finally summoned back to the presence of Whistling Elk. The old chief now was looking tired and frowning bitterly at the medicine man, Vermillion Paw, who stood to the side with several war leaders, arms folded beneath his blanket and eyes fastened on the amulet around Sam's neck.

Sam couldn't imagine what was coming but was secretly wishing he had just been able to sing a little in church.

In sunny Santa Fe Dennis had found work in a wagon yard, had learned to speak some Spanish, made friends with several enterprising businessmen, and had just filled their little rooms with flowers to celebrate the arrival of his beautiful baby son, delivered by Chloe the night before. Excited neighboring women were everywhere, helping with the baby, bringing food, tying little luck pieces to Chloe's bed and in general giving the cramped quarters a festive air. In the evening their men came bringing wine and a few guitars, filling the air with soft songs and many toasts to the future of Dennis Sadler Jr., although his father insisted the child be given the middle name of Cole.

Chloe beamed at her baby and reluctantly allowed some of the few childless women to hold him, a gesture which was supposed to increase their fertility by exposing them to the miraculous touch of new life. Happiness was hardly the word for its parents. Only one thing stood in the way of near total bliss. Chloe, no matter how she tried to suppress it, was lonely for Hattie, lonely and now dying to show her mother her beautiful grandchild. Dennis suffered no such pangs, he would have liked to have seen Cole and Cathy again but the thought of returning to Kansas left him shaking his head, muttering, "Hell, no! Not on your life!" But Chloe's eyes kept finding his. Their love had slowly deepened and their togetherness had grown in spite of the many friends they made. Neither was now totally whole without the other, and she had discovered her needs slowly became his.

In the days that followed both kept alert to remarks from new arrivals, especially those coming from the north. What were conditions on the trails? What was the mood of the tribes? What effect was the war having on travel? They heard nothing to encourage them but they continued to listen, even though Dennis was determined to go into business for himself here in Santa Fe, where he felt his prospects would always be better than in Kansas. Chloe, if quiet and patient, remained thoughtful, even though motherhood became her and did wonders for her body. She appeared a little more rounded and hence more beautiful. Dennis couldn't believe he was married to such a beauty, everywhere people gazed at her and smiled. Beautiful women were prized in Santa Fe and Chloe had become so stunning many men, often strangers, took off their hats and bowed gallantly as she went by.

After her baby their lovemaking blossomed again with a new intensity. They would lie in each other's arms for hours, repeatedly making their bodies one and only stopping to joke good-naturedly when the baby cried for attention. It was a good life and their little garden in back was resplendent with rare flowers and exotic scents, though Chloe sometimes awoke in the dawning with Hattie's face before her and half-finished prayers on her lips. There was no way for mail to travel between them and so her imagination, driven by concern for her mother's safety and tormented by constant rumors of Indian trouble to the north, kept Chloe looking into her husband's eyes until Dennis took her in his arms. "I understand Chloe . . . I know . . . soon as it's safe for the baby we'll try. Meanwhile you got to brighten up . . . Hattie would want you to."

She smiled and settled on his lap, feeling warm and even vaguely comforted as her breasts, larger and fuller now, were fondled and kissed by her man, who seemed stronger and more in love with her than ever. As this memorable spring arrived, its pleasant days followed one another in a mosaic of sun-filled moments, often brought to a close by startling sunsets and melodic nights. Chloe sometimes felt life was almost too perfect to go on.

* * *

Lee was right about one thing. They were going to be freed, but not before certain promises were extracted. They were to be given one moon to deliver the presents, supplies that must include a hundred guns, and Sam had to return at that time to state where this tribute could be collected. Sam translated the chief's words for Lee, who cautiously raised the question of returning the captives. He did not ask for what his eyes told him was now impossible, that all the captives be in good health. But it didn't matter for no words of Sam's could move Whistling Elk, who threw several dark looks at Vermillion Paw, to make concessions. Instead the chief pointed to the angry warriors around them, shouting in Comanche. "My people want war! You want peace? Make sure you not come to Whistling Elk's camp with split tongue!"

Sam was beginning to panic. "Wat ah tell him . . . Ah doan know nuthin' 'bout no presents . . . he wants me to come on back y'here and tell him where dey at."

There was a tenuous moment of silence. Finally Lee muttered, "You have damn little choice to my reckoning, we're getting a month to deliver . . . maybe it can be done."

Sam's eyes resembled a frightened frog's. "Mebbe? What ah suppose to tell him?"

"Tell him we'll do it . . . better add our hearts will be very glad and our presents bigger if we can have our people back."

Sam looked like a man sinking in quicksand, snatching a last look at the world. "Ah done said dat a'ready . . . he gittin' mad."

"Say it again."

Sam gathered his breath and uttered some hesitant words in Comanche but Whistling Elk cut him off, pointing to the north and shouting, "You go! One moon you come back! Whistling Elk has spoken!"

They left with Lee looking behind them. "That's one stirred up touchy sonofabitch, those bastards are so anxious for a fight they smoking at the mouth."

"You don't 'spect ah'se comin' back y'here, do you?"

Lee was silent for a moment. "Not by choice . . . but you can't tell, he holds all the cards, he's got those captives. Right now he doesn't trust us, if we don't make good on this deal we're probably in for the goddamnedest uprising you've ever seen."

"Ole Sam ain't gonna see it . . . ah'se leaving."

Lee grunted, turning to look back again. "You know that medicine man seemed to take a shine to you."

Sam rolled his eyes toward him. "Ah knows . . . dat one is bad trouble . . . ah smell it."

The two troopers rode along behind, making subdued remarks to each other. "Glad you volunteered?" queried one.

"Yeah, it convinced me my wife is right."

"What she right about?"

"I'm plum crazy."

Hattie had become a prominent figure in the devastated settlement, now an army and civilian campground, as well as the outpost marking the end of civilization in Kansas. Even Cheatem couldn't deny she was probably more help in the aftermath of this calamity than a mule train full of missionaries. All the women except Flora had become fond of her and turned to her when others, wearied of listening to them bemoaning their plight, slipped away. Alice followed her around simply because Hattie stayed active, kept young Skeeter and old Ben grumbling but moving, and seemed a match for every problem that arose. After a few days the wounded man, whose wife had been rescued, and who wasn't sure she was fit to live with again, came complaining he wanted her sent back to her family in Missouri.

Hattie stared at him. "Yo' her husband . . . you gots to send her back."

"I ain't her husband no more!"

"How you 'magine dat?"

"I gave her a chance to make a little love last night and she run away. Dang woman ought to be grateful . . . bin bedded by a parcel of stinking bucks and now can't appreciate a decent man . . . her husband to boot."

Hattie moved up to him until her face was only inches from his. "Yo' forgittin' dat woman bin raped! She doan want no man fussin' wid her for a spell."

"Why the hell not?"

"Cause it don't feel right no mo'. Dem devils done mess it up."

"Well, she best come to her senses . . . I ain't keeping no woman that ain't there when I want her." He looked like he was going to stomp away but then swung about, irritably confronting Hattie. "How come you know so damn much about all this?"

Hattie's answer was loud, angry, bold. "Cause ah bin raped! Dats how!"

The man stared at her for a moment, his face strained by doubt. "By savages?"

"No, by a white man!"

"What the hell kind of white man rapes a nigger?"

"One dat talked a mite like you!"

Hattie was also the one who noticed a face peering from across the river and sent Skeeter to tell Captain Quarles Lame Fox was back. The Shawnee came into camp at the captain's bidding, but after eating and resting reported little except the land was empty and the game plentiful. He looked doubtful about staying, but Quarles, knowing his value as a scout, convinced him he had little to fear now, for many of the people that might have recognized him were dead. Also, Quarles was now growing restless, the peace delegation was not back and its fate was beginning to trouble him. It was enough that he had to face Cathy each day and watch Cole wasting away on the cabin floor. It was difficult to determine whether the man was recovering or not, for after a few good hours his fever would race up again and he would groan in agony for half the night. Cathy looked pale and ready to collapse from exhaustion, so much so that Cole, in his few waking and rational moments, began urging her to go somewhere and rest.

Because of the growing tension it was a joyous moment when Lee led Sam and the two troopers back into camp. Quarles couldn't wait to hear their report but was quickly puzzled and increasingly concerned when he did. One month! That was ridiculous; where would they find adequate supplies in a month?

He would have been far more concerned had he been in the great camp on the Arkansas, for there the council had been resumed, and Vermillion Paw, backed by many of the war leaders, was demanding the *tahbay-boh* be attacked at once. The whites had no presents, their promises this year were no better than those of last. They would use this moon to bring more soldiers into the land of the Nerm. If they had presents they would have sent them and not a peace delegation. Vermillion Paw finally ended on a small but disturbing and almost ominous point. Why was the black man wearing Bad Eyes's powerful medicine amulet? No medicine woman would have willingly given that powerful medicine source to one outside the tribe. Probably it was stolen from her after her murder.

The dark rumblings of the war leaders had Whistling Elk climbing wearily, with bitter expression, to his feet. "We are a great people! We have told these enemies we would wait one moon. Are our hearts, our words, no better than theirs? I say one moon passes quickly, if they have not sent word where their presents await us by then, we will strike all their settlements and paint the prairie red with blood."

He threw a handful of medicine grass on the fire, and as it flared he spread his hands over it palms down. There were many grim and unsatisfied faces, but the council of war was over. The great gathering rose slowly, and though the mood was one of uneasy resignation, within moments all but Vermillion Paw had strode away. He stood looking at Whistling Elk until the chief looked back. "The spirits are not with you," the medicine man muttered.

"You are not with me, my brother. Beware . . . do not speak for the spirits."

"The signs are bad. Whistling Elk will need strong medicine."

Whistling Elk smiled grimly, nodded, and walked away. He needed strong medicine all right, not only against his enemies. Somehow thoughts of Black Otter kept sweeping like shadows falling lightly across the back of his mind.

57

No one questioned Quarles's decision. Even Dillby agreed nothing else made sense. Henry had to return to Leavenworth; he had the best chance of impressing upon the army, and through it the government, the critical need to deliver the supplies. Even so, based on the record there was little hope of assembling suitable amounts and moving them west in a month. With the endless paperwork involved and authorizations required, three months would have presented problems enough. Only the government's promise to cooperate fully in recovering the captives had a few believing with sufficient expedition it could be done.

In the face of this optimism, which to Lee seemed wishful thinking, the scout found himself hard put to conceal some nagging fears. The mood of that Arkansas camp still hung in his mind. Whistling Elk alone was keeping that horde of bellicose warriors at bay, but the whole camp reeked of explosive rage. The taste for war was in those people like grain in wood. Lee didn't believe the old chief would be able to keep his promise of a month, nor would it be the first time, he warned Quarles, Indian warriors, ignoring tribal agreements, slaughtered trusting and unsuspecting whites. He convinced Henry this very camp could be in jeopardy.

Quarles, forced to leave right away but swayed by Lee's warnings, left orders for the camp to be evacuated at once and its occupants moved back to Salina. With his many concerns his departure was hectic enough, but he struggled to find time to see Cathy before leaving. She greeted him with unconcealed despair. "We can't move

Cole, you said yourself traveling over rough ground . . .
he'd bleed to death."

Quarles was standing close to her, his voice muted.
"There's no longer a choice. I'm sorry. It's too dangerous to stay here."

Cole was awake and watching them, noticing Quarles
taking her arm as he said, "Your husband has been in the
hands of the Almighty for days now and is still with us
. . . if he makes it to Salina perhaps they can do more for
him there."

Cathy held his eyes with hers. "What will I do if . . ."
She glanced down at Cole and, seeing him watching, let
her breath fall away. "If he can't keep his food down. It
seems harder for him all the time."

Quarles, noticing her eyes flicking to her husband,
released her arm, aware his grip might seem somehow
possessive. Stepping back he cleared his throat to say,
"You'll have to do the best you can, believe me we'll all
be praying." He had a wild desire to hug her but she was
holding her body back to discourage this gesture she
could sense coming. She needed comforting but not
from this strange, even enigmatic, man, who with knowledge of her flesh was now appealing to her spirit,
appealing or perhaps trying to enlist it. At least she
couldn't accept his comfort with her husband looking
on. She followed him to the door, in spite of her mixed
feelings she did not want him to go. But this was only
one more emotion that left her inarticulate and a stranger to herself. She was drained beyond belief by Cole's
agonizing decline and a feeling of death at her elbow.
When she returned, Cole was looking up at her. "He's a
good man," he murmured weakly.

"I know," she breathed back.

Surprisingly, in spite of the effort, he was struggling to
say more. "He's tried his best."

"I know," she repeated.

He kept struggling until he had enough breath for a
few final words. "So did you. Thanks." He said no more
but his eyes fell on her with gratitude, love, and something else he couldn't or wouldn't work into words. A
cold sensation moved along her spine and stopped at the

level of her breast. In some mysterious way, in that mystical keep of the heart, beyond logic, instinct, and even that strange light death throws upon the dark corners of life, Cole had just grasped what happened between her and Quarles, and now wanted her to know he saw it as proof, not a betrayal, of their love.

Henry left with an escort of six troopers, instructing a young lieutenant, now commanding the company, to prepare the camp to move, providing it with protection as it traveled east. But moving the camp was to prove no easy matter. Many of the volunteers, whose kin were now known to be in the village on the Arkansas, refused to go. They lobbied for an immediate attack on that enormous assemblage which Lee dismissed as insanity. Dillby, who openly acknowledged Hattie was a greater source of spiritual strength for the rescued than himself, went about pleading for harmony in their continuing hour of trial. Nevertheless there was much confused talk, even about the ranch, though Cathy, remaining indifferent to the dispute, pretended to be gathering a few things to take along. In her heart she knew Cole would never survive the trip. Feeble as he was he lay looking up at her with a gutsy look of resignation, a frightening sign that he also knew.

Cheatem had changed the burnt slats on his lumber wagon, which otherwise survived every attack, and offered it to Hattie. With Skeeter driving, it would carry all the rescued women and the two children in as much comfort as could be arranged. Old Ben piled some blankets on the edge of the tailgate. "Gonna sleep right y'here . . . see none dem ladies fall out."

But as the morning turned to afternoon and the afternoon to night the wrangling in some parts of the camp became oddly matched by a deathly silence in others. Still by dark the issue was far from settled. Though the young lieutenant's plan was to begin the military exodus shortly after dawn, two things happened during the night that changed the feverish arguments and quarrelsome judgements of the camp.

* * *

Cathy knew Cheatem was only trying to help. He was explaining to her how they could swing a hammock on a wagon and cut down on the jolts, though little could be done about the swaying motion or quick drops. Cathy listened listlessly, staring out a nearby window, watching stars appearing on a far horizon. She had just left Cole, still feeling his holding her hand to his cheek, squeezing it meaningfully as he let go. Something in that gesture reminded her of his embraces when leaving in days gone by. Somehow she knew he was telling her something, something she would understand then or later. But now her eyes were idly fixed on Cheatem's hands as he lifted them over his head, showing how high a hammock needed·to be slung, when a deafening shot, almost behind her, rang out. Silas dropped his hands and ran to the nearby hall where Cole had been lying. "Jesus! God Almighty!" he sputtered. "Poor Cole done shot himself!"

Incredibly, Cathy didn't, couldn't, move. She sat there, not in the paralysis of shock but held by something deeper, something too vast and engulfing for her emotions to register. It was a moment she knew was coming, a moment when the shock of death had to be endured, accepted, allowed to lay its terrible finality upon her heart. But now in this moment she found its crushing weight unbearable. As she did with all things she had to fight it. She could hear Hattie and Skeeter and Ben reaching the hall and exclaiming their shock but still couldn't move. She looked out into the night and saw her husband tall and strong, turning to smile at her from a distance, waving goodbye until through her tears she saw him disappear, leaving her with only memories to help her through a lonely and now deficient world.

Lee heard of it before dawn but he could do no more than grimly shake his head, sighing as Henry's face swept before him. Sober thoughts arose about his old friend. Something dark and inevitable had long hung about that situation. But in this dawning bigger problems were besetting him. During the night a group of fifty volunteers opted to approach the camp on the

Arkansas, hoping to somehow get the captives back. The young lieutenant pleaded with them not to go, saying they might trigger devastating attacks on every settlement in Kansas. But the young officer didn't have the arguments to stop them, though Lee almost did.

Lame Fox had awakened him an hour before, the Shawnee's face dark with concern. The camp was being watched, he had spotted Comanche scouts huddled over a hidden fire a mile to the south, false coyote howls heard earlier had drawn him in that direction. There were not many of them but they smelled of trouble.

Lee sent him back to see if any large parties were close by, then went and found the lieutenant trying to reason with a heavily bearded volunteer who seemed to be leading the imminent departure.

"You won't have to go far to find them," said Lee. "They're already here!"

There was a strange silence. "What damn nonsense is that?" exploded the heavy beard. "They nigh a hundred miles yonder."

"Not anymore, our scout says they've been watching this camp all night."

"Well, I'll be go to hell!" shouted the bearded man. "What the devil scout is this?"

"Lame Fox, a Shawnee who ain't been wrong yet."

"Where is he?"

"I sent him out to keep an eye for large parties. So far he's only spotted a handful of scouts."

The bearded man spit and stamped the ground. "Shit, I don't believe it! We 'uns is heading out anyways."

"It's a free country," said Lee, "but don't forget there ain't no peace agreed upon until those supplies show up. Right now they're in a sweat to fight, don't give them any excuses or you'll wish your daddy had sent you to sea."

A furious wind was sweeping the Arkansas and the Comanche headmen stood in their blankets, quietly confronting each other. Whistling Elk had not broken his promise, but Vermillion Paw, backed by a host of war leaders, refused to trust the *tahbay-boh*. "Let our wolves watch them as the eagle watches the snake," said the grim medicine man. "If they send for more blue coats or start to arm their camp we will strike as the eagle strikes. The serpent-tongued whites have betrayed the Nermernuh for the last time."

Belatedly informed that scouts had been sent out and couldn't be readily recalled, Whistling Elk's voice was almost strident. "Let there be no fighting," he shouted. "If the spirits call for war we must fight together and with the wisdom of the pipe to guide us."

"It will be as you say, Whistling Elk," a war leader answered, "but our people are angry and our young warriors wish no peace with these despised enemies."

"One moon!" declared Whistling Elk angerly. "Have I not promised one moon, either we will have many riches and a promised peace or we will know their words, like their hearts, are false and destroy them in war?"

The high wind had increased its whine and, roaring down the valley, swept the harsh scathing words away.

Though they pressed their horses as hard as he dared, and changed mounts in Salina, it still took Quarles's party over five days to reach Leavenworth. There he found the fort near deserted and the general gone. The officer of the day said all able-bodied men had been sent east to join Grant in the Mississippi Valley, and the commanding general was out visiting recruiting points and overseeing new telegraph lines connecting them to the fort. He was expected back in two days. With a week gone, Quarles tried to get the adjutant, a red-faced blustering major, to start ordering and collecting supplies to be taken west. Within minutes the major, turning huffy, made it clear he was not to be ordered around by a mere captain. Quarles, worn by anxiety, fatigue, and nearing exasperation, demanded they find and read Secretary Stanton's telegram. This sobered his florid face and brought the major's nervous hands up to grip his lapels. "Captain, exactly what supplies are you after? If you fancy this post is well stocked you're mistaken. We've actually had to send foraging parties out to requisition food."

Quarles wanted to lean over and pound his fist on the

desk. "Goddamn it! Surely you have some blankets, pots, pans, some old guns, even some nails or barrel hoops, things they set a store by."

"If you can find any of that stuff around here, take it. My guess is you'll have to requisition your needs from Ohio. There's a large Union depot there."

Quarles sat down, staving off exhaustion. "Major, we have three weeks to get ten or twelve wagonloads of goods west of Salina. Nothing now in Ohio is going to help us."

The major tapped his fingers quietly on the desk. "I'm sorry. Perhaps the general will have some ideas. As I've said he'll be back in a day or two."

Quarles stomped out of his office. The helplessness of individuals trying to move large bureaucratic institutions was hardly new to him, but the tragedy now sitting in the offing transformed his helplessness into guilt. He had to find a way to muster support from sources of power, something he mistakenly thought he had. But again he could sense it was this damn war, with its death lists and burning towns and villages holding the country and its leaders in a vise of fear and self-doubt. A handful of people on a distant prairie was little more than a tiny moth, hardly visible around a conflagration consuming a nation. But to Henry Quarles that handful of people was counting on him for survival, counting on a man almost as helpless as themselves.

58

The heavy wind that paused to groan when not shrieking across the Kansas plains was the perennial herald of violent spring storms. In its train came torrents of rain, relentless downpours that swelled the streams and turned the few beaten trails into corridors of mud. It didn't discourage the grim volunteers, who left single file, their ponies picking their way across high ground, but the military, trying to move the bulk of the camp, hadn't sufficient teams to drag wagons through the quagmire forming about them. Cheatem's lumber wagon sunk to its axles, and the few draft horses available couldn't pull it out. "Gonna have to wait till it dries out a bit," advised Lee, putting an arm about the worried young lieutenant. "Meanwhile we best stay here where we've got some cover."

The lieutenant nodded in the direction the volunteers left in. "Wish that crowd had stayed put."

"No sense in stewing over 'em." Lee paused to shake rain from his hat. "Wouldn't be surprised to see 'em back."

"Think so?"

"Yeah, likely they're headed for trouble . . . probably quicker than they figure."

The young lieutenant rubbed a worried face. "Jesus! I hope they don't start a rumpus we're gonna have to finish."

Lee tried to smile but it came hard; the lieutenant's words were too close to his own thoughts.

They buried Cole just before the rain struck and Cathy sat listening to Hattie pray for his soul, later leading the ladies in "Rock of Ages," the one hymn everyone seemed to know. She hadn't wept a great deal, but interest in what was happening about her simply vanished. She looked out into space and stared at Dillby without seeing him. He prayed over the grave and once more made an attempt to approach Flora. But she turned away, her bitter expression seeking and finally finding Alice who now avoided her at every turn. Charity, holding a blanket around her, sat mumbling to herself. It was a depressing scene and Cheatem's attempts to lighten the mood by offering some berry wine he had bought from the volunteers repeatedly failed.

Finally it was Charlotte Barry who drew all eyes when she settled by Cathy and hugged her silently. Many noticed it was the first deliberate gesture the Barry woman had made since her rescue. Cathy limply let herself be hugged, seeming content to allow long moments go by until Charlotte whispered, "I know, I understand . . . they killed my Tod too."

Cathy, closing her eyes, felt Charlotte's wet cheek against hers, and slowly turned her body to surrender to the other's embrace. After a few moments Cathy was quietly hugging Charlotte back, and Hattie, knowing what was needed most at the moment, motioned the others away.

It was luck that brought Quarles to a tavern outside the fort, where he went needing a stiff drink and time to think. Rain had started drumming down and the place was crowded. After half an hour word got around that he had just galloped in from a trouble spot in the west, and looking up he caught a pleasant-faced young man with a bowler hat approaching him. The stranger extended his hand, saying unabashedly, "Briggs, *Chicago Sentinel,* may I join you, Captain?"

Quarles nodded to an adjacent chair. The young man removed his hat as he settled, placing it gently on the table. "Heard you just got in from that settlement Injuns overran a while back." Henry nodded again. "Can I ask you what's going on out there?"

Quarles lifted his drink and threw it down in one swallow. "You hunting a story?"

"I'm a reporter."

"Well you can report I'm having the goddamnedest time raising supplies to keep a murderous swarm of Indians from killing some defenseless settlers!"

The young man stared at him, confusion nettling his brow. "Now just a minute. Isn't that the settlement Secretary Stanton wired Leavenworth about?"

"You've got a good memory Mr. Briggs. Better than most around here."

The reporter's eyes suddenly widened and nervous

tension edged his face, revealing his sensing he had hit upon something big. "Holy hallelujah, Captain, why don't you wire Stanton back? He's no clerk! He'll get you your supplies!"

"How am I supposed to wire him, I've no authority to talk to the secretary of war, I'd be ordered to go through channels."

"Channels hell! Look, Captain, I need a story, if I help you do I get one?"

Quarles looked at him curiously, a slight irritation creasing his face. "Just how in hell are you going to help me? You figuring on wiring Stanton yourself?"

The young man smiled conspiringly. "No, I'd have less chance of reaching him than you."

"What then?"

"You give me an exclusive story on this whole affair and I'll have someone wire him that no politician dare ignore."

Quarles leaned back in his chair. "And just who might that be?"

"My paper."

The volunteers were slowed by the rain. In three days they made only forty miles. Some of them were experienced enough to know they were bucking the odds, if there were scouts about their leaving was known and they were probably being shadowed, removing all chance of surprise at the Arkansas village. Still they struggled ahead, their determination sustained by thoughts of kin, especially womenfolk, in Comanche hands. The bearded man read prayers before each cold dark camp, and every morning the men wrung water from their blankets and packed them in slickers tied to their saddle. Hot coffee was the routine breakfast and noon saw their one meal of jerked beef and hard biscuits.

Tiring and chilled to the bone, many began falling sick, but there was no time for doctoring. In truth, concern centered more on their horses than on themselves. Several individuals had to stay awake at night on guard duty, and even so a few head had already disappeared. For their owners it was a calamity. No one needed to be told without mounts they were lost. Though the bearded man cautioned everyone against shooting until they had to, hoping to keep their approach as secret as possible, the sight of even a few men riding double forced him to order any figures seen around the picket line at night to be shot on sight.

That was to prove a fatal order.

The Comanche scouts followed this struggling party with ease. They remained at a distance but at night crept closer, noticing the many horses held on a single long rope. The horses had few opportunities to graze and after a day or two appeared listless, stamping their feet and swishing their tails in futile efforts to chase legions of flies brought on by the rain. The scouts had been told not to attack but watch these whites and report all hostile movements. This they had done, sending a messenger to say an armed party of fifty or sixty was making its way southwest toward their village.

But if the words of their war leaders were rarely flouted the lure of good horseflesh was a constant temptation for Comanche braves. The dull days of tracing this party usually throbbed with excitement by nightfall when the prospect of stealing its horses arose. Among their tribal skills even their enemies would have granted them the palm for rustling ability. On their first try they had managed to cut away two mounts without a suspicious glance from guards posted only a few yards away.

Their leader, a warrior called Little Hawk, decided of his five scouts, one son of a chief, the honor of stealing more *tahbay-boh* horses should go to those most deserving of it. His first choice was a young warrior who had skirted along the exposed and therefore more dangerous eastern flank of the column, his second was the chief's son. This second choice would have needed explaining only if it had not been made.

But it was a night when the volunteer leader himself was on guard and pacing restlessly up and down the picket line. He was aware the missing horses were a tribute to Indian subtlety and guile, many of them crafty light-handed thieves able to evade the most vigilant guards. But tonight he had set a trap. A few horses were not on the picket line but on long halters. Though tied securely they appeared to have come loose from the line and were starting to drift away. Any horse thief who spotted them would assume they could easily be led off. Though the bearded leader was pacing back and forth he stayed secretly attuned to these mounts, advising other guards when they saw him shooting to immediately join in.

It was the chief's son who first spotted the seemingly wandering horses and, ignoring his young companion, who tried to restrain him until they got closer, moved quickly to claim them. The young warrior stayed anxiously beside him but as the horses began to shy at their approach he saw the halters tightening and, gripping the chief's son's arm, tried to pull him down. But it was too late. A fusillade of gunfire broke out and the two braves were flung to the ground as several leaden slugs tore through their bodies.

For Little Hawk it brought a crisis. He had been warned not to attack, repeatedly cautioned by several war leaders to simply scout these intruders. Now he had the death of a chief's son to explain. His remaining three braves fixed doubtful eyes upon him. His medicine had proven weak, his council faulty, his reputation as a potential war leader tarnished. One said they should return to their village, there was no need to track this party further, it was clear where they were going. Another said it was up to Little Hawk to explain the disastrous outcome of this ill-starred attempt to steal a few horses.

Little Hawk finally stood and made the sign for returning home. He would explain this fateful event and its threat to his standing in the tribe his own way.

Lee was secretly being seized by a sense of urgency. They were well into their second week and though the rain had continued from time to time the ground was slowly drying out. He began advising the lieutenant, whose name was Grimes, to send back at least the women and several others who had taken sick in the long spell of damp weather. But the young officer pointed to the volunteers who had not left with the foraying party, and who had decided to stay, awaiting the outcome of this effort to rescue more captives. Lee studied him for a moment. Something curious had happened to this young man. Quarles's final order to move appeared to have lost its imperative quality. Somehow the long delay caused by heavy rains had brought an obscure but discernible shift in his manner. He was no longer as tense and anxious as he once seemed. But if the young lieutenant was content to await events, Lee was bent on making him think ahead. "Lieutenant, I still figure you'd be best off packing all noncombatants east while you've got the chance."

"Could be you're right," allowed Grimes, but Lee sensed a strange hidden reluctance siphoning energy from his words.

Lee, growing concerned as well as confused, rested one foot on a small barrel and leaned over the young officer. "Have you calculated the fix you'd be in if they showed up here and euchred us into a running fight? Be best if we were shut of any that would slow us up."

After a moment's silence Grimes only muttered, "Possibly you're right." He looked about him as though hardly comfortable with this concession, but finally said, "All right, I'll have Hattie get some of the ladies ready to go."

Lee backed away, trying not to smile, but he had heard the *some* in the lieutenant's remark, and a puzzle that had been clouding his mind for some time was now partially solved.

It was his many trips to see Charlotte that finally offered Lee a solution to the puzzle. The lieutenant spent a lot of time talking to Hattie, but Lee, with the eyes of a trained scout, noticed how many times the young officer's glance settled on Alice. Alice at first appeared not to notice, but that was short-lived. Now when the lieutenant appeared, sauntering down the slope presumably to visit Hattie, Alice was suddenly by her side.

But Lee's moments with Charlotte, though now more rewarding, did little to reduce his uneasiness. Quietly sinister concerns were mounting. Half the month had passed and no word had come from Quarles. Lee finally got Charlotte to stroll short distances with him in the evening, a closeness made possible only because he seemed shy, even withdrawn. She got no hint he was anxiously if secretly battling fears harder to suppress each day.

Little Hawk had more to worry about than he thought. When word came to the great camp on the Arkansas that a party of armed men were coming in their direction, over a hundred warriors left camp to meet them. Whistling Elk insisted on going along, unless the whites started it he wanted no fighting. He had promised them a moon to deliver the supplies and wanted no hot heads destroying what he sensed might be the last chance for peace. Though it confused many of his tribesmen, Whistling Elk had good reasons for his caution. He was as incensed as any of his people at the perfidy of the *tahbay-boh*, but he had heard rumors of Sioux and Cheyenne chiefs being invited to Washington and returning awed by the white man's numbers and arms. Perhaps it wasn't true, but eastern Indians, who for decades had been drifting west before the spreading tide of whites, carried tales that whispered it was. And then there was his dream.

Little Hawk, held to the truth by the other warriors, confessed the chief's son had been killed trying to steal horses, but quickly added these mounts and others had to be taken to keep the *tahbay-boh* from swiftly striking the village and making a rapid escape. Whistling Elk looked at him askance but the damage was done. The listening braves, enraged at the pointless deaths, raced out to surround the approaching volunteers and a fight broke out. It was to lead to tragedy for the bearded leader, bravely trying to make a stand and at the same time signal a desire to talk. He was one of the first struck down, leaving his followers surprised and scrambling in near panic to defend themselves. But the mission was over, pluck and determination had failed, within an hour they began a ragged retreat toward the camp. Whistling Elk, both furious and dismayed, saw the war leaders decending on him. Reluctantly he faced them, no longer able to deny their angry demands that all warriors on the Arkansas be brought up. It was to be war after all, a war beginning with that strange settlement of *tahbaybohs* on the Smoky Hill being swept from the earth.

59

Briggs was as good as his word. His Chicago office wired Stanton that his earlier promise to aid negotiating for captives and promoting peace needed urgent fulfilling. Stanton, Lincoln's outspoken, arrogant but doughty cabinet member, was unfortunately at McClellan's field headquarters, fuming at the military stalemate, and couldn't be reached. But word soon circulated among the agencies, and informers for the Washington press saw a chance to make the unpopular Stanton look unconcerned about settlers he had promised to help. It resulted in a boon for Henry Quarles since Washington, often a bedlam of plotting and fiercely ambitious figures, had at its center one of the coolest and judicious minds in history. The crisis on the far western frontier, stirred now by a host of news releases, was soon on the desk of the composed if beleaguered president. His reaction was immediate. A dispatch went out that day.

Commanding Officer
Fort Leavenworth

Dear Sir:

*All resources of the U. S. Government are to be
committed to the aid and relief of the settlement
presently reported in danger and possibly under
siege on the Kansas frontier. Please consider this
authorization for any and all necessary measures.*

Abraham Lincoln
President of the United States

Quarles couldn't contain either his surprise or elation,
but his joy was soon tempered by a realization half the
month was gone. Even with a presidential mandate it
would take days to collect the supplies, assemble drivers,
teams, wagons. At a minimum he would need twelve
days to reach any satisfactory delivery point.

The situation was still critical. The Plains Indians
were in a vengeful mood, another miscalculation by the
whites and the full fury of those deadly nomadic horsemen would set the border ablaze. Massacres reported
along the Platte to the north proved hostilities once
started were not easily ended. He was only glad, as he
turned in for a few hours' sleep after an exhausting day,
that he had ordered Grimes to move those at the
settlement, including a woman he had left but whose
image would not leave him, eastward to Salina and
safety.

To Lee's chagrin the settlement was only at that
moment preparing to ship its first wagonload of sick and
any women willing to go, or too mentally confused to
remain, eastward to Salina. But it was not a painless
effort. Several unforeseen complications arose to ham-
per every move the young frustrated Grimes made.
Flora refused to go without Alice, even though they
wouldn't face each other to discuss it. Alice wouldn't go
without Hattie, and Hattie wouldn't leave without
Cathy, who was not ready to abandon Cole's grave. She
sat for hours looking at the little cross marking the site.

Around her people passed silently or watched from a distance, speculating on her future.

Cheatem, silenced by events but always conscious of her sensuous figure, still nurtured a fantasy of her one day turning to him, taken by his glowing ambitions and some measure of wealth, things he was convinced ultimately outweighed love in a woman's mind. Naturally he would have to be patient through this period of mourning, but Silas was always good at thinking ahead. Hattie caught him staring at Cathy through a side window. She shook her head as she laid a kettle on the stove. "What's yuh lookin' so hard at?"

Silas strove for nonchalance. "Cathy. Sure is a pity. But she's young, she'll git over it."

"Folks git over eatin' and breathin' too, but t'aint easy."

Silas turned around, spontaneously slapping his chest. His expansive mood had brought a slight sheen to his eyes. "What she needs is a real savvy upstanding man."

"Den she don't need you!"

Cheatem threw her a sullen glance. "You might be surprised." But he walked away, once again realizing this woman could pester or deflate him at will. It seemed goddamn unfair. In the distance he saw the young lieutenant approaching, and from the stream side caught a glimpse of Alice, breaking away from some women she was helping to wash and quickly heading for the cabin. That young female was rounding out nicely; if she ever got away from that bitch of a mother she might deserve a little attention.

Grimes came to count the women preparing to go. He wanted to put the sick on the wagon last and was hoping no further complications would keep the now crowded lumber wagon from starting out the following morning. He was uneasy at the way the scout, Lee, had started looking at him, as though he knew Grimes could have sent many of these civilians back days ago, but was delaying for lack of some rationale to keep Alice behind.

But the many problems the women presented at least gave the young officer a screen to maneuver behind, and he came now intending to use it. After checking numbers and names with Hattie he turned to Alice. "I wonder if I could have a word with you."

Alice smiled, her expression coy but affirmative. He led her a few feet from the cabin and started to move along the bank. "I was hoping your mother might somehow agree to leave, do you believe there's a chance?"

Alice, sensing his eyes moving over her with a faint hint of interest, began quietly appraising him in return. It wasn't the first time he was in her thoughts. She was reasonably sure by now it was her and not her mother he was interested in. It was a relief to know men not only noticed her again but fancied her. At a distance, in uniform, standing before his troops, he seemed formidable enough, but up close, walking beside her, speaking tensely and obviously a little nervous, he struck her as only a young man secretly shy of approaching a girl he was attracted to, and barely able to hide it. Alice was no longer the innocent young child instinctively frightened by men attracted to her budding body. Being stripped and handled by the burly warrior had not only left her burning with resentment, it had also given her a less squeamish feeling about men coming close. In fact in a perverse way she even began to enjoy his evident discomfort, his persistent clumsy efforts to protectively take her arm. "Lieutenant, why don't you just order my mother to leave?"

He coughed to clear his throat. "Normally, that might be permissible, but separating a mother from her daughter could require explanations."

"I'll do the explaining. I don't want to go with her."

He struggled to look troubled by the issue, but as she suspected his mind proved elsewhere. "How old are you?" he asked suddenly, his voice growing slightly hoarse. She knew why the question and when she failed to answer at once he queried gently, "Fifteen? . . . sixteen?"

"Sixteen," she responded, watching his relief at the answer. "Do you always ask young ladies their age?"

"Well, I was just wondering . . ."

Now a pixie quality was alive in Alice's eyes. "You were wondering if it was safe to court me?"

"Well, not exactly . . ."

"Ah, then you just wanted to kiss me?"

He heard the teasing quality in her voice. "Perhaps."

She turned around and started back toward the cabin. "I can't leave without Hattie, but you don't have to pretend to visit her to see me."

He had to run a few steps to catch up. "Are you saying I can call on you?"

Alice couldn't remember a moment she enjoyed more. "Lieutenant Grimes . . . wouldn't you say you've already started?"

That night Lee managed to keep Charlotte with him when darkness enveloped them in a grove just above the settlement. Had his mind been free it would have been an ideal time to slip an arm around her, conveying at least some hint of the affection he felt for her. But he was deeply worried. All his senses warned him too much time was passing; the fate of the volunteers was unknown and no messages had come from Quarles assuring the crucial supplies were on their way. No matter how he tried to shrug it off a whisper of menace was in the air and he was too seasoned to pretend it was imagination. Men who survived years in the wilderness only did so because of a nose for trouble.

Charlotte, aware of his constant attention, knew that this strange man desired her, but was thankful until now he hadn't touched her. Somehow she needed time to restore the sanctity of her body, the feeling it was hers to give as her emotions chose. Being taken by that young brave now seemed unreal; he was inept and mechanical, she was too much in shock at Tod's loss to realize what was happening. Unknown to Lee, she stood there hugging herself in the dark, not knowing he was too worried to grasp this opportunity for some gesture of intimacy. Unknown to him she felt grateful he was apparently content to wait until she signaled her consent. It was ridiculous to pretend she was over her love for Tod, but it would have been deluding herself not to admit she needed the support of a warm, kindly man, one who would help restore her faith in herself, and in men. Secretly she sensed the one standing next to her in the dark was just such a man. He was not pressing her, but obviously wanted her to know he was there, attuned to her feelings, willing to wait. After a tense moment she reached up and meekly kissed him on the cheek.

Lee, realizing they had crossed some barrier, one he had sensed but didn't know how to scale, put a comforting arm around her and started moving into the settlement again. He was glad now he hadn't tried to kiss her, which, had he not been preoccupied with the dangers surrounding them, he fully intended. She was a beautiful woman, with a soft yielding nature. Her love was worth waiting for, certainly restraining himself for, in fact going to any extremes for. Thomas Zacklee, a veteran scout, usually as independent as the wind, and as confident of life as a mountain lion gazing on a valley of dozing sheep, was in love.

With a reassuring squeeze of her hand he left Charlotte at her shelter, making his way to his own quarters, not knowing the figure looming up in the darkness, and making him reach for his gun, had come to put grim realty into his long-hidden fears.

Lame Fox had been distantly following the volunteers and their furtive Comanche scouts, and knew the party was caught in a running fight with a large force of warriors appearing from the south. He knew they were retreating toward the campsite and, if suffering some losses, were fortunately not facing enough Indians to overwhelm them. Wisely they were firing and falling back, making stands where the ground favored them, exploiting the known Comanche aversion to frontal assaults. But they were in trouble, trouble they were bringing to the settlement, trouble that could mean disaster.

His only friends had to be warned. He started back to the settlement as swiftly as possible, racing in the darkness to be there as far ahead of the struggling volunteers as possible. He came up to its outskirts and found only a few campfires burning low and a sentinel leaning against a dark stump glancing up at a brilliant canopy of stars. With ease he slipped around to the women's quarters where he spotted two figures moving in the night. He watched them separate and one start up the slope for the tent area before the burnt-out hall. He could tell by this figure's gait it was Lee.

Lame Fox hurried until he reached the top of the slope. There he jumped out to confront Lee coming up.

Lee had his gun out and leveled on the frightening figure appearing before him as he gasped, "Lame Fox! What the devil are you doing here?"

"Bad trouble!" grunted the Shawnee, stepping close and making signs. "Comanches come soon." As Lee lowered his gun he read in his signs and in the Shawnee's breathless broken English the plight of the volunteers. Lame Fox ended grimly with "Much trouble come when sun rise!"

Lee didn't hesitate, there was no time to waste. He sought the square shape of the military tent and entered it brusquely, shaking Grimes awake, his voice cutting through the dark interior. "Better get humpin', we got to fort up!"

Grimes came around blinking at the dim light thrown by a candle Lee was lighting. "Fort up?" he mumbled, then gruffly pulled himself to a sitting position. "Why?"

"Injuns coming."

Grimes's feet hit the ground. "Injuns! Jesus! How many?"

"Don't know . . . best get ready."

The lieutenant was reaching for his pants, shouting to the sentry outside the flap. "Have the bugler sound a call to arms, have all sergeants report here!"

"Yes, sir," the sentry shot back, and within minutes the whole camp came alive, soldiers and civilians alike looking to their guns and staring at the darkness, wondering what new torment or agents of death it concealed.

Only Lee realized that one matter couldn't wait. He

pulled Lame Fox aside and whispered to him. Lame Fox swung away, then turned back to face the scout with an expression of fear weirdly mixed with defiance. A third party observing them would have thought they were in a deadly debate, with Lee only managing to win after several bitter exchanges. But Lame Fox, his face turning granite with foreboding, finally slunk back into the darkness and disappeared, leaving a thoughtful Lee looking after him, hoping he hadn't sent the shaken Shawnee to his death.

60

Captain Quarles was more than a conspicuous figure around the fort. His comings and goings were watched by everyone; even the general stayed aware of his movements. Unfortunately no effort on behalf of others satisfied him. The general had given him two aides to write and dispatch his orders, but he glared at them, temper barely in check, at any minor delay. The troopers that had returned with him were out busy requisitioning wagons, though Henry, swearing under his breath, turned many back, not finding them sturdy enough for a long trip over poorly cut trails.

A sticking point was the guns. The general was flatly against giving Indians any firearms, and only Lincoln's letter enabled Quarles to requisition old rifles and even muskets abandoned by Confederate soldiers in battles along the Ohio. But it required three days to bring them by rail, and only the fact that he received two hundred instead of the hundred requested was any consolation. The general overcame a sullen peeve at being passed over when his summary inspection proved few of the guns were in good operating order. "Bunch of junk . . . army probably glad to be rid of them," he commented, but Quarles had no time for exchanging views with a superior officer whose cooperation was hardly by choice. Yet no urging or prodding on his part helped; supplies arrived with infuriating slowness. Blankets, pots and pans, mirrors, knives, and large iron nails so treasured by Plains Indians slowly accumulated. Canvas and such trivial items as beads, vermillion, and tobacco, were the last packed, and a small barrel of whiskey, which the general now only "advised" against, was finally carefully anchored beneath the driver's seat on the first wagon.

Drivers could have well been a problem but when a bonus of fifty dollars was offered a group of whip-cracking teamsters, contracted by the government to haul military equipment but unpaid for six months, were soon inquiring about the job. Quarles looked them over carefully, explaining to each the risks Indian country held for wagon trains, making it clear these goods were to be delivered to a hostile tribe that had spilled its share of white blood. A few grunted, then awkwardly edged away, but most, having faced cannon fire on the job, simply spit, swore contemptuously at the thought of mere Indians, and signed.

When Quarles, leading his heavily loaded train of ten wagons, pulled out of Leavenworth he figured he had ten days to get far enough west of Salina to unload at a place suitable for those dangerously aroused hostiles and their brooding chief, Whistling Elk. He only hoped Grimes, moving the camp eastward for safety, had not made the Indians suspect the supplies were not coming and these whites departing to avoid their wrath. Once again he thought about Cathy, about her dying husband, about the strange intimacy between them, about the terrible way life put good people in painful dilemmas, trapping them between insoluble suffering and that infinite loneliness life without love means. There was nothing honorable about what he had done, but honor was intruding now. She was a woman watching her husband die,

destined to see part of her life ending at some lonely
grave. Though he could not drive her image from his
mind he knew now his desire for her, and the torment it
already promised, should remain his burden alone. She
belonged to another, she had given herself to save that
other, and though he had possessed her physically her
real gift, her love, belonged to Cole. He could only
despise himself for not respecting that sooner. He was
that kind of man.

Shortly after dawn Lee could hear shots in the distance. He had slipped out beyond the perimeter of the
camp, studying the terrain to the southwest. He was
cursing himself for not insisting Grimes move the sick
and all noncombatants eastward sooner. Now no wagon
dare leave the protection of the camp. He was wondering
how many of the volunteers had been lost; Lame Fox
had reported they were badly outnumbered. Then in the
scant light he saw a flash of gunfire halfway to the
horizon. They were coming, what was left of them, and
behind them would be the maddened warriors Whistling
Elk had promised to keep at peace for a month. But that
month was fast disappearing, in his reckoning only seven
or eight days were left, if Quarles were not well on his
way by now a desperate situation was fast in the making.

The sun was well up when the volunteers reached the
camp. They came in exhausted, some lightly wounded
but grieving pitifully about the seriously injured that had
to be left behind. When the last one straggled in Lee
decided at least one third of the party had been lost, a
serious reduction in the camp's earlier strength. Grimes
could hardly conceal his fury they had gone at all. He
ordered what help he could for them and even asked
Hattie to bring across any women who might be helpful
dressing wounds. But he refused to greet them, he left
that to Lee whose reception was cutting and brief. "Well,
you've brought them here, let's hope some damn fools
like yourselves can get 'em to leave again."

By noon the camp was surrounded by painted warriors, peering at them beyond rifle range and occasionally

shaking bows decorated with scalps in defiance. But they weren't attacking. Everyone in camp carefully sought cover and settled down to watch. After an hour Grimes approached Lee, who was instructing those volunteers still able and willing to fight which positions they should hold. A dread silence hung over most of the camp and Lee's voice carried further than he knew.

"What do you think?" queried the young lieutenant coming up.

Lee shrugged and stared at him. "You wouldn't like what I think."

"Well, let's have it . . . saying it can't make it any worse."

"They're waiting," said Lee, nodding toward the distant line of painted figures.

"Waiting for what?"

In his mind's eye Lee saw once again the hordes of warriors milling about Whistling Elk's camp and his mouth grew taut as he replied. "For the biggest damn bunch of redskins this side of hell to get here. When they do, you better put any more questions you got to them."

Lame Fox was a troubled and increasingly harried man. Lee had made him promise to race directly to Quarles, report the camp's plight, and plead with him to hurry. This time no intermediators were to be trusted, no strangers relied upon to take seriously the word of a shadowy Shawnee and race to Leavenworth with dispatch, even desperation, to tell of dangers now facing the settlement. Lee understood Lame Fox's anguish at the thought of returning to a scene where death might easily be waiting, but the Indian knew this country well and had the best chance of getting there in the shortest time. The peril the Shawnee was running had to be weighed against the disaster that threatened their entire camp. Once there Quarles would certainly protect him; getting there would be his only risk.

But it was risk enough for Lame Fox. He skirted Salina and raced eastward, wondering to himself why powerful spirits he often prayed to and strove to live in harmony with had left a proud Shawnee warrior with no friends except these whites, who were forever stumbling into trouble, forever forgetting the land they coveted belonged to others, forever blaming Indians for their misfortunes, never sensing the trouble lay in avarice and the acquisitive nature of their ways. In truth, he was growing deathly sick of whites and the misery and fear they had reduced him to. Galloping hurriedly through the countryside, feeling the wind upon his straining face, it was impossible not to think of days when, as a young brave, he had proudly painted himself for war and followed renown Shawnee leaders into the *Kain-tuck-kee,* the dark and bloody ground, to see other tribes, including the mighty Cherokees, retreating before them into the mountains. But time had swept those glories aside, life in the sham world of the whites had become tasteless, empty, devoid of honor and pride in one's tribal feats. He now lived like an animal and like any animal his life held no sanctity for men. Lame Fox saw himself as just another wolf with a bounty on its pelt, for which his life would be readily forfeited. It was not a role a proud Shawnee warrior should be made to play in the twilight of his years, and Lame Fox, staring at the horizon ahead, suddenly decided he would play it no more.

Whistling Elk stared at the charred remains of the settlement they had now camped in view of. Here and there temporary shelters had been thrown up and two rows of tents ran along the slope leading to the river. There were still bluecoats here and what remained of the hapless party they had just driven back with heavy losses. The whites were tenaciously holding on to this forlorn spot but for what purpose defied him. There were only a few sleeps left in that moon of peace promised them, and Vermillion Paw, backed by many war leaders, was urging an all-out attack. In a day or two the great gathering of warriors left on the Arkansas would be arriving and the issue could not long be delayed. Whistling Elk knew his people could and would destroy this handful of *tahbay-bohs,* satiating their long-smoldering anger by torture and the ripping off of scalps. But would that remove the sinister cloud on the horizon, the one he once dreamed threatened the tribes and that no medicine could dispel?

At night the warriors, restless and hot for war, set up a line of drums and danced wildly, burning off the energy hatred of these stubborn whites had engendered. They screamed in frenzied joy, acting out in pantomime their revenge for what they considered an endless string of betrayals and false promises. Whistling Elk sat watching their wild gyrations and listening to crazed yells that betrayed his people's primal thirst for blood, for vengeance, for slaughter. Strangely it made him meditative. What would be their destiny, these horse warriors of the Plains he had risen to lead. Raised in an ethos of violence and drugged by superstition, they seemed never to grasp the menace that lay in the calm, calculating ways of the whites. He saw Vermillion Paw standing in a ghostly light thrown by leaping fires, his eyes fixed on the spectacle before him. Vermillion Paw was a powerful medicine man, in this hour of war fervor he would sway their hearts, their minds, gaining the power of their deep hatred for his words. When the moment of decision arrived he would be a force to be reckoned with.

Whistling Elk, sensing the whites beyond were watching this grim revelry, wondered if they knew they were looking on a dance of death, where the imaginary figures being slain in mock assaults were themselves. He lit his pipe and stared into the night. Perhaps they did, perhaps the dark silence that hung over their camp meant they were looking toward the leaping fires, the maddened dancers, and quietly wondered at their destiny too.

Lee couldn't get over the way Hattie refused to show fear. She kept talking to the "ladies" to keep their spirits up, refused to let Skeeter and Ben act dejected, and would allow no panicky talk when the beat of drums rose from the hostile camp, visible in a flickering light thrown by spreading fires. He kept forgetting she had already killed two Indians, one the bloody chief, Black Otter. Still the sight of her carrying a shotgun clashed with what he knew to be her nature.

"Always figured you to be a great Christian, Hattie," he said lowly, standing next to her in the dark.

"Das right!"

"Must know you look mighty unchristian with that gun."

"Das right!"

"Didn't think Christians were suppose to shoot people."

"Dey not, only de devil."

"You figure anyone getting in your way is some sort of devil . . . that it?"

"Das right!"

It was a strange conversation but it was only an attempt to deal with the growing tension. There was nothing to be done. They had set up what defenses they could, distributed as much food as they could prepare, and as much ammunition as could be spared. Their ammunition supply turned out to be far less than thought, yet nothing could be done about that either.

Hattie cleared her throat to finish her remarks. "Righteous folks always git dangerous when evil come 'round." Then, turning to Alice, "We best git 'nough water . . . likely we be needin'."

Alice coming closer found Lee's face in the dark. "Where's Lieutenant Grimes?"

"Reckon where he belongs . . . with his troop."

"He coming by?"

Lee was curiously long in answering, his hand going up to rub his mouth thoughtfully as he made out her features in the night. "He's a busy man, Alice, he's got that parcel of Indians to worry about. Wait a few hours and if nothing happens and you still want to see him try fetching him yonder by the guidon."

Lee moved away to the other side of the ranch where he knew he would find Charlotte. She looked up in the darkness to find him standing next to her. Somehow it seemed natural to enclose her in his arms. She didn't resist for he kept his lips on her forehead and she, sensing he would go no further, hugged him back warmly, her body feeling good against his. After a few moments he murmured, "Frightened?"

"Yes."

"Well, they're not attacking us, and right now we figure we've got them outnumbered. If things look right we might try moving east in the morning."

She stayed very close, clinging to his jacket, and suddenly some deep need in her rose to meet some long wanting in him, making them one for a single fleeting moment before he nuzzled her hair and gently released her. But it had happened. Lee felt her closeness had just communicated something her tongue could not, but it was enough. He had lived long enough to know a woman's warmth was the postilion of her heart.

But the setting was all wrong. There was no forcing the terrible foreboding from his mind. The tribesmen camping beyond were but a small fraction of the number seen on the Arkansas, surely more were coming. Unless Quarles arrived with those supplies this whole camp was in deadly peril. His eyes caught the dim forms of women, almost like ghosts, shifting about him. Were Charlotte and these pathetic souls to be subjected to a second gauntlet of rape and torment? His mind ran to Cathy. Did Henry know this woman he was so attracted to now faced the fate of Flora or even the witless Charity? Perhaps Lame Fox had reached him, perhaps he now knew the dire straights they were in and was hastening a wagon train west. Perhaps.

He stared into the night, rising on his toes to view the distant Indian camp, his eyes catching figures weaving and leaping about, contorting jerkily to the drums. Years in the wilderness had taught him to recognize warriors preparing for war. This scene left no doubt. He settled back again sobered, brooding over how much depended on Lame Fox. There was no limit to what he would have given to know where that Indian was at the moment, for the fate of this beleaguered camp might well be riding on the fortunes of an old, scarred, renegade Shawnee who was bearing their solitary cry for help through the night.

☆ 61 ☆

Though Lame Fox had made a swift if furtive trip eastward, a few miles from the fort he rode into the brush and dismounted. From the back of his saddle he took a pouch that contained odd remnants of his earlier life, items he'd kept for years, parts of himself his spirit could not let die. There were small packages of red and yellow face powder, finger bones he had taken from enemies in his youth, worked into ear pieces reaching almost to his shoulders. There was a sharp knife to shave his skull, leaving only a scalp lock tinted with white. Recalling the magic medicine designs of his once great nation, he wet the powder and painted his face completely red, then streaked it with bold angular lines of yellow, making his strange dark eyes seem reptilian pits in a mask of hideously clashing hues. Finally he found the scalp of red hair taken from the fat man he had killed in the grove. This he tied to his waist and with a few strokes of yellow and red across his chest and forearms, he tied the pouch to his saddle again and remounted. Lame Fox, the great Shawnee warrior, was now ready to enter the white man's fort.

Captain Quarles couldn't imagine what was causing the commotion at the gate. He was anxious to get underway, they had covered the long stretch from the quartermaster shed and were about to exit at the main gate when the first wagon signaled a halt. He rode forward rapidly, shouting to the sentry as he came up. "What's the hold up here? We've got to get moving!"

The sentry saluted and pointed to a mounted figure his companion had a gun trained on. "Sorry, sir. This dangerous-looking buck wants to enter. Indians aren't allowed in the fort. I've sent for the sergeant, should be cleared up in a minute or two. Sorry, sir."

While the sentry gestured and talked Quarles glanced at the figure being discussed, and suddenly discovered its grotesque face staring at him. In that same moment his heart skipped a beat as he realized he was looking at Lame Fox covered with war paint. Shock and momentary confusion robbed him of breath to speak but finally he sputtered, "Lame Fox! What in Christ's name are you doing here . . . dressed like that?! Are you crazy?"

Lame Fox rose up in his stirrups. "Me Lame Fox, Shawnee warrior." His eyes swept the great sweeps of space surrounding the fort. "This land of my people . . . bones of my fathers sleep here. Lame Fox belong here, his spirits speak in wind, the suns of his youth journeyed across this sky. Lame Fox sent here by great spirit. Lame Fox belong this land."

Quarles pulled his mount over to the Indian. "Now, listen to me. Don't say any more, you could be in a helluva lot of trouble." Acting with more assurance than he felt he explained to the puzzled sentries that Lame Fox was an army scout returning from extended duty. He hadn't recognized him at first because of his disguise. But he would take charge of him. The sentries, if not satisfied, were glad to get this dangerous-looking Indian off their hands. They saluted to Quarles and returned to monitoring traffic through the gate.

During that first night Alice had wandered through the dark camp looking for Grimes. She finally stumbled into a guard post which, informing her Grimes was at his command tent, abruptly escorted her back to the ranch. She heard again they were going to try and move the camp eastward at dawn, a feat that made the only soldier she got to talk sound jittery. Strangely enough she herself had experienced so much fright lately she was becoming noticeably inured to it. If the camp was going to fight she was going to fight too. She had enough of being stripped by savages, her face painted, her body ravished. Incredibly she was still a virgin, but virginity no longer seemed important. The young girls and unmarried women who had been raped were suffering as much from public knowledge of their violation as they were from the physical abuse that accompanied their assaults. To her these women seem unjustly cursed, unfairly judged, held accountable for the sanctity of their bodies when powerless to preserve it. She had seen some of the horrors that befell her mother, Charity, and others. They had left her mute, stunned, sickened beyond the ability to feel. She still had to repress scenes from that first night in captivity, finding them too shattering to accept as reality. But the aftermath proved an equal if different and more insidious kind of shock. These women found their own people becoming awkward and embarrassed in their presence. Everyone knew they had been the playthings of brutish men, their bodies abused by filthy hands, churlish primitives with dung in their hair subjecting them to unspeakable humiliations. Alice knew that had she been raped at the time she would have been helpless, but she wasn't helpless now. One of her reasons for seeking Grimes was to get a pistol. The thought came into her mind as she heard women in the shelter, with the Indians in sight again, asking for handguns. Rather than face captivity a second time they preferred death by their own hand.

Alice was not only resentful but angrily disturbed by her mother, who kept demanding they be taken to safety, who kept upbraiding Grimes in his absence for not moving eastward sooner, who now screamed at Alice for not obeying her and Charity for not acting rationally. Only Hattie seemed able to keep smiling at her, if only occasionally running out of patience and saying, not unkindly, "Hush up, de Lord need time to rest. Can't lissen to yo' complaints when come time to hear mine."

Hattie was surely a blessing and secretly Alice near worshiped her. But she was determined to find Grimes, the young lieutenant was beginning to play a strange, perhaps critical role in her mind. If these last few dreadful days had appalled her they had also matured her. She had been viscerally shaken by her nude captivity but also in some way curiously released, thrown into life again with a mind aged well beyond her years. Her skin was still childlike smooth, her eyes bright, but those cruel scenes observed and endured in the hands of savages had given her a new outlook, markedly cynical and irreverent. Nothing she believed before her captivity seemed valid any longer. The settlement didn't need, as she had been taught, her mother or Charity to lead it; when trouble came it needed Hattie. The religion Dillby preached hadn't done for these women what Hattie's simple presence did. For all her mother's talk about the power of virtue it was a fragile thing, disappearing when ignorant heathens forced your legs apart. Now Alice wanted Grimes and she wanted a gun; the only other thing she wanted she had quietly wanted for some time, to see Chloe again. Hattie's daughter, unlike herself, would surely be pining for her mother, and one day returning to her. Alice could only smile bitterly at the thought, for she knew now she would never pine for Flora, the mother who felt her better off had she been raped.

What Quarles began shouting at Lame Fox didn't upset the Indian half as much as Quarles himself was rocked by what the Shawnee shouted in return.

Henry was choleric. "You must be out of your mind coming here painted like that, have you forgotten why you left?"

They were in a small grove, quarter of a mile from the gate. The wagon train was coming up behind them.

"Lame Fox Shawnee warrior, not weasel moving only in dark!"

"Weasels in daylight don't last long." Henry irritably swung around, glancing at the wagon train. "Why in hell are you here anyhow?"

"Bad trouble at camp!"

"What?"

"Many Indians come to camp."

"Many Indians? . . . camp? What the hell are you talking about? They're in Salina!"

Lame Fox told Quarles how the lieutenant delayed leaving, how the volunteers set out for the Arkansas and ended up drawing hostiles to the settlement. As he finished Quarles was pounding the saddle horn. "Why in hell didn't that goddamned Grimes follow orders and pull back! Jesus! Does anyone use his head anymore?"

They sat staring at each other, the pressing question in Henry's eyes missed by the Indian who failed to read it. Quarles had to voice it, in truth he actually skirted it by asking about Cole. "How's that Sadler fellow?"

"He dead."

Quarles took a deep breath and looked away.

Suddenly Lame Fox sensed anxiety replacing anger in the other and was confused by the change. He lifted an arm, pointing it west. "Friend Lee say you come quick, maybe big attack come soon."

Henry pulled back and started toward the wagon train, his voice suddenly cold, hard, his eyes down, looking inward, his face creased with concern. "We'll come as quick as we can. You get the hell back and tell them to fort up ... find some way to convince the Indians we're coming ... do everything to avoid a fight!"

Lame Fox watched him ride off and grunted to himself. Once again a white man was sending a Shawnee warrior to do his bidding. Lame Fox swung his mount about and disappeared into the brush. He was going west again but this time not to save whites ... this time he would serve his own embattled race.

The camp's attempts to move east that morning only proved the wildly charging horsemen, who chanted their death songs before every foray, were too agile, too shifty, too clearly masters of the quick and deadly strike, to make retreat to Salina anything but a costly nightmare. After two attempts Grimes decided to fortify the camp as best he could and await results. After all the truce still had a few days to run. He might be stirring up trouble a little patience could avoid. But Lee argued waiting was a mistake and spoke against the decision. "Can't you see they're waiting for reinforcements, when they get here they'll be calling the tune." He looked about him as though wishing he had more authority than a mere scout. But finally, shaking his head, he settled with, "We better start praying ole Henry is getting close."

With tension nearing its peak, the camp, now being constantly watched by Indians beyond rifle range, found itself in for some strange days and even stranger nights. Alice was still trying to get Grimes alone, though not in daylight when he was always bustling and busy with defense, but at night, particularly late night, when she had hopes of catching him resting in his tent. Her determination finally paid off and she, eluding a smoking sentry, slipped through the flap and muffled his surprise by placing a soft, scented hand over his mouth. The young lieutenant couldn't believe she dared appear there at such an hour, but he couldn't deny she was settling on his cot beside him, and, as a seeming precaution, wetting her fingers and pinching his single candle out.

"Jesus, what the devil are you doing here?" he whispered.

"Visiting you," she whispered back.

His speech sounded a tick slower, his voice slightly lower as he gasped, "What if you were seen?"

"I wasn't."

She heard his breath being drawn in again to speak. "I should be calling the guard."

"You won't."

She felt his arm going around her and tentatively gripping her shoulder. "You're pretty cocksure of yourself, aren't you?"

"I need a few things from you."

"From me? What?"

"A pistol."

"You came here for a pistol?"

"A handgun."

She sensed him studying her in the dark. "Aren't there handguns at the ranch?"

"They don't belong to me."

He could smell the fragrance of her young body in the still air of the tent's interior. Something told him she wasn't there for a pistol but on a different kind of quest, a quest as old as human craving. They were two young people in a perilous situation, a chance bullet or a tomahawk blade might suddenly end all dreams, all sensual, no, all sexual expectations, with or without love. The young, confronted with death, tended to grasp what they could of life. He had seen it in the quick desperate hedonism possessing young men marching off to war. He was close enough to his own youth to remember that great mysterious unknowing concerning the opposite sex, that preoccupation that hung like an internal sun heating the sap of youth, bringing a secret but relentless lust to boys and an inarticulate, sometimes painful yearning to girls. He sensed it was working now. She couldn't see it but he was smiling grimly to himself. He had read in military histories of women in ancient cities, besieged and about to be overrun or taken, offering themselves to defending soldiers so as not to die virgins or have their virginity swept away in an orgiastic frenzy of the foe.

Alice would have been mildly shocked at his thoughts, for that night fell into different focus for her. She had seen what happened to captured women and knew it might still happen to her. She had been raised with a vow to give her virginity only in love and under the sanctions of God. But somewhere in her mind, conflicting with this belief, was the thought of her virginity being taken by these grotesquely painted savages, whose filth nauseated her and whose thirst for blood might leave her crippled. How coming here might solve this problem, reconciling these stark realizations feuding in her brain, she didn't know. She was here on instinct, knowing she was making herself vulnerable to Grimes, but hoping the company of a young male of her own race would allow nature and normality to point the way. Oddly enough she wasn't afraid, even when he lifted her chin, bringing her lips even with his, bending over to kiss her. She was still not afraid when he put his hand under her dress, though now she squirmed and murmured in faint alarm. He cautioned her to remain silent, for a guard was only a few yards away. About that she knew he was right and kept mute while he went on kissing her. Soon she felt him undoing her clothes and somewhere in

her mind a warning to resist flared up. But she was
beginning to feel a strange warmth in his closeness and
her mind was beginning to spin. What did she really
want? Did she even know? A minute or two later the
warning rose again but had to fight its way through
strange exciting sensations rippling through her loins. It
came one final time as she feebly resisted a slow settling
on the cot, but by then something more powerful than
will was surging through her body like fire and it was too
late.

62

The troubled moon of waiting was over. Whistling Elk
knew from scouts galloping in and shouting from exhausted ponies that the great mass of warriors gathered
on the Arkansas, chanting hatred for the *tahbay-boh* and
itching for war, would be around him by sundown. The
chances for peace were slipping away. The swift destruction of this camp they had pinned down with a few
determined assaults would only be the beginning. Vermillion Paw and a swelling number of war leaders were
demanding bloody attacks along the entire frontier.
Once again talk of driving white men from the great
sweep of buffalo range was causing the eyes of the people
to shine; once again Whistling Elk, haunted by his
dream, would stare uneasily into the council fire, knowing his warriors could and would overwhelm and destroy
this and many other small settlements. But what lay
beyond that? Would the dark cloud grow as they struggled to destroy it?

Discouraged, embittered by endless white duplicity,
yet reluctant to see the last hope of peace disappear,

Whistling Elk secretly decided to send word to the whites that the moon of waiting was over, the messenger he told to return and say where the promised supplies would be must now appear. If he did not war would break out like thunder in the night. It was not the Indian way to warn enemies of attacks but if it was to be war, warnings couldn't save this settlement.

He looked about him. Here and there medicine men were chanting over their drums as squaws feverishly filled large numbers of boiling pots. Great cuts of meat were being cooked with herbs and wild roots, preparations to feed what would soon be over a thousand warriors. When cooking squaws usually chattered among themselves like excited crows, but the prospect of impending hostilities now kept many mute, withdrawn, watchful. Like himself, they glanced toward the white camp and listened to Vermillion Paw chanting a medicine song, calling upon the spirits to give the people strength.

Lee could no longer stand and simply wait. A constant nagging fear that Lame Fox hadn't reached Quarles, that one of a thousand things had happened to the Shawnee, troubled him. He kept suggesting to Grimes that he slip off in the darkness and race to find the wagon train. Henry had to know how very desperate things were. Somehow they had to learn if the wagons were even coming and if so when. Time had run out, in his heart he knew unless the wagons showed, an overwhelming attack was imminent.

Even his visits to Charlotte when darkness fell were becoming a trial, for though his mind refused thoughts of her being in captivity again the specter was mounting. Seeing Charlotte brought him closer to Cathy, for the two had become inseparable. As Hattie said, "Folks un'nerstand misery dey got to share." Cathy rarely spoke but even she was beginning to realize they were in dire trouble. She saw Lee with his arms around Charlotte and sensed, though Charlotte didn't allow herself to be kissed, she was comforted by his closeness. A pang shot through her as she thought of Cole but was kept from

crying when thoughts of him brought to mind his pride
in her as a fighter. An image of his encouraging smile
when she took a stand on things flashed through her
mind. What would Cole expect of her here? Now?

Lee made no mention of his decision to leave and race
eastward to find Quarles, but felt forced to whisper to
Charlotte he might not be able to visit for a spell.
Charlotte, betraying only a moment of fright, gripped
him more tightly with a near inaudible gasp. The painful
question of "why?" rose to fill her eyes, but its only
possible answer kept it from being asked. She knew now
what danger they were in. Yet that moment resolved
something in her mind, for she slowly raised her lips to
his and left them parted for his kiss.

Henry Quarles rode alongside the train in a continual
sweat. His eyes, if sunk from fatigue, were still raging,
his language harsh, profane, yet nothing he said or did
could speed these wagons up. Long before he got to
Topeka he was quarreling bitterly with the teamsters,
experienced men who knew horses couldn't be driven at
his pace and not founder. With the spring runoff in spate
water bedeviled every low spot and the ungraded trails
were in miserable shape. Wagons kept breaking down
and if a steady sun meant stops for water, rain brought
mud. No one needed to tell him how late he was going to
be, nor did he need telling what the delay could mean to
Cathy and the other women. The tragedy it promised
was daily inflicted on his soul, sickening him with dread
when not inflaming his temper.

It was in Topeka when he first heard rumors that a
great uprising was expected on the Kansas border that
spring. The governor of Kansas had advised settlers to
pull back as far east as possible for he lacked troops to
protect them. The war was still going badly for the
Union and the frontier had to shift for itself. This was
hardly news to Quarles, but biting into his lower lip he
stared at the western horizon, knowing when the storm
broke it would strike first at a settlement with what
remained of his broken life, and that strange female
whom he fantasized might repair it, its first victims.

But he had to keep hoping. Perhaps Lame Fox was there assuring them he was coming. Perhaps the Shawnee's report of approaching wagons would keep the natives hungry for this bounty and their minds off war. Perhaps. But what was it about Lame Fox that now rankled in his brain, was it that ridiculous warpaint and defiant talk or was it something more, something jarring his long-held belief that Lame Fox was little more than a surly, occasionally drunken lackey of the whites? Then after a moment or two he rose up in the saddle with a start, for he knew now it was a scalp of red hair he spotted hanging from the Indian's belt. Lame Fox was brazenly announcing to the world he had killed a white man.

The arrival of great parties of braves riding into the Indian camp was accompanied by a din that could be heard inside the ranch house. Drums began to sound and more fires were lit, but most of all the great screaming of squaws, as they saw their favorite braves or war leaders riding by, made the distant scene resemble noisy spirits coming together in a ritual of endless shrieks. But it soon had its more menacing side. Warriors rode up to peer across at the white camp, some shaking their weapons, mouthing epithets that distance defied hearing. Grimes, watching them approach, was still disturbed by an earlier argument that day with Lee, who had since disappeared.

He had made his stand as clear as any officer could. "I can't give you permission to leave, we may need you. A command can't operate in this country without a scout."

"This command needs them wagons a hell of a lot more than it needs a scout. Some of the volunteers can fill in in a pinch."

"Those volunteers aren't under contract to the army, you are! Permission denied."

Permission to stand helplessly by and watch a calamity building didn't rate very high in Lee's reckoning. He slipped along the back of the camp, taking his horse as though moving it to a better grazing spot, then, acting as though ordered to circle the camp and check its perimeter defense, he mounted, maneuvered the mount behind a stand of brush, and disappeared.

Grimes, suspecting he was gone, winced at the sorry job he was doing since taking command. He should have moved the camp east when Quarles left, or at least sent the women and sick back. Upon first seeing Indians he should have kept battling his way toward Salina. Instead he depended on a truce that the frightening sight developing before him now warned hung by a thread.

Finally there was Alice.

An officer and a gentleman was the noble code he swore to upon leaving military school. Was he really either? Though he had told himself a thousand times she came there wanting him, whether she knew it or not, it didn't help. She was sixteen, with the confused courage of a young girl's first heady venture into life. Yet he was still puzzled. If innocent she had been wonderful to make love to, departing without a word or gesture to hint the tryst was a commitment she expected to be honored.

But in the last hour events had crowded even Alice from his mind. The camp, watching the warriors gathering beyond, was increasingly tense and watchful, with sergeants coming by for final orders on defense and volunteers urgently requesting remaining ammunition be fairly divided before any fighting began. In the late afternoon a small band of warriors, led by a war leader, came across the no man's land between the camps and raised a spear in a sweeping motion, the ancient request for parlay. Grimes, suspicious of their intent, and lacking experience in dealing with Indians, turned to Cheatem, who was nervously striding up. "What do you think?"

"Best send someone out there . . . talkin's better 'n fightin'."

Grimes rubbed his forehead, catching sight of Alice watching him from a distance behind Cheatem. Then, ordering a corporal's guard to accompany him and instructing them to form a square behind him, he straightened his tunic and went forward to meet the yellow- and black-faced war leader who sat his horse, scowling at him as he approached.

Alice was not sorry for what happened in the tent that night but it had changed her. She found herself less in awe of other women, even Hattie, less in fear of other men, even Comanches. She had gotten her handgun and had put an issue to rest in her mind. Now she was no longer Flora's daughter. That night made her something else, a woman in her own right, not a wildly searching girl incensed at the burden of virginity. This was no country for virgins. She watched Grimes marching toward the painted braves, his shoulders back, his gaze apparently engaging theirs. What happened in the tent seemed to matter little now, what mattered was something far different, something she was waiting to see.

The war leader had been chosen because he spoke some English, but he resented the task. He sat watching Grimes looking up at him, requesting the reason for a parlay. He rose in the saddle and pointed to his own camp. "Chief want Medicine Stone to return . . . want hear his words."

"Medicine Stone?" Grimes looked confused.

"Black man," he gestured to his neck, "have medicine stone."

Now it was clear, they wanted Sam. Grimes looked uncertain for a moment. "Why you want this man?"

"It is for Whistling Elk to say."

Grimes looked about him. He could see warriors to the east and west circling his camp, somewhere they had crossed the Smoky Hill, for one or two mounted figures could be seen approaching the opposite bank. Something told him weakness was a mistake. He tried to look indifferent to their predicament, saying with as little emotion as possible, "We will consider your message. Tell your chief we hope for peace until the many wagons with presents come. Tell him our hearts are good and filled with friendship. The great father in Washington wants only peace."

The war leader grunted cynically. "Medicine Stone must come to our council before the sun sleeps. Whistling Elk has no more words to speak." Pulling his mount about, he rode away.

That afternoon there was also tension in the camp of the hostiles, but it wasn't to last. Vermillion Paw and his many war leaders couldn't refuse Whistling Elk's request for a parlay, it was the ancient right of a chief, but even old Elk knew it was to be their only concession. The council was a distressful one, with many war leaders sullenly declaring they had waited too long, the spring buffalo hunt had been seriously delayed, a long summer hunt would now be necessary as few lodges had the robes and dried meat required to live through the long icy winter. Whistling Elk argued that the parlay should take place the following day, but grunts of impatience and even insurgency were too loud and numerous to ignore. Vermillion Paw's eyes looked solemnly across the fire to hold those of Whistling Elk. "Before the sun sets, my brother, we must know what falseness still lies in their hearts. If it is not as they promised the sun will rise on their scattered bones."

The disgruntled council finally settled on a war leader to ride out and offer a parlay, and, if it failed, declared dawn to be the fateful moment for an all-out war.

By riding all night and into the following day Lee kept driving eastward, his sustained pace made possible by exchanging horses with the few isolated settlers, who refused to abandon their claim and flee east, and who, hearing he was trying to stop an Indian uprising, gladly cooperated. But upon reaching Salina without meeting the wagon train he knew it would take at least a week to get the promised supplies anywhere near the settlement. He finally encountered Quarles a few miles east of Salina, and while shocked at the deeply lined, ashen face of his old friend, he immediately sensed Henry had resigned himself to a critical and perhaps disastrous delay. They couldn't put wings on these wagons, they could only pray one more wheel didn't break or one more horse give out. Quarles was tempted to open the whiskey barrel but Lee cautioned against it. "We got to keep our minds on pushing ahead . . . bad as you need it now if we don't find a way to get back there a hell of a lot faster than I'm thinking, all the whiskey in the world isn't gonna make us forget what we're going to find."

The whole camp watched as Cheatem led Sam up to where the company guidon sat before Grimes's tent. Sam had taken his medicine stone off but brought it along clutched in his hand at Cheatem's request. Hattie, mute with concern, was following them at a good fifty feet, her eyes fixed upon Grimes, who stood studying Sam as he came up. Skeeter straggled behind her.

"Here he be," said Cheatem, nodding at Sam.

Grimes took a step forward and cleared his throat. "They're asking to talk to you. Any idea why?"

Sam's gaze held steady as he confronted Grimes but his voice revealed the tension building within. "Deys waitin' fo' dem supplies . . . dey wants me to tell 'em where dey at."

"You speak some Comanche, don't you?"

"Sum."

"Then you got to tell them the supplies are coming, they just have to wait."

Sam took a step back and looked ruefully toward the Indian camp. "Dey bin waitin' a powerful long time. Dem supplies is mighty, mighty late."

Grimes threw him a look of faint annoyance and shook his head. "We don't have any choice . . . somehow you've got to keep 'em talking till those supplies come."

By now many onlookers were drawing close enough to

hear. Cheatem, looking about, grunted and nudged Sam. "You game to go, son?"

Sam looked back at Hattie who was now almost beside him. "Is ah'se goin' alone?"

Cheatem shifted uncomfortably, drawing in his breath. "Well . . ."

"I'll go with you," declared Grimes.

Cheatem used the breath he had gathered to quickly caution the grim-faced Grimes. "Don't believe the commander of the camp should be putting he'self in the hands of them savages."

Several bystanders, overhearing, spoke up in agreement.

Hattie was next to Sam now. She had him by the arm. "You go talk to dem rascals, Sam. Ah knows you scared but look 'round you . . . dey everywhere . . . like ants 'round spilt molasses. You as safe dere as here. Don't forget de Lord watchin'."

Sam's expression hardly suggested the Lord's attention brought much relief. He kept staring at the Indian camp as though it were a face he didn't trust. "Well, you willing to go it alone?" demanded Grimes.

Sam hesitated just long enough to hear Skeeter and a sergeant, along with one or two volunteers, offering for the sake of the camp to go with him. But Grimes was growing irate at Sam's reluctance. He turned to Skeeter. "Do you speak any Comanche?"

"No, suh."

Grimes swung to the crowd surrounding them. "Anyone here understand Indian lingo?"

When no one responded, he half shouted with an unmistakable ring of authority. "It doesn't make sense to jeopardize a single person if it won't serve any purpose. Sam, they asked for you . . . you going or not?"

Sam eyed Hattie, whom he could see was ready to answer for him, then hurriedly fixing the medicine stone around his neck replied, "Ah'll go over, mebbe chat wid dem, if ah doan git back doan send no mo'."

A little cheer went up from those who heard, but no one was fooled. Sam was entering a hostile camp, boiling with warriors painted and itching for war, with nothing to offer but confusion and even doubts about a wagon train that secretly was assailing and depressing them all.

Lame Fox made his way west along the Smoky Hill, avoiding settlements and even homesteads, only once coming unexpectedly upon some children playing near the stream. They ran from him screaming in terror. He could tell from his reflection in the water that his warpaint was still showing and his scalp lock still giving his head a wolfish outline. He was surprised to see any whites left in this threatened land, but that was their way, always a few defying death from a tomahawk or at the torture stake, creeping ever westward no matter the risk. He wondered at his own people, depending on scattered, fiercely independent tribesmen for survival, forever fighting but never grasping that constant warfare brought faltering manpower. Finally they would be overtaken, as was he, by a malign fatalism as their medicines no longer brought spiritual strength. Though bitter and angry at heart he felt desperate, dispirited, achingly alone. A sense of doom near strickened him. The great affliction he had watched strike his race burned like acid in his brain. His whole life had been witness to the despoiling and depraving of every familiar tribe of his youth, allies and enemies alike. All memories of past glories, alive now only in legend, made more insufferable this scourge of white power spreading like a pestilence over the land, inexorable as nightfall, a nightfall that offered no dawning.

In spite of misgivings about his possible reception a vague kinship with these Comanches and Kiowas had worked its way into his mind. It was a strange sensation, for however formidable these tribesmen seemed, his heart told him they were destined to go the way of the Shawnee, the Cherokee, the Ottawa, those heroic tribes who thought to stop the whites and were now dead or pariahs in their own land.

He studied the sky. A spring storm was coming. A lone warrior approaching a strange tribe should come armed with many presents, but he had no presents, though perhaps he had something far more precious . . .

something fortune might allow him to offer. Finally, topping a scrub-dotted mound he stared upriver and spotted the two camps in the distance; still, remote as they were, he realized at once a furious battle between them was taking place.

Stepping gingerly, but struggling to keep his expression friendly, Sam made his way into the hostile camp, where before a huge fire he spotted the long, drawn face of Whistling Elk. Around the chief were a multitude of painted faces, some fearful to behold. One, painted black with white stripes in a radial pattern extending from red-daubed eyes, he knew was Vermillion Paw, for the medicine man's gaze was fixed, as before, on the medicine stone around Sam's neck. For a moment he wondered if wearing it was a mistake.

Whistling Elk drew himself up as Sam approached. An explosive array of warriors, standing before a throng of squaws, children, and even a few surviving captives, waited for him to speak.

The old chief struck the ground with his spear. "Now we will hear your words Medicine Stone, tell us if your heart spoke true in the last moon!"

Sam rubbed his hands together and glanced anxiously at the solemn countenance of the old chief. His command of Comanche, though poor, was good enough for all he could say. "Supplies come . . . they late but they come . . . me friend, speak with straight tongue."

A roar of anger went up from the crowd and Vermillion Paw took a step forward. "The word of the *tahbay-boh* is like a moan of the wind, heard for a moment then forever forgotten."

"Big supplies . . . big presents coming," stammered Sam, glad he had thought of another term to describe the expected goods.

"When?" The reptilian voice of Vermillion Paw hissed across the fire.

Sam bit down on his lip, his tongue growing thick in his mouth. His body felt cold and clammy with the realization he was dealing with renowned killers angered beyond talk. Knowing the Comanche mind he dared not lie; they would surely hold him until proven right or wrong, and if wrong insure him a hideous death. In spite of rising panic he remembered his camp was depending on him to stall an attack as long as possible. In desperation he decided his only chance was Whistling Elk. "Great chief," he began, "fighting not bring presents . . . fighting make big chief in Washington mad . . ." He decided he had to gamble. "Wait two, three suns . . . all good."

Vermillion Paw roared angrily, "The quiver of a liar is never empty of lies!"

"We wait no longer!" thundered the mass of warriors, beginning to break loose and surround Sam. He felt himself being seized and rushed toward a stake in the middle of the camp. Within moments he was tied fast to it, his stupefied expression hardly able to register fear. When he looked out he could see his own camp in the distance and wondered if in the failing light they could see the mortal straits he was in. It was over an hour before he realized, when a slew of vulgar quips and jests was shouted in his direction, that they had tied him there to watch the assault on his own people, to be a witness to their slaughter at dawn.

Grimes, with his field glasses, knew all too well what had happened to Sam. He put the camp on immediate alert, making it clear an all-out attack could come at any moment. There was no panic. A certain grimness had seized the camp, recrimination and even the solace of prayer now seemed pointless. The frontier was historic killing grounds, warfare was endemic, many by now knew a people and their culture had to die to bring peace. Grimes, grave but also resolute, brusquely went about ordering measures that had to be taken. Any sick able to sit up were armed and placed under whatever cover was available to add fire power to the defense. Women who volunteered were given guns and told to defend the bank along the stream. With the spring spate the water seemed high enough to slow the charge of even the best mounted braves. There was no sleep that night and not only because of rising tension seeping through the stark-faced defenders but the clamor and outcries from the hostile camp, where a thunderous war dance was taking place, came through the night like ghastly tocsins of doom. In the light of leaping fires warriors could be seen gyrating and pounding the earth, some with hawk bells tied to their legs or shaking skulls filled with gravel high above their heads. The heavy chanting and the piercing screams of squaws came through the night air like the plaintive cries of souls roasting in hell. Hattie summed up the feelings of many about her when she sighed, "De devil over dere . . . 'n he comin' here . . . we gots to pray de Lord git here furst."

Such was the turmoil that no one heard a distant storm building in the west.

Bathed in sweat, both Quarles and Lee pulled the fresh horses into additional harness. With horses rapidly acquired in Salina they now had teams of six, with a relief six tied to the rear of the first two wagons. Knowing the pace of the train was hopeless they rashly decided to take two wagons and rush on ahead, ordering the others to follow up their trail. Both estimated three days of relentless driving would still be needed to draw near the settlement, but there was no other choice. Lee, cautioning Quarles to watch the horses, animals could and did drop dead when forced too long, swung onto the first wagon and, using the rein ends as a whip, brought them down with a loud crack on the straining teams and with a jolt they were under way. Quarles followed him, angry he had not thought of this means of reaching the hostiles sooner, of at least getting proof of honest intentions before them and perhaps avoiding a tragedy that could mean annihilation of a settlement. They were already long overdue and every moment made calamity more certain. His lips had been moving for several minutes before he realized, while nervously glancing at the western horizon, he was praying to himself.

Sam spent a chilly and almost fatal night. The insults were soon followed by stones and the slash of bows. His grimmest moment of trial came when Vermillion Paw approached him, one hand extended to rip the stone amulet from his neck. "You can't take the medicine stone," he called out in Comanche. "The spirits say it must be given."

Vermillion Paw's face was surly, disdainful, yet he was careful not to anger the spirits. "It will be mine when the wolves suck marrow from your bones."

"It will still not be given."

Vermillion Paw stamped the ground as he brought his grotesquely painted face within a foot of Sam's. "Then you will give it to me! One who speaks with false tongue should not hold a sacred medicine stone of the Nerm!"

Sam obeyed some instinctive urge to resist. "The spirits told Bad Eyes to give it to me, now they are silent."

The medicine man, muttering in rising rage, shook a red stick covered with black feathers in the air. Then he shouted a string of weird-sounding words as his hand reached for Sam's throat. "The spirits tell Vermillion Paw to take it back!" With that he ripped the stone away and left Sam startled and slumped against his bonds. But suddenly not only Sam but many of the warriors standing about turned shocked eyes on Vermillion Paw. He had broken the gravest of taboos. Uncertain murmurs began to ripple through the camp. Whistling Elk, hearing them, started moving toward the helplessly bound Sam, who by now was regarding Vermillion Paw with a puzzling look. Surprisingly Sam was feeling a curious sensation of relief. This powerful medicine man had just put himself in a dangerous and vulnerable position. Any bad luck striking the camp now would be charged to his reckless breaking of the medicine taboo. Sam knew he might be dead soon, but now even his death would not, in the eyes of the tribe, stave off the wrath of any angry spirits, might even make it more certain. The superstitious tribesmen, grunting to each other, were suddenly restive. Uneasily they eyed the stone in Vermillion Paw's hands. Watching them, Sam sensed in some vague way this turn of events might help him stay alive.

Whistling Elk came up in time to hear Vermillion Paw rasping in a voice that could have been vehemence

masking a worm of guilt, "Tomorrow's sun will be your
last, the spirits do not serve liars who come with false
hearts."

Sam's gaze stayed locked with the other's. "The spirits
gave me that stone . . . you took it away . . . tomorrow
we will both look upon the sun and wonder who the
spirits favor."

Long after Vermillion stomped away, awkwardly carrying the stone which caught and held every eye he
passed, Whistling Elk remained standing there.

Sam tried to think of something to say, but he was too
breathless after the draining scene just ended. It was
Whistling Elk who spoke, but his words were strange,
cryptic; they left Sam staring into the night. "You brave
man . . . bravery is friend in war, but medicine stone has
no friend . . . it holds power of the spirits . . . it is why
my people hope."

It was some time before he noticed a flickering light
playing along the horizon to the west. It came in diminu-
tive streaks as though some feeble spirit was struggling to
climb the edge of night.

64

In the hours before dawn the storm to the west seemed to
stall, rumble internally as though building power, and
hurl long spears of light both north and south, revealing
the massive weather front approaching.

Within the settlement that night there was more than
one crisis. Grimes had to stand eye to eye with Hattie,
accompanied by Skeeter and Alice, who, with the hostile
camp finally quieting down and only low fires to be seen,
were preparing to sally over to release Sam.

Grimes's anger matched his amazement. "You'd only get yourselves killed and him to boot!" He could see they were armed, determined, only Skeeter looking apprehensive.

Hattie held her shotgun as familiarly as she might a broom, but there was no mistaking her intent. "Y'all gonna save him?"

"If we get the chance, we will!"

"If ah gits the chance . . ."

Grimes stopped her with both hands in the air. "Please, get back to your posts, it's dangerous to be standing in the open like this."

Nothing more was said but as they reluctantly backed away the lieutenant again sensed how tenuous was his hold on these people. He noticed Alice staring at him expectantly, as though watching to see how he acquitted himself in the coming attack. She surely didn't look like a girl who had lost her way, she was gripping the handgun he had given her as though more than ready to use it. Incredibly it made her seem desirable again in a way he never imagined. Did he still have something to learn about women? He was still pondering this when he heard a voice rising in the hostile camp.

Whistling Elk was not surprised to see Vermillion Paw climbing a large boulder before the camp, preparing to make his medicine chant in the false dawn, telling the warriors the spirits were with them, their hearts must be strong, victory was assured. The warriors came out of the shadows and gathered before him, their multitude filling half the camp. It was a strange moment, for Whistling Elk didn't believe the seizing of the medicine stone had been forgotten, if unease among the people couldn't be seen it could be felt. The old chief would have liked an excuse to delay fighting until the storm passed but there was nothing to discuss, the attack had been carefully planned. Each war leader knew where to strike and all were anxious to open the assault.

Sam looked on, praying for the storm to break and perhaps for a time thwart the attack. Indians didn't like to fight in heavy weather, it spoiled the vision and softened the bowstring. But if the storm hadn't struck, the air was brittle with its menace. Something about the dark roiling sky made Sam feel lightning was drawing itself into a spring about to be released. Vermillion Paw came down from his boulder and the war leaders moved out to take their positions. But the mood was now unsettled, quirky. Somehow the shadowy silence seemed ominous, the air eerily calm. When with that sound of crinkling paper, with which thunder begins, a sudden burst of lightning flared forth it near blinded those looking up. A giant blue and yellow fork knifed into the earth just west of the camp. It was followed by a second. This one stuck the camp, hit the boulder Vermillion Paw had just left, and with a ear-splitting crack shattered it. The entire camp looked on in shock and near paralyzing awe. It was an appalling moment. Vermillion Paw had missed death by seconds. A great moan went through the crowd. Whistling Elk, striding forward, shouted to the stunned warriors, "Come back! Let the storm spirit pass, the time to fight will come!"

It was too violent a storm to last, but for a quarter of an hour its fury reminded the praying Dillby how God taught the law to kings. Winds of near hurricane force swept the land and thunder turned the earth into a vibrant drum. Lightning speared down in frightening patterns, streaking across the plains and giving rise to impaling claps of thunder that reached and convulsed the heart. Sheets of rain, coursing down in diagonal waves, blotted out the landscape and left one feeling alone in the midst of many.

Lame Fox, holding up in a heavy stand of brush, weathered the storm by sitting on the ground and holding his head between his knees. He knew his eyes had not deceived him. These two camps were armed against each other, fighting was about to break out. But he knew such an appalling downpour couldn't last, it would end or taper off by daybreak. But now he had crucial decisions to make, decisions upon which life or death depended. Like all old men he was resigned to what little was left of life, his hopes now were for the afterlife. He had heard as a child the lodge of the great spirit was open only to those who lived bravely and died honorably; lesser souls fell to the great cannibal owl. Warily he reached for his medicine bundle. How bravely had he lived? How honorably could he die? The feel of his tightly stitched bundle brought little assurance. He decided to put on fresh paint and redress his scalp lock. In war warriors drew sacred medicine symbols on their bodies and painted on faces enemies would fear. As the storm abated Lame Fox laid out his meager possessions and squatted over them, chanting a little medicine song to the spirits, telling them in as firm a voice as he could muster he was an old warrior, a brave old warrior preparing to die.

With the teams straining and Lee driving them on long after darkness, increasing the danger of stumbling on to soft shoulders or planting hooves in gopher holes, they now figured they had cut half a day from the trip. But there was still a ways to go. Even though they regularly changed and briefly grazed the horses, the animals were beginning to droop, their heads lolling back, as though trying to glimpse the shouting faces and stinging whips that mercilessly drove them on. Both men slept beside their wagons for four or five hours a night, but conversation was sparse; there was only one thing to talk about and it was growing harder and harder for hopeful comments to sound convincing.

"Two more days," grunted Lee, climbing once again to the wagon seat.

"Two more days to what?" responded Quarles testily, as mounting his wagon he brusquely pulled the whip from its socket.

"To something we're bound to remember, one way or the another, for the rest of our lives."

When the storm finally rolled off to the east, leaving many tents and wickiups flattened and the ground soaked, war leaders once again moved forward for the attack. But the mood of the warriors had changed, though they followed their leaders and again surrounded the settlement, their eyes were heavy with doubt, their minds on the shattered boulder. Such a happening had never been recorded in tribal history, but then neither had the breaking of a medicine stone.

Vermillion Paw, aware he had missed death by moments, now stayed back, his faith in his medicine shaken, his error in snatching that medicine stone apparent. A medicine man breaking a sacred taboo was a pathetic figure with a perilous future. His high standing in the tribe was already vanishing and his very life might now be forfeited to appease the spirits. He must find a way to return the amulet to the captive Sam, who was still tied to the stake. He saw Whistling Elk glancing grimly in his direction. It was to be a black day for Vermillion Paw, only a great victory here, proving he had not brought tragedy to the tribe, could save him.

The fighting started on the right where the volunteers were stationed but soon swept around to the stream where Hattie and a growing number of women began blazing away. The soldiers were attacked last, but Grimes saw warriors charging into the ranks and taking the forward positions in hand-to-hand fighting. Yet the settlement was no longer made up of green immigrants and unblooded soldiers or volunteers. The defenders, if openly scared, even desperate, were now laying down a cool, deadly fire. Bold warriors pressing the fight began to die. There was no way to get behind the defenders and attempts to get across the stream, further swollen by the storm, were driven back as Hattie's shotgun roared repeatedly over several rifles barking out in the murky dawn. The war leaders began to hang back; something was wrong. Yesterday's warriors would have overwhelmed this settlement in a frenzy of vengeful slaughter, but today the furor that rose with that first charge couldn't be sustained. It was too costly to delay, snatching their wounded and their handful of dead they retreated beyond rifle range, with more and more warriors glancing toward the camp, toward Whistling Elk who was watching from a distance.

Grimes, relieved to find his side had suffered very few casualties, saw Cheatem running and ducking low as he came up the rise. He swore under his breath. He didn't like people abandoning their posts on any pretext. "What the hell are you doing here?"

"It's them damn women, they're still talking about rescuing Sam. Best keep an eye out for them!"

Grimes shook his head, groaning in irritation. "I'm supposed to command soldiers, not goddamned crazies," he muttered, but his eyes were pinned to the distant line of braves. He nodded toward them. "What d'you think?"

Cheatem, taking a step closer, peered out beside him. "Dunno, but something's wrong . . . they ain't fighting like they mean it!"

"Mebbe just keeping us guessing."

Cheatem shrugged. "Ain't a heap to guess 'bout. They hold all the cards."

Grimes sighed and glanced at the silent settlement behind him. "Well, guess we're just gonna have to sweat it out."

"Reckon we do . . . seeing there ain't no choosing."

Whistling Elk knew there was trouble, the kind of trouble that numbs the mind and burdens the heart. The warriors were convinced Vermillion Paw had angered the spirits. It had them fearing defeat and perhaps death, which in war makes both more likely. Now he must rally their hearts again, if not to fight, to stay together. Braves left camps stricken with bad omens. He could see them looking and, as moments passed and the sun's halo lightened the sky, coming toward him. He knew they were anxious for words that would dispel the nagging doubts draining their will to fight. But he himself could feel the pall that had seized the camp and his heart told him evil spirits hovered over this dawning. Did he have any inspiring or even reassuring counsel to offer? He stood before them, a man facing fears without corporeal form but more real to these warriors than the sight of the earth taking shape in the gathering light. It was a moment he would always remember, for it was a moment he looked about to catch, outlined against the rim of the sun, a figure approaching, boldly entering his camp, a figure he recognized with shock as the one who appeared in his medicine dream many years ago.

Lame Fox walked like a man in a trance. He knew he should be making gestures of friendship or holding his hands up in a sign for peace. But something told him the more brazen his approach, the less risk he ran. He was simply moving as the spirits willed him, head high, striding forth until he was only fifty feet from Whistling Elk. In truth his bizarre appearance saved him. Had he come dressed as a Ute or an Osage he would have been seized and clubbed to death, but his shaven head and strangely painted face marked him as too alien to these parts not to arouse curiosity, perhaps even fear at that eerie and unsettling moment.

Whistling Elk, overcoming his emotional jolt, saw the impact the appearance of this stranger had on the people and quickly summoned the breath to speak. Since this was not a Comanche he began with sign language. "Who are you and why do you come unbidden into our camp?"

Fortunately Lame Fox's winter with the Omahas had sharpened his use of sign, for now his life depended upon it. "I am Lame Fox, great warrior of the Shawnee. I come to join you, to warn you of the white man's ways."

"Shawnee? Who are the Shawnees?"

"A great tribe who once ruled where mighty rivers ran and great mountains were filled with game."

The braves began to mutter. Who was this queer-looking figure speaking of things beyond the knowledge of the far-traveling Nerm? The crowd was rapidly swelling as they came up and pressed forward to see more clearly the strange garb of Lame Fox. Only Whistling Elk, suspecting him to be a messenger from the spirit world, kept friendly eyes upon him. The chief was searching for ways to convince his people that Lame Fox should be treated with respect, but this was no time to

reveal his medicine dream. After so many years of
silence he wouldn't be believed. Yet, he had to protect
this spirit; instinct told him the fate of the camp depended upon it. Tragically this visit came when their
medicine was proving weak, the people shaken, a state
brought about by the stupidity of Vermillion Paw. But
the very thought of the medicine man made him glance
around, suddenly feeling his heart jump as he heard
shots ring out and slugs came whining across the camp
like invisible wasps seeking victims to sting.

Grimes was not the only one watching the Indians
drift to the other side of their camp and gather about
Whistling Elk, apparently held by some happening he
couldn't see. Since the firing stopped Hattie had been
quietly circling and mounting the rise. She was watching
too. Behind her now were Alice, Skeeter, and Cathy, all
armed. Had Grimes remembered Cheatem's warning he
might have noticed them slipping behind a boulder
almost as close to the bound and struggling Sam as he.
But the strange noises rising from the throng of warriors
held his attention, for he suspected something beside
Whistling Elk was holding them, arousing them, making
them sound puzzled, vexed, on the edge of anger. If he
noticed the area around the stake was momentarily clear
it didn't strike him as offering a realistic chance to rescue
Sam. It wasn't until he saw Skeeter and then the three
women racing forward that he grasped a rash and
perhaps suicidal attempt was being made to recover
Sam. His first impulse was to shout at them but realized
at once this was pointless, shouts could not stop them
now. Swearing profanely he pulled his side arm from its
holster and raced after them.

The warriors may have been distracted but squaws
lingering on the deserted side of camp began screaming
and pointing to Skeeter as he reached Sam and started
cutting him loose. Warriors, whirling about, immediately rushed back toward the stake, whooping and
shaking rifles or war clubs in the air. By now the women,
coming up behind Skeeter, were kneeling around the
stake and firing at the oncoming braves, making them

duck away and instead move to cut the rescuers off from the settlement. If Grimes thought the attempt impossible it was only made so by a fateful incident none could have predicted.

Vermillion Paw had also been watching that stake. He wanted to return that damnable medicine stone, place it around Sam's neck, and hope it would redeem him with the spirits. He had just started a stealthy approach to the bound captive when he saw Skeeter and the women coming to release him. He couldn't permit Sam to escape until he took back that stone. Though only armed with his medicine knife he flew at Skeeter, stopping him from quickly finishing the job and allowing them all to flee.

Skeeter, forced to stop cutting rawhide thongs to grapple with the medicine man, discovered his assailant was not strong but madly determined to hang a stone around Sam's neck. He succeeded although twice Skeeter thrust him away and once slashed him with his own knife, but it wasn't until Alice, rising up, shot him through the temple that it ended. But the damage was done, the moments they needed to retrace their steps were gone, Sam was free but his freedom was going to be short-lived. Grimes reached them so breathless he could hardly speak. "You damn fools!" he sputtered. "How the hell you going to get back?"

Sam, stiff from being tied up for so long, sank to the ground, but Skeeter and Hattie pulled him to his feet and headed toward the settlement. Cathy's voice was suddenly shrill with warning. "Look! We can't get through! They're cutting us off! Look out, they're shooting! Get down!" Bullets began whizzing about them and though Alice started to shoot back Grimes seized her arm and waved Cathy's rifle down. "Stop! They'll massacre us! Put down those guns!"

Hattie, refusing to lower her shotgun, struggled to aim it at those blocking their way. It was a moment Alice would always remember, for it was in that terrible moment a bullet struck Hattie high in the chest and drove her back into Alice's arms.

Grimes, trying to signal surrender, took a slug in the

shoulder before Whistling Elk's sonorous voice brought the firing to a halt.

In the terrible silence that followed, the braves swiftly moved up to close around them, seizing their guns and staring at Vermillion Paw's body on the ground. Alice and Cathy were left glancing tensely at each other as the first warriors up roughly claimed them. They were captives, the stark point driven home by the prurient glint in the eyes of the warriors and the gloating cackle of squaws coming up to confirm it.

65

Lame Fox saw them surrounded, knew who they were, but stayed back out of sight. If the tribe discovered he was known by these whites they would suspect he had come to spy, posing as an Indian from a faraway tribe. There was no mistaking the edginess or suspicions of these tribesmen; fearing evil spirits were about, they already half believed he was one.

He saw Hattie on the ground with Sam and Skeeter bending over her, Alice and Cathy being led away by squaws after warriors claimed them, Grimes desperately but futilely trying to signal Whistling Elk he wanted to talk. He could see figures over by the settlement appearing from everywhere and looking on. It was a moment suddenly disturbed by feelings he thought he had rejected, feelings he had determined to leave behind when vowing to return to his own race. With some relief he heard Whistling Elk calling to the war leaders gathered around Vermillion Paw's body. The old chief wanted a council to be held at a spot further back in the camp, beyond view of the settlement. At his command a new fire was started there. To Lame Fox's delight, for standing alone he was easy to single out and perhaps recognize, Whistling Elk beckoned him to join them.

Before the war leaders approached the council they ordered all prisoners moved further back from the stake. It was too close to the settlement. Lame Fox, watching them coming up and eyeing him warily, thought it best to settle close to Whistling Elk. But he felt his breath leaving him with a start when he caught sight of Sam and Skeeter gently lowering Hattie to the ground not thirty feet away. He put his head down and quietly chanted a little prayer to the spirits, his voice so low Whistling Elk sitting beside him did not hear.

Cathy couldn't believe what was happening to her. She felt them pulling her clothes from her body and saw Alice already nude and being driven into the shelter of two wickiups joined together. She saw Grimes being herded to the rear of the camp and caught a glimpse of Sam and Skeeter, unable to carry Hattie any further, lowering her to the ground near a circle of heavily painted men squatting together. While stripping her the squaws snatched away her locket, clawed off her wedding ring, and cut locks from her hair. Fortunately they didn't use the heavy switches many of them carried, but she could feel them running their rough hands over her smooth body until one old hag snapped at them and immediately she found herself thrust into the shelter and made to sit next to grim-faced Alice.

Neither woman spoke. Cathy was too aghast at finding herself nude and at the mercy of these menacing faces. Alice, aware of what was coming, was too shaken and embittered to talk. For a moment the naked girl wondered where Grimes was. That he might see her nude didn't bother her, but was he to witness her being humiliated and raped for hours as were her mother and Charity?

Finally Cathy helplessly gasped, "Why won't they give us something to cover ourselves?" She was hugging herself, cupping her breasts. "I'm freezing."

"They will when the men are through with us."

"Oh, my God!"

"Cathy, don't plead with them . . . it won't help."

Cathy looked around, still shuddering. She was trying not to think of herself. "Poor Hattie," she half whispered, "what will happen to her?"

Alice only answered after several moments. "Afraid she got hit badly . . . wasn't conscious when they pulled me away." She heaved a resigned sigh. "Well Cathy, you heard her, she wanted to save Sam or die with him. Believe she's going to get her wish."

Cathy covered her face with both hands to shut out this appalling plight. "The wrong people die."

They sat in silence until Alice brought her knees up and wrapped her arms around them. Settling her head on her kneecaps she murmured, "Cathy, you should have stayed with Charlotte, perhaps I should have too; this country is too goddamn evil. It's no place for women wanting only to live and love . . . we don't belong here."

Cathy stared at her, rubbing her naked thighs, trying to warm them. She knew Alice was only talking to keep their spirits up. "And where do we belong?" she asked feebly.

Alice's painful glance reached for the horizon. "Some place safe for children, where flowers can be raised and men who love us, making their way in the world, come to us for comfort when that way is too hard."

Cathy almost broke into tears. How had this poor child matured so quickly, what had befallen her in so short a time to leave her with the mind of a woman of many years? This was truly a terrible country, for when it didn't rob you of life, it robbed you of what made life worthwhile, that innocence nurturing a few short years of dreams and confident expectations called youth.

The council was soon torn by conflict. No one mourned the death of Vermillion Paw but it convinced many the spirits were angry, that evil forces were around exacting punishment for the medicine stone. Several of the war leaders demanded all captives be put to death, for one had killed Vermillion Paw and might be that evil force. Others simply said they had come to kill whites, why were they waiting? A few, surprised that Lame Fox was sitting in their council, pointed at him with the pipe stem and frowned at Whistling Elk. "Do you welcome this one who speaks of weird places unknown to us, and asks us to believe things our hearts cannot?"

The old chief pulled himself up knowing this strange visitor, if indeed he was a messenger from the spirit world, should, if allowed to speak, be able to protect himself. Yet his secret hope was that this alien warrior, so like the one in his dream, would serve his own cause and strengthen the case for peace. He was ready to help him in any way he could. He spent a moment gazing about the circle before saying, "Many strange happenings have troubled this day. We have found our medicine weak in battle, we have seen the lightning shatter a great stone, hoping it is not the rage of spirits threatening to shatter our people. This visitor will speak and bring us a message. I, Whistling Elk, say on this day of so many evil omens we should listen to him." He settled on the ground, gravely signaling that the pipe should be passed to Lame Fox.

The Shawnee's heart almost stopped beating. He was now going to address this council of skeptical faces and not a few outright glares of distrust. Obviously Whistling Elk thought he had come with a message. But what could he say? Did he have words to offer these incensed warriors, dressed for war and fearing the presence of demons? Did he have some bit of wisdom to deliver? Worst of all, could he possibly stand up and speak out without drawing the attention of Sam, Skeeter, and Hattie settled just beyond? The pipe had reached him, he took it and stared at it in despair. Moments of silence linked themselves together until Whistling Elk turned to him and with a strange light in his eyes muttered, "Speak!"

Lame Fox came to his feet, looking into his heart and finally realizing he had only one bit of wisdom he could offer these faces. It would not be popular, it might even be fatal, but whatever happened he had to die with honor, he could not go to the great spirit with false words on his lips.

It was the middle of the night but the two or three hours Quarles had slept was all his restless mind would allow. Lee heard him up and brewing coffee and rolled out of his blanket. "We've got to get some rest," he mumbled, sitting up.

"I'll get plenty of rest when I'm dead," snapped Quarles. "Now I've got to get there or go out of my mind!"

Lee's tone was sobering. "These horses are near played out, another day and they're finished."

"Can't help it." He threw a glance at the dusky forms of hobbled animals munching grass in the dark. "There's a few still pulling well enough to get us close by morning."

"That what you fixin' to do?"

"Lee, we're more than a week overdue . . . it might already be too late, if we don't get there soon it won't matter."

Lee shook his head, knowing now what Quarles intended. They were cutting to one wagon, taking their six best horses and making a last dash for the settlement, or as close as they could get. He knew the risks it involved, those six horses would be their last chance, if even one or two foundered they were finished, the great effort had failed. He might have argued with Quarles but in his heart he knew Henry was right, time was the enemy, already too much had passed. Besides, he had been suppressing something far too long. If Henry's agony over Cathy was more visible it was no less painful, or gnawed less cruelly at the heart, than his over Charlotte.

Lame Fox, peering toward the horizon, appeared to be having trouble with his eyes. They seemed to be staring out into space though actually he was looking back in time, witnessing again that day when his people had thought to defeat the whites. He was recalling a youth filled with stories of medicine men predicting victories that never came and brave warriors falling in battle and leaving squaws to slash their flesh and keen shrilly into the night. Standing in this camp was like going back in time. Here again were tribesmen talking of defeating the whites, trusting to medicines and spirits that the whites merely laughed at. The many warriors gathered here would surely destroy this settlement but it would be like killing one ant from an ant hill. Lame Fox knew the numbers of whites that lay to the east; he knew the plains tribes, however brave, however determined, faced impossible odds. In spite of his fury at his own treatment by the whites his heart told him tomorrow's world would be white. The Indian world was vanishing along with its protecting spirits and sacred medicine chants like a handful of dust in the wind.

At first the war leaders watched Lame Fox in open disbelief if not scorn, but as he began to relate the story of Tecumseh, a Shawnee legacy carefully handed down by his tribe, a few began to listen with interest. The tale of many tribes coming together to defeat the whites appealed to their vengeful mood, but the ultimate defeat of this multitude of warriors had many huffing and turning away. Words of defeat were not welcome to their ears. But when Lame Fox began to tell them about himself, about living near a fort where he had seen hundreds of soldiers gather, that there were countless such forts to the east, they shifted uneasily. When he finished saying white soldiers without number were fighting each other today, but this fight must end and those soldiers would join together and march toward buffalo plains, toward the very ground on which they sat, the rattling of weapons rose in a response more ominous than words.

Around the circle the war leaders were rising in anger, one finally crying out. "Are your words meant to bring fear to our council?"

Lame Fox kept his eyes on the growing fire. "They are meant to spare you the fate of my people."

Another war leader, pointing meaningfully at Whistling Elk, roared across the circle. "What is this message . . . this wisdom Whistling Elk tells us you bring?"

Lame Fox saw Whistling Elk looking at him in desperation but could only answer, "I bring the wisdom of old man coyote who surrenders the path to the grizzly and learns to live with his enemies."

"That is coward's talk!" shouted a war leader. "We are not coyotes, we are warriors! This is not wisdom you bring! It is talk of peace! Peace with the false-tongued whites . . . peace that deprives us of honor as it has the many goods promised us."

Lame Fox saw no words of his could soothe this rising wrath, but suddenly he no longer felt frightened. He had vowed to speak the truth and if threats to his life were mounting he was determined to die with honor. "When wars are fought only for men's pride—peace is truly wisdom." He was preparing to sit again but these brave words were hardly out of his mouth when the real menace hanging over this scene struck. His eye caught Sam and Skeeter, and Hattie with her head resting on Skeeter's leg, staring directly at him, and Sam's mouth moving as though fighting to be heard.

Sam and Skeeter, forced to carry Hattie back, placed her unconscious body on the ground as gently as they could. Their attention was so centered on their beloved aunt they hardly noticed a council forming only a few yards away. She had a bloodstain high on her chest and her breathing was irregular, but Skeeter, balling up his shirt, forced it under her dress to stop the bleeding. Sam, speaking Comanche, managed to get some water from a watching squaw. He discovered the medicine stone around his neck again and spoke up when he caught a squaw eyeing it with respect.

The water revived Hattie enough to look up and see her nephews bending over her. "Where we at?" she murmured.

"We captives," answered Sam. "Doan try to speak, you hurt."

Hattie tried to look around. After some effort, in spite of Sam's urgings to lie still, she managed to raise her head and Skeeter slipped his knee under it. "Where's Alice, Cathy? . . ."

"Dey here . . . squaws took 'em 'way." Sam wondered if she had forgotten about Grimes.

She could be heard mumbling under her breath for a few moments. "What dat yuh sayin'?" asked Sam.

"Ah'se prayin', best you do too."

There was a long silence before Hattie looked up again. "Who dat talkin'?"

"Dey counciling over dere . . . likely studyin' wat to do wid us."

For a moment, though now squirming some in pain, she seemed to be musing to herself. "Ah knows dat voice . . . sure as fish come fried, ah do." Sam and Skeeter were relieved to hear a touch of irritation in her voice. They sensed it a good sign. She poked Skeeter in the side. "Hep me up, ah gots to see."

"You best stay down," cautioned Sam. "It's only some old fool gittin' misery off his chest." But glancing toward the council he sensed the warrior standing was not a Comanche, for he was making great use of sign. The sight held him for a moment, for there was something strange yet familiar about that figure. Without thinking he gave Hattie his arm and she worked herself up until she could see across to the council. There was a long spell of silence before Hattie whispered, "Ah know who dat is . . . mercy, ah sure do."

"Who?" said Sam looking on with her.

"Dats dat red scamp, Lame Fox! Wat in Jehovah is dat sinner doin' y'here?"

≫ 66 ≪

Whistling Elk was first puzzled by the captives calling out to Lame Fox, but soon like others he was twisting about, still curious but also annoyed by the intrusion. Lame Fox knew the calling would only stop when the captives were aware it was endangering his life. But how was he to tell them? Surely some of these war leaders knew enough English to grasp what such words implied.

Whistling Elk came to his feet staring at Sam, noticing the stone about his neck, but finally swinging his eyes back to Lame Fox. "It is forbidden to disturb our councils! Do these foolish ones know you?"

"Many from the east know me."

"Tell them to be quiet before our war clubs teach them the wisdom of silence!"

Lame Fox realized asking for quiet wouldn't help. They were lying there helpless, fearful of being killed. Discovering him addressing this council surely made them think he could save them. Only when they realized he no longer served their side, had left the whites and all connected with them, would they understand he was now an enemy, and grim as the Indian's future might seem he had chosen to share it.

But this was not easily done. "I will take them your warning," he said, stepping around Whistling Elk and moving solemnly toward the captives. They watched him coming with eyes brightening with hope.

Hattie even fought for a smile. "Don't know how y'all got here . . . but sho glad to see you," she grunted. Luckily the bullet, striking her sternum, had been deflected toward her shoulder and was lodged in the socket. She was in visible pain but by twisting her knee and hip she kept her weight off that side. "Wat dey done wid Alice and Cathy?"

Lame Fox kept his voice low. "They prisoners same you."

The warmth they momentarily displayed began to fade. "How come you here?" asked Sam.

"Me Indian, my skin red, me belong here."

Hattie lifted her head. "You ain't fixin' to help us?"

"Lame Fox is Indian warrior, not homeless dog begging from white man's lodge."

There was a long empty silence until Hattie, glancing toward the council, muttered, "You sayin' you is now one of dem sinful heathens?"

Lame Fox stared down at her, pain in his aged face. "Me Shawnee. White men destroy my people, take our land, leave us homeless, no pride, no hope. Now I fight for my brothers whose land the whites have come to steal. Lame Fox no longer takes the faithless hand of the whites."

Hattie grimaced in pain, her fingers gripping the bulge made by the rolled shirt above her breasts. "Lordy, Lordy, de devil sure done got into you!"

The Shawnee raised his head defiantly. "Old woman not know . . . she not Indian . . . her skin not red."

"You lucky yours ain't black." Hattie now had to squirm to look up at him. "You doan know what dem whites done to us?"

Lame Fox shrugged impatiently. "Whites bad . . . do all bad things . . . kill game . . . destroy earth . . . speak with false tongues."

Hattie raised one hand feebly. "Dey not all bad or we folks wouldn't be y'here."

The Shawnee stamped his foot, this was taking too long. "Lame Fox goes the Indian way!"

"Lame Fox done made a stupid choice."

Lame Fox stared down at her, aware the council behind him was watching, probably by now convinced he was no spirit. He had to say something to prove he was one of them soon or surely find himself a captive too. "Only foolish ones, wanting presents, fooled by false promises, think whites good? Indian grief has taught us much, even papooses know they bad!"

Hattie let out a deep breath and settled against Skeeter's thigh. "Ah ain't sayin' dey good or bad, only thing ah'm sayin' . . . and you best tell yo' friends . . . is dey gonna win!"

"You not know that."

"Yes, ah do . . . so do you."

Lame Fox looked away to hide the twinge tightening his face. Queerly but undeniably Hattie's words knifed into him, reaching and joining a nagging conviction he had been struggling to suppress. Suddenly he heard himself saying, "I cannot tell them that."

"You doan got to say it."

"You have other words to say?"

"Tell 'em to make peace."

"They not listen, it too late."

"Tell 'em if dey doan listen it sure as gospel gonna be too late."

"Only one with power can speak so. I have none, already they think me a bad spirit."

Sam, quietly studying the Shawnee, knew he was hearing the truth. He had caught some of the comments rising at the council and knew the war leaders were suspicious of Lame Fox. More critically he sensed time was running out for all of them. Whistling Elk was on his feet again. The expression on his face spelt trouble. Suddenly it dawned upon Sam there might be a way to help Lame Fox, for surely this almost pathetic figure was all that stood between them and death.

Standing up he deliberately waved an arm to draw attention, then as ceremoniously as he could he lifted the medicine stone from his neck. Using his grasp of Comanche, for he wanted all at the council to hear, he placed the stone about the Shawnee's neck, saying, "Here, Lame Fox, the spirits have whispered that you be given this stone as a gift. Its powers are now yours, its strength yours until they whisper to you it must go to another."

A string of startled gasps arose from the council. After what had happened to Vermillion Paw this was not a gesture to ignore.

Grimes was beside himself with anger. Time after time his judgement had proven bad. Impulsively joining that crazy attempt to rescue Sam had led to six of them, including himself, becoming captives instead of one. Worst of all three women had been taken, including Alice! He knew all too well what happened to women in the hands of Comanches.

There was a stinging sensation where he had been hit in the arm. Luckily it was only a flesh wound but it had gone unattended and blood was staining his tunic. He was taken to the back of the camp and there tied to a stake driven into the ground. He could no longer see the chief. He wanted desperately to talk to him, to barter for Alice's freedom, but they threw him down roughly and turned their faces away when he spoke. After a time he noticed some squaws gathered about a makeshift shelter, and by watching them realized they were drawn by something within. It was almost half an hour before enough of them moved away to allow him a glimpse inside. His breath stopped in his throat as he caught sight of Alice and Cathy sitting naked. Had their humiliation already started? Now somehow he must get to the chief. He began to shout but that only brought angry squaws wielding heavy switches who beat him around the head until he fell silent. Then maddened they began to strip him too. He felt his belt being torn from him as two big squaws clawed at his boots until they were off. His socks and undershirt disappeared; soon he was near nude himself. The squaws, laughing at his pale skin, knew by evening the sun, already well into the sky, would turn it a blistering red. Then they would rub sand and ashes into his burning flesh to hear him scream. Cackling, leaving him with only his torn underpants, they returned to the women.

He could only crumble on the ground consumed with fury until misery replaced it. He discovered the rumpus around him had drawn Alice's attention and she could now glimpse him in the distance as he could her. What must she be thinking? But suddenly breaking into his thoughts was a tumult of irate voices. Further forward in the camp the Indians had started arguing violently among themselves. Something had happened. He couldn't see the source of the clamor but in his mood he could only believe events had taken another turn for the worse.

The council had been thrown into a wild dispute. Lame Fox, returning with the medicine stone, was suddenly staring into space again, desperately searching for a way out of his plight. It didn't help that these truculent faces were startled by Sam's move. Whistling Elk watched him returning, eyeing the stone but now aware Lame Fox was acquainted with these captives, an ugly turning for a stranger professing friendship. Yet the ways of the spirits were never known, the stone and lightning shattering that boulder were still connected in the people's mind. For a time it would give Lame Fox some power.

But would he use it wisely?

"Hear me," finally began Lame Fox, an audible quiver in his voice. "Victory in battle does not make up for defeat in war. No victory here will discourage the whites from fighting again. They will appear like lice on an old buffalo robe, like locusts when the land is dry, they will outnumber the buffalo, even stars in the sky. Do not lead your people down that trail of sorrow."

"We are not afraid to die!" cried a war leader.

"Your deaths would be a small matter," answered Lame Fox. "Your people will lose their freedom, they will live on barren land, they will eat only food whites throw at them, they will be told worshipping the spirits is forbidden. Make peace while you can, make peace while you can bargain for some things you hold dear."

"There can be no peace for us without honor!" shouted a war leader. "They have lied to us, why should we believe more promises made in return for peace?"

"The whites have not always kept their promises, but then neither have we. I have spent much time in the white world, it is a cruel world, but in it are men of honor. They speak with straight tongues."

"Not to us!" cried a war leader. Now they were all rising to shout at Lame Fox who could no longer be heard above the clamor. The outburst was so deafening it drew the attention of everyone in camp and many in the settlement beyond. Finally Whistling Elk rose and spread his arms in a motion for silence. Slowly, hesitantly if not reluctantly, the war leaders settled down. In the end only the old chief and Lame Fox were left standing.

"We are a proud people!" said Whistling Elk, his sonorous voice reaching beyond the council. "Lame Fox, we find your words strange, our hearts do not welcome them. Twice we have been promised supplies that never came. Only a moon ago we were promised wagons full of goods that never appeared. We have been promised guns, ammunition, blankets, knives, and many metal things. Tell us, Lame Fox, where are these men of honor? Where are the wagonloads of goods? Where are the reasons we should seek peace?"

Lame Fox suddenly felt a curious light opening in his mind. With a queer surge of excitement he realized he could have an answer no one else was aware of; he alone saw Quarles's wagon train leaving Leavenworth many days ago, only he knew they were surely coming. Certainly by now they were getting close. He turned to Whistling Elk and drew himself up like one confident enough to cast earlier fears aside. "There are reasons, my brothers, and they will speak to your heart . . . the promised wagons are coming!"

It should have been simple after that, but it wasn't. The war leaders, momentarily silenced by the Shawnee's words, could not so easily dismiss their anger. Several were on their feet again, one roaring out, "You say the wagons are coming . . . have we not heard that before?! Tell us, O great wise one," mockery was now tainting his voice, *"when* will these wagons come?"

"Soon."

Even Whistling Elk knew that answer would only increase their skepticism, rekindle their rage. "Have your eyes seen these wagons?" he asked Lame Fox warily. At the Shawnee's disclosure he had secretly felt his chances for peace had improved, but now hope was fast disappearing, these war leaders would not wait another day.

"Yes," responded Lame Fox a bit too hurriedly, his confidence beginning to wane at the hostile reception to what he believed would be received with gratitude. "I saw them many days ago."

"Then why are they not here?" cried one of the war leaders.

Lame Fox forced himself to shout, "They will come!"

There was an eerie silence as the war leaders began muttering to each other. Finally one stepped forth to address Lame Fox. It was clear from Whistling Elk's expression the decision was no longer his. The war leader's voice was grim with warning. "We have heard your words, but the time for pipe talk is over. If your wagons are not here by the next sunrise you and all those taken from these false-hearted whites will die."

It was a dreadful night. Sam, aware of what was coming for Alice and Cathy, managed, at Hattie's urging, to catch Whistling Elk's ear long enough to plead Cathy was the woman of the man bringing the wagons. To harm her might turn his heart against them. Whistling Elk stared at him, eyes half closed in doubt, but he could not allow the ravishing of one female to jeopardize whatever chance this tenuous hope of peace had.

That evening women were neither abused nor raped but nothing could keep the warriors from parading their captives around fires built where those in the settlement could see. Grimes too was dragged forth and made to walk behind Alice and Cathy. For some reason, Sam and Skeeter were allowed to stay beside Hattie. Something of the spell of the medicine stone still hung over Sam, and his knowledge of Comanche probably made him seem less alien. Not that they were out of danger, but they had not been claimed yet and the despondent forms of Grimes and the two white women were holding the eyes of this embittered camp, resentful it must wait yet another night to vent its wrath.

Grimes tried not to look but he couldn't help seeing Alice and Cathy walking nude before him. He was struck at once by Cathy's sumptuous figure, her full breasts and rounded hips. Alice looked like a slimmer version, but there was no denying the woman in her was coming to fruition, its sensuous promise already apparent. He himself was practically nude, the squaws having ripped away his army drawers, leaving them hanging about him in tatters. Both women, seeing him as they rounded the fire, gasped at the sight of his scarlet flesh, a scorching red that was painful to look at. When finally they were herded into the shelter together and made to sit down something strange happened. Suddenly their nudity didn't matter any longer. They were three human beings deprived of their dignity but aware the human body is not a source of shame. Within moments they were no more conscious of each other's bareness than small children being bathed together.

That night was a night of agonizing hopes and harrowing fears for many, with Whistling Elk being the last to sleep. He had finally called a few warriors aside and after an uneasy whispering session had mutely watched them disappear into the night. After a while he threw some medicine grass onto a dying fire and sat chanting to himself for almost an hour before turning and quietly rolling up in his robe.

67

Quarles and Lee had forced the horses forward during the night, neither mentioning it but both aware the animals were coming to the end of their tether. They had perhaps an hour left, then the desperate dash and even more desperate hopes must end. Equally disheartening and increasing with every moment was the feeling the sky was growing lighter at their backs. Dawn was coming, somehow daylight would make defeat final and further striving pointless.

They were probably only eight or ten miles from the settlement but the teams were beginning to stumble and swerve into each other. The lead team, all important in keeping the pace, was beginning to pull apart instead of together, a sign of faltering muscles. Lee could no longer use the whip. The horses had nothing left, further punishment would only hasten the end. His resigned glance at Quarles said the issue was over. They had come as far as determination and desperation could carry them, now the consequences of failure had to be faced.

Neither believed the settlement still held out, surviving in spite of impossible odds. Visions of Cathy and Charlotte as captives, enduring the fate of Flora and Charity, were impossible to dispel. They climbed down from the wagon and started working the harness from the horses. Whatever chance the animals had for life lay in letting them settle in whatever postures of exhaustion they could manage. Streaks of faint pink were slowly weaving into the eastern sky as they finished with the animals, and Lee quietly warned they'd better start watching for signs of trouble, this was still hostile country. Quarles couldn't bring himself to worry about safety, certainly not his own. He was wondering how fast they could walk to the settlement, search for evidence of its fate, perhaps find tracks showing where the Indians had gone, likely taking their captives with them.

Lee stared at him, sensing his thoughts, even sharing them but realizing such a course had its risky side. "I'm game . . . but we've got to keep a sharp lookout. Damn if I don't feel redskins hunkerin' down hereabouts a'ready!"

It took them several minutes to work into a backpack supplies they wanted to take along, but just as they were about to leave, Lee grabbed Quarles from behind and pulled him down.

Quarles, jolted by Lee's seizing him, twisted his head about, exclaiming, "What the hell! . . ."

"Look yonder," hissed Lee, pointing southwest. The sky was only beginning to brighten but one could easily see puffs of dark smoke rising in the morning air.

"What's that?" Quarles's voice came low, almost a whisper.

Lee's answer was slightly higher but stamped with concern. "Injun signals . . . don't like it."

"Signals? . . . signaling what?"

Lee let an audible breath out and shook his head.

"Must have seen something . . . if I was betting my last dollar I'd bet it's more 'n likely us."

At the camp daylight approached like a knell of doom. Even as first light appeared Sam watched stakes going into the ground and wood and buffalo chips being gathered at their foot. The tribe was going to make the deaths of its captives a grimly festive affair. Above all, the cruel tormenting would be visible from the settlement. Cathy and Alice would survive for reasons hardly less hideous than public cremation, but Sam was reasonably sure Grimes would be the first to die, though Lame Fox might well soon join him. The Shawnee was no longer safe at Whistling Elk's side. Now two braves stood over him as he sat alone, dismal if resigned.

Hattie had started to run a fever but remained conscious and refused to stop praying for their salvation. Sam and Skeeter tried to quiet her, Sam whispering passing warriors were not above silencing her with a tomahawk if her voice, constantly breaking out, began to irritate them. Sam nursed no illusions. He knew warriors routinely dispatched wounded captives, no energy was wasted keeping enemies alive. Suddenly he saw Grimes being dragged from the shelter, the still nude Cathy and Alice rising behind to watch him go. Grimes was trying to struggle free, losing what was left of his torn underpants in the attempt. But he was soon thrust up against the foremost stake, with Indians of all ages and sizes excitedly gathering around to watch his death throes. To his credit he was not dying like a frightened child, mute with fear, but shouting at the top of his lungs, demanding to speak to Whistling Elk, telling them they'd pay for his murder a hundredfold. That only a handful even partly understood him didn't matter; the young lieutenant was raging enough to convince even those coming to mock they weren't killing a coward. From the shelter Alice kept looking after him, tears of outrage rising in her eyes. She knew once they lit the fire she could no longer watch. Cathy took her in her arms and they both sank to the ground to pray.

The war leader who came with the pipe to light the fire

was making signs to the four directions while Whistling Elk, standing on a nearby mound, drew his robe about him, his heavy face like granite in acceptance of defeat. War was now inevitable, that tiny flame in the war leader's hand would ignite a conflagration that would commit his people to a bloody stand against the whites, a stand which could decide their fate. Being a warrior who once loved combat, the faint tinge of valor in this moment should have brought a sense of exaltation, but instead a cold tentacle of fear brushed lightly against his heart.

It was his young squaw coming up behind him who tapped his forearm and pointed to the east. "Look," she murmured, raising a hand up to ward off the brighter sky in that direction.

Whistling Elk swung about and peered eastward. In the distance, against the coming dawn, he could see tiny dark puffs just clearing the horizon. It made him swing hurriedly back, shouting to the crowd about the stake. "Stop!" he cried. "Stop! Our brothers have sighted a wagon!"

They had only traveled a short distance when they heard galloping horses, hoofbeats coming rapidly in their direction. They ducked into the brush but Lee knew it was pointless. They were on foot, doubtless already spotted, those smoke signals could not be ignored. He decided to brave it out. He rose and watched a heavily painted warrior riding up to him, halting and making the sign for where they were headed. Lee, a fair hand at sign himself, answered they were bringing a wagonload of goods for Whistling Elk's people, but that their horses had broken down and they were going for help.

The brave grunted and ordered Lee to mount behind him. Another warrior pulled Quarles up and without further exchanges they returned to the wagon. Here Lee and the brave dismounted and the warrior was quietly shown the guns and other supplies the wagon contained. When Lee saw the trace of a smile on the warrior's face he immediately used sign again to say another wagon was left a day's ride back, then added eight more were on their way.

The heavily painted brave began shouting excitedly to the other warriors, who dismounted to take ropes from the wagon and tie them to the wagon tongue. Others tied pieces to the wagon itself. Pretty soon ten horses were ready to haul the heavy wagon forward and without comment Lee and Quarles were waved onto the wagon seat again. Something in the warrior's manner told them they were momentarily out of danger and were finally going to ride this blessed wagon into the Indian camp after all.

They came into camp with Whistling Elk standing forward, waiting for them. No one spoke until the warrior who led them there dismounted and spoke with the aged chief. The warrior's words were brief but they brought a look of triumph to Whistling Elk's heavy features. Some of war leaders began to come up, their eyes noticing and gradually brightening at the contents of the wagon.

Lee and Quarles climbed down, both staring at Grimes still bound to the stake. Their relief at seeing the settlement beyond was tempered by the sight of Alice, guarded by some squaws, standing nude in the background. Another figure was standing just behind Alice, Quarles instinctively knew it was Cathy and, even without looking, realized she was nude too. It made him turn away and settle on one knee, looking at the ground.

She, anxiously watching the wagon arrive, noticed him doing this and realized at once he wanted to spare her the shame of appearing naked before him. She smiled in spite of herself—he was that kind of man.

In time a tenuous peace was arranged, ostensibly until all the wagons arrived, but many knew the threat of war was past. Grimes was released from the stake, Alice and Cathy were given blankets to cover themselves, and Quarles was allowed to look at Hattie's wound. Within the hour warriors were sent to get the wagon left behind when the last dash was decided upon. People from the settlement began to call over, Cheatem waving the guidon as though celebrating a victory.

No one realized that day that the old frontier was dying. With peace restoring safety to travelers Dennis and Chloe made their way north with their infant son. It was an uneventful trip, the only excitement coming at the Arkansas crossing where they met the old prospector again. He had tried Saint Louis but the lure of open spaces was in his blood. He tagged along, a companion making trail life easier and, though doubtful their raw settlement would end his wanderlust, finally offering to give it a try.

It proved the luckiest decision of his life. When Sam finally decided to find his silver mine again the old prospector jumped at an invitation to go along. He helped make up a strange party of four, with Dennis coming along as heir to Troy's interest and Lame Fox, who elected to rejoin the white man's world, and whose winter with the Omahas had given him great familiarity with the mountains, finding himself invited because Sam secretly wanted experienced eyes alerting him to any intruders such as the Utes.

They came back in two months knowing they were wealthy. Within a year mule trains were bringing out high-grade ore that the government bought up to meet the nation's mounting demand for silver coins. Much of Sam's earnings went to Hattie, who used it at once to build another church. She had been holding prayer meetings by the river for some time, with more and more people showing up. Dillby, with his own church in ashes, asked permission to preach to Hattie's congregation and received it. When her church was finished she asked him to be its pastor, but insisted a cross with the savior be placed near the top of the steeple, and that no denomination ever be mentioned in its name. "Dis a house of God," she explained. "Everybody welcome, everybody belong." It got to be known as the Church of God, though many old timers quietly referred to it as Saint Hattie's.

That church would witness many occasions that gave

the settlement its history. The marriage of Major Henry
Quarles and Mrs. Cole Sadler, and that of Tom Zacklee
and Mrs. Charlotte Barry took place there. Almost two
decades later the son of Mr. and Mrs. Dennis Sadler and
the daughter of Colonel and Mrs. Quarles would be wed
there. In 1890 funeral services for the founder of the
church, Mrs. Hattie Boggs, were held there with the pall
of mourning and a sense of loss lasting most of the year.
Still the town grew and Alice Grimes started a library in
honor of her husband, a general of cavalry lost in the
Spanish-American war. There was no lack of gossip
either. Silas Cheatem, seeming less prominent and even
a bit helpless without the Boggses, slipped off for California one night, though it was not known for weeks that
Flora Hunt had gone with him. They were last heard to
be working themselves upward in San Francisco society.

But civilization and the twentieth century slowly came
to engulf the old Smoky Hill country. The church by the
river became hemmed in by buildings stretching skyward, housing commercial endeavors or offices of law.
Still, for those who remembered and stopped to look, the
crucifix could still be seen near the steeple top, with
Christ looking outward toward the plains, where savage
fighters, painted for war and haunting the night with
medicine chants and the rousing beat of drums, once
roamed.

In 1968, Calvin Boggs, great grandson of Hattie
Boggs, was elected mayor. He kept a picture of an old
Indian chief over his desk. It was never positively
identified but children from the nearby reservation,
gathered before it by their teachers, often giggled and
whispered to each other it was Whistling Elk.

Magnificient Western Sagas by

DAVID WILLIAM ROSS

"Ross has painted a fascinating American
era with a brilliant brush."
Sunday Oklahoman

SAVAGE PLAINS
78324-X/$5.99 US/$7.99 Can

The Sadler family's fight to save a group of slaves
has made them fugitives. And in the raging frontier fires engulfing settler and tribe, the Sadlers'
true destiny awaits them. For here they must
suffer and learn . . . or here they will surely die.

And Don't Miss These Other
Adventures of the American West

WAR CRIES
78024-0/$5.99 US/$7.99 Can

EYE OF THE HAWK
72232-1/$5.99 US/$6.99 Can

BEYOND THE STARS
71471-X/5.95 US/$6.95 Can

Buy these books at your local bookstore or use this coupon for ordering:
....
Mail to: Avon Books, Dept BP, Box 767, Rte 2, Dresden, TN 38225   E
Please send me the book(s) I have checked above.
❏ My check or money order—no cash or CODs please—for $_____is enclosed (please
add $1.50 per order to cover postage and handling—Canadian residents add 7% GST).
❏ Charge my VISA/MC Acct#_____Exp Date_____
Minimum credit card order is two books or $7.50 (please add postage and handling
charge of $1.50 per order—Canadian residents add 7% GST). For faster service, call
1-800-762-0779. Residents of Tennessee, please call 1-800-633-1607. Prices and numbers are
subject to change without notice. Please allow six to eight weeks for delivery.

Name_____
Address_____
City_____State/Zip_____
Telephone No._____   DWR 0996

REMARKABLE ADVENTURES OF THE AMERICAN WEST

by

JOHNNY QUARLES

SPIRIT TRAIL

77656-1/$4.99 US/$5.99 Can

Fleeing ghosts and chasing dreams, a gunslinger
seeks the future in a forgotten Indian past.

FOOL'S GOLD

76813-5/$4.50 US/$5.50 Can

An unforgettable adventure of heroes and legends,
of losers and loners in glorious pursuit
of an impossible dream.

NO MAN'S LAND

76814-3/$4.99 US/$5.99 Can

"Johnny Quarles is breathing new life
into an old genre."
Charleston Gazette

SHADOW OF THE GUN

77657-X/$5.50 US/$7.50 Can

Buy these books at your local bookstore or use this coupon for ordering:

Mail to: Avon Books, Dept BP, Box 767, Rte 2, Dresden, TN 38225   E
Please send me the book(s) I have checked above.
❑ My check or money order—no cash or CODs please—for $_____is enclosed (please
add $1.50 per order to cover postage and handling—Canadian residents add 7% GST).
❑ Charge my VISA/MC Acct#_____Exp Date_____
Minimum credit card order is two books or $7.50 (please add postage and handling
charge of $1.50 per order—Canadian residents add 7% GST). For faster service, call
1-800-762-0779. Residents of Tennessee, please call 1-800-633-1607. Prices and numbers are
subject to change without notice. Please allow six to eight weeks for delivery.

Name_____
Address_____
City_____State/Zip_____
Telephone No._____   JQ 0596